PRAISE FOR RAMSEY CAMPBELL

'Britain's most respected living horror writer' *Oxford Companion to English Literature*

'Easily the best horror writer working in Britain today' *Time Out*

'Campbell is literate in a field which has attracted too many comic-book intellects, cool in a field where too many writers – myself included – tend toward panting melodrama . . . Good horror writers are quite rare, and Campbell is better than just good' Stephen King

'Britain's greatest living horror writer' Alan Moore

'Britain's leading horror writer . . . His novels have been getting better and better' *City Limits*

'One of Britain's most accomplished horror writers' *Oxford Star*

'The John le Carré of horror fiction' *Bookshelf*, Radio 4

'One of the best real horror writers at work today' *Interzone*

'The greatest living exponent of the British weird fiction tradition' *The Penguin Encyclopaedia of Horror and the Supernatural*

'Ramsey Campbell has succeeded more brilliantly than any other writer in bringing the supernatural tale up to date without sacrificing the literary standards that early masters made an indelible part of the tradition' Jack Sullivan (editor of the Penguin encyclopaedia)

'England's contemporary king of the horror genre' *Atlanta Constitution*

'One of the few real writers in our field . . . In some ways Ramsey Campbell is the best of us all' Peter Straub

'Ramsey Campbell has a talent for terror – he knows how to give you nightmares while you're still awake . . . Only a few writers can lay claim to such a level of consummate craftsmanship' Robert Bloch

'Campbell writes the most terrifying horror tales of anyone now alive' *Twilight Zone Magazine*

'He is unsurpassed in the subtle manipulation of mood . . . You forget you're just reading a story' *Publishers Weekly*

'One of the world's finest exponents of the classic British ghost story' *Sounds*

'For sheer ability to compose disturbing, evocative prose, he is unmatched in the horror/fantasy field . . . He turns the traditional horror novel inside out, and makes it work brilliantly' *Fangoria*

'Campbell has solidly established himself to be the best writer working in this field today' Karl Edward Wagner, *The Year's Best Horror Stories*

'When Mr Campbell pits his fallible, most human characters against enormous forces bent on incomprehensible errands the results are, as you might expect, often frightening, and, as you might not expect, often touching; even heartwarming' Gahan Wilson in *The Magazine of Fantasy and Science Fiction*

'Britain's leading horror novelist' *New Statesman*

'Ramsey Campbell is Britain's finest living writer of horror stories: considerable praise for a man whose country boasts the talents of Clive Barker and Roald Dahl, M. John Harrison and Nigel Kneale' Douglas Winter, editor of *Prime Evil*

'Campbell writes the most disturbing horror fiction around' *Today*

'Ramsey Campbell is better than all the rest of us put together' Dennis Etchison

'Ramsey Campbell is the best horror writer alive, period' Thomas Tessier

'A horror writer in the classic mould . . . Britain's premier contemporary exponent of the art of scaring you out of your skin' *Q Magazine*

'The undisputed master of the psychological horror novel' Robert Holdstock

'Perhaps the most important living writer in the horror fiction field' David Hartwell

'Ramsey Campbell's work is tremendous' Jonathan Ross

'Campbell is a rightful tenant of M. R. James country, the genuine badlands of the human psyche' Norman Shrapnel in the *Guardian*

'One of the world's finest exponents of the classic British ghost story . . . His writing explores the potential for fear in the mundane, the barely heard footsteps, the shadow flitting past at the edge of one's sight' *Daily Telegraph*

'The Grand Master of British horror . . . the greatest living writer of horror fiction' *Vector*

'Britain's greatest horror writer . . . Realistic, subtle and arcane' *Waterstone's Guide to Books*

'In Campbell's hands words take on a life of their own, creating images that stay with you, feelings that prey on you, and people you hope never ever to meet' *Starburst*

'The finest writer now working in the horror field' *Interzone*

'Ramsey Campbell is the nearest thing we have to an heir to M. R. James' *The Times*

'Easily the finest practising British horror novelist and the one whose work can most wholeheartedly be recommended to those who dislike the genre . . . His misclassification as a genre writer obscures his status as the finest magic realist Britain possesses this side of J. G. Ballard' *Daily Telegraph*

'One of the few who can scare and disturb as well as make me laugh out loud. His humour is very black but very funny, and that's a rare gift to have' Mark Morris in the *Observer*

'The most sophisticated and highly regarded of British horror writers' *Financial Times*

'He writes of our deepest fears in a precise, clear prose that somehow manages to be beautiful and terrifying at the same time. He is a powerful, original writer, and you owe it to yourself to make his acquaintance' *Washington Post*

'I would say that only five writers have written serious novels which incorporate themes of fantasy or the inexplicable and still qualify as literature: T. E. D. Klein, Peter Straub, Richard Adams, Jonathan Carroll and Ramsey Campbell' Stephen King

'Ramsey Campbell is the best of us all' Poppy Z. Brite

'The foremost stylist and innovator in British horror fiction' *The Scream Factory*

'One of the century's great literary exponents of the gothic and horrific' *Guardian*

'A national treasure . . . one of the most revered and significant authors in our field' Peter Atkins

'No other horror writer currently active is engaging with the real world quite as rigorously as Ramsey Campbell' Kim Newman

'Ramsey Campbell taught me how to write . . . There's an intensity and clarity to his worldview that's quite beautiful' Jeremy Dyson

'When it comes to the box of nightmares into which we all reach for inspiration, Ramsey reaches deeper than anyone else' Mark Morris

ABOUT THE AUTHOR

Ramsey Campbell has been given more awards than any other writer in the field, including the Grand Master Award of the World Horror Convention and the Lifetime Achievement Award of the Horror Writers Association. In 2007, he was named a Living Legend by the International Horror Guild. He is the author of over fifteen novels, short stories and a collection of nonfiction. He lives on Merseyside with his wife Jenny and his pleasures include classical music, good food and wine, and whatever's in that pipe.

For more information visit www.ramseycampbell.com

THIEVING FEAR

Ramsey Campbell

Published by Virgin Books 2009

First published in hardback in Great Britain in 2008 by PS Publishing Ltd

First published in paperback in Great Britain in 2009 by
Virgin Books
Random House, 20 Vauxhall Bridge Road
London SW1V 2SA

www.virginbooks.com
www.rbooks.co.uk

Addresses for companies within The Random House Group Limited can be found at:
www.randomhouse.co.uk/offices.htm

The Random House Group Limited Reg. No. 954009

A CIP catalogue record for this book is available from the British Library

ISBN 9780753518113

The Random House Group Limited supports The Forest Stewardship Council [FSC], the leading international forest certification organisation. All our titles that are printed on Greenpeace approved FSC certified paper carry the FSC logo. Our paper procurement policy can be found at www.rbooks.co.uk/environment

Typeset in Sabon by Palimpsest Book Production Limited,
Grangemouth, Stirlingshire
Printed and bound in Great Britain by
CPI Bookmarque, Croydon CR0 4TD

2 4 6 8 10 9 7 5 3 1

For Jeannie and Tony
without a grain of gluten

ACKNOWLEDGMENTS

As usual, Jenny had to suffer the book with me as it crawled into being. Mat and Sharika put up one of my characters in their flat, while another borrowed some elements from Tammy's and Sam's. Parts of the first draft were written in Venice (where I fear the hotel room afforded little writing space), in the Byzantium Apartments in Troulos on the island of Skiathos, at Fantasycon in Nottingham, the Festival of Fantastic Films in Manchester and the H. P. Lovecraft Film Festival in Portland, Oregon. My thanks to Steve and Justin of the Portland White House for their hospitality – what they call a bed and breakfast I'd describe as a small and very splendid hotel – and to Andrew and Linda Migliore of the Festival for much stimulating fun. I also have a special thank you to Huw Lines for the cry.

THIEVING FEAR

TEN YEARS EARLIER

'Good night,' Ellen called to Hugh, 'brilliant teacher.'

A boat chugged on the river beyond the cliffs before Hugh said 'Night' from the brothers' tent as if he wasn't sure his cousin Ellen had meant him.

'Good night, famous artist,' Ellen called to Rory.

The sound of the engine had dwindled towards the Welsh coast by the time Rory responded 'Aren't we getting too old for this?'

Charlotte wriggled around in her sleeping bag to face Ellen in the dark. 'He means camping out,' she said loud enough for Rory to hear.

'You mustn't let our aunt and uncle know you think that even if you do,' Ellen called to Rory.

'He won't. Go on, say good night,' urged Hugh.

'I don't need my little bro to tell me what to do.' In a voice more childish than he'd sounded when he was half his sixteen years Rory added 'Nighty-night, sweet dreams.'

'Don't let him take away the magic,' Charlotte murmured. 'He's only being like boys are.'

'Hugh isn't,' Ellen said lower still. 'Anyway, good night, equally famous writer.'

'And good night, caring person,' Charlotte said to Ellen.

If this sounded feeble by comparison, at least it was true. Three short stories in the school magazine and half a dozen chapters of a novel not even printed out from her computer hardly entitled Charlotte to be judged a writer, even if she might like to earn the name as much as Hugh wanted to teach and Rory, though he would never admit it, to be hailed a painter. 'Wake up older,' she called.

'And wiser,' said Hugh.

'And prettier,' Ellen supplied.

'And with all your eyes open.'

'How many of those have you got, Rory?'

'Watch it, Hugh, or we'll be thinking you've got an imagination.'

'Now, boys,' Ellen said, 'don't spoil the summer. Let's just enjoy our lovely night.'

They'd recently finished gazing at the sky while it filled with dark and stars. When Rory pointed out galaxies nobody else had noticed, Charlotte had suggested they were ghosts composed of light from the distant past. She might have been happy to continue lying outside on the grass if the vista of infinity hadn't made the ground feel infirm, an impression gradually dissipating now that she was snug in her padded cocoon. At least the tents were as far from the edge of the cliff as the campers had promised Auntie Betty once she'd finished failing to persuade Rory to camp in the back garden. 'We'll look after the girls,' Hugh had said in case that helped.

Charlotte was drifting into sleep as these memories grew blurred when Ellen spoke. Her voice was loose with slumber, so that it took Charlotte some moments to guess the word or words: hardly 'Pendemon', since that meant as little as a dream; possibly 'Pendulum' if not 'Depends on . . .' She peered across the narrow space between the bags and was just able to distinguish that Ellen was facing her with eyes shut tight. Even more indistinctly Ellen protested 'Don't want to see. Won't look.'

'Don't,' Charlotte advised, and might have said it louder if it would rescue Ellen from her dream. Perhaps Ellen was attached to the experience, because with an emphatic wriggle she presented her back to her cousin. 'Keep it to yourself, then,' Charlotte said and returned to her search for sleep.

Oddly, Ellen's words left her feeling watched. The brothers had been silent for a while, but the darkness was finding its voices: the croak of a frog on the common, the cry of a midnight bird over the river. A breeze tried the flap of the tent before rattling a clump of gorse. Was Charlotte hearing a frog or a crow? The harsh sound was more prolonged than she would have expected from either. As Ellen stirred uneasily Charlotte took the chance to say 'What do you think that is out there?'

Ellen had no view, though she expelled a breath that might have been a wordless plea for her to be left alone. Perhaps Charlotte's question had come close to rousing her, unless the noise close by on the common had. In a moment the pair of croaks was repeated. Could the speaker be uttering them behind a hand? That would explain their stifled quality, and speaker seemed to be the right word, since she could imagine that the repetition contained two syllables. It sounded like her name. 'All right, Mr Punch,' she called. 'Let's have those dreams you were talking about.'

She was turning over when he repeated the utterance. Was Hugh asleep? She would have expected him to second her request if it had been audible in the boys' tent. 'Shush now, Rory,' she said loud enough to make Ellen shift with a rustle of the fabric of her bag, but he scarcely let her finish before he croaked her name again. If she remonstrated any louder she might waken Ellen. She eased the zip down on her sleeping bag until she was able to slide out and untie the bow that held shut the flap of Betty's and Albert's tent. As she ducked through the opening and raised her head she was greeted by her name.

Now she understood why Hugh hadn't intervened. Rory wasn't speaking from their tent but somewhere closer to the cliff. The trouble was that he had nowhere to hide on the expanse of turfy common. He must be lurking over the edge, beyond which the black river underlined the Welsh coast that glittered as if a section of the sky had fallen to earth. 'I know where you are,' she called, impatient with the joke. 'Come back before we both catch cold.'

In fact the grass beneath her bare feet seemed no colder than the inside of the sleeping bag had been. Might Rory be sickening for something, though? When he spoke her name again as if he couldn't think or couldn't bother thinking of another word, she realised why she'd mistaken his voice for a crow's before she was quite awake; it kept catching in his throat, perhaps on phlegm. 'Give it a rest,' she urged. 'You don't want to fall down the cliff.'

This put her in mind of the girl who had thrown herself off, unless she'd slipped while running along the edge nearby, above the rocks. According to their uncle's version of last year's local newspaper report, she had been bullied at school – at least, she'd told her parents that she couldn't stand how she was being watched. Charlotte felt as if she were gaining years of maturity to compensate for the ones he seemed happy to give up, because she was striding across the blackened grass to find him rather than abandoning him to his silly fate. She was almost at the cliff when she faltered, throwing up her arms for balance or from frustration. The clogged voice had named her yet again, but it was at her back.

As she twisted around, the sky seemed to reel like a whirlpool brimming with stars. How had he managed to sneak past her? The common was deserted all the way to the twin elongated pyramids of the tents, and beyond them for at least a quarter of a mile to a dim hedge bordering a dimmer field. 'Throwing your voice now?' she suggested before realising how he could. No wonder it was so harsh and indistinct if he was using a cheap microphone. Of course he must have hidden a receiver somewhere in the grass.

It was almost at her feet. By the time it finished dragging out her name again she was within inches of it. The voice sounded more congested than ever, so that she wondered if soil had got into the receiver. Her T-shirt rode up her thighs as she crouched, having distinguished a gap in the turf where Rory had cut into it to hide the receiver. She dug her fingers into the overgrown gap and lifted the large square of turf.

More than turf rose to meet her. As she teetered on her heels, Charlotte only just kept hold of the metal object she'd found. She straightened up and did her best to bring it with her, but it was embedded in earth or turf or some more solid item. She stooped to tug at it with both hands, and almost toppled into blackness. She wasn't holding a receiver. It was the handle of a trapdoor.

She let go as she stumbled backwards, and the trapdoor fell open with a thud. A smell of earth seeped out of the blackness as she tried to see what she'd opened up. The sky seemed to blacken and sag with her concentration, but she could see nothing beyond the square outline without standing over the hole. She planted her feet on either side of a corner opposite the trapdoor and peered down.

The hole was full of blackness. She thought there might be steps, except that the dim slope looked too featureless, more like a heap of earth. She was able to discern two handfuls of pebbles separated by a slightly larger pair of stones some way below ground level, but she was distracted from examining them once she observed that the handle was on top of the supine trapdoor. It had been on the inside, and so the door must have been partly open when she'd groped underneath. As she pondered this she heard her name.

The voice sounded close to falling to bits. She could almost have imagined that it or his breath was catching on the substance of the speaker's throat. If she meant to retrieve Rory's device she would have to climb into the hole. She might have left the receiver to rot if the slow thick crumbling voice had given her a chance to think or feel. It was intoning her name without a pause, and growing so loud that she couldn't understand why it hadn't roused Ellen or Hugh. The vibration was shifting the earth where the receiver was buried, a few inches lower down the slope than the collection of pebbles. It was even dislodging the earth around the larger pair, which appeared to swell up from the dimness.

Charlotte peered at them as she gripped the stony edge of the hole in order to descend and took hold of the handle of the trapdoor. She was taking her first step into the dark when she noticed that the stones weren't just moving but widening. They were eyes, watching her without a hint of a blink. The smaller pebbles were stirring too, poking up to reveal they were fingertips. The discoloured hands were reaching to help her down or drag her into the earth.

As she recoiled the ground seemed to give beneath her. She was terrified that it was spilling into the hole until she realised her bare feet had lost their purchase on the grass. One skidded over the edge and met a bunch of cold objects that responded by writhing eagerly. She kicked out and flung herself away from the hole, almost sprawling on her back. She was thrusting her hands under the trapdoor to lever it up when the voice repeated her name.

The thud of the trapdoor laid it to rest, but its clogged yet mocking tone suggested she hadn't escaped. The panic that she'd barely managed to suppress overwhelmed her, and she backed away so fast her ankles knocked together. She no longer knew where the trapdoor was. She had no idea where she was going except backwards until, with a swiftness that snatched all her breath, the common vanished together with the further landscape of fields and distant houses as if earth had closed over her eyes. She had backed off the edge of the cliff.

Its side rushed up past her like a mass of smoke, and then her feet struck ground, too soon. She was on a ledge close to the top, which meant she had a long way to fall. She staggered against the cliff to rest her face and hands against the clay while she tried to be sure of her balance. The ledge was dismayingly narrow as well as slippery with sand. 'Can someone come?' she cried before she had time to wonder who might respond. 'Can anyone hear?'

She could – a muffled restless sound, and then a louder and more purposeful version. She wasn't sure it was made by the flap of a tent until Ellen called somewhat sleepily 'Was that you, Charlotte? Where are you?'

'Here,' Charlotte shouted and turned her shaky head to see. It wasn't a ledge, it was a path that led straight to the top. As she scrambled upwards, a shape loomed above her. 'What on earth are you doing down there?' Ellen said. 'Were you sleepwalking?'

Charlotte didn't answer until her cousin took her hand and helped her over the edge. The common stretched as blank as innocence to the tents. She murmured her thanks and stayed close to Ellen while they padded across the grass. She could see no sign of a hidden trapdoor in the area where she remembered it to have been, and how could none of her cousins have been disturbed by a voice as loud as the one she'd seemed to hear? 'I must have been,' she decided and instantly felt better.

This appeared to be Hugh's cue to call 'Where are they? Which way did they go?'

'Listen to it,' Ellen said with an affectionate laugh. 'It's a good job we didn't have to rely on the boys, isn't it, Charlotte?'

'What's wrong?' Rory demanded. 'We were asleep. I was down the house.'

'Charlotte's been walking in her sleep.' Ellen led her into the tent and waited while she wriggled into her sleeping bag. 'Let's get you snug so you can't wander off again,' she said, zipping the bag up tight. For a moment, until she controlled herself, Charlotte found the tent and the bag and Ellen's concern almost as oppressive as the notion of climbing down into the dark.

ONE

'Shall we walk along the beach for some more exercise?' Ellen said.

They were at the end of the road that led from Thurstaston to the cliff. Above the Welsh coast the sky was padded with white clouds that kept displaying and repacking the sun. As sunlight outdistanced a mass of shadow that raced across the common alongside the road, the grass seemed to breathe the light in. A child cried out beyond the thorny hedge that had just turned more luminously green, and it wasn't until a man shouted 'Shemp' that Charlotte realised the child had been startled by a dog. By then Hugh had told Ellen 'Good idea before we have to drive.'

Ellen raised her almost invisible eyebrows and then narrowed her bluish eyes and pressed her full lips together as if searching for a way to render her round face less plump. 'You're supposed to say I don't need any exercise, Hugh.'

His long face tried on an apologetic smile as he passed a hand over his cropped scalp before patting his prominent stomach. 'I meant I did. You need to keep fit in my job.'

Rory shook his head, wagging his black ponytail. His face was even longer than his brother's and bonier as well, which emphasised his large sharp nose. His habitual wry but weary grin, so faint it was close to secretive, scarcely wavered as he said 'Say what you see or you'll never be a writer.'

'I'm not one,' Hugh said as though he'd failed to grasp that Rory wasn't addressing him. 'You're the artistic lot. I'm Supermarket Man.'

'That's art if you do it right,' Rory said. 'Everything is.'

'You're just as important as the rest of us, Hugh.' Perhaps in a bid to heighten his tentative smile, Ellen added 'More than I can be just now.'

'You've been crucial to people who needed it,' Charlotte assured her. 'So are we having our last walk on the beach?'

Rory's shrug might have been intended to dislodge her wistfulness. He turned fast along the path that skirted a caravan park. An assortment of steps up which several large dogs and their less energetic owners were scrambling led to the beach, where the tide had pulled the river back from the cliffs. Halfway down Ellen glanced around at Charlotte, then hurried after the brothers, her slightly more than shoulder-length blonde hair swaying as if to deny she'd had a question for her cousin. They were all on the beach by the time she murmured 'I shouldn't think anyone's had time to look at my little novel.'

'Not so little,' Hugh protested.

'Not so novel either,' Rory said.

'You've been reading it, then,' Ellen said like a gentle rebuke.

'Some of it,' he said and glanced away from the unfurling of a swathe of windblown sand. 'I liked the bit where you had some old character muttering silently. Good trick if you can bring it off.'

'I thought it was pretty original,' Hugh said. 'The whole book, I mean.'

'You've never heard of anybody having nightmares that turned real before.'

'Not old folk giving them to people who mistreat them.' Hugh bit his lip before asking Ellen 'It couldn't give you any problems if someone you didn't want to hear about it heard about it, could it?'

'Gosh, that's a mouthful. Who would they be?'

'They couldn't say at the industrial tribunal you'd been making stories up about old people being treated badly, could they?'

'It would have to be published first, Hugh. I'm sure they'll see I was telling the truth.'

'You haven't said what you thought of it yet,' Rory told Charlotte.

She'd kept feeling that the conversation was about to converge on her. 'To be honest, Ellen –'

'That's what I want you to be. I absolutely do.'

'I think it needs some work.'

'You're saying you can publish it if she works on it?' Hugh enthused. 'That's great news, isn't it, Ellen?'

'I don't know if she's quite saying that,' Ellen said and gazed at an approaching rush of sunlight that snagged on clumps of sedge.

'I'd have to see your revisions before I could be too definite. I'll email you when I'm back at my desk.'

'That's still great news, isn't it?' Hugh insisted. 'You won't be paying her anything on account yet then, Charlotte.'

'No contract for the first book till it's publishable, that's the directive that came round last month.'

'Even for family?' Perhaps sensing that he'd gone too far, Hugh made haste to add 'I was only wondering if you were hard up, Ellen. You could have my thousand and pay me back whenever you can.'

'You can have mine too by all means,' Charlotte said.

'It wouldn't buy her much in London,' Rory seemed to feel he should reassure Ellen. 'Hardly worth getting the train for.'

Charlotte thought that was a remark too far. 'I didn't come for the will,' she said, 'I came for the funeral.'

'Then you're no better than the rest of us. You can stick my handout in the bank as well, Ellen. I'd rather still have Albert and Betty, and I don't need it for the stuff I'm playing at.'

'You're all too generous. You treat yourselves and don't worry about me. I'll make do if I have to.'

Charlotte refrained from pointing out to Rory that she'd spoken at the funeral – Albert's, who had died less than four months after his wife. Some of his colleagues had reminisced about working with him at the library to which he'd donated his collection of old books, and a bearded guitarist rendered a twenty-first-century folk song about giving oneself back to the earth. Other librarians read favourite passages of Albert's from *The Pickwick Papers* and *Three Men in a Boat*, earning muted amusement that sounded dutiful, and then it had been Charlotte's turn. She'd kept panicking while she rehearsed the eulogy in the shower or on the roof terrace above her flat, but as she climbed into the pulpit she'd seen that she just needed to talk to her cousins. She reminded them of the word games their uncle had relished inventing, the one where you had to say an even longer sentence than the previous player, and the game of adding words to a sentence spoken backwards, and the conversations made up of words in reverse, when Betty had vacillated between tears of frustration and of helpless mirth . . . 'Rebmemer, rebmemer,' Charlotte had finished, prompting mostly puzzled looks and a few guarded smiles from her uncle's friends and token laughter from her cousins. The all-purpose priest had brought the proceedings to an end with a Cherokee homily, and as curtains closed off the exhibition of the coffin while speakers emitted one of Albert's favourite Beatles ditties, the congregation had vacated the unadorned chapel to accommodate the next shift of mourners. Charlotte and her cousins had to represent the family outside the crematorium, since their various parents were either abroad or estranged from Albert since he'd closed into himself after his wife's death. Charlotte had felt uncomfortably presumptuous, especially since the rest of the occasion was so lacking in ritual. 'We all came, that's what matters,' she belatedly said.

'It's like we've never been away,' Hugh said. 'Nothing's changed along here except us.'

'What are you using for eyes?' Rory was amused to ask. 'Everything has. Not a single grain of sand's the same.'

'I shouldn't reckon even you can see them all.'

'I'm saying there's not a solitary bloody thing that hasn't moved or grown or died or come or gone.'

Charlotte had a sudden notion that neither of the brothers was entirely right. 'Depends on . . .' she almost began and wondered why the phrase should feel unwelcome. She gazed along the miles of cliff that stretched to the mouth of the river. Spiky tufts of grass turned towards her in a breeze as if sensing her interest, while the cliff face that sprouted them appeared to stir, acknowledging her concentration. A flood of shadow lent a darker substance to the cliff, and she was trying to decide why its presence had grown oppressive when Rory said 'Have we walked enough of us off yet?'

'Up to Ellen,' said Hugh.

As she responded with a gentle frown Rory said 'I've had tramping through sand, that's all. Bungs my senses up.'

Charlotte didn't notice the path, a series of zigzags lying low in the grass on the cliff face, until he turned towards it, and then she remembered falling onto it out of her teenage dream. 'Beat you to it,' she declared and strode upwards.

The cliff crowded into one side of her vision and then the other as the path, which was only inches wider than her waist, changed direction. Tufts of grass caught her feet or emitted whispers of restless sand. The cliff top would be safer, and only the low wadded sky made her feel as if she were under a lid. She remembered lying in the tent that night, unable to stay asleep for the thought of closing a trapdoor on herself and utter darkness. She tried to leave the memory behind as she climbed onto the open common.

A gorse bush scraped its thorns together as a wind dissipated through the grass. The clump of about a dozen bushes was the only vegetation other than the green expanse that stretched more than a quarter of a mile to a hedge, and Charlotte was wondering why the view should contain even the hint of a threat when Hugh stepped up behind her. 'This reminds me of the last time we camped out,' he said.

'It should. It's where we were.'

He tramped past her and gazed about before rubbing his scalp as if that might electrify his brain. 'I don't think I know where I am.'

Rory joined them and shook his head at his brother. 'How could you get lost up here?'

'Charlotte did last time.' Less defensively Hugh asked her 'Have you sleptwalked since?'

'Has she what again, Hugh?' Ellen clambered onto the common and tucked her dishevelled blouse into her jeans. 'Don't all look at me,' she begged.

'Sleptwalked, sleepwalked, I don't know. Does it matter that much?'

'Not enough to have an argument about,' Charlotte said. 'I was the one who did it, after all, just that once.'

'I'd have expected you of all people to care about words.' With no lessening of reproachfulness Ellen said 'I was the one who looked after you. Shall we walk?'

Charlotte couldn't help peering at the grass as she followed Ellen. She recalled how a slab of it had risen in her dream, and felt as if the memory wouldn't go away until she identified the spot. Of course she was on edge only because of the funeral, and at first she was glad to be distracted when Hugh spoke. 'We had a bad night too.'

'He means we kept waking each other up. We were asleep when you girls were on the wander, though.'

'Good gracious,' Ellen said as their aunt used to. 'What were you boys up to in your bags?'

'Just dreaming,' said Hugh.

'Nothing to blush about, then.'

'It wasn't,' he said, though her question had mottled his cheeks. 'Just I couldn't find my way somewhere.'

'I couldn't see where I'd got trapped somehow,' Rory offered. 'Might have been a house with no lights in.'

'It's not like you to be so unobservant.'

'He said I was asleep,' Rory retorted, though Ellen's comment had been affectionate. 'Your turn.'

'I was saving Charlotte, if you remember.'

As Charlotte thought the answer had been too quick and glib, a mass of blackness seeped out of the earth all around them. Although it was the shadow of a cloud, it made her feel shut in. 'We're heading back, yes?' she said and set out for the gate through the distant hedge. Even when sunlight washed away the shadow, she could have fancied that darkness was pacing her and her cousins under the earth.

TWO

'You may call your witness, Miss Lomax.'

Just one, Ellen thought as she pushed back her chair – just one former inmate of the Seabreeze Home had agreed to testify on her behalf. She didn't blame the others for refusing. They'd been through enough, and so many were living on little but memories that she didn't want to make them recollect the bad ones. At least they weren't speaking up for the Cremornes as Peggy appeared to have promised she would, if she wasn't playing one of her wily games. As Ellen opened the door of the committee room she was eager to read her face.

Six straight chairs kept company in the corridor, beneath an interbellum photograph of Southport Pier, but only two were occupied, by Muriel Stiles and a nurse. 'Thanks so much for coming, Muriel,' Ellen said.

The old woman took some moments to tilt her head up, which failed to unwrinkle her neck. Her wide loose faded face was so preoccupied that Ellen had the fleeting fancy that the crowded photograph of sedate revellers, an image of enjoyment curbed by moderation and flanked by wars, could be a childhood memory that Muriel was reliving. It reminded Ellen of a flashback inset in a panel of a comic. She would have scribbled down the image if she'd had a notebook, but Muriel was giving her a shaky smile. 'Don't worry, Muriel,' she said. 'I won't let anyone upset you. Just say what you remember.'

She held the door open as the nurse ushered Muriel into the room. The tribunal was seated at the far end of the long table, on the left side of which the Cremornes guarded their lawyer. To Ellen's and quite possibly to Muriel's dismay, the nurse steered his charge in that direction. 'This side,' Ellen told him in less of a murmur than she would have preferred.

Virginia Cremorne interlaced her fingers and sat forwards with a prayerful expression on her small sharp face as Muriel sank onto the chair opposite. 'How are you keeping, Muriel? You're looking as fit as ever.'

Jack Cremorne pinched his shiny brown moustache between finger and thumb as if he meant to remove a disguise from his large perpetually suffused face, then fell to gripping his chin as he said 'Nice to see you again, Muriel. A pity you felt you had to leave us, but we hope you're managing to settle in where you are now.'

Surely they shouldn't be allowed to speak to her that way. When Ellen sent the tribunal a glance that was rather more than enquiring, the chairman said 'Is Miss Stiles ready to proceed?'

Ellen turned further towards Muriel. 'Can I just ask you –'

Both women on the committee parted their lips – like a ventriloquists' contest, Ellen might have noted – but it was the chairman who said 'Miss Stiles will need to take the oath.'

'You'd think someone didn't want people telling the truth,' Jack Cremorne suggested to his wife.

Ellen would have expected the chairman to issue a rebuke, but he only held a Bible out to her. She handed the diminutive book to Muriel, who extracted the card that bore the oath and performed it with such force that Ellen was reminded how she'd often told tales of her days in amateur dramatics. Muriel carried on pressing the Bible to her bosom until the chairman had to ask for the book. 'By all means proceed,' he said.

'I'm just going to ask you a few questions about things Mr and Mrs Cremorne have been saying about me, Muriel. Did –'

'We aren't the only ones that say them,' Virginia Cremorne said.

'They were said to us,' her husband amplified.

'That will be addressed,' said their lawyer.

'May I speak now?' When the chairman delivered a weighty nod of his saturnine squarish head, Ellen asked Muriel 'Did you ever see me steal from any of the residents?'

'I certainly never did.'

'Did any of the other residents?'

'Objection,' the lawyer said. 'Hearsay.'

'Now, Mr Bentley, you know that isn't how it's done,' the heavier and more plainly dressed of the committeewomen said. 'You'll have your turn.'

'If I may be allowed to finish my question,' Ellen said, starting to feel like a lawyer, 'did any of the other residents say they had?'

'Had what?' Muriel said and glared at the Cremornes. 'We didn't have much. I didn't get half of what I paid for. Cold in bed and starved at dinner.'

As Virginia Cremorne opened her outraged mouth, Ellen tried to retrieve her theme. 'I was asking if they said they saw me steal.'

'She'll be tying her tongue in a knot if she carries on like that, won't she?' Muriel said to the chairman. 'They said they saw me steal,' she repeated and attempted to do so at speed. 'I used to be able to say those,' she conceded at last. 'The things you miss at my age.'

'Miss Stiles,' the chairman said, 'if you could do your best –'

'Only trying to cheer the show up. You three look as if you could do with it or you'll be as bad as this pathetic pair.' To Ellen she said 'Nobody saw you because you never did.'

'Thank you, Muriel. And as far as you know, was I ever drunk on the job?'

'You had a glass of wine at my eightieth, didn't you? Everyone did except for this pair, who couldn't be bothered to come.'

'It should be in the records that I wasn't on duty that day,' Ellen said to the tribunal. 'I went in for Muriel's party.'

'Some of the staff that were on had a lot more to drink. Pam was so squiffy she dropped Hilda in the bath.'

'The person concerned is no longer employed by us,' Jack Cremorne informed the panel.

'How about bullying, Muriel? Was I ever guilty of that to your knowledge?'

'You were not. You were the one who cared for us most and that's why you said what you had to. Standing up to people isn't bullying.'

Though Virginia Cremorne uttered less than a word, it was enough to provoke Muriel. 'I'll tell you an example,' she declared and turned from the panel to Ellen. 'What was the blackie's name again?'

Ellen thought it best not to draw attention to the term. 'Daniel, you mean.'

'That's him. A big black buck, that's what they used to call them,' Muriel said with some defiance. 'Doris kept saying he'd sneak into her room at night and do things to her, but he made out she was imagining it and this pair said she must be. If you ask me they were scared he'd sue them because you can't say anything about anyone these days unless they're white.'

'I really must point out,' Virginia Cremorne said, 'that the person referred to –'

'Don't bother telling them you fired him. That wasn't till this girl followed him to Doris's room one night and found him touching her. He got hold of her and tried to throw her out while she was asking Doris about it. I heard it all, and I'll tell you what else, don't talk to me about drinking. That stuff he used to smoke in the back garden and some of the rest of them did, that was worse than any drink.'

'That's entirely news to us,' Jack Cremorne said. 'Isn't it, dear?'

The lawyer held up his skinny hands between the couple and inclined his balding but unruly head towards the chairman. 'In any case the people mentioned aren't the subject of this enquiry.'

'I see that, Mr Bentley. Have you any further questions, Miss Lomax?'

'Would you say I neglected the residents, Muriel?'

'I would not,' Muriel said and squinted at the tribunal. 'She cared so much about us she lost her job reporting the place to the authorities when this pair wouldn't listen.'

'Thanks, Muriel. No further questions.'

Muriel was gripping the edge of the table as an aid to standing up when the lawyer said 'I won't detain you long, Miss Stiles.'

As her wrists continued to tremble once she'd subsided onto the chair he said 'You've told us a number of things you didn't see Miss Lomax do. Can you tell us anything you actually saw besides her enjoying a glass of wine at the party Mr and Mrs Cremorne were kind enough to have the home put on for you?'

'I said how she dealt with that animal in Doris's room.'

'I understood you to say you only overheard what may have happened. I think the incident proves my clients were quite willing to take action whenever there was the need. Was there anything you saw with your own eyes?'

'There was plenty. I saw what was his name, the one with the face like a bloodhound, Billy kicking Anna's legs because she wouldn't go to bed and saying she'd hurt herself falling. And I saw –'

'May I ask you to confine yourself to Miss Lomax? This hearing is about her.'

'I'll say everything I said all over again if you like. And I'll tell you this, she was the only one we trusted out of the lot of them. Even the ones who never did anything to us wouldn't speak up for us.'

'Very well, if that's all. Thank you, Miss Stiles. I can see it's been a strain.'

Muriel seemed as confused by his ending the interrogation as the Cremornes were pretending not to feel. The nurse was helping her up when she leaned towards Ellen. 'Can I wait and see how we did?'

'If you wouldn't mind waiting outside,' the chairman said.

Muriel stared as if she wondered what it had to do with him. 'I will,' she told the nurse.

As the lawyer held the door open for them he called 'We're ready for you, Mrs Nash.'

So Peggy had shown up. A nurse wheeled her forwards as Muriel hobbled out of the room. Did she mean to make a point of not recognising Peggy, or was she taken aback by the wheelchair? Peggy greeted the Cremornes and then peered with her magnified eyes through her glasses at the tribunal. 'Where do you want me sitting?' she said.

'It looks as if you already are, Peggy,' Ellen remarked with a gentle laugh.

'I'm not speaking to you.'

'That could pose a problem,' the chairman said. 'Please sit wherever you're comfortable.'

'I was at the Seabreeze,' Peggy said and stared at Ellen before telling the nurse 'Put me here.'

As she settled at the end of the table facing the tribunal, the lawyer said 'Mrs Nash, can I just establish you're here of your own free will?'

'Don't insult me. My body may have let me down but there's nothing wrong upstairs.'

He handed her the oath to take and followed it by asking 'Is it the case that you're still living at the Seabreeze Home?'

'You know I am.'

'I have to ask you these things for the record. Could you tell us how you came to take up residence there?'

'I met my husband Gerald when he was posted to Nairobi in the fifties. He wasn't like most of them. Most of his troop, they looked down on us and let us know it. The sergeant, he was the worst of the lot. He –'

'Forgive my interrupting,' the chairman said, 'but may we move this forwards? There's another hearing scheduled for this afternoon.'

Peggy's mouth drooped open with outrage or because she'd lost her verbal grasp. 'Can I ask what happened after Mr Nash's death?' the lawyer prompted. 'When you decided to seek residential accommodation, and I appreciate that was years later, did you encounter any problems?'

'Half a dozen of them, and that was just here in Southport. Homes that didn't have a vacancy after all when I turned up.'

'And you feel that was because . . .'

'Have you really got to ask that too? Because of what I am.'

'To put it delicately, an ethnic lady.'

'That's not what I see when I look in the mirror. I just see me.'

Having opened her mouth at the hint of an unwelcome memory, Ellen had to find something to say. 'Everybody's ethnic,' she murmured. 'You shouldn't hijack words.'

'Perhaps some people have more of a reason to care about them,' the lawyer said. 'And how were you made to feel at the Seabreeze Home, Mrs Nash?'

'They treated me like anybody else.'

'Which I take it you're saying was excellently.' When Peggy gave several vigorous nods the lawyer said 'But you'll be aware there have been problems recently with the running of the home.'

'Some of the staff weren't up to standard all the time. The night manager should have kept more of an eye on them. You were right to boot her out,' Peggy told the Cremornes. 'Except the worst of the lot was the one that snitched on her workmates. She only did it so people wouldn't notice how bad she was herself.'

'To be clear, the person you have in mind –'

'She knows who I mean. She's trying to bully me now, looking at me how she does.' Peggy fixed Ellen with a gaze she seemed to think was reciprocal. 'I wouldn't be surprised if she's tried to disguise herself,' she said. 'I don't remember her that size.'

Ellen felt as if her face had swollen up with fever, clamping her lips shut, as the lawyer said 'For the record, you're referring to Miss Lomax.'

Peggy's gaze flickered, only to intensify. 'Is that what she's calling herself?'

'And you believe Mr and Mrs Cremorne had reason to fire her.'

'That's opinion, Mr Bentley,' the chairman said. 'Please concern yourself with evidence.'

'What's the basis of your views, Mrs Nash? What are you saying Miss Lomax did?'

'Stole, for a start. When all the money went from Veronica's purse I saw how guilty that one looked. And one night I saw her with a little whisky bottle when she thought I wasn't looking.'

This was enough to activate Ellen's unwieldy face. 'I found it,' she said. 'I was taking it to the night manager.'

'You'll have your chance, Miss Lomax. Any further observations, Mrs Nash?'

'You've seen how she bullies people. She's doing it now.'

'Please don't feel intimidated. You're among friends.' As Ellen looked away from her, only to wonder why she should have, the lawyer said 'Your witness, Miss Lomax.'

Ellen's lips felt thick and not entirely stable as she said 'First of all, Peggy –'

'I've told you, I'm not speaking to you,' Peggy said and stared at the tribunal.

'Excuse me, but you just did, and I have to point out –'

'She's trying to confuse her,' Virginia Cremorne protested. 'She'll have her not knowing what she's saying.'

Ellen turned her awkward face towards the chairman. 'How am I supposed to question her like this?'

'You should have thought of that before,' Jack Cremorne said. 'If you believed you were in the right you'd have bet some money on a lawyer.'

'This is most irregular,' the chairman said. 'If Miss Lomax poses the questions, Mrs Nash, will you give me your answers?'

'We'll see what she has the cheek to ask.'

'Peggy, you said I was trying to divert attention away from some behaviour of my own. What kind? You surely aren't accusing me of sexual abuse.'

'Mrs Nash, you said –'

'I heard her. Couldn't not. I've never known anyone to drone so much. Used to put me to sleep while I was awake and keep me awake when I was trying to sleep.' Having ventilated this, Peggy said 'There are other kinds of abuse.'

'And which are you saying I was guilty of?'

'Miss Lomax would like to know –'

'I can still hear her. It's like hearing a cow moo.' Peggy rested her gaze on the chairman while she added 'Here's the truth and she won't like it. She made up that tale about Daniel to get him kicked out.'

'Why would she have done that?'

'Because she didn't want him there any more than she wanted me.'

'The previous witness agreed with Miss Lomax's version of events.'

'Are you talking about Muriel Stiles?'

Ellen hoped Peggy's tone had antagonised the chairman more than he made audible. 'That was the lady, yes.'

'She didn't see anything. She only heard Doris making a fuss, and everyone knew poor old Doris dreamed up half of what she said. We'd be sitting in the day room and she'd say the man on television wanted her to get undressed.'

'She could be a little flustered sometimes,' Ellen told the panel, 'but she wasn't that night. I'd remind you that Mr and Mrs Cremorne took the situation seriously enough to send him on his way.'

'Only because she saw her chance and backed Doris up,' Peggy said. 'Maybe she hated him even more than me because she had to work with him.'

'Forgive me, Mrs Nash, but we need to be clear for the record. You mean like you in the sense of . . .'

'Black.' With enough force to capitalise all the letters Peggy repeated 'Black.'

Ellen had to draw a breath as shaky as her mouth to catch her voice. 'That really isn't true.'

'Is she trying to paint me as white as she wants you to think she is?'

'I'm saying I've never said or done anything against her, and this is the first time she's ever said I have.'

'Too frightened to while you were at the Seabreeze,' Virginia Cremorne muttered.

'The light went off in my room one night,' Peggy said, 'and that one told everyone she wouldn't be able to see me in the dark.'

Ellen managed to produce a parched laugh. 'That wasn't how it happened, Peggy. If you remember, I was changing the bulb because nobody else could be bothered, and I simply said I couldn't see you in your chair because you were so far from the door.'

'Were there witnesses?' the chairman said to one or both of them.

'They're some of the ones she got fired.'

'Is this documented, Mr Bentley?' When the lawyer admitted the opposite the chairman said 'Please continue, Miss Lomax.'

'Is there anything else you want to say about me, Peggy?'

'I don't want anything to do with that one at all,' Peggy told everyone apart from Ellen.

'Have you even got a problem with my name?'

Peggy clutched at the wheels of her chair. 'Can I go now?'

All at once Ellen was sure it was crucial to ask 'Seriously, aren't you able to say it?'

'Why should I?' Peggy appealed to the chairman.

'I think perhaps you should just for the record.'

'It's Lomax.'

'That's what you've heard people calling me today. What did they call me at the Seabreeze? You must remember, surely. Like the gentleman told you, it's for the record.'

'Little Miss Innocence. Little Miss Better Than Everyone Else.' To the Cremornes Peggy said 'Do you know what Doris used to call her? Little Saint Whosit. I wouldn't call her little anything.'

Ellen had to shrug the insult off to reach the point. 'Saint what, Peggy? What's my name?'

'That's all Doris said,' Peggy informed the panel. 'I told you she didn't know what was going on or who anyone was half the time.'

'I hope that's enough,' Jack Cremorne said. 'Aren't you ever going to stop bullying our residents, Ellen?'

'And don't anybody run away with the idea I didn't know her name,' Peggy said, 'except I used to call her Lemon and she never knew.'

'Are there any other matters you would like to raise, Miss Lomax?'

'I think I'm finished.'

She was almost certain that the chairman gave her a sympathetic look. 'Thank you, Mrs Nash,' he said. 'We appreciate the effort you've made to speak to us.'

'It's a pity more didn't. Jack and Virginia have enough problems without this.'

The Cremornes seemed less than wholly grateful for her parting comment. They watched the nurse wheel her out and the tribunal murmuring to one another. Ellen tried not to appear too hopeful or the reverse while she gazed out of a high window at a treetop entwined with powerless coloured light bulbs. Eventually Jack Cremorne said 'Any idea how long you're likely to be? Our parking's nearly up.'

Ellen was sure this provoked the chairman to say 'I'm afraid we'll have to defer judgment until it can be put in writing.'

'It isn't only us that wants to hear,' Virginia Cremorne objected. 'You can see Miss Lomax is anxious.'

'I think you'd best be seeing to your car,' the lawyer murmured.

He conducted them out and held the door open for Ellen. Peggy had been wheeled away, but Muriel was keeping her vigil beneath the photograph of quieter times. As the Cremornes marched off with their lawyer, Ellen said 'We have to wait.'

The words made her feel clumsy before Muriel whispered to the nurse 'What have we got to wait for?'

'Sorry, Muriel. I meant me.'

Muriel's whisper was even more piercing. 'Why have we got to wait for her?'

'You haven't. I'm the one who has to wait. Not here, for them to make their minds up. They haven't time today. There are other people they have to see.'

Ellen might have expected those to have arrived, but perhaps they were watching along the corridor. 'I'll tell you the decision when I know,' she said.

She felt weighed down by her mass of words and Muriel's vague patience and the tardiness of the tribunal. 'I'll keep in touch,' she said and turned away, to find that they and the nurse were alone in the corridor.

The impression of a watcher was no more than a lingering smudge on her consciousness. She hurried to the end of the corridor, but the wide stone stairs to the ground floor were deserted too. She was taking the first step down when she faltered with a hand on the chill banister. Muriel's whisper was loud enough to be heard in the committee room. 'Who was the fat girl? Did she think she knew us?'

THREE

'Hate the title.'

Charlotte thought she heard or otherwise sensed the faintest rumble of a train worming underneath the basement office. She looked up from the printout of *Take Care* to find Glen Boyd leaning over the partition around her desk. His high straight black eyebrows gave him a routinely eager expression confirmed by his bright-blue eyes, and in general his lean face seemed pared down to essentials: broad blunt nose, wide lips slightly parted for the next remark, round prominent chin sporting today's crop of stubble. Three furrows were sketched on his forehead, underlining how his short bristling hair had started an early retreat. Perhaps that came with the senior editorship of Cougar Books, Charlotte reflected as she said 'You do or I should?'

'How about both?'

'Too English, do you think?'

'Hey, I've nothing against the English,' Glen said while his accent grew more nasally Maine. 'I wouldn't be here if I had.'

'So what is it about it you don't like?'

'Sounds like a caution manual. Caution doesn't sell our kind of books.'

She might have asked what kind he was saying those were, but she wanted to know 'Apart from the title, what did you think?'

'If she can give us enough of a rewrite I'd say we might take a chance on her.'

Charlotte felt disloyal to be surprised. She had been taken aback by how childish some of the writing was, the characterisations in particular. Though she knew there was nothing more pitiless than authorship when it came to betraying any hidden immaturity of the writer – that was why she'd abandoned her own literary plans – she hadn't been ready to discover it of Ellen. 'How much are we talking about?' she said.

'She has the idea, now she needs to make it work. As long as it's nearly the weekend, why don't I tell you more over a drink.'

Perhaps she was too close to the book or its author, and her inability to see how to improve it was why she'd begun to feel shut in. 'I'm free,' she said.

'I'll see you at the elevator in five. Here's a title for you in the meantime. *Bad Old Things*.'

The long-suffering residents of the Pantaloon Rest Home could hardly be described as villainous, even if maltreatment eventually provoked them to wish their infirmities on their tormentors so passionately that their shared imagination did the rest. Charlotte boxed the stack of pages in the file on which Ellen had painstakingly inked the title and her name, and then she stuffed another typescript into her shoulder bag before tidying her laden desk.

Glen was summoning a lift in the corridor narrowed by lockers. A threesome of their colleagues from the erotica imprint Ram followed him and Charlotte into the windowless grey cage and stood in a corner. 'Beats me,' Fiona was saying to Tasha and Niki, who appeared to share her position. As the doors lumbered shut Charlotte thought for an instant that someone else had slipped between them, but only a shadow could have been so thin. She could think a shadow had dimmed the indirect lighting, which was already meagre enough.

On the ground floor various Cheetah personnel – editors from Koala and Antelope and Little Deers – were spilling out of the other lift. Beyond the lobby New Oxford Street was crowded too. The side street along which Glen turned beneath a curved blue strip of August sky was deserted, but she'd had little chance to relish any spaciousness when he stopped short of Charing Cross Road. 'Here's my favourite,' he said.

Presumably he wasn't addressing the doorman outside Shelves, who inspected her bag and Glen's briefcase before Glen led the way to the cellar. The wine bar earned its name at once, constricting the steep staircase with bookshelves full of dilapidated volumes. At least the bar was relatively roomy, though it smelled of the musty volumes on the shelves that covered practically the whole of the walls up to the bare brick ceiling. Three businessmen with loosened ties were taking peanuts with their white wine at the bar. A balding man whose grey hair was as dishevelled as the rest of him was inspecting the books with such dissatisfaction that Charlotte guessed he was a bookseller. 'Shall we get a bottle of red?' Glen suggested.

'If you'll be drinking more than half.'

'However it works out,' he said and, once they were ensconced at a corner table, gently fended off the share of the price she tried to hand him.

'That's fine, Glen. That's even finer. You have some.' When he moved the bottle of Argentinean Malbec to his own glass Charlotte said 'Why is here your favourite?'

'I like dreaming how it used to be. You could publish anything that took your fancy and if it tanked, nobody would give you too much of a hard time. I think I'd do a better job than some of those guys, mind you. No wonder all their picks are buried down here, books you never heard of by writers nobody remembers, and I'll bet most of them weren't even known while they were alive.'

This seemed to intensify the smell of stale books, and Charlotte couldn't help reflecting that their authors must be even dustier – indeed, little more than the substance. She felt stifled enough to admit 'I've a confession to make.'

'Tell me anything you like.'

'It's just that Ellen Lomax – we're related.'

'I don't know any rule at Cheetah saying people can't be too close.' Glen waited for the unkempt bookseller to shuffle to a further bookshelf and said 'I'd say she's less exceptional than you, whatever she is to you.'

'Cousin,' Charlotte said and made her smile quick.

'It could work to our advantage,' Glen said, holding up his glass until she raised hers. 'You can say whatever she needs to hear.'

'Anything in particular?'

'Hey, no call to get protective. She wants to be published or she wouldn't have sent us the book.' He replenished the glasses, though Charlotte had by no means emptied hers, and said 'You won't be making her do anything we mightn't have to do ourselves.'

'I don't think I follow.'

'That's because officially you aren't hearing this till next week. Now we're part of the Frugo Corporation we need to look at books the way they do.'

'Which is . . .'

'Instead of buying books and then figuring out how to market them we have to turn it round. Unless you're sure how we can market it, don't make an offer.'

'Is that how they buy products for their supermarkets?'

'Same deal, or will be. They want Cheetah to produce books they can sell in every branch. They're going to be expanding into books there too.'

The room felt darkened and shrunken, but perhaps that was her state of mind. She found his comments so dispiriting that the only positive response she could offer was 'My cousin Hugh works for Frugo in Yorkshire.'

'Maybe soon the whole world will be working for them.' Glen added a laugh that seemed resigned to cynicism and said 'Your family for sure.'

'Not my cousin Rory. He'd starve first.' She took a mouthful of wine before asking 'So how do you think we can market Ellen's novel?'

'You tell me.'

'Well, I think it reads as if she knows her subject and cares about it too.'

'No, I mean sell the book to me. I'm a buyer. Thirty seconds or less.'

Charlotte felt boxed in by the dull dim faded volumes and his insistence. She didn't know how many seconds it took her to think of saying 'It's about people getting their own back.'

'That could sell. What kind of people?'

'Old folk who've been treated badly because there's nobody to look out for them, and so they have to discover their own power.'

'I'm just hearing old. I guess we're stuck with that, but why should I want to read about old guys in a home?'

'Because there are a lot of people in that situation?'

'No use going for my better nature. I'm shopping for product, not donating to charity. Don't hand me a collecting box.'

'Because your parents might be like that one day? Yours and everyone's.' His relentlessly expectant look had begun to peeve her. 'You might too,' she said.

'No point in giving me a hard time. We're talking fiction here. Guilt never sold that if it ever sold any kind of book.'

'It's about how you'd like to be when you're old,' Charlotte said in some desperation. 'Not as helpless as you'd be afraid to be. Able to fight back.'

'Me, I just want a quiet retirement on all the money I'll have made with books that sell. And by the way, your time ran out a while back.'

'You're supposed to be enthusiastic about her book,' Charlotte said and downed some wine to douse her anger. 'Your turn.'

'Hey, I'm only trying to show you how we'll have to think. I'm your friend, remember. Every book will need to have a concept we can package. Let's find one here.'

Charlotte was distracted by the bookseller, who had lifted a large book of English landscapes off a shelf only for the yellowed photographs of vanished views to sprawl out of the binding. As the man thrust the handful of images between the dilapidated covers and dumped the infirm volume on the shelf she said 'You start.'

'Try Sorcerous Seniors Strike Back. Magic's always going to sell, people need fantasy even if they know it's bullshit, and there's your revenge theme as well.'

'Don't you think it sounds like a comedy?'

'Sure. It should. That's what it needs to be.'

Charlotte had found Ellen's attempts at humour painfully facetious, by no means an unusual reaction to manuscripts she had to read but in this case uncomfortably personal. 'You think she could bring that off,' she said.

'I guess you'll do whatever it takes to show her how. Keep it black. Shock the readers, even the ones that think they can't be shocked. Get them arguing. Make it a book everyone will have heard of and won't want to say they haven't read.'

Charlotte wasn't sure how much of his enthusiasm could be ascribed to the wine, especially when he said 'Take the nurse who ends up incontinent. It's like your cousin doesn't want to admit she's writing about it. I'd want to see him suffer a lot worse. In public would be better too.'

'You don't think that's too basic.'

'The word is don't risk sales by aiming too high.' Glen laid a hand on her wrist while he said 'Listen, you're the editor. Tell me to shove my suggestions if you've got other ideas.'

'I wouldn't be so rude.'

'Hope you don't think I am,' he said before transferring his hand to his glass. 'The guy they turn blind, now. I figured they could do it to him when he's speeding in whatever snazzy car he owns.'

'Won't that seem too vindictive?'

'Depends how much they had to put up with. How about the woman who's in her second childhood gets raped by him? Or even a gang rape. Just so we've enough reason to wish the worst on the bad guys.'

Charlotte felt as if someone were wishing claustrophobia on her. Even if the cramped inadequately lit place that Glen was stuffing with ideas was her mind, the low dim room shrunken by the mass of books had become far too similar. 'Your title makes it sound as if that's them,' she said.

'*Bad Old Things*?' Having savoured it like another mouthful of wine, he said 'Nothing wrong with them being wicked if they were treated bad enough. The guy that ends up crippled like the woman he keeps tripping up, maybe they should make him get outrageous with his stick.'

She wondered if he would ever propose a change that she might simply agree with. 'That's a bit incorrect, isn't it?'

'Then maybe your cousin should target the public that's sick of correctness. If anyone objects, that's publicity too.'

'I'll have to see what she thinks.'

'Well, sure, and there's another point you need to put to her. I don't believe the story yet. It needs a better gimmick.' Glen emptied the bottle into his glass when Charlotte covered hers. 'Try this,' he said. 'Someone new moves in and sees how they're all being treated, and she turns out to be a witch.'

'Perhaps she could be the thirteenth resident.'

'I love it. Great idea. Now you're on the wavelength.'

Charlotte had been joking if not hoping the proposal would strike him as a step too far. As she strove to hold her expression neutral she felt watched, not just by Glen. The bookseller was kneeling in front of a shelf, and everyone at the bar had their backs to her. Peering about only seemed to bring the book-laden shelves closer, and she could have imagined that the earth around them was pressing them inwards – that the dimness adumbrated a seepage of earth. She could almost have thought that its smell was overtaking the odour of books. She was fending off the impressions as Glen said 'We ought to be writing some of this down. I'll email it to you tomorrow, all I can remember.'

He drained his glass and raised the empty bottle. 'Shall we celebrate?'

'I think I've had enough, thanks, Glen.'

'Better eat, then,' he said and recaptured her wrist. 'Let me buy dinner.'

She felt as if he were shackling her under the earth. 'Can we make it another time?' she murmured. 'I wouldn't mind heading for home.'

'Whatever's good for you. Let's make it soon, though, yes? How's next week?'

'I should think it's fine.'

'Look forward to it,' he said or advised, relinquishing her wrist. As she stood up he said 'Not finishing your drink?'

'It's yours,' Charlotte said and hurried to the stairs, where a musty breath caught in her throat. The open air was less of a relief than she had anticipated; the length of blue sky looked clamped by the roofs, brought low by them. 'See you on Monday,' she said as soon as Glen appeared, 'and thanks for everything.' As he set out for the car park she turned towards Tottenham Court Road, only to remember that the train was underground. She didn't need to understand her yearning to be in the open and closer to the sky. The train was quicker than the bus, and once she was home she could go on the roof.

FOUR

Hugh had just managed to locate the nightwear section on the upper floor of Frugo when his supervisor beckoned him with a pudgy indolent finger towards the beds. 'Is it all right if I leave you now?' Hugh said.

The older woman mopped her brow with a handkerchief, and her daughter gave her a sympathetic glance. 'Thanks for the tour.'

As Justin folded his arms above his prominent stomach, his expensive pale-blue shirt from Frugo Dude puffed out a spicy scent of Conqueror deodorant. His even paler eyes peered at Hugh from beneath a black fringe combed low on his wide smooth forehead. Their earnestness seemed designed to contradict his other features – nose snub enough to be accused of cuteness, inadvertently pouting mouth, face rounded by at least one additional chin. 'What was that supposed to be about,' he said, 'the scenic route?'

'The more they see the more they might buy,' Hugh thought and less distinctly said.

'I don't remember that in our mission manual.'

'Maybe I should put it in the suggestion box.'

'It'll have to wait. You've done enough wandering all over the show when you're meant to be stacking your shelves.' As Hugh felt his face grow patchy with resentment Justin said 'If there's any problem I should know about, I'm here.'

'It's you. It's how you take breaks whenever you think nobody's looking and suck up to management while other people are getting on with their work. And half the time you never finished a job so I had to finish it for you, and then you took all the credit and got the promotion I should have got.' Even if he found the nerve to say any of this, what would it achieve beyond losing him his job? 'I don't know my way around the new floor yet,' he said.

'Then you should have paid attention when we all walked through.' Justin expelled a breath that twitched a spider's leg of hair in its nasal burrow and said 'Better skedaddle back to your wine.'

For a moment Hugh forgot where the escalator was, and then he saw the restless rubber banister between two wardrobes at the far side of the maze of beds. As the lower floor spread into view, he was borne towards a customer leaning on a trolley and a stick in front of the poster for the month's wine promotion. The man wore a short-sleeved shirt, white except for the armpits, and trousers even more generously proportioned than himself. 'Where's this?' he greeted Hugh by asking.

'Happy to show you,' Hugh said by the book.

He could have imagined that excessively thin footsteps were accompanying the customer behind him, but of course the stick was. When he halted in front of the wine shelves at the far end of the widest aisle, the last rap sounded vigorous enough to be knocking on a trapdoor. 'What's your best deal?' the man said.

'Frugo's Own Extra Special White and Red Peruvian Sauvignon is half price this month, and there's an extra five per cent off six or more.'

'Give us a dozen. Make it red.'

Hugh planted six in the trolley, only to expose the empty shelf behind them. There were none among the cases he'd loaded onto his float in the stockroom. 'Let me see if we've got more,' he said and slapped his forehead harder than he meant to, having turned the wrong way along the aisle of soft drinks.

The door to the delivery lobby was beyond the bottled waters. The staff lift was empty except for a crumpled left-hand rubber glove resting on its wrist as if the shrivelled brown fingers were groping up through the stained floor. Nevertheless the windowless grey cage had scarcely begun its descent with a creak that sounded older than the building when someone muttered Hugh's name.

He twisted around so fast that his feet nearly tripped him. Of course he was alone, and the nearest thing to a speaker – the emergency phone embedded in the metal wall – was beside the controls to the right of the door. The voice had sounded less muffled than buried, and oddly directionless. It must have been on the public address system, calling him in the basement as well as through the store. He was still trying to identify it when the doors crept open.

The stockroom extended under the whole of the supermarket, but in every direction the view was obscured by boxes and cartons and cases piled higher than his head. Some of the gaps between the stacks of merchandise were so narrow that a single float blocked them. Cartons blinkered his vision as he stepped away from the lift, and he spent a few seconds trying to determine where liquid was dripping. It was the shrill blink of a faulty fluorescent tube across the room. 'Anyone in here?' he enquired as the lift shut with a surreptitious clunk. 'Was someone paging me?'

Although nobody responded, he had the impression that he wasn't alone in the basement. Why would any of his workmates refuse to answer? Perhaps they were up to something they would rather keep quiet – perhaps a couple of them were together. Hugh blushed as he lifted the phone from the wall beside the lift and used the intercom. 'This is Hugh. If anyone wants me I'm fetching from the stockroom.'

His own dislocated voice surrounded him. Although the speakers were up in the corners of the room, he could have thought he was hearing a stifled echo somewhere in the maze of merchandise. It distracted him enough that he forgot to end the call before replacing the receiver, and the amplified clatter filled the basement from four directions at once. The idea that Justin must have heard his incompetence made his face hotter, and for a moment he didn't know which way to turn.

The wine was stored at the back, extending from the left corner. He dodged through the maze as fast as he could, because the room felt cold as stone that had never been touched by the sun. The concrete floor, which was grubby with shadows, appeared to be shivering on his behalf. It owed its eager instability to the twittering of the light, which also made the cartons that hid his section restless. Their hulking shadows kept up a primitive dance along the adjacent wall, in the refrigerator cabinets full of Frugo Fusion items for the delicatessen: Fruit Dim Sum, Chicken Tikka Masala Pizza, Thai Style Sushi, Tandoori Smoky Bacon, Black Pudding Pizza, Gnocchi Stroganoff, Gumbo Pizza . . . Sweet 'n' Sour Steak 'n' Kidney Pie had been withdrawn for lack of popularity, though it might be relaunched with a shorter title. Hugh had to clear his head of the clamour of names before he was able to locate a case of Peruvian Red in the middle of a stack.

He was replacing the cases he'd had to shift when he seemed to sense movement nearby. He could see nothing new over his shoulder, even if the piles of cartons looked anxious to topple, undermined by the unsteadiness that the light imparted to the floor. Hoisting the case of wine, he tried to take the most direct route to the lift, but more than one aisle was blocked by wheeled floats. He was somewhere in the middle of the labyrinth of merchandise when he heard his name.

It was much closer than any of the corners of the room, yet he couldn't tell where. It felt directionless enough to be inside his head. Was the mutterer hiding to one side of him or behind him or beyond one of any number of stacks of boxes in front of him? Hugh could have imagined it was beneath him, and when he glanced at the floor it seemed to stir like troubled mud. Only shadows did, but he still recoiled, and the weight of the case propelled him several extra steps backwards until he stumbled aside. The stockroom felt colder than ever, as if all the refrigerators had opened wide, and he fought to overcome his shivering so as not to drop the wine. He hitched the case higher on his chest and made to step forwards, and then he realised that he couldn't see the lift. Indeed, he no longer knew where it was.

Had he turned around? As soon as he did, he didn't know how far. He was surrounded by boxed barbecues that helped emphasise the subterranean chill. He hugged the case and glared about at stack after stack upon stack of boxes standing monolithically inert. The longer he stood there the heavier the case would grow, but he felt as if its weight and his disorientation were capable of paralysing him. Surely he ought to be able to work out his position by locating the different lines of stock, except that his growing panic seemed to flatten all meaning out of the descriptions on the cartons, which might have been printed in an unknown language. He had to move, and so he staggered sidelong away from the nervous light, only to realise that he no longer knew which side of the oppressively crowded room he was making for.

He hadn't felt so helplessly trapped inside his brittle skull since discovering that he was useless as a teacher, when less than a fortnight in front of a classful of teenagers apparently determined to break him had left him terrified even to get out of bed. That was as near to a breakdown as he ever wanted to venture, and he'd given up his place at training college to seek another job, any job. However dismaying his failure had been, the vindictiveness that had caused him to fail was worse, and now he felt surrounded by a version of it that resembled a memory he very much preferred not to revive. The concepts of left and right had deserted him, and the ideas of ahead and behind were losing significance. He couldn't see the lift when he dodged to one side and then to the other while the jerky light plucked at his vision as though encouraging him to prance back and forth, to lose his way even more thoroughly. Nothing made sense outside his skull, and that was a dark cramped place in which he had no idea where to turn. He was clutching the wine to his chest, both for fear of dropping it and because its solidity was the nearest thing to even a hint of reassurance, when he heard a voice.

He pivoted towards the side of the room where its owner was lurking, whichever side that was. As he regained his hold on the case of wine, which had almost slipped from his aching arms, the muffled voice was answered by another. Both were female, unlike the one he'd previously heard. 'Where are you?' he shouted.

They didn't acknowledge him, unless their amusement did. Hugh sidled a few paces, which only aggravated the confusion all around him. 'What's funny?' he protested. 'Why won't you show yourselves?'

His panic might have driven even Hugh beyond politeness if the girls from the cosmetics section hadn't strolled into view at the end of an aisle. He could have taken them for contestants in a slimming competition, not to mention one for blondeness. Tamara turned sideways to hold a round-bottomed pose for a second. 'Seen enough, Hugh Lucas?'

Without copying the posture Mishel said 'That's all we're showing of ourselves to you.'

'I didn't mean that,' Hugh declared, but his vehemence didn't stop his face from growing hot and, he knew, mottled. 'Who was calling?'

The girls stared at him and even more incredulously at each other. 'You were,' Tamara said.

'I don't mean just now. Who was saying my name?'

'On the intercom?' Mishel said with every appearance of concern.

'I suppose.'

The girls burst out laughing. When she could Tamara said 'That was you.'

'I didn't mean then,' Hugh pleaded, sidling to keep the girls in sight as they lost interest in him and returned to the aisle they'd emerged from. In a moment he saw why their voices had started out muffled. The girls hadn't been hiding from him. They'd been in the lift, which was beyond them.

He dashed along the aisle as if the case of wine were dragging him. He kept his gaze on the metal doors while he jabbed the button and struggled to hold onto the case and poked the button again. When the doors parted at last he staggered in and leaned on the case against the wall as he groped to send the lift upwards. He was labouring to face them when they opened once more, revealing the lobby and Justin. 'Where did you get to?' Justin demanded. 'I've been having to hold your customer.'

'I couldn't find –'

'Just give me that.'

Justin seized the case and drummed his fingers on it while Hugh typed the exit code on the keypad by the door. As he marched out, Hugh was at his heels. 'There you are,' the customer said in case Hugh needed to be told. 'We thought you'd got lost.'

'Sorry,' Hugh blurted.

'No need to go red in the face about it. He's the one doing the carrying.'

'Plenty of shelving whenever you're ready,' Justin said.

At least Hugh's resentment overcame his panic as he returned to his shelves. If he found out who'd been trying to distract him he would bring their behaviour to the attention of the management, although shouldn't it have been noticed? The incident was so much like a dream that he ought to be able to put it out of his mind. Once Justin ushered the customer to the Loads o' Loaves aisle Hugh managed to give up his grudge too. He was close to emptying the float onto the shelves, and feeling as if he'd regained the control he had inexplicably lost, when Justin reappeared. 'Fancy being helpful?' he said.

'I think I am.'

'Well, here's your chance to prove it.' Justin looked satisfied with his quip. 'We're losing Selma from edibles. Ate a left-over roll she should have binned at the end of trading, and you know that's the instant sack.' He stared at Hugh as if to emphasise a warning. 'You'll be taking over tinned foods,' he said. 'Just don't start taking after your brother.'

FIVE

'Yo Yorkshire! That was Bradford band Benign Lumps with their new single "Crutches", and this is Sabyasachi Chatterjee with the Sabya Show on Moorland Radio. In the studio with me I have Rory Lucas, Yorkshire's most controversial artist. Rory's sculpture *Can Do* has been on the airwaves lately, and that's why we have him here today to discuss his work and any other arty topics you want to phone about. Was that a face, Rory? Don't you like me calling it a sculpture?'

Rory hadn't been aware of betraying a reaction. 'I don't care what anybody calls it so long as they look for themselves.'

The presenter ducked to a clipboard, giving Rory more of a view of his slick black precisely parted hair. 'You haven't always gone in for this style of work, have you?'

'I've not just piled up litter on the moor, you mean, Sabyasachi.'

'Call me Sabya.' At the hint of conflict his eyes gleamed with anticipation, though his voice stayed suave. 'You were top of your art class at school, weren't you?'

Rory might have borne this kind of regressively nostalgic

comment from Betty or Albert, but not from a radio host. 'I did what they wanted,' he said.

'We all have to start by toeing the line if we want to get anywhere, don't we? That's what I tell my daughters. So then you went to art school.'

'Down to London where they think the world is.'

'Quite a lot of art is, isn't it?'

'It's everywhere. It's even here.'

A smile that might have been wryly appreciative flickered across Sabyasachi's full lips. 'I go down to see the exhibitions. I've got family in Brick Lane,' he said. 'Now here are the Refreshing Tissues from Leeds with their latest single.'

As he set the disc off he raised a mobile phone. For all Rory knew the impassioned conversation might have been about him, since he couldn't recognise a word. His incomprehension made him feel enclosed, not just within the fat white walls but inside his head. 'Yo Yorkshire,' Sabyasachi said as the song ended with a flourish of guitars. 'Refreshing Tissues with their single "Left Behind". My guest this afternoon –'

'We are the shadows on the land,' Rory couldn't wait to say, quoting the refrain of the song. 'That goes for art too.'

'Don't they say art's longer than life?'

'You mean it's older. Old paintings, you can't see how they really were. Even if they're restored, that's not how they were to begin with. Everything changes, you as well. We don't need art, we just need to look and listen and feel and get a sense of how we really are.'

'Careful or you'll be talking yourself out of a job.'

'It's not a job, it's what I am. It doesn't have to be a job as well.'

'You mean you don't need to earn a living while Yorkshire Arts is giving you a grant.'

'As long as they're offering I'd be a fool not to take it.'

'Plenty for our listeners to talk to you about. So the year after you left art school your first exhibition got good reviews, but here's a caller. Rory, you need to put your headphones on.'

They felt like earmuffs, even when they acquired Sabyasachi's voice. Rather than bringing it closer, they surrounded Rory's ears with an aloof version of it. 'Hello Mike from Batley. What do you want to say to Rory Lucas?'

The caller sounded even more muffled. 'Are you having a joke on us all, Mr Lucas?'

'I –' Rory swallowed hard, but that didn't render his own voice any less remote. Feeling both cut off from it and confined by it was so much of an obstruction that he hardly knew what he said to overcome his inhibited silence. 'Life's a bit of a joke.'

'I'll wager it looks that way to somebody that's being paid to do the kind of thing you're doing.'

Rory struggled to outdistance the hindrance of his dislocated voice. 'You'll have been to look, then.'

'I don't need to see it to know it's rubbish.'

'No, that's what it was.' The retort seemed to lose force by surrounding Rory at a distance. 'That's what it was,' he had to repeat, 'before I recycled it.'

'There's bins for that. You'd be better off if you got a job emptying them, and a lot more important, us taxpayers would say.'

'No you wouldn't. The money would just be spent somewhere else you'd probably moan about by the sound of you.'

'Thank you, Mike. Mike from Batley,' Sabyasachi said and mouthed 'No need to shout.'

Rory had been trying to project some strength into his oppressively detached voice. 'Do I have to wear these?' he complained mutely. 'Can't you put it through the speakers?'

'It doesn't work like that,' Sabyasachi not just mimed but grimaced before saying, 'Here's Eunice from Holmfirth. You're on the air, Eunice.'

'What's his name, this vandal you're giving all the publicity?'

'Rory Lucas is my guest today. Did you have –'

Rory tried to fend off their dulled voices with his own. 'Do you know what vandal means?'

'People like you and the people you're attracting that vandalise our landscape.'

'Isn't that you if you've been to look?'

'Don't you dare say I find it attractive,' the caller said with a kind of stifled shrillness. 'We aren't given any choice when we're on the motorway. We have to see that rubbish heap and what people did to it.'

'What's that?' Rory was jolted into demanding.

'Don't you know? I thought you said you had to look for yourself.'

'Fine, don't tell me. I'll see later.' Rory felt hemmed in by his own muffled petulance. 'Whatever's happened, it's change,' he made the effort to declare. 'That's life.'

'You just said it was a joke. Don't you care about anything?' the caller said and transformed the question into a statement with the full stop of an emphatic plastic click.

'Eunice? We seem to have lost Eunice from Holmfirth,' Sabyasachi told anyone who ought to know. 'Here's Brenda from Bingley instead.'

There barely seemed to be: just a mumble buried in the headphones. As Rory reached to adjust them Sabyasachi mouthed 'Don't take those off.'

'I can't hear.'

'Brenda says you didn't answer.'

'That's because I didn't hear.' Rory yanked the headphones lower on his ears and felt more shut in than ever. 'Didn't answer what?' he supposed he had to learn.

'What you were asked,' a flat distant female voice said.

'I told you I couldn't hear you.'

'I didn't ask you anything.' As Rory decided she'd lost any right to politeness she added 'Eunice from Holmfirth did.'

'She rang off.'

'I'm sure we'd all still like to hear what you care about,' Sabyasachi said.

'Plenty.' Rory might have been more specific if he hadn't needed to say 'What?'

'Not books, Brenda said. You don't destroy them if you care about them,' the presenter added, possibly quoting the caller. 'You'll be thinking of his piece called Read, or was it Read?'

'It was both. Pronounce it how you like, and I didn't destroy anything.'

'Hold on for a minute, Brenda,' Sabyasachi said as a technician wearing a grey wool cap over her ears removed Rory's headphones and donned them. 'Hearing me?' the presenter said.

'Like you're in my head. Nothing up with these.'

As she boxed Rory in with the headphones Sabyasachi said 'Just fixing a glitch, Brenda. He's all yours.'

'Sounds pretty destructive to me, drowning *War and Peace* in an aquarium.'

If anything her voice seemed to have receded, inflaming Rory's frustration. 'Did you see it for yourself? Some people said it changed how they thought about books.'

'I wouldn't waste my time, but my sister saw your other silly business with the wheelchair.'

'That would be Age,' Sabyasachi supplied.

'Age isn't that senseless, and if it ever is he oughtn't to be making fun. Another fish tank with a wheelchair going rusty in the water.'

'It was the most talked-about piece in the exhibition,' Rory felt defensive for saying.

'I'll bet you couldn't broadcast what they said. You don't like criticism much, do you? Shouldn't it make you look again like you keep telling the rest of us to?'

'I do it all the time.' After a pause clogged with silence Rory said 'Is she still there?'

'I think you scared her off.' Sabyasachi patted the air, though Rory hadn't been conscious of shouting. 'Next up is Hugh from Huddersfield,' the presenter said. 'Have you a question for Rory Lucas, Hugh?'

'Where do you get your ideas?'

The voice was so faint that Rory wasn't sure he'd identified it. The invisibility of the caller made him feel as if the failure of one sense had robbed him of another. The sight of the pale boxy room didn't improve matters, nor did Sabyasachi's professionally expectant face. Rory tried closing his eyes, but not for long. 'Wherever other people don't,' he retorted while his lids sprang open as if he were fleeing a nightmare.

'Can't you say where, Rory?' It was indeed his brother, who appeared to think he could help by adding 'Your thing with the tins, didn't you get that from someone working in a supermarket?'

Rory was distracted by the notion that straining his ears had brought him more than Hugh. 'I'm taking all the blame,' he said.

'But didn't you say putting tins on the shelves was a kind of art too?'

Rory couldn't judge whether Hugh aimed to make his brother's work more accessible and populist or was hoping for some kind of acknowledgment. 'That's the truth,' he said.

'Then do you think –' Hugh seemed distracted, perhaps by an ill-defined sound. 'Do you think your things you've been talking about could be about the family?'

'You'll have to tell me how.' This was meant to dismiss the idea rather than invite an explanation, and Rory didn't wait for one. 'Are you at work?'

'No, at the house. Why?'

'I thought someone was calling you.'

'Weren't they saying our name at your end?'

Rory felt bound to say to Sabyasachi 'In case you're wondering, we're brothers.'

'Nothing wrong with family. Hugh, how are you saying Rory's work is about them? Is that including you?'

'I –' Hugh faltered, perhaps from embarrassment. 'I'm at Frugo,' he admitted, 'and our cousin looks after old people and the other one does publishing.'

'Tins and age and books,' the presenter said. 'Well, Rory, it sounds as if you secretly care about something.'

Rory didn't want to claim this as a reason to appreciate his work. 'Are you still hearing that, Hugh?'

'I can't,' Sabyasachi said. 'Have you any more insights for us, Hugh?'

'He's always been artistic.' Hugh's voice had begun to fall short of its intentions before he said 'Rory, I think I still can.'

'We'll need to say goodbye if you've got a crossed line.'

'Hold on,' Rory said and cupped his hands over the headphones. 'Do you want me to come and see you, Hugh?'

'No, you stay there. It's publicity.'

'When I'm done, I mean. You don't sound quite right to me.'

'Nothing's up at all. You ought to find out what they've done to your thing with the tins.'

'If you aren't talking about his work there are callers who want to.'

'I'll come and visit soon and we can go out for a meal or a drink,' Hugh said and was gone.

'Hugh there from Huddersfield speaking up for the family, and now we have Alf from Netherthong. What's your point, Alf?'

Rory watched more than heard Sabyasachi say all this. If there was another voice in the headphones, it sounded buried deep. Only the presenter's expectant look told Rory the caller had finished. 'What did he say?' he was reduced to asking.

Sabyasachi gazed at him before murmuring or mouthing 'You had to get your brother to come to your defence.'

'That's bollocks. I didn't know he was ringing up.'

Sabyasachi patted the air again as if cuffing a child, which left Rory's senses feeling even less reliable. 'Thanks, Alf, and now it's Daphne from Heckmondwike.'

Any voice was so muted that Rory couldn't even identify it as female. Perhaps he was hearing less than a voice inside his head – nothing but the echo of his name. When he grew aware of the presenter's waiting gaze he had no idea how loud he demanded 'What is it this time?'

'You don't seem to want to hear anything you don't like.'

'You're saying that or she is?' When Sabyasachi raised his eyebrows and his upturned hands Rory said 'It's bollocks either way.'

The presenter used both hands to tamp the air down. 'Be as lively as you like, but can you keep an eye on the language?'

The prospect of being restricted still further made Rory's brain feel shrunken. He snatched off the headphones but refrained from slamming them on the ledge in front of him. 'I talk how I talk, like I work how I work.'

'Daphne says that's almost a poem. Maybe you should try your hand at that.'

'Everyone should. Everyone's an artist. You just need to open up your senses.'

Sabyasachi touched his left headphone, apparently to indicate that he was reciting the call. 'In that case why do we need you.'

'You don't,' Rory said and walked out of the studio.

'A final bit of controversy there from concept artist Rory

Lucas,' Sabyasachi said through the speaker above the receptionist, who gave Rory a pink smile bordering on straight-lipped. 'Yo Yorkshire! This is the Sabya Show every weekday afternoon on Moorland Radio. My next guest will be Prue Walker, great-grandmother and founder of Wrinkles Against Racism . . .'

As Rory left the concrete building, which was so featureless it might almost have been designed to deny perception any hold, he saw the Frugo supermarket across the business park. If Hugh had been at work Rory could have looked in on him. Perhaps he'd found a girl at last, hence his reluctance to be visited. Unlike Rory, he hadn't discovered that he didn't need them.

Six lanes of traffic were racing back and forth across the moor under a blue sky and flocks of giant clouds. Rory climbed into the aR tSeVe rYwh eRe van and drove onto the motorway, where drivers peered at the letters stencilled on the sides and rear doors of the vehicle before signifying comprehension with an enlightened grin or an aggravated scowl. As he headed west, sunlight flooded across slopes aglow with heather, and someone else might have fancied it was celebrating his approach. Once the motorway began a protracted descent into a valley he saw *Can Do* on the horizon.

It looked dully familiar. It never had before, and he tried to see it from the viewpoint of a new spectator. At this distance the jagged mass against the stately clouds resembled the ruins of a castle or of some less identifiable building. Closer, colours formed within the outline, eventually betraying that the bulk was constructed from thousands of tins. The viewer would experience a shift of perspective, having grasped that to be separately visible at that distance the tins must be unusually large. They were the biggest cans of paint Rory could find, and he'd lost count of the number of times he'd loaded the van before driving up on the moor to paint every tin the colour of its contents and glue it into place. He'd done his best to see that the arrangement was completely random, but perhaps that was an impossible task. There was an inadvertent pattern, so simple a child could have produced it. Wasn't childlike desirable? Weren't those the perceptions he believed everybody should recapture? Childish was the word that occurred to him just now, perhaps because he felt dispirited by his introversion. He was driving out of the valley, past a herd of sluggish trucks, before he observed that someone had sprayed paint over his work.

Wasn't this a kind of life? The trouble was that when he drove off the motorway, along the road that passed by *Can Do*, his mind felt as distanced as ever. He parked as close as the road would take him and stepped down from the van. The turf and especially the heather must be springy underfoot, but the sight of the graffiti was dulling his senses. The scrawl didn't even include words, let alone any meaningful image or use of colour. It was the kind of random anonymous doodling that showed up on derelict buildings, a mass of drooling pallid purple loops. Didn't they add to the enigma that *Can Do* presented to any distant spectator? Might this enliven a few minds? He turned to shade his eyes and peer at the traffic coursing up and down the landscape, but it was pointless to look for signs of interest. He felt as if the graffiti had infected his work with their meaninglessness, unless they were a kind of comment. Perhaps they demonstrated how uninspired and uninspiring his work was, and not just this example. Should he revert to being uninspired in a way that pleased the public? Once he might have painted the landscape, until he'd seen that paintings were as redundant as photographs, pathetic samples of reality if not attempted substitutes for it. Nevertheless he was surveying the moor in case it could entice his perceptions out of the dark undefined place into which they seemed to have sunk, when he thought he heard his name.

He'd turned his mobile phone off at Moorland Radio, and it was still dormant. Nobody was hiding behind *Can Do*, though more graffiti were. They weren't even visible to traffic, which added to their meaninglessness. He was standing in the shadow of the discoloured piles of metal when the voice repeated 'Rory Lucas.'

Was it just in his head? It seemed muffled enough. As he dodged around the cans, darkness sped across the moor towards him, flattening the heather and the grass. A wind must be up, although he couldn't feel it. His senses had flinched inwards, away from the voice and its implications. His imagination must be playing tricks. He'd stimulated it too much.

A glossy crow sailed up from the undergrowth at the edge

of the road and flew straight at him. He was wondering how it could fail to see him – if it took him for part of *Can Do* – when he realised that it was a plastic bag. Ordinarily he would have appreciated the visual pun, but just now it disturbed him. Was he smoking too much skunk to keep his senses primed? He'd never known the effects to linger the next day. He didn't enjoy hallucinating unless he'd set out to achieve it, still less the useless experience of hearing voices. As the airborne litter subsided in the clutches of a patch of heather he tried to hear the voice again, to prove he could produce it and silence it at will. The effort shrank his consciousness until he lost all awareness of his surroundings, but he wasn't certain that he heard his name in his head. Then he grasped what he was doing – attempting to rouse a hallucination before he had to drive. The notion dismayed him as much as the idea that the voice was lying in wait to take him off guard, and he fled to the van as another flood of shadow rushed towards it. He was glad Hugh hadn't wanted him to visit. He would feel safer at home.

SIX

Ellen felt as if she were being scrutinised not just by Mrs Stevens but by the framed photograph on the desk. She was about to favour it with a remark when she heard sounds overhead: a heavy thud followed by a cry. The proprietor of the Peacebrook Home didn't react, and nobody seemed to have gone to the aid of the injured, even once the cry was repeated with additional anguish. 'Should I go and see what's happened, do you think?' Ellen was driven to ask.

'There'll be no need for that, thank you.'

Mrs Stevens sat back in her generous leather chair, and the lower reaches of her sleeveless blouse bulged as though celebrating her last meal or many of them. Her small face was set in plushy flesh that underlined her diminutive chin with a larger version, while her pale arms were so plump they hardly seemed defined. Ellen had been reflecting that at least she was slimmer by comparison, but now she was worried about whoever had fallen. The cry came again, and she was on the way to standing up despite the proprietor's reply when she heard an exaggerated voice that she guessed was a nurse's. 'Have you knocked your table over again, Thora? There it is for you. We'll have to see about getting it screwed to the floor, won't we? Why don't you come down and sit with the others now. Your quiz show that you like is on soon.'

He sounded as smug as Mrs Stevens had settled into looking. If Ellen had turned the situation into a test, she had no idea how she'd fared. As she sank back onto the chair its creak made her feel yet more examined. 'Sorry,' she said sooner than she'd planned to speak.

'Ah,' Mrs Stevens said, perhaps with satisfaction. 'What for?'

'I wasn't meaning to imply nobody was dealing with it.' When Mrs Stevens only gazed at her Ellen said 'I suppose I did, but I was wrong.'

'Nothing wrong with being conscientious.'

'I'm that, I hope. I'd look after your residents the way I'd look after any of my family.'

'Do they need it?'

'My family?' The proprietor's question seemed both irrelevant and oddly ominous. 'They're fine,' Ellen said. 'My parents are forever travelling and my cousins are all working.'

'If more people cared for their families there'd be less need for us.'

Since she was resting her fingers on top of the photograph, Ellen wondered if she had the couple – a young white man arm in arm with a young black woman – in mind. 'Yours?' she said.

'Why, do you see a problem?'

'I hope not. No, of course not. Certainly there shouldn't be.' Ellen thought she was saying too much and then not enough as the proprietor's gaze failed to change. 'They're your children, are they?' she said, which earned no response. 'Adopted?' she tried saying.

'Why are you asking that?'

'I don't mean both. It needn't be either.' Ellen felt as if she were strewing her words in her path. 'I don't even know why I said it. Forget I spoke.'

Mrs Stevens turned the photograph away from Ellen. 'They're my son and his partner.'

'Of course, I should have known.'

'Why should you?'

'Tell me if I'm trying too hard,' Ellen said and worked on a laugh. 'I just want to make sure you don't get the wrong impression.'

'You are.'

'Well then, I'll stop.'

'And I will,' Mrs Stevens said, caressing the top of the frame. 'I'm afraid you aren't suitable for the post.'

Ellen's face felt puffed up with dismay. 'Because of what I just said? I'm sorry if I was clumsy, but surely I wasn't rude.'

'How much more of my time are you proposing to waste, Miss Lomax? I'm surprised you attended the interview.'

'I don't believe in letting people down.'

Mrs Stevens shook her head as if Ellen's remark were an insect to be driven off, and her lower chin quivered while the smaller one stayed unsympathetically firm. 'Just in taking them for fools,' she said.

'I really don't think that's fair. How have I done it to you?'

The question appeared to topple the proprietor. Without taking her gaze from Ellen, she leaned sideways out of her chair. Her face seemed to swell or sag in that direction as she reached down for a newspaper, which she brandished like a warning to a dog. It was the *Knowsley Globe*, a local weekly. 'Seen enough?' she said.

'I haven't. If there's something I –'

Mrs Stevens leafed through the paper so vehemently that Ellen was surprised the pages didn't tear. Not much less than halfway through she turned it towards Ellen with such eagerness that it left several pages behind. 'Here you are,' she said in a kind of triumph.

Ellen saw the photograph first, such as it was. She'd hidden her face from the photographer outside the town hall because Muriel's comment had made her feel worse than plain, but she looked as if she had been trying to conceal her identity. How fat a face was her fat hand not quite able to cover up? The headline beside them snatched her gaze away. TRIBUNAL UPHOLDS DISMISSAL OF CARE HOME WORKER, it said.

The report insisted that the panel had convicted Ellen Lomax of racist attitudes and intolerance of disability and bullying a vulnerable elderly witness. Having parted her thick lips with her outsize tongue, she managed to mumble 'It isn't true.'

'We've always found it reliable.'

'How can they print this when I haven't even been told?'

Mrs Stevens tidied the newspaper and folded her arms. 'I don't think they have to ask your permission to publish the news.'

'Not the paper, the tribunal. They haven't told me anything.'

'Dear me, someone has been thoughtless.'

'Yes, the paper. How could they put in all that and not interview me?'

'Perhaps they tried.' When Ellen uttered something like a laugh Mrs Stevens said 'Our son works for them. You'll have to excuse me now. I've an applicant to see in a few minutes.'

Ellen worked her stiff lips until she was able to say 'You never were going to give me a chance, were you?'

'I wanted to see how far you'd take it so I can advise my colleagues in the business.'

Ellen rose to her feet at a speed that she tried to find more dignified than ponderous. As she plodded out of the room she felt weighed down by the proprietor's gaze, but as she closed the door she found that Mrs Stevens had crouched forwards, face drooping as she pencilled comments on an application letter. Ellen was tramping along the hall when a voice above her said 'Are you the new girl?'

A woman was clinging to the banister two-handed while she lumbered downstairs. Although she was mostly enveloped in a voluminous long-sleeved floral dress, Ellen saw that her legs were twice as wide as her feet. 'I'm sorry, I'm not,' she said. 'I won't be working here.'

'Didn't you like our home?'

As disappointment shaped her mouth it threatened to infect Ellen's. 'So long as you do,' she said and had to turn away.

'I wish you wouldn't go. You're a jolly sort, I can tell. Some of these thin ones are a bit grim.' The old lady took a step that trembled the stairs and said 'Us fatties ought to stick together.'

She only meant that Ellen was less scrawny than whoever she found lacking in humour, but Ellen felt as if a memory that she preferred not to revive were lying in wait for her. 'Sorry, I'm not welcome,' she mumbled and was on her way to the front door when she caught sight of herself in a mirror across the lounge. Several seated residents turned to watch as she leaned through the doorway. She looked smaller than a child, but her head was swelling out of proportion, pumping up her cheeks so that they dwarfed the rest of her face. The expansion had spread lower than her shoulders before she recoiled, to be addressed by Mrs Stevens along the hall. 'Wrong door, Miss Lomax. Nobody wants you in there.'

'I hope you find a suitable replacement,' Ellen said with the remains of her dignity and let herself out of the house.

Had the afternoon grown humid, or was that her body? As she crossed the car park the sunlight felt treacly on her skin. She wanted to be home, to look up the phone number of the tribunal, but she could have mistaken her urgency for fever. Her skin was crawling with moisture by the time she reached the road to Hesketh Park.

Crossing the park on her way to the interview, she'd imagined walking through all its seasons to her new job. She'd wished she had a notebook for scribbling her observations: a girl being led by the hand past the duck pond by a boy stripped to the waist for some kind of action; a Crazy Golf course so miniature that you couldn't call it crazy, just mildly deranged. This no longer seemed inspired, and as she passed the aviary beyond the vandalised greenhouses she was distracted by a rooster puffing itself up. It reminded her of her appearance in the mirror, and so did the chubby-cheeked jovial moon on the front of a small blue engine carrying toddlers along a path. Perhaps she could do without a notebook.

Three-storey blocks of apartments faced her side of the park, but hers was at the far end of a side street. The numbers of her cousins' first initials admitted her to the square white concrete lobby. Mrs Sharp from the left-hand ground-floor flat kept replenishing a vase on a table with flowers from her plot behind the block. The current bunch was as white as the solitary envelope beside the vase. Although it hadn't been there when Ellen had picked up her mail – bills and offers rendered personal by computers – it was addressed to her. Someone had ringed the address with an incontinent blue ballpoint and scrawled more than one sputtering version of a word beside it.

MISDELE was succeeded by MISDILIVERED, so forcefully that several of the letters were italics.

The item had been posted first class several days ago. Ellen tore open the envelope and unfolded the single sheet, which was apparently all it took to sum her up. The Appellant's attitude to a disabled witness was judged to be unsatisfactory. Her approach to this witness went some way beyond cross-examination and, given the age and frailty of the witness, could only be described as bullying. The Appellant displayed tolerance of racism and exhibited racist tendencies of her own. By the unanimous decision of the Tribunal, the appeal of the Appellant is dismissed and the decision of the Respondent is upheld.

The sheet bore a telephone number, but what would calling it achieve? The impersonal language had left her feeling exposed, unfamiliar to herself, guilty of behaviour she hadn't been aware of. What else was she unwilling to acknowledge about herself? She was refolding the page rather than screwing it up in her fist when she saw Mrs Sharp's Punto puttering into the car park. She didn't want to talk to anyone just now. She ran upstairs, at least until she reached the last flight, and arrived panting on the top floor.

Her family were waiting in her hall, or rather Rory's portraits were. He'd made prints for his cousins and Hugh while he was at art school. Each of them was gazing past the artist as if they were seeing the future, but now their fixed stares seemed more ominous; she might almost have imagined that they'd noticed an intruder. Ellen shut the door and halted in front of her own portrait, where her faint reflection on the glass doubled the image. Whichever way she moved she was unable to fit her present face within the younger model. Why was she wasting time? She ought to be checking whether she'd heard from Charlotte.

The computer occupied much of the desk beside the bookshelf full of Cougar titles in the main room. She switched on to find there was indeed an email from her cousin, headed *Take Care?* It was hundreds of lines long, and she sent them racing down the screen as she tried to find their point. Cougar might want her novel, but not under that title. Charlotte's senior editor Glen had suggestions for improvements – many of them, though some were Charlotte's. Ellen felt heady with elation and yet heavy with the prospect of so much extra work on a story she'd been sure was finished. In particular she could have done without Glen's choice of words or Charlotte's decision to quote them unedited. 'Right now your work feels bloated. Try to slim it down.'

SEVEN

As Charlotte looked away from the poster of a flooded St Mark's Square the restaurant manager said 'Have you gone?'

'To Venice? Only in my dreams.'

'She ought to make them real, shouldn't she, Fausto?' Glen said and pointed at her with the grappa bottle. 'You could be there quicker than it took us to eat dinner. You can sink into the past like nowhere else I know.'

The thought of being shut in an aeroplane for hours made the small noisy Venetian restaurant feel cramped. 'Sink looks like the word,' she said.

Despite the lamps reflected in the water, she could easily have taken the black expanse for mud that was about to engulf the dim basilica. The impression seemed to darken the lanterns on the tables and to shade the manager's already swarthy face, unless her remark had pained him. 'I meant it's not the best advertisement,' she said.

'Our daughter took it. We asked for it so big.'

'It's a great photograph. She must be talented.'

'Your family's creative too, right, Charlotte?'

'Some of us are.'

She meant to leave herself out, but the manager was grinning at Glen. 'Is she another of your writers?'

'I'm just a colleague.'

'Hey, less of the just.'

'*Bella*, anyhow.' The manager pinched a kiss from his lips to flick towards Charlotte. Perhaps he was indicating the grappa, since he added 'On the house.'

'*Bella* for sure, Fausto. The end to a perfect evening.'

The manager gave Charlotte a comical frown. 'Don't say it is the end.'

As he sidled away between the tables, pulling in his proud dinner-suited stomach so as not to dislodge a pink-check tablecloth, Charlotte murmured 'Another in what sense?'

At first she wasn't sure that Glen had heard, given the Vivaldi that had joined the uproar, having lent the restaurant its name. He rested his gaze on her before saying 'A girl I was seeing wanted to write us a book. It didn't work out.'

'Sorry to hear it.'

'I should have known you shouldn't get too close to your writers.'

'Are you saying I am? Gosh, that's more than enough.'

He'd replenished her liqueur glass to the brim. As he refilled his own he said 'Not so long as you can be an editor. How's work progressing on your cousin's book?'

'I've sent her the suggestions.'

Glen stoppered the grappa, none too firmly. 'Any comeback yet?'

'She's had a new idea.'

'Fine if it works with ours. Sounds like we triggered her imagination.'

'An idea for another book.'

'OK then, sounds like she's productive. Don't forget your drink.'

Charlotte had a sip of brandy to fire up her enthusiasm. 'Four people share some kind of magical experience but they don't realise till years later when it starts to affect all their lives.'

'Go on,' Glen said and more than matched her sip.

'That's all so far. Maybe she doesn't want to risk developing it till she's had a response.'

'We need to see how she shapes up with *Bad Old Things*. If she fixes that I guess we'd want to option her next novel. Did you talk to her?'

'Not yet.'

'You could tell her that. Could be it's what she needs.'

'All right, I will.' Charlotte felt as if she'd neglected her cousin, although she had been waiting to speak to Glen. 'I'll call her now,' she said. 'I'll be outside.'

Ellen's soft voice couldn't have competed with the din, but as Charlotte unfolded her mobile beside a dormant streetlamp under the nine o'clock sky she realised how oppressive she'd begun to find the boisterous dimness. If there hadn't been so many people spilling off the pavements of Camden Road, outside would have been more of a relief. The phone had almost rung enough to rouse the answering service before the simulated bell subsided. 'Is that my author?' Charlotte said.

'Would you want it to be, Charlotte?'

'I wouldn't have written all that to you otherwise.'

'I knew really. Thanks for spending so much time on me. You're not still at work, are you? You sound shut in.'

'I'm not. I'm outside a restaurant.'

'Not dining alone, I hope.'

'I've just had dinner with Glen. I mentioned him, my senior editor.'

'You don't mean old.'

'Four years older.'

'That's not too bad, is it? He's the one who's giving you ideas. What did you think of my new one?'

Charlotte glanced around, but nobody was eavesdropping. 'I was wondering what kind of magical experience.'

'The kind you don't know was one till it's got inside you and changed you. That's part of the point, the people it happened to didn't notice.' Ellen paused and said 'I hoped you might help me work it out.'

'Glen thinks we need to concentrate on your novel first, so you'll have some kind of track record.'

'I wouldn't want to cause any friction.' Before Charlotte

could absolve her of the possibility Ellen said 'Will you have time to help me if I need you?'

'You know I'm here whenever you do,' Charlotte promised, only to wonder 'Now, do you mean?'

'Of course not now. I don't like to think I'm interrupting your date.'

'*I* did that. So what would you like me to do?' Charlotte thought it best to add 'About your book.'

'Can I send you bits when I think they're done?'

'Absolutely.'

'And if you still don't think it's right . . .' Rather than continue Ellen said 'I'll try not to let it take up too much of your time. I'll be giving it all of mine.'

'You mean you've given up looking for another job.'

'Wherever I tried they'd be able to check what was said about me. It won't do me any harm to stay out of sight for a while.'

Passers-by were crowding close to Charlotte, but nobody was peering around the streetlamp beside her. 'Why, who's been saying what?' she protested.

'Do you mind if I don't talk about it? Let's just say I wouldn't look suitable for the kind of job I used to do. Maybe I've been denying I'm what people say I am.'

'If it's anything bad I very much doubt it. Honestly, Ellen, you should tell me so we can deal with it together.'

'Just tell me if you think I'm a writer.'

'If you're willing to do all the work I'd say you must be.'

'Then I definitely must, because you're a lot more of one.'

Charlotte would have met this with a modest smile if they had been face to face. Before she could think of a verbal equivalent, Ellen said 'I was going to ask if you still don't think I've got it right, would you have time to rewrite it for me?'

'Let's hope that won't be necessary. Let's see how well you can do.'

'Have there ever been cousins who collaborated on a book? By Charlotte Nolan and Ellen Lomax.' A silence suggested she was dreaming of the prospect until she said 'Would you get half the money?'

'Of course not, Ellen. I'm being paid to edit.'

'Do you think I'll be seeing some soon?'

Charlotte heard how casual Ellen was trying to sound. 'As long as you're happy to work on the changes I'll look into what can be done.'

'We'll stay in touch, shall we? Not just us.' Ellen might have paused for thought, but all she said was 'Anyway, I've kept you away from your date long enough. I hope you'll be pleased with me.'

With that she was gone. Charlotte folded up her phone and dodged through the crowd to the Vivaldi. How had she overlooked the lowness of the ceiling? The room hardly seemed to have space for so much clamorous dimness, let alone for her. She might have indicated that she would wait for Glen outside if he hadn't been sitting with his back to the door. As she struggled alongside the table he reached for the grappa. 'Anything to celebrate?'

'Maybe, but do you think we're finished here? I'm feeling a bit closed in.'

'Let's chase that, then. I've got the check.' When Charlotte made to take out her purse he said 'No, I mean I got it.'

'Well, thank you for a very pleasant evening.'

As they emerged into the crowded thickening darkness he said 'Can you use a coffee?'

'If I'm buying, Glen.'

'Everything's bought,' he said and steered her by the elbow towards Kentish Town.

As they left the crowd beyond a side street where three-storey houses propped up the black sky, he let go of her arm. He turned along a narrower street and then down one that might be narrower still. All at once his height dropped inches, followed by twice that. 'Going down?' he said.

Charlotte tried to find the sight of his lean face smiling up at her as comical as he might intend, but it made her less than eager to descend the steps. 'This is it, then.'

'It's worth a whole lot more than I paid for it back when.'

'I wasn't putting it down,' she said and ventured onto the first step.

It was dark in the cramped stone yard at the bottom, and darker beyond the door Glen unlocked. As she waited for him to switch on some light Charlotte had the unwelcome fancy that he was about to encounter an intruder in the blackness. She heard a beeping that suggested Glen was trying to summon help on a mobile phone, but he was switching off an alarm. In another moment the hall lit up, and he looked out of the doorway. 'Are you OK on the steps?'

She felt less so with each one she took. 'I didn't drink that much,' she said, wishing that were the problem, whatever it was.

The click of the latch reminded her how she was shutting herself in. The short hall was decorated with Cougar posters as if, she felt unfair for thinking, Glen anticipated a visit from their bosses. Past the bathroom and a bedroom where a double bed lay low in the dark, the main room managed to contain a leather suite and a home cinema system with a plasma screen, as well as bookshelves and a hi-fi and a desk bearing a computer. Glen crossed the room to a panelled kitchen largely occupied by fitted units and a pine table with six chairs. 'Sit anywhere you're comfortable,' he said.

'Can I open the curtains?'

'Handle whatever you like.'

Was she hoping for a sunken garden? When she parted the black curtains they revealed French windows, but these opened onto a subterranean brick enclosure where a round metal table and four chairs were surrounded on three sides by boxes spilling blossom. 'What do you think?' Glen called.

Charlotte retreated to the farthest leather chair in case at that distance the enclosure could be mistaken for the edge of a darker garden. It couldn't, and she was thrown by her desire for the illusion. 'It's neat,' she had to say. 'You must be quite a gardener.'

'I'm not. My girlfriend was.'

'Oh dear, are you going to have to learn?'

'That's one option. You any good with that stuff?'

'I don't think any of my family have much to do with the soil.'

'Pity,' Glen said and stayed quiet while the percolator did its work.

Charlotte's last remark echoed like an unwelcome voice in her head for no reason she could grasp, unless it was reminding her that she was under the earth, except that she was nothing of the kind. 'You've made a lot of your space,' she said.

'It's my burrow for sure. The girl I mentioned, she used to say it was like some animal's home in a fairy tale. Guess which animal.'

'I really couldn't say, Glen.'

'OK, well, you haven't seen it all yet.'

Before she could think of an answer he carried in two mugs, each advertising a Cougar million-seller. Having handed Charlotte *How You Can Save the World*, he planted *Know Everybody's Secrets* next to the chair he took opposite her and sat forwards. 'Anyway, let's get to the important stuff,' he said. 'Your cousin, yes?'

'I'd very much like to offer her a deal.'

'We haven't seen any rewrites yet, have we?'

'She's committed to them, and I'll give her any help she needs, on my own time if I have to.'

'We may not have so much of that, the way things are shaping up.' He took time to swallow a mouthful of coffee and said 'So you don't think it's going to call for too much of a favour.'

'I think together we can come up with a book that'll sell the way you thought it could.'

'I guess that's good enough for me. I'll back you when you talk it up. How much are you looking to offer?'

He'd lowered his head as he put down his mug, and yet she felt watched. 'As much as we reasonably can,' she said.

'Go ahead, give me your figure.'

As he raised his eyes she had the disconcerting idea that it wasn't his attention she had been sensing. Of course nobody was spying through the windows behind him; there was certainly no room for anyone to hide beneath the sill. 'We've been paying twenty-five for some first books, haven't we?' she did her best to concentrate on saying.

'Maybe, but I'd expect a whole lot more for that now, more than I figure you're going to give me.'

She felt not just eyed but trapped. The room seemed to have grown constricted, whether by its contents or the earth that must be pressing against the walls of the apartment, and dimmer. She tried a gulp of coffee, only to feel the caffeine seize her by her nerves. 'What would you suggest?' she said.

'I'd say ten tops.' Perhaps he sensed her disappointment on Ellen's behalf, because he added 'Did she say any more about her next book?'

'She asked me to help her develop it.'

'So what's your take?'

As Charlotte searched her mind she felt as if she were reaching down into a lightless place where she was awaited. That was just a dream she'd once had, but it made her feel more confined than ever, unless Glen's insistence did. 'I haven't had a chance to work on it yet,' she said. 'I'm sure it has potential. Don't call me unprofessional, but maybe it's too late in the day right now for me to give it what it deserves.'

'Listen, forgive me. This was meant to be a fun evening, not an editorial session. Let's make the most of our free time while we have it,' Glen said, leaning forwards to take her hand. 'OK, maybe I should put your mind at rest. Why don't you pitch twenty for both books at the meeting and I'll back you on that.'

She might have felt more at ease if she'd known why he had apparently changed his mind. 'Well, thank you,' she said, 'and Ellen thanks you just as much.'

'Hey, my pleasure, but we're the only ones here.'

She was instantly convinced he was wrong, and struggled to dispel a sense of being spied upon as he squeezed her hand before gradually letting go. 'So what's yours?' he said. 'Another drink? Some music? All that and more?'

She gathered he was talking about pleasure, an experience that seemed to be receding from her at speed. Of course the darkness just beyond the light wasn't crushing the apartment smaller and dragging it down into the earth, but she needed to be in the open – much better, on her roof. 'Would you mind if I called it an evening?' she said as evenly as she could. 'I've got some reading still to do before I go to bed.'

'That's perfectly fine. I have myself. Need a taxi? Want me to walk you to the station?'

'You get your reading out of the way, Glen. Maybe I can work on Ellen's idea while I'm walking.'

'Ever the professional,' he said and ushered her to the street. As she turned to say good night he clasped her hands and dealt her a kiss more lingering than she was quite prepared for. When she flexed her fingers he released her and backed down a step.

'Thanks for everything, Glen. See you on Monday,' Charlotte said and managed not to rub her hands on her skirt until she was hundreds of yards away. She wasn't trying to rub away Glen's touch, nor was she fleeing the sight of his jerky descent. She was simply anxious to leave behind the image of a figure reaching up to draw her into the dark.

EIGHT

Hugh had almost finished stripping the left side of aisle thirteen of tins when Tamara and Mishel sauntered out of the cosmetics section. At first they seemed content to pose at the end of his aisle, so that any passing customers might have taken them to be promoting dietary aids and blondeness, and then Tamara said 'You're being very fruity, Hugh.'

He was able to believe she had the contents of the tins in mind until Mishel enquired 'Are you fond of fruits, Hugh?'

'Some.' When the girls pouted to prompt him he admitted 'I like pears.'

Tamara unleashed a delighted squeal. 'I'll bet.'

'Not in tins. Too sweet for me.'

'He likes them out in the open with nothing on,' Mishel declared.

Hugh felt his cheeks begin to flare red. 'It's the syrup I don't like,' he tried saying.

'He doesn't like that slimy gooey stuff,' Tamara spluttered. 'You haven't told us pairs of what, Hugh.'

'I'm talking about fruit.' The heat spread over his face as he grabbed cans in both hands to add them to the stacks on the floor. 'I thought you were,' he mumbled.

'Oh, we are,' Tamara said. 'Don't you like dates?'

'Only at Christmas.'

'That's too long to wait for one, isn't it, Tam? You must like passion fruit, Hugh.'

'I've never had it.'

Even before they greeted this with cries of sympathy Hugh realised he could have phrased it better. He turned his blazing face to the shelves and lifted down tin after chilly tin, which didn't prevent Mishel from asking 'Don't you like a nice juicy melon?'

He had the impression that she was aiming her prominent breasts at him, but nothing could happen if he stared straight ahead. 'No,' he muttered.

'Now you're sounding like a lemon, Hugh.'

'An old prune, more like,' said Mishel.

'I think he's being a prickly pear.'

Hugh thought he saw a way to join in. 'At least I'm not an ugli fruit.'

There was silence while he shifted two armfuls of cans, and then Mishel said 'That's verbal abuse, that.'

'If a customer called us that we'd have security on them.'

Hugh thought they'd found a different way to tease him until he saw that their faces were stolidly blank. Beyond them his supervisor had come into view and perhaps into earshot across the wider aisle. 'I thought we were having a bit of fun,' Hugh protested.

'What kind of fun were you after?' said Mishel. 'Yes, you may well blush, Hugh Lucas.'

'You've got plenty to blush about,' Tamara said.

Justin pressed his small mouth thin as if to purge it of cuteness as he stalked across the aisle to plant his hands on his thick hips. 'Exactly what do you think you're doing, Hugh?'

'Being rude to us,' Tamara said.

'We were just joking and I was defending myself.'

'Oh, poor Hugh, having to defend himself from girls,' Mishel cried.

'You'd think we'd been assaulting him. Go on, Hugh, show us on the security tape.'

'There's verbal assault,' Hugh blurted. 'You just said.'

'It looked more like flirtation to me,' Justin said without approving. 'Does anybody want to report anybody here?'

He stared at Hugh as the girls did, and Hugh's face grew hotter still. 'Not if nobody else is,' he said.

'Ladies?'

They turned their heads towards each other and eventually shook them. 'Maybe not this time,' Tamara said.

'If he behaves himself,' said Mishel.

'Better control yourself,' Justin warned as Hugh opened his mouth – indeed, gaped. To the girls he said 'You'll have some work to do, will you?'

'We're on our break,' Tamara told him.

'Better take it somewhere else, then.'

As they ambled away the girls stuck their pink tongues out at Justin, so lingeringly that Hugh wondered if they were challenging him to draw the supervisor's attention to them. He was close to giving them what they apparently wanted, on the assumption that for once he'd understood a girl, when Justin said 'I'll ask you again. Just what do you imagine you're doing?'

'What you said to.' When Justin pursed his lips tinier, Hugh tried 'Clearing the shelves.'

'Go on.'

'I would be if you weren't distracting me,' Hugh mouthed, grabbing cans of kumquats.

He deposited them and was reaching for the next when Justin demanded 'What do you think you're doing now?'

Hugh raised his empty hands, which made him feel arrested with no idea of his offence. 'What you said again.'

'How stupid are you trying to be? I told you to tell me what you're doing.'

Hugh felt as if the interrogation had become a cramped maze with no light to show the way out. 'Clearing the shelves,' he repeated, attempting to laugh. 'I said.'

'I didn't realise I was so amusing.' Justin's gaze felt like a burning glass on Hugh's face, and stayed relentless as he said 'Which?'

Hugh jabbed his hands at the shelves, to no avail. 'And which are you trying to tell me those are?' Justin said. 'Don't do that, it's unhygienic.'

Hugh lowered his hand instead of passing it once more over his scalp. 'Fruit,' he felt ridiculed for having to say, 'and at the other end –'

'Have you really forgotten what you were told to do?'

'Clear the left side of aisle thirteen.'

'And what are you telling me this is?'

For a moment Hugh didn't know which way to turn, and then he peered along the aisle at the number of the checkout desk framed by the shelves. 'It's thirteen.'

'You're not having a laugh, are you? What side?'

'Left. I said.'

Justin unfolded his arms, puffing out a scent of Conqueror deodorant, and stretched his plump fingers towards the emptied shelves. 'And what do you call this?'

Hugh felt as if the aisle had been added to the dark maze that was his brain. 'Left,' he said doggedly.

'Well, it's not. It's right, which is wrong.'

Hugh gazed in dismay at the thousands of cans on the floor and complained 'It depends which way you're facing.'

'You keep your back to the front of the store. You face the back.'

Hugh had the unpleasant impression that Justin's words were turning around and around in his brain. He was close to accusing Justin of wanting to confuse him when the supervisor said 'You tell me what clearing them was going to achieve if you can.'

'I've no idea. You never told me why I was moving the stock.'

'You could have asked, or don't you care enough about your section?'

Hugh remembered Justin giving him the task before hurrying away to chat to a manager. 'You're moving right fourteen to left thirteen and vicey versa,' Justin said. 'See the sense now?'

'I think so.'

'Try being sure. Go and have your break and come back with your ideas sorted. There's enough of this in your family without you.'

'Enough of what?'

'People playing silly buggers with cans.' Justin paused not

quite long enough to give Hugh time to respond. 'And you'll need to get a move on with this,' he said. 'We can't have anybody sleeping on the job.'

For some reason this unnerved Hugh. He turned away to hide his aggravated confusion and hurried along the aisle. He'd just realised that his haste was taking him away from the staffroom when his mobile rang. Staff were forbidden to use their phones in the public area and the storeroom – indeed, mobiles weren't supposed to be switched on. Hugh spun around to see that Justin had left the aisle, but which way should he head to elude the supervisor? The ringtone – the theme from *Sesame Street* – seemed to be leaving his thoughts no chance to cohere. He needed to be outside the supermarket, and so he dashed towards the checkouts. He sidled past two heaped trolleys beside the thirteenth desk and dodged a security guard, who gave him an unnecessarily suspicious blink.

Beyond the car park the sullen brows of the moor were crowned with a puffy strip of white clouds beneath a thinner sky. Hugh quelled the ringtone and read the named number. 'Ellen,' he said.

'Is that Hugh?' Before he could ask who else she expected to encounter on his phone she said 'What have you been saying about me?'

He couldn't help his defensiveness. 'What have you been hearing?'

'I only rang up yesterday to see how people were. I wasn't looking for anyone to bail me out. I said after the funeral I had money in the bank.'

'You thought you'd be able to find another job, though, didn't you?'

'I've got one. Charlotte's getting my book bought and the one I'll write next too.'

'A proper job, I meant.'

'This is a proper job. It's every day. I'm even working now, on Sunday.'

'Well, so am I,' Hugh was provoked to retort. 'Someone has to, and the ones with families like to spend Sundays with them.'

'Oh, are you? I was going to ask if you'd seen Rory lately.'

'Not since we all met.'

'We shouldn't keep losing touch. If you weren't working I'd have liked you to check up on him.'

'Why, what's wrong?'

'Probably nothing. Most likely just me stuck in my caring mode. It was only that he offered me his grant, and when I said he mustn't be so silly he tried to give me half.'

'I'm not sure why that's bad.'

'I expect you're right. He was only being generous even if he doesn't want anyone to think he is. I just wondered –'

Hugh thought he heard his name or one like his beneath the rumble of traffic on the motorway. If he was being paged, the store would have to wait. 'What?' he urged.

'If he'd given me his grant, what was he going to live on? Do you think he's in a bad way somehow?'

'I didn't when I spoke to him. Maybe he knew you'd have to turn him down and so you'd find it harder not to accept half. Or maybe he's got money in the bank like you.'

'I'm sure that's it, one of them. Thanks, Hugh. You've helped,' Ellen said. 'So what did you actually say to him about me?'

'Just what you said about how we should all look out for each other.'

All at once Hugh wondered if she was hoping he'd said more or would now. He could tell her that he cared about her most of anyone he knew. The thought of admitting it kindled his face, but if he ever meant to risk it, shouldn't he try while she couldn't see him? He was struggling to part his nervous lips when Ellen said 'You should have known if I wouldn't take your money I wouldn't take his either.'

Hugh hadn't told his brother about offering a loan. It didn't seem worth establishing the truth now that he'd lost the opportunity to tell her how he felt. 'Is there anything else I can do to help?' he said.

'Not that I can think of. Should you be getting back to work?'

'I've a few minutes yet of my break. It's a pity you aren't closer,' Hugh said before his daring deserted him. 'Rory could have a go at taking your photo. Will Charlotte?'

After quite a silence Ellen said 'Why would anyone want to do that?'

'Why wouldn't they?' Much more loudly Hugh said 'To put on your book.'

'I hadn't thought of that. Some books don't have a picture of the author.'

'Well, yours definitely should. Don't you want people to know you? You want to get all the publicity you can. Make sure people see a lot of you.'

'There's too much of that, I'm afraid.'

She must mean she already felt visible – because of the business with the care home, of course. Hugh closed his eyes to help him dare to murmur 'There's nothing wrong with you, anything but. You're just how you ought to be.'

Perhaps she didn't hear. His eyes jerked open, because he'd begun to feel as if he were dreaming of being watched. 'Were you ready to get back to your writing?' he belatedly wondered. 'You don't need me in the way.'

'Don't underrate yourself, Hugh. We all admire you for doing what you can. I know I do.' Before he could at least return the compliment if not strive to improve on it Ellen said 'Maybe you should have another go at teaching now you're more mature.'

'Once was enough. I'd rather not feel like that ever again, not knowing what I was doing and not wanting anyone to know. I'm best off staying where I know my way around.' To head off any further impractical advice he blurted 'Aren't you going to tell me what your other book's about?'

'Four people spend a night somewhere, I'm not sure where yet, and something magic gets inside them.'

'That sounds like –'

Three words sufficed to let him hear that he was addressing a silence so hollow it seemed to gape beneath him. Had Ellen's phone run out of power, or could she have rung off because she didn't think he was creative enough to help? He pocketed the mobile, having switched it off, and glanced at his watch to see black scraps of digits form themselves into the next minute. He hadn't time for a coffee, and his useless labour was waiting to be reversed. He tramped past the vista of checkouts rendered more identical by dozens of overalls as yellow as a Frugo sign, and succeeded in feeling decisive by the time he reached the empty shelves and the floor piled with stock.

'Back you go,' he muttered as he handed items forwards. At least this restrained his frustration, so that he didn't slam cans into place. Long before he'd finished, the whole of him was as hot as the girls had made his face, not to mention as prickly as the pear Tamara had accused him of resembling. It took him most of an hour to restore the shelves to their earlier state. He stood back at last and closed his eyes, and thought he'd done so for at most a few moments when Justin said 'Do you know what you're doing now?'

Hugh opened his eyes to find he didn't know which side of the aisle he had been working. The discordant colours of the tins seemed to clamour in his head. He felt as if his stomach had given way, or the ground beneath him had. Perhaps his confusion was evident, unless Justin lost all patience. 'Clear this,' he said, snatching a can of spaghetti off a shelf behind Hugh and planting it on the floor, 'and bring everything round from the back.'

That couldn't go wrong, Hugh vowed, and set about emptying the shelf. He didn't notice when he was left alone, perhaps because he still felt watched. Surely that was only a symptom of his fear of making another mistake. The girls had confused him, and then Ellen had distracted him – some aspect of her call had. He mustn't think about that now; he had to concentrate on his task. All that mattered was not to forget which shelves he was turning back to front. There was no room for anything else, especially imagination, in his mind. Just now the job was his life.

NINE

As the doors of the lift drew shut a hand stayed them. It was Glen's. 'More coming,' he said as he stepped in. 'Make room.'

He wasn't speaking to Charlotte. He seemed not to have noticed her at the back. She would have thought the lift was full, despite the notice claiming that it held twelve people. Two secretaries dutifully retreated, backing her into a corner, and a pair of editors joined the crowd. The lift was unquestionably packed now; what was it waiting for? If it was overloaded she wouldn't mind taking the next one. Then the doors lumbered together, so sluggishly that they could have been admitting someone else.

Of course they hadn't. There were just eleven people – no, twelve including Charlotte. It cost her some seconds to count the immobile backs of heads and the equally inexpressive profiles beside her, but apparently that wasn't long enough to stir the lift. Was it stuck? Should she ask, since everybody else seemed to be ignoring its paralysis? No, it was sinking at last, and in a few seconds – more precisely, twenty or so – she would be out of the windowless cage, out of the surreptitious light as grey as the walls. Meanwhile she was reduced to watching the secretive heads, which she could have fancied were determined to overlook some intruder, staring resolutely forwards while he wormed across the floor. The notion was so grotesque that she refused to look down, to establish that no face was grimacing up at her. Nobody was there, either in the lift or under it – nobody was dragging it downwards so lethargically that the air befogged by the light would be used up before they ever reached the basement. Her companions hadn't stopped moving because they were unable to breathe; they weren't about to topple against her, pinning her in the corner. They were swaying only because the lift had shuddered to a halt, although the doors weren't opening. Was it between the floors? Charlotte took a shallow effortful breath so as to wonder aloud, and then the doors crept apart, revealing the underground corridor. The foremost rank of passengers stepped forwards, and as she succeeded in drawing more breath the people in front of her gave her some room. By the time they reached the doors she was almost treading on their heels.

She had never been so conscious of how much the lockers narrowed the corridor. Even the extensive office felt pressed smaller by the ceiling, and once she was seated the partitions that surrounded the desks took away more spaciousness. She was trying to concentrate on opening the day's envelopes and packages as she saw Glen return to his compartment. 'Morning, Glen,' she said and turned her wave into fanning herself. When he looked at best puzzled she said 'Too many of us in a box.'

'Everyone's important here. We all have to get to work. I don't believe anyone else had a problem.'

'I won't again,' Charlotte promised herself more than him. 'I wouldn't mind a bit more elbow room on our way upstairs, though.'

'Not much chance we'll be alone in there,' he said and wheeled his chair over. 'We'd better talk now.' As she turned her chair towards him in the flimsy alcove he murmured 'I'd have called you if I had your number.'

'Shall I give it to you now?'

'You can if you like,' he said and rested a hand on her arm, but only for a moment. 'You may not want to. Let me tell you first of all you've got a knack for pitching projects.'

'Well, thank you.'

'I've seen you do it upstairs but I guess I never appreciated just how good you were.'

'Thank you twice.'

'But I've been thinking over the weekend, I don't believe even you can sell your cousin's book upstairs by yourself.'

'Then it's a good job I won't be trying, yes?'

'You won't.' This was close to a question, and so was 'You've decided to wait till she sends us some rewrites.'

'No, I mean I'm glad I'll have your support up there today.'

Glen inched his chair towards Charlotte. 'What did you say to her?' he said in a low voice. 'You didn't tell her it's bought.'

'I wouldn't before it is.' Charlotte was starting to feel penned in. 'I might have implied that with both of us behind it we shouldn't have much of a problem,' she admitted.

'Yeah, well, that could be one.'

'I don't think I follow.'

Glen clamped his hands to his thighs and leaned so close that Charlotte smelled harsh coffee on his breath. 'Are you trying to make this as hard as you can?'

She didn't retreat, not least since there was very little room. 'No, I'm trying to be pleasant,' she said.

'Hey, me too. OK, let's be professional as well.'

'I thought I was.'

'Maybe I wasn't on Friday, so I apologise.'

'Glen, you've nothing to apologise for. I had a good time and I hope you did.'

'Sure, but remind me never to talk terms after an evening like that. Like I said, you're great at firing people up, but I've had the weekend to think it over. Call me unprofessional, only maybe you were too if you told your cousin she could expect a contract ahead of the pitch.'

'I already said I didn't say that. What are you saying I should have said?'

'You're going to need to tell her to show us some rewrites before we can make a decision.'

'We agreed that wasn't necessary. You can't have changed

your mind that much.' Charlotte's voice had begun to sound as boxed in as she felt. 'Is this about Friday night?' she said so quietly that she almost didn't hear herself.

'What about it?'

'Wasn't I as friendly as you wanted? I really did have work to finish. You were saying that's the attitude we need to have. If you think supporting Ellen's book is doing me a favour –'

However she might have continued, Glen cut her off. 'I won't be,' he said. 'That's all that matters here.'

'I won't ask you, then. I'll see if I'm as good at pitching as you say.'

'Let me tell you as a friend, that's not a good idea.'

'Why isn't it?'

'Because if you try I'll block you. I have to look out for my imprint, and that book isn't ready for us.'

'Suppose I can persuade everyone?'

'You won't persuade me, and I'll kill it.' Glen laid one hand on her desk and waved the other beside her, hemming her in. 'Listen, nobody can afford too many failed pitches round here any more. I'm thinking of you. Don't risk your job.'

Just now it was answering him that Charlotte didn't dare to risk. He steered the chair away and glanced at his watch. 'Time we were moving,' he said. 'Let's not be the last to take our seats.'

She had another first novel to propose, by an author who felt fiction ought to help her readers help themselves. 'You haven't turned against *How Not to be Afraid of Anything* as well, have you?'

'Nothing wrong with your judgment when it comes to Disney Hall. I'd be happy to pitch her book myself.'

As he trundled his chair to his desk, Charlotte grabbed her handbag and made for the lift. Her determination to act efficient and professional lasted as far as the subterranean corridor. How crowded might the lift grow on its way to the top floor? Although she'd jabbed the button she hurried along the corridor, which was cramped enough. She had almost reached the door to the emergency stairs before Glen called 'Don't you want to ride with me?'

'I don't feel like riding with anyone just now.'

'We all need to be part of the team,' he said, but Charlotte pushed the door open and stepped out of the corridor without looking back.

She'd thought the concrete stairs were wider. There appeared to be just enough space for two average people to pass. That had to be enough for her, however windowless the passage was. She ran up the flight to the bend between floors, not so much accompanied as beset by the flattened echoes of her footsteps. She was turning the bend when she thought someone below her spoke her name.

She didn't recognise the voice, though it seemed somehow familiar. She took a step backwards to peer around the enclosed bend. If anyone had called her, they must have been on the other side of the door; the voice had sounded at least that muffled. She wasn't about to waste time on finding out, because the prospect of descending the stairs seemed to shrink the passage. She turned her back and made to take two stairs at once, and then she grabbed the solitary banister so hard that she felt one of its supports grind within the wall. The higher flight of stairs was narrower.

It must be an illusion. Her confrontation with Glen had left her feeling penned in, that was all. As she dashed up the stairs the light appeared to flicker, and she was afraid it was about to shut her in total darkness. However insubstantial the footsteps crowding around her might be, they felt capable of robbing her of breath. She stumbled onto the ground-floor landing and gazed upwards. Though it had to be another illusion, the next flight looked narrower still.

She dragged the door to the lobby open, to be confronted by personnel piling into a lift. Someone beckoned her and made just enough space for her, but she waved him and the lift away. She was heading for its twin when she wondered how much of her state she was causing. How could she expect to relax until she'd spoken to Ellen, if then? The editorial meeting wouldn't start for ten minutes. She hurried past the reception desk into the street, where the sunlight rendered Ellen's number on the phone almost invisible. It had barely started to ring when Ellen said 'Gosh, have you bought me already? You must start awfully early.'

Charlotte found she was nervous of being overheard, though the pavement was deserted except for a traffic warden stooping to a parked car. 'Ellen . . .'

'I'm up too, writing. I have been for hours. I keep waking up with ideas.'

'As long as you're enjoying it and you're being productive.'

'I know I haven't sent you any revisions yet. I've nearly finished the chapter where they meet the one who's a witch. Charlotte?'

Was there a hint of panic in the last word? Charlotte hoped she wouldn't aggravate it by saying 'I'm afraid we're going to need more than that.'

'Well, of course you are,' Ellen said and laughed. 'A whole book.'

'No, I mean before we can make the deal. I'm really sorry. I shouldn't have been so eager to cheer you up.'

'I can live.'

'Oh, Ellen. How are you for money?'

'I wish people wouldn't keep asking me that sort of thing. I'm fine. I'm not spending as much as I used to, and don't start worrying about that. It'll do me good.'

Charlotte thought she would have preferred to be attacked for hastiness rather than hear Ellen striving to be positive. 'When do you think you might be able to send me say half a dozen chapters?'

'I'll see if I can by the end of next week.'

'Don't rush, but once I have them –'

'You'll send me my contract.'

'I'll do everything I can.'

'I'd better get started, then.' With scarcely a pause Ellen said 'You won't want a photo, will you?'

'Of what, sorry?'

'What is right. Of your cousin. Some books don't have them.'

'I certainly hope you'd want to do publicity if we can fix it up. All our authors do.'

'Let's get the book written first. And thanks for looking after me.'

In a moment Ellen was less than invisible. Charlotte dropped the mobile in her bag and turned away from the traffic warden, whose reproving frown she could easily take to heart. An empty lift was waiting in the lobby, and she hastened herself in. As the doors took time over closing and the grey cage dawdled upwards she had to quell the notion that the space around her was no larger than the inside of her skull.

TEN

'What's that bitch think she's up to? Who does she think she is?'

'Who are you calling one of those, Rory?'

'Who do you reckon, Hugh? Who do we both know?'

'Not Ellen.'

'Not her, no. She may be stupid in some ways, but nobody's got any reason to say she's a bitch that I know of. Cares too much for her own good about some things, like what people think of her. Have another go.'

'I don't see why you'd be talking about Charlotte.'

'What are you muttering about? Don't you want me hearing?'

'I said Charlotte. I mean, not her.'

'You've not heard what she's done to Ellen, then.'

'What?'

'By gum, I heard that all right. Didn't know you cared that much.' Rory gave Hugh's face time to grow hotter than the sunlight had rendered it before he said 'She's making Ellen change her whole book.'

'She'll be helping her, won't she? That's her job.'

'Shut my gob, are you telling me? I bet she'd like that, but I didn't think you would.'

'None of us would. I said she'll be doing her best for Ellen.'

'I didn't get half of that. You aren't making any sense to me.'

'It's noisy under the bridge. Wait till I'm over,' Hugh shouted, hurrying along the pavement above the road that girdled Huddersfield. In the midst of the thunder of lorries he thought he heard a shrivelled laugh. Pedestrians weren't allowed down there, and he was glad to be well clear of any driver who sounded like that. As he reached the brink of the street that sloped into the town, the mobile enquired 'Am I allowed to speak yet?'

'You never heard me say you weren't.'

'No, I heard you going on about someone that was under somewhere.'

'I didn't say that either,' Hugh protested more nervously than he understood.

'Carry on. You'll have me senseless before you're done.' Without giving Hugh time to respond Rory said 'Let me guess, you were standing up for your favourite girl.'

'She's not my favourite,' Hugh declared too vehemently and too loud. He felt desperate to hide his face as he tramped down to the pallid sandstone buildings around the railway station, although there was nobody in sight to observe him. 'All I'm saying,' he said, 'is Charlotte must know what she's doing.'

'Why?'

'She's paid to.'

'Money makes everything right, is that right?'

'Not everything, of course not, but it won't do Ellen any harm.'

'You reckon if you pay someone you buy the right to tell them how to create.'

'Charlotte won't be forcing her, will she? Maybe knowing she's worked for her money will help as well.'

'I'm losing you again. Where have you got to now?'

Hugh had turned under a railway bridge towards the town centre. 'I've something to do,' he said as he passed into the shadow, 'and then I could come and see you this afternoon if you're not too busy creating.'

'Trying to sound mysterious? That's not you.'

'I'm not trying to sound anything,' Hugh said, only to hear his voice grow close to subterranean. 'I just need to do some research.'

'Thought you'd found yourself someone there for a moment. What are you digging into?'

'I've had an idea for Ellen's next book.'

'Want to be like her cousin, do you? Want to tell her what to write.'

'I am her cousin,' Hugh said and felt absurdly obvious. 'You're wrong about the rest of it. I can't tell her what to do.'

'Sounds like you'd like to.'

Hugh almost retreated under the bridge to hide his progressively mottled face. 'I just want to give her my idea.'

'Let's hear it, then. Surprise me.'

'You mustn't tell her. I will when I've looked into it. Promise.'

'You're still the little brother, aren't you, Hugh? All right, promise. Hope to die.'

'I've thought where her thing that changes people's lives could be.'

'Let me guess. Where we all went back for a walk.'

'You still won't tell her, will you?' Hugh pleaded, feeling more obvious than ever. 'If it's no use there's no need for her to know.'

'Your secret's safe with me. Maybe you should tell her before she thinks of it herself.'

'I'll see what I can find out first, and then are we getting together?'

'I'm losing you again. Is who what?'

'Am I coming to see you?' Hugh demanded loud enough to rouse a muffled echo at his back, though he would have assumed he was too far from the bridge.

'Let's skip it this week. I'm best left alone till I've got a new project on the go. Right now I just feel locked up inside myself.'

Hugh might have pointed out that they hadn't met since the weekend of the funeral. He was opening his mouth when Rory said 'Anyway, you've got your own idea to work on. See to that and forget about me.'

'Forget my own brother? I don't think so,' Hugh said, though mostly to himself. He returned the deadened mobile to his pocket as he crossed the road to Cybernet, the closest Internet connection. It was housed in the lobby of the old Empire cinema, the upper storey of which still exhibited sex films in a club. But the doors to Cybernet were locked.

He was registered to use the computers in the central library too. All the same, for a moment he felt robbed of the route he'd planned to follow. On the way into the town the shops grew larger and more expensive, as if striving to be worthy of the old pale stone they occupied. Three headscarved women, Muslims rather than just Yorkshire housewives, were sitting on the library steps to watch two men pore over a giant game of chess on the flagstones outside, to the accompaniment of calypsos performed on a steel drum near a pub. Beyond the doors at the top of the steps another flight divided at a landing to climb both ways to the reference library. Art was stuck to the wall above the stairs – two trails of outsize coloured arrows, one side identified as RIGHT, though the other was unnamed. It meant nothing to Hugh, and as he made for the lending room he wondered if it would to Rory. Once a librarian who'd slimmed her accent down had booked him in, he took his place halfway along a line of shallow computer booths. A faint metallic calypso greeted the appearance of the Internet, and he sent Metacrawler in search of Thurstaston.

Which of the references would help Ellen? Thurstaston Rugby Club seemed unlikely to inspire her, and the same went for a yacht club. Thurstaston Bird Hide suggested concealment and secrecy, which she might take further than he felt able to. Thurstaston Country Park, Thurstaston Tea Parties, Thurstaston Gardeners' Association . . . He was beginning to think he'd been too eager to give Ellen ideas until he found a reference to Thor's Stone. He called it up at once.

It described a block of red sandstone twenty-five feet high, twice as wide and almost three times as long, which stood in a stone amphitheatre on Thurstaston Common. Traditions suggested that it had given the area its name and that it was a Scandinavian altar on which animals – perhaps humans too – had been sacrificed. One Victorian commentator described it as 'red as blood'. Less than a hundred years ago children would decorate an adjacent fairy well with flowers, and even now local pagans celebrated the midsummer solstice and other occasions at the stone. Never mind rugby and cups of tea – there was magic in the landscape. Perhaps Ellen should use the common instead of the cliff top, though that was less than a mile from the stone. He returned to the list, on which the next item was Thurstaston Beach.

This brought him a gallery of black and white photographs. While some resembled his memories – yachts bowing to a wind, sandpipers stooping along the shoreline or flocking like a pennant of windblown smoke above the estuary, an elaborate sandcastle defying the waves – the shapes of the cliff were unfamiliar, and the clothes of such people as appeared in the photographs dated them to the early years of the last century. One image had strayed in by mistake or as a cameraman's joke: the stretch of cliff that Hugh and Rory and their cousins had climbed after the funeral. Hugh inched the photograph up the screen to reveal the legend. *'Site of Arthur Pendemon's House.' Photo by Stanley Neville, 1926.*

Hugh stared at the picture of a convex stretch of cliff beneath a bloated cloud as dark as a winter midnight and tried to make sense of the caption. If the year referred to the date of the photograph, surely it was misattributed. This section of the cliff could hardly have survived unchanged for eighty years, especially when the other photographs showed such an altered landscape. How useful might Ellen find the notion, though? Perhaps there was more that she could use. He recalled the search engine and typed 'Arthur Pendemon' in the search box. At least, he thought he had until he read 'Stygie Orbswnim'.

He had to laugh, loud enough to earn him a frown from his turbaned neighbour on one side and a grunt from the white-robed greybeard on the other. While the grotesque words suggested a secret name or formula, he'd simply managed to miss every key, hitting adjacent ones instead. He erased the gibberish and set about taking his time until he saw that he'd typed 'Serjyt Owm'. Didn't he care about helping Ellen? He looked for the arrow like a nameless direction sign and held down the key until it swept the parodies of words away, then he ducked to the keyboard, peering about in search of the letters he needed. At last he glanced up for the thirteenth time to see the name in the search box. He clicked on the button to start the search, or rather he tried to. The cursor went nowhere near.

He skated the mouse around its mat to free it from the invisible obstruction and made another snatch at the button on the screen, but the arrow veered aside and did its best to vanish off the edge of the monitor. 'Wrong way,' Hugh muttered and watched the arrow sidle downwards as he tried to raise it. 'Wrong again,' he declared. 'All right, you little rodent, let's see you go left.' Was he losing his way among his words? 'I said left, right,' he exhorted through his teeth and assumed they were keeping his volume down even when he gritted 'Wrong' like a ventriloquist until the librarian with the lurking accent bustled over.

'Excuse me, what's the problem?' she murmured. 'You're disturbing people.'

'This is disturbing me,' Hugh complained as he saw his neighbours staring at him. 'It won't go where I want it to.'

The librarian leaned forwards while staying ostentatiously clear of him. 'You want to search for this, do you?'

For an absurd moment the question sounded like a warning. 'Of course I do.'

'Then there you are.'

She'd clicked on the search button before she finished speaking. 'Thanks,' Hugh said as she returned to the counter, having called up more than a dozen references to Arthur Pendemon. Hugh clicked on the first – at least he did his utmost to, but the mouse had still more ideas of its own.

'Wrong. Wrong. Wrong again, you little swine,' he tried to whisper, but his monologue grew louder and threatened to become less polite. Well before his neighbours started glaring at him he'd had enough. He could hardly ask the librarian to wield the mouse, and all the other terminals were in use, although was the computer the problem? He sent the chair stumbling backwards and blundered away from the source of his feverish embarrassment, looking, at nobody. Even the automatic doors that had admitted him no longer worked for him. He was making to haul them apart when he realised what the librarian had just called out to him. 'Isn't anything right round here?'

he blurted as he dashed along the counter to the exit doors, which swung open at once.

He could easily have imagined that the word over the arrow above the stairs was a joke at his expense. The three women had vacated the steps outside the building, but the men were still at their chess. One used both hands to move the black knight backwards, a sidling retreat that bewildered Hugh. He needn't feel compelled to take so devious a route, but a flurry of metallic drumming wouldn't let him think. He felt as if his confusion were being observed, which made it worse. Straight ahead seemed to be the safest direction, though he hardly knew where he was going until a roof closed over him.

It belonged to the market, where he'd often been as a child. He remembered the smells of cloth and Asian spices, and the stalls piled with exotic vegetables and bright clothes, and the motto above one stall that announced WE CAN ALTER ANYTHING, but he seemed to have forgotten there was no direct route through. At each junction he had to dodge one way or the other to find the next aisle that led forwards. Soon he would be out and capable of seeing which way to proceed, but why couldn't he now? As he hesitated at yet another intersection boxed in by boxy stalls he realised where his haste was leading him. He was heading away from Cybernet, even if the place was open now. Worse, he was heading away from home.

He had only to retrace his steps, but which way had he come? He turned around, though not too far, to see the last junction. 'Stupid,' he muttered and thought it best to say 'Not you' to a pair of Indian grocers who were eyeing him across their stall. He retreated to the junction and almost ran along the next aisle to the blind end. 'Which way now?' he wondered, surely not aloud. This way and then this, past WE CAN ALTER ANYTHING, followed by the opposite direction, although shouldn't that be showing him the exit? It must be this way instead, but that led to an aisle where Hugh had to twist around more than once before he could decide which route to take out of it. His decision brought him back to WE CAN ALTER ANYTHING, which was approximately in the middle of the market. Surely he could use the other exit and head home around the outside of the building. 'Back again,' he told the grocers, whom he suspected of conducting an unsubtitled discussion about him. He bore his blazing face out of their sight and along the side aisle before backhanding his forehead to brush away sweat if not to rub his brain alert. This didn't restore his sense of direction, since he carried on turning blind corners until he grasped that there couldn't be so many between him and the exit or even, he was beginning to dread, in a building the size of the market. Indeed, he was being told WE CAN ALTER ANYTHING again, and had that befallen his mind? The smell of cloth grew stale in his nostrils as if he were being tracked by someone in disagreeably old clothes. He backed away from the sign towards the entrance opposite the library, but as soon as he left the aisle behind he lost his sense of where the next one led. He fled into it anyway, and its staggered continuation, and please not many more. A stalled intersection and another, both of which made him feel like a rat in a maze as the heat trapped beneath the roof parched his mouth, and WE CAN ALTER ANYTHING, and an airless junction smelling of dusty cloth together with something mustier, which hardly explained why he felt watched. Of course stallholders were observing him, however surreptitiously. Why hadn't he asked one of them the way out before he was too shamefaced to admit the need and too panicky to speak? The Indian grocers were undoubtedly discussing him. That dismayed him less than his having somehow wandered back to their stall, and he was retreating when the stocky slick-haired man said 'Pardon me, what is your name?'

Hugh might have ignored the question and kept moving if he'd had any idea of where. 'Who wants to know?' he felt childish for retorting.

'My wife.'

His portly partner took this as her cue. 'Are you looking for somebody, please?'

'Who would I be looking for?' Belatedly aware that this could sound insulting, Hugh had to admit 'The exit, that's all.'

The couple had a brief though passionate untranslated dialogue, and then the woman lifted a flap in the counter. 'Come along with me.'

She was vanishing around a corner before Hugh moved, and

he was afraid she would be out of sight by the time he reached the junction. She was waiting more or less patiently for him, however, and he followed in her faintly spicy wake until a fourth turn brought them out of the market on the far side from the library. As he blinked both ways along the narrow street Hugh felt more lost than ever, unable to recognise left or right or to determine what became of them if he turned around. 'All right now?' his guide said and peered at him. 'Where are you wanting to go?'

The answer was almost too desperate for words. 'Home,' he begged.

'Just stay there.'

She trotted into the market and was lost to view before Hugh thought of a response. Did she mean he shouldn't have left home while he was in this state? He was trying to prepare to venture one way or the other in the desperate hope that some familiar landmark would restore his bearings when the male grocer emerged from the market. His frown made Hugh wonder if he intended to deal with some slight to his wife, especially since he complained 'You still have not said your name.'

'Hugh Lucas,' Hugh felt powerless for confessing.

'Rakesh.' The man delivered a terse soft loose handshake and turned away. 'Come quickly now.'

'Where?'

Rakesh renewed his frown over his shoulder. 'You are on the corner, are you not?'

'Of what?' Hugh pleaded, feeling yet more disoriented.

'Of the road.' Having gazed at him and seen no comprehension, Rakesh added, 'The road where we live.'

In a moment, far too tardily, Hugh recognised him. He and his wife and twin daughters lived at the far end of the terrace opposite Hugh's. 'I'm sorry. I'm really sorry. I didn't know you at first,' Hugh babbled and, as his face grew hotter, couldn't stop. 'It's just that I'm, you know, you saw how I am.'

Rakesh gave him a last slow blink before facing forwards. 'I will take you home.'

He led Hugh to a white van speckled with rust above its wheels and watched closely until his passenger was strapped in. A devious series of turns led to the ring road, which the van hardly sooner joined than left. As he drove past a factory into the sudden shade of trees Rakesh said, 'I hope our girls will not see you like this. You should be careful of whatever you are doing.'

It was clear that he had drugs in mind. Hugh would have denied ever touching them – at least, the single joint he'd shared with Rory had left him coughing tearfully for several minutes – if the foliage hadn't loosed the sun, bleaching his vision. As the van swerved into a street and then another the pallor drained away, reinstating the shapes of houses along with their sandy colour. 'Do you know where you are now?' Rakesh said, halting the van.

Clothes flapped on lines in the narrow front gardens, dancers pranced on plasma screens in more than one front room. As Hugh released the seat belt and clambered clumsily out of the vehicle, he heard a sitar racing up a scale, pursued by the drumming of a tabla. He was home. He thanked Rakesh, who watched him hurry up the weedy path through the weedier garden to the house at the windy end of the terrace. When he unlocked the door he tried to find the house – hall and two rooms downstairs, three rooms and a bathroom above – reassuring in its simplicity. There was surely no space to get lost in it, and he did his best to believe that only the sunlight had distracted him during the journey. That didn't quite explain why he had absolutely no idea which way he'd just come home.

ELEVEN

He shouldn't keep putting Hugh down, Rory thought. It was such a habit that Hugh seemed to expect it if not invite it, but it did neither of them any good. When had Rory fallen into it? Perhaps once their parents had betrayed they found Hugh's teacher training worthier of respect than Rory's ambitions, and their refusal to own up only made it worse. 'You do whatever makes you happy, Rory,' their mother would say, to which their father invariably responded 'Nobody can do more than they can.' There was no arguing with this, or rather if he tried to they would deny that they'd meant to criticise him and look unfairly criticised themselves. He'd suspected that they wished he had Hugh's discretion, which he would call timidity if not cowardice. The worst row had been over the house, when they'd implied he was being racist for suggesting that they wanted to move not just south but somewhere whiter than the district had become, though it hadn't been Rory or indeed his brother who'd kept acting pained by the sight of a sari outside their property or the least hint of spice in the air. 'You boys can have it all to yourselves,' their father had said as if, having forgiven Rory for disappointing his parents again, they had to treat him just like Hugh, while their mother declared 'They need their own space at their age.' They hadn't had much in their student accommodation, but once their parents moved to the Norfolk seaside, all the room in the house had begun to seem less than enough. Living with Hugh was the problem – with his oppressive eagerness to please, his insistence on putting his brother first whenever possible, his dogged willingness to help in any way he could and quite a few he couldn't, his mottled embarrassment at being proved inadequate. Rory had given none of those as reasons for moving out within a year, and he wouldn't have admitted leaving behind so many temptations to disparage his brother. Nevertheless he could hardly bear knowing that their parents saw his move as evidence that he felt like them.

At least he had the view from the twelfth floor of the tower block across the fields east of Leeds. The vast sky was an inexhaustible prospect all by itself – at least, it used to be. Just now it was emptily blue except for three clouds raising their curly white crowns above the horizon and a diagonal vapour trail as blurred as the muffled thunder of the aircraft. This ought to be more than enough to engage his imagination, but he felt as if that were falling short of the view.

He would like to blame the letters in the local newspaper. Certainly they made him feel resentfully defensive, shut inside himself. All the same, when he headed for the kitchen in case coffee was able to electrify his brain he sat at the table and read them once more, the entire black-bordered column of them that might have been announcing if not celebrating his death as an artist. In the first letter Name and Address Supplied had a joke that the writer must imagine nobody else had cracked: 'Can Do? Can't Do, more like.' Below this Name and Address Supplied wanted to know why the grant hadn't been spent on building a rubbish tip and added 'Hang on though, it was.' Their neighbour, Name and Address Supplied, complained that *Can Do* was a bad example to the young and an invitation to graffiti. Rory might have retorted that graffiti were a species of change and that without change there was no life and that life was the art of the universe, but how much of this was he sure he believed? The final letter, from Name and Address Supplied, maintained that public money should only support real art, which apparently was art that everyone could enjoy, and condemned Rory for robbing real artists. Perhaps his work was nothing more than an excuse for words.

Argument was life too, he tried to think as he filled a mug with muddy coffee, but he seemed to be causing his audience to retreat into their attitudes, which made him feel too close to the same state. Perhaps he should revert to exhibiting in galleries, where at least people came prepared to find art. That seemed like despairing of renewing anyone's view of the world. Not long ago he'd felt that anything at all, however banal and everyday – even the concrete kitchen full of metal surfaces – could set off his perceptions on a voyage of discovery that he would want to share with as many people as he could, and now he had fewer creative ideas than his drudge of a brother.

No, that wasn't quite the case. He'd had the same idea as Hugh for Ellen's next book. How much use was Hugh likely to be? She needed input from someone with imagination – someone besides Charlotte, given how she was confining hers to whatever she thought would sell. She ought to be helping Ellen's writing look professional, not telling her what to write.

Rory took a gulp of coffee as he passed the garden furniture that did duty as a dining suite in the main room. This felt like a joke that had died of old age, and so did the plastic chairs cushioned with toddlers' cartoonish quilts, not to mention the shelves composed of bits of a dismantled van and only just able to carry their load of art books. Even the taste of coffee seemed not just stale but shy of reaching him. Perhaps guilt was in the way. Hugh might at least deserve some credit for thinking how to help Ellen, but if Rory became involved, Hugh would have no chance.

That needn't happen. He could tell Hugh anything he found and let him pass on the information. The credit would mean more to Hugh than to him. Perhaps letting Hugh take it would free his own imagination from the dull dark mood that had settled over it – perhaps thinking of others would free him from the prison of himself.

As he sat at his desk in front of the window, a plane as silent as a snail drew its lingeringly disintegrating track across the sky. Rory was surprised not to hear it, since it was quite low. He switched on the computer and logged onto Frugonet and sent its engine in search of Thurstaston Cliffs. There were at least a dozen references, the first of which informed him that the area was composed of glacial drift, boulder clay up to one hundred feet thick on top of Triassic sandstone. He didn't see how that was of use to Ellen, but she might like the idea that the substance of the cliffs was full of erratic rocks. He was imagining a swarm of rocks crawling through the earth when the next sentence made clear that they had simply been transported by ice. They often contained crystals, and perhaps she could develop that. Erosion had scattered many of them on the beach.

Next came old news of a drowning at Thurstaston, of a teenager who had either fallen or thrown herself from the cliff. He remembered hearing of the incident, which had happened near the place where they'd all camped out and not long before they had. The girl – Mary Botton, a name that must have been a gift to any tormentors – had been plagued with nightmares for supposedly the first time in her life, after which she'd kept complaining that her schoolmates were watching her and wouldn't stop.

Rory found himself rereading this without understanding why and then gazing at it until his vision lost focus. He had to blink hard to rid his eyes of blankness, but this didn't enliven his brain. What was he expecting the report to convey to him? Perhaps if he didn't nag at it the point would become clear, though he felt oddly uneasy about leaving it uncomprehended. He seemed to sense it lurking among his thoughts as he clicked on a reference to Thurstaston Mound.

This showed him a site called *Lost Landscapes of Britain* and a nineteenth-century painting, which it would have taken him a while to recognise as depicting Thurstaston without the title: *Twilight Vigil at Thurstaston Mound*. What the silhouetted figure was engaged in besides pointing with his stick at an inflamed sunset above the Welsh mountains across the estuary, Rory couldn't guess. Was that a bird or some other night creature swooping over the still water? The painter had omitted to put its reflection in. Was the figure meant to be indicating it or somehow attracting it with the long gnarled stick? All that Rory could be sure of, given the view that included the mouth of the river, was that the dark mound, which must have stood at least fifty feet high, had once occupied the edge of the stretch of cliff top where he and Hugh and their cousins had camped.

Where had it gone? He didn't know if he was more troubled by the question or by the significance of the painting, nor why either should concern him. Perhaps the painter's other work might help him interpret this one. Rory searched for Allan Gemini and was rewarded with a handful of listings, the first of which led to a site of *The Occult in Art*. The page that opened was devoted to the artist, displaying the Thurstaston image and three others. *Stargrave in Winter* showed a village square illuminated only by the pallor of snow, in which a dozen or more dark figures stood ankle-deep, their postures so awkward they might be frozen or intended to be symbolic or both. *Night over Moonwell* depicted a distant village where no lights were visible in the left half, beneath a sky that was utterly black except for a massive moon and an oblique tendril of luminous white cloud that looked close to connecting the village with the satellite. *Goodmanswood in November* was a forest dimly glowing from within as though the fallen leaves had absorbed the last of the daylight, while the branches appeared to be straining to draw down the first stars or the dark gulf between them or something beyond. Rory didn't care for the paintings – they seemed sly, reluctant to own up to meanings that he suspected were aimed at an audience as secretive as they were – but he supposed he might mention them to Ellen, although they'd offered him no insight into the image of Thurstaston. He took another mouthful of coffee, only to feel he was searching for the taste. He swallowed to be done with it and went back to the listings for Thurstaston Mound.

The next one teased him with a sentence and the start of another.

> Pendemon's house used to stand on the cliff below Thurstaston Mound. His reputation seems to have been why the local people made no attempt to rescue him from . . .

Rory fumbled with the mouse, and the list was replaced by a site. The title appeared first, at the top of an empty window. *A Battle of Magicians: Arthur Pendemon versus Peter Grace.*

That sounded like background for Ellen, and he grew nervously impatient as the page failed to load. Once he'd set the computer refreshing the page he gazed past it at the unrewardingly eventless sky. The sentence and the fragment he'd already read took grudging form at the foot of an otherwise empty screen, and he had to assume they were waiting for some image to occupy the space. When the indicator at the bottom of the page showed that about half the document was loaded, he scrolled upwards, to find nothing but emptiness all the way to the top. Should the document be full of pictures? His inability to imagine them felt too close to losing all his creativeness. He scrolled down in the hope that something had arrived above the words, but now the page was absolutely blank.

'Try again,' Rory snarled and jabbed the refresh button. It took him a while to be convinced that this had an effect, and longer to identify it. The screen had turned yet more featureless. Even the title had disappeared from the upper margin of the document. He raised his aching gaze to rest it on the sky, and the blank came with him.

It felt pasted to his eyes. The floor and ceiling and the walls on either side of him were blurred presences that he could hardly claim to be seeing. When he tried to look at any of them, the blank did away with them. Worse still was being unable to see his hands unless he held them out to either side of him, where they appeared as undefined lumps whose colour he had to remember more than discern. He felt disembodied and yet shut up in his body, the worst of both worlds. He closed his eyes and clenched his fists on the desk while he did his best to live with however many minutes the blankness took to dissipate. At last he risked slitting his eyes. Even when he stretched them so wide that they stung he might as well not have opened them.

It must be a migraine. The condition had affected more than one of his classmates at college like this. Rory had suspected them of finding an excuse to miss lectures, but he wouldn't have scoffed at them now. He groped at the vague colourless bulk of the computer tower to switch it off – he couldn't see to shut the programmes down first – and then he clutched at the desk to help himself up. By shuffling with his feet almost together, and by making contact with several items of furniture that his blindness scarcely let him feel, he managed to reach the door. He slid his hand along the wall to guide him to his bedroom, where his shins bumped into the mattress and let him crawl onto the bed.

As he lay on his back he had the unpleasant notion that the blankness was a slab laid over his eyes. He was hoping to sleep off his state, but he was still trying to sink into unawareness when he seemed to feel a large insect struggling in his hip pocket. It was the vibration of his mobile, which he must have inadvertently silenced at some point. He fumbled it out and pressed it to his ear. However many times he said 'Hello?' he couldn't distinguish a response; even his own voice was sounding mostly in his skull. Had losing one sense infected another? 'I can't hear you,' he said desperately. 'I'll call you back later.' As he moved the phone away from his face he thought he heard a voice, but it sounded far away under the blankness. It didn't speak again as he killed the call and scrabbled at his pocket with the mobile before attempting to grow calm. Perhaps the voice that had seemed to speak his name was deep in him.

TWELVE

As Charlotte made to send the longest email she'd ever had to write, Glen came back from lunch with an author. 'Might be good news,' he said.

'I'm glad,' she felt required to say, though she had no idea for whom.

'How have you been spending this sunny afternoon?'

His breath betrayed how he'd spent much of his. She didn't need reminding how she was buried away from the sun. 'Just being an editor,' she said.

'Hey, me too,' he said and squinted at her email to Sextus Sexta Sexagesima, lead singer with Ban This and now author of *Praying is the Piss*, in which a rock group called Shag the Pigs used magic to become the most successful band of all time. 'Did you send this?'

'I'm about to.'

He reached around her shoulders and scrolled with the mouse, a gesture she found more presumptuously intimate than touching her might have been. 'OK, don't,' he said soon enough.

'Is he another author we've had second thoughts about?'

'I was talking to the big man upstairs and he thinks you shouldn't edit this at all. Some books need to breathe, he said. If you try to fit them into how you think all books are meant to be you could end up suffocating them.' He continued to expose her email as he said 'I guess some of the spelling may need fixing if it's not intentional. Maybe some of the punctuation, though I don't believe they changed a comma of John Lennon's books. Leave all the words he's made up, but the title could use work.'

'I won't argue with that.'

'One word should do it.'

'*Praying is the Pits*, you mean? It might still offend some people.'

'We're going to offend plenty. Let's use it, not pretend we can avoid it. I'm saying we should call it *Praying is Piss*.'

Charlotte might have laughed, if only to discover how amused she was. 'Have I heard the good news?' she wondered instead.

'Maybe you can make this work for your cousin. Don't tell me you weren't hoping it might be about her.'

Charlotte was recalling that he'd also drunk a good deal the last time he'd been enthusiastic about Ellen. 'I won't,' she said, 'but how?'

'Hey, where did your imagination go? While they're sold on magic upstairs you ought to make your move. How are her books looking?'

'I thought she was supposed to be working on the first one.'

'Better make it both. Right now they're saying they like two-book contracts for first-timers or they don't think it's worth the risk. She should give you a pitch you can wow them with, then as long as her new chapters shape up I'd say she's sold. They're hot for her upstairs.'

'You mean you've been talking about her?'

'Don't worry, I said she was your author and I didn't say she was your cousin. Maybe we should keep that between us for a while.'

He'd leaned closer to say so, and Charlotte felt oppressed – by his nearness, by the partitions around them, perhaps most of all by his inconsistency. 'Why don't you ask her how she feels about working on both books,' he said.

'I don't think many authors work on more than one at once.'

'A great reason for new ones to learn to, I'd say. The more ways they can compete in today's market the better it'll be for all of us. It's not like she's on her own, is it? She'll have her cousin if she needs help.' He straightened up with a comical wobble that might have been intentional. 'I'll leave you to call her,' he said but lingered to frown at the screen. 'Don't send that by mistake.'

'I'll see if I need to say any of it.'

While it seemed disagreeably likely that she wouldn't, the delay gave her the illusion of control. As Glen gave up playing overseer she freed the desk phone and typed Ellen's number. He was rearranging papers in his cubicle by the time Ellen said 'Hello?'

'Me.'

'Charlotte. I know you're waiting for my chapters. They're coming soon, I promise.'

'Do you think you might be able to let me have a synopsis of your next book as well?'

Ellen hesitated and then sounded oddly wary. 'Can I do a bit of research first?'

'Certainly you can, only how long do you think it'll take?'

'I've thought where I can set it. It's near enough for me to go and have a look.'

Charlotte wasn't sure if she heard or otherwise sensed movement beneath her. The muffled subterranean activity had to be that of a train, and of course she hadn't felt the floor shift like a lid. 'Have I guessed where?' she said.

'I wouldn't be surprised.' Ellen paused for some kind of effect and said 'Thurstaston.'

Another train must be worming under the office, but Charlotte was more aware of having mouthed the name as Ellen spoke it, as if it were a prayer or some other kind of invocation. 'I'll finish this chapter and then I'll send them to you,' Ellen said. 'I was working on it when you rang.'

'Don't let me interrupt any more. I'll look forward to whatever's coming.'

At that moment the computer screen turned black. It had simply grown dormant, though it put Charlotte in mind of a window overwhelmed by a sudden fall of earth. She wasn't going to let it remind her of the earth that must be pressing against all the walls. She nudged the mouse to restore her words on the monitor. 'Enjoy your research,' she said as a farewell.

THIRTEEN

Ellen was about to ask the children what they were doing on the swings when she saw that the house was for sale. A family must be viewing it, since a man was staring down at her from the attic bedroom that she and her cousins had shared until their aunt and uncle had begun to worry they were too mature. He seemed to take Ellen for an intruder, spying over the hedge with crime in mind. She could assure him that she'd spent several of the best weeks in her life here, except that it didn't quite live up to her memory: the trees and bushes that had turned the garden into a maze full of dens had been cut back, and where were the vines that had elaborated the adventure? The elder relatives must think this was the way to sell it, and at least the will donated the proceeds to a children's home. Ellen blinked her eyes more or less dry for a last sight of the house, and turned away as the man at the top told the children not to swing too high. None of this would help her with her book.

The row of houses overlooked a gravel track for walkers and cyclists alongside a bridle-path, beyond which fields and woodland stretched to the brink of the cliff. Ellen might have found the gap in the hedge and made straight for the field where she and her cousins had pitched camp, but after almost two hours on a pair of trains preceded and succeeded by buses, she needed a walk. The low unbroken cloud stained grey and black had none of the stale heat she'd brought with her. As she tramped a mile to the visitor centre she felt coated with humidity, which gave her little chance to think about her book.

The occasional cyclist overtook her so discreetly that they made her feel followed by someone she couldn't hear, and the odd head peered down at her – riders, of course. On this weekday afternoon the visitor centre was almost deserted. Ellen plodded along the corridor decorated with children's essays about nature to the Ladies', where she splashed her face with handfuls of cold water. She managed to splash the mirror above the sink, distorting her reflection, which appeared to sag and spread. She hurried out of the building rather than waste time wiping the glass.

Ought she to walk along the beach or the top of the cliff? It might be cooler near the water, and perhaps one of her characters could find something magical left by the waves. She crossed a field where a woman in a singlet and equally enormous shorts was competing at inertia with her breathless dog. A shady path led alongside a caravan park where the immobilised vehicles were as white and silent as monuments. At the end of the path an uneven series of steps cut out of the earth and ribbed with sticks descended to the beach.

The river had withdrawn, baring an expanse of sand several hundred yards wide. Yachts crept across the estuary, beyond which the sea bristled with the crosses of a wind farm. Down here the piebald mass of clouds seemed even lower, capable of resting on the edge of the cliff as it had settled on the darkened mountains across the river. Perhaps it was the reason why the beach was unpopulated, which she ought to welcome. She didn't want anyone interrupting her thoughts.

She headed downriver. This would take her below the area where she and her cousins had camped, and perhaps where her characters would do the same. What might they see? Perhaps million-selling novelist Carlotta might think that the pebbles strewn alongside the foot of the cliff and at the water's edge resembled fairy treasure, jewels turned to stone. She would observe the green crewcuts of tussocks protruding from mud exposed by the tide and wonder what species of heads was buried there. Ellen found the notion disconcerting, and tried to concentrate on how Roy, an artist garlanded with awards, saw the beach. Besides noticing that the sand retained the forms of waves, he might well reflect that the countless scattered shells were tomorrow's sand, along with those patches of cliff that weren't protected by foliage. Indeed, a breeze was troubling the bushes in their sleep, and Ellen thought she glimpsed wind-blown sand catching on shells ahead. Could care-home owner Helen spot an object glistening, no, glittering among the pebbles? It might have fallen out of an eroded section of the cliff, but Ellen found that she preferred to locate it by the water, where a wave could rearrange the delicate chain of some unfamiliar and unusually luminous metal into a shape like a magical symbol. By rescuing it Helen would discover that a pebble was attached to it, or rather that a perfectly globular stone was – a stone so uncommon that you could gaze into its depths and never name the visions it brought to mind. 'Have that to show your children,' Helen might say to Hugo, British Headmaster of the Year, as she passed him the charm.

Had Ellen said the line of dialogue aloud? She had to glance over her shoulder to confirm she couldn't have been overheard, but she ought to be concerned about the way her book was reshaping itself. The characters hardly sounded like people who would camp out on a cliff. They would have to be friends who met at weekends for a bracing walk of the kind she could do with taking more often. Roy and Carlotta would need to handle the magic stone before Hugo accepted it on his pupils' behalf. What effect did it have on the friends? Perhaps it granted each of them their deepest wish – so deep that none of them had ever put theirs into words. Or might they not be wishes, the unadmitted feelings that became altogether too real? She was driven to tramp faster, as much as the soft sand allowed, but she couldn't outdistance the idea. She felt as if her imagination were in danger of lifting a lid on it, calling it up from the dark.

What might her characters wish for? Hugo would be anxious for his pupils to behave, which meant he might secretly dream that they did exactly as they were told. Roy's dream could be that any work he imagined, no matter how impossible it seemed, would become real in every smallest detail. As for Carlotta, what would a writer dream other than to write the most successful book of all time? Helen's dream had to be that all the old folk in her care would stay healthy for the rest of their considerable lives. So much for the wishes, but how would they go wrong?

Hugo's pupils might grow absolutely obedient, unable to act without his direction, inside or outside the school. How unremittingly responsible for them would that make him? Carlotta's book would be so successful that everyone she met insisted on questioning her about it, until her home and her phone and her computer were so besieged that she hadn't a moment of her own. The unnatural health of Helen's residents might suggest to their offspring that they were refusing to die, and Ellen fancied that some of the children would take matters into their own homicidal hands. As for Roy, anything he visualised would become real, including whatever he feared. How would he stop this, if indeed he could? How could any of them control elements buried so deep in their minds that they might not even be able to identify the material until it was too late?

This was certainly an unnerving notion. It even made its author uneasy, down here alone on the beach. Perhaps she should save working on it until she was home; she had more than enough to take back to her desk. She could walk faster now that she didn't have to think. If she'd had enough of the beach, the nearest escape route was up the path where Charlotte had walked in her sleep.

This put her in mind of her own dream that night, of being trapped in a house that had smelled stuffed with clay – a house as dark as the inside of a skull and yet not dark enough for her. In the dream she'd thought any of the windows would be as bad as a mirror, but she was distracted from the memory by the creaking of the cliff beside her, or rather of the shrubs that covered it. A trickle of sand emerged, presumably dislodged by the same imperceptible wind, and she veered away from the cliff. She ought to be able to walk faster on the pebbles than on the sand.

The stony trail bordered the mud at the edge of the water.

The mud was as gloomily brown as the exposed clay of the cliff, and scored with ruts that she could take for scratches gouged by giant fingernails as their owner had sunk into it. Rocks of the same increasingly omnipresent colour protruded from it, some wearing wigs of moss or seaweed, some warty with barnacles. The tops of a few had been hollowed out by waves and held water as if, Ellen thought, they were fonts for a primitive baptism or a more mysterious ritual. Did she need to quell her imagination until it was safely home? The calls of seabirds had begun to sound like the cries of children in a panic if not worse. They seemed oddly muffled, so that she wondered if any mischievous children were lying low in the rusty hull of a boat at the foot of the cliff, but it was full of clay and rocks. Ahead of it she saw the rounded bulge up which the trail snaked towards the dark stained lid of the sky, and she was making for the path so hastily that she almost failed to notice a movement within the cliff.

There was a hole in the clay, about the size of her head and slightly lower. She had the unwelcome notion that a face had peered out of it before withdrawing like a worm. It could have belonged to an animal, since the hole went deep into the cliff. It could hardly have grinned at her, displaying a mouthful of clay. She tramped towards it, holding her shaky breath, to quash the impression. Something moved as she did, back there in the dark.

Was it a rabbit? As she stooped with some reluctance to peer into the burrow, its denizen advanced to meet her. It was no wild animal, and Ellen recoiled, almost sprawling on her back. The tenant of the burrow shrank away just as vigorously, and when Ellen risked ducking for another look she was able to distinguish that the face was her own.

The reflection wasn't flattering. Surely it was blurred by the dimness or by the surface that was acting as a mirror. Had erosion exposed some uncommon species of rock? Ellen crouched, gripping handfuls of thigh, until she was certain what she was seeing. A mirror was buried at arm's length inside the cliff.

She was able to discern most of the oval frame and some of the handle, which was propped among the subterranean roots of a tree or bush, but her image in the smudged glass remained puffily shapeless. She couldn't really look like that. To prove it she planted one knee on the yielding sand, which made her feel yielding too, and reached into the burrow.

She hadn't fully grasped the implications of an arm's length. She had to grope blindly inside the narrow tunnel, catching earth under her fingernails, until she could almost have imagined that someone was inching the mirror out of reach. Her cheek was inches from the cliff, which filled her nostrils with a heavy smell of clay. She wobbled on her knee, and as her shoulder bumped against the cliff, her fingertips nudged a flat surface – the glass of the mirror. By stretching her arm as straight as it would go she was able to touch the handle among the bony roots. She strained her thumb and forefinger to dislodge it, and the bunch of scrawny objects shifted in response.

Ellen sucked in a breath that tasted of clay. The next moment she lost her balance, and the side of her face slammed against the cliff. Beyond the impact she thought she could feel the thing she'd mistaken for roots flexing itself, rediscovering liveliness. Perhaps it was preparing to seize her by the hand. It took her a dismaying effort to remember that she had another one – that she could use it to fling herself backwards. She barely saved herself from falling as her arm emerged from the passage. She wasn't certain that she saw the five discoloured twigs move, but the mirror did. It tilted just enough to trap her face, displaying how deformed it was, not only by terror, if indeed that could be blamed at all.

She didn't quite scream. She released an ill-defined cry that made her lips feel as unhealthily swollen as her entire face looked. It failed to rescue her from her nightmare, because she wasn't asleep. The mirror tilted further, turning her reflection into clay, and for a crazed moment she was tempted to reach for it again, to examine her face until she was sure of her appearance. Or might the remnants of a hand adjust the mirror? When she realised she was waiting for this – waiting like an animal pinned by headlight beams – she floundered away along the beach.

She couldn't use the path up to the field. It passed directly above the burrow, from which she could imagine an arm thinner than flesh sprouting to clutch at her feet the instant she strayed close. As she fled towards a road that descended to the shore, the sand kept slipping aside, twisting her ankles, until she had to hobble like an old woman. Eventually the beach grew firmer, but it was a trick: when she trod on it her feet sank deep into packed sand that was well on the way to becoming mud. She felt as if it were dragging her weight into her legs, swelling them out of proportion, except that they were no heavier or more unmanageable than the rest of her. Surely only her toil and the heat as thick as the low clouds were weighing her down. When she held out her hands as if beseeching an invisible companion, she was almost certain they were more or less the size and shape they ought to be.

Nevertheless when she finally arrived at the road up the cliff she was wary of encountering someone at the top – anyone at all. She didn't want to be near people while she couldn't tell the difference between humidity and her own sweat or as long as a thick smell of clay seemed to cling to her. The road was deserted, and she put on speed once it flattened out alongside the field where she'd slept. A hedge blocked her view, but the occasional gap let her see that the field was unoccupied. If anyone was hiding, so they should, given how their hand had looked. While Ellen wished she hadn't had that thought, she gave in to whispering the rest of it. 'Worse than me.'

Perhaps she imagined the muffled distant voice – if it was both, how could she hear it? – but she couldn't doubt its message, which felt buried in her skull. 'No,' it said.

FOURTEEN

The schoolchildren on the back seats of the bus found Hugh's ringtone hilarious. Even though they were sharing the kind of cigarette Rory had once offered him, they made him feel childish. Perhaps he ought to substitute the Frugo ringtone, the melody of 'We're cheap so you'll be cheerful'. As he cut the *Sesame Street* theme short Ellen said 'Can you talk?'

'What's going to stop me?'

'You aren't busy at work.'

'I won't be there for . . .' He peered at the two-storey houses packed together on either side of him. Surely he'd slept off his bout of disorientation, which must have been some kind of summer virus, even if he was glad that the bus stopped at the end of his road. 'We've got plenty of time,' he promised Ellen as well as himself.

'Can I ask you a question, then?'

'Anything,' Hugh said and held his breath.

'What do you remember about Thurstaston?'

This was so much less intimate than he'd hoped or feared

that his breath emerged in a kind of tentative gasp if not exactly a sigh. 'What sort of thing?'

'I don't want to prompt you. Whatever comes into your mind.'

'Us all being together. I wish some of us could be more often.'

'Just some?'

'I see quite a lot of Rory. Not so much lately.' Hugh tried to detain his retreating pluck by admitting 'It'd be nice to see you.'

'Do you think so?' With a weightiness he didn't understand Ellen said 'You're kind.'

'I'm not. I mean, I hope I am, but I'm not being now.'

'Anyway, we're talking about Thurstaston.'

Hugh felt rebuffed if not rebuked. 'So what do you remember?'

'I said I didn't want to prompt you.'

'I expect we all remember Charlotte sleepwalking best,' he said and risked adding 'I wouldn't have minded if it had been me.'

'Why not?'

Her voice had grown sharp, and Hugh's was ready to falter. 'Never mind. Just a silly idea.'

'Tell me anyway.'

Hugh could see no way out except to speak. As his face continued reddening he mumbled 'I might have wandered into your tent. That'd have been my excuse.'

He didn't realise the schoolchildren were listening until they dawdled giggling past him and looked back from the stairs to aggravate his mortification. 'Go away,' he blurted. 'Leave me alone.'

'I'm sorry if you think I –'

'Not you,' he pleaded as the children piled downstairs. 'They've gone now.'

'Who? Are you sure?'

'I saw them go. Just kids being like kids are – well, we weren't, I don't think.'

'Listen, Hugh.' As he wondered what she was urging him to listen for she said 'I appreciate what you were saying before, truly I do, but this isn't the right time for me just now. I can't expect you to understand, but will you try and be patient with me?'

'Maybe if you told me what's –'

'Trust me, Hugh, it couldn't be wronger. Just let me say it's not your fault. It's nothing to do with you.'

He couldn't claim any right to feel excluded. As he uttered rather less than a word of agreement she said 'Any other memories?'

Hugh had no idea how she could use it, but he wasn't a writer. 'Just a dream I had when we were sleeping there.'

'You remember that.'

'I just did. I was in some house with no lights and I didn't know which way to go.'

'Where did you need to?'

'Out.' Even if this was for her book, he regretted having brought it up. 'Away,' he said.

His brusqueness failed to truncate the memory of knowing he wasn't alone in the darkness as thick as the clay it had smelled of. He'd sensed that any way he turned would deliver him into the clutches of whoever was waiting, so silently it seemed they'd given up the need to breathe. He was sure his outstretched hands would touch a face, if it was recognisable as such. Perhaps it would bare its teeth in delight, if they could be exposed any further, and widen its eyes as his fingertips groped at them, although that was assuming it still had – 'I'm there,' Hugh gasped.

'Where? Hugh, where are you?'

'My stop,' he said and struggled to laugh at the misunderstanding, not least to overcome the panic she seemed to have communicated to him. If this was how it felt to be as imaginative as his cousins and his brother, he should be glad that he ordinarily wasn't. He had never looked forward so much to his supermarket work, the more mechanical the better. He clattered downstairs just in time to halt the bus beside a shelter surrounded by the hailstorm of its glass. 'I'm off,' he said.

'Should I let you go?'

Beyond the concrete path into the retail park Frugo was visible across hundreds of emptied cars. 'Not unless you want to,' he said. 'I've got minutes yet.'

'I haven't upset you, have I? I wouldn't want to.'

'It's like you said, there'll be a better time. You can tell me when.'

'I meant about your bad dream.'

'Forget it,' Hugh said and glanced around to see that nobody was observing how mottled his face had grown as he struck out across the car park. 'I found out something for you,' he managed to admit.

'Will I like it?'

'I don't know.' He had the sudden wholly irrational notion that he should invent a discovery rather than tell her the real one, but of course he was incapable of any such invention. 'Where we all slept,' he said, 'it's the same.'

'I should think so, but I don't think Rory would.' He couldn't tell if she was disappointed in him or with the information as she added 'Does it make much difference either way?'

There was only one, Hugh thought, and that was straight ahead. The gaps between the cars didn't constitute a maze, or if they did he could see his route. He oughtn't to feel distracted by saying 'It's been like that for, I don't know, a hundred years?'

'Watch where you're going, son,' a driver apparently felt entitled to protest as he backed a van almost too large for its parking space into Hugh's path.

By this time Ellen was repeating 'Like what, Hugh?'

'The cliff where we were, it was the same shape eighty years ago. All the rest has changed but it's still sticking out like there's something inside it. You'd wonder what's keeping it that way.'

The van hadn't made him late for work, but he kept an eye on the supermarket while he dodged around car after parked car. He was so intent on it that he had to make an effort to grasp Ellen's question. 'What are you suggesting?' she hardly seemed to want to know.

'Will the rock be harder? That's just me being unimaginative. I'm sure you can think of something, I don't know, more magical.'

'It isn't rock, it's clay.' Quite as sharply she said 'How do you know about it?'

'Found it on the Internet for you.' At last he was clear of the labyrinth of parked cars. 'I've got to go in now,' he said.

He sounded like a child summoned by a parent. Had Tamara

and Mishel overheard him? They'd just emerged blonder than ever from Hair You Are. As they sauntered to the nearest Frugo entrance Ellen said 'Let's speak again soon. Shall I let you know how my book goes down with Charlotte?'

Hugh found her turn of phrase inexplicably ominous, but he said 'I'd love you to.'

The girls shared a glance about this and loitered as he made for the entrance, pocketing his mobile. 'Girlfriend, Hugh?' Tamara said.

If he hadn't been struggling to forget his dream he mightn't have mumbled 'Are you offering?'

The girls produced identical momentary frowns. 'Justin warned you about that,' said Mishel.

'Stop doing it to me, then.'

'She was asking if you'd got your girlfriend there.'

'Might be.'

'How long have you been with her, Hugh?' Tamara said.

'I haven't.' To fend off their instant sympathy he said 'I've known her a lot longer than I've known you.'

'Lucky her,' Tamara said without quite winking at Mishel. 'Have you told her how you feel about her, Hugh?'

They were passing the checkout desks. Hugh might have terminated the interrogation by taking a longer route to the staff quarters, but the ground floor seemed bewilderingly crowded, not least with children for some reason out of school. He couldn't escape Mishel's contribution to the survey. 'Don't you want her knowing you care?'

'She'd know how he feels just from looking at his face. Ooh, I don't know what kind of feeling that's supposed to be, though.'

Was it betraying more nervousness than he preferred to understand? He trailed the girls to the Staff Only door beside the shelves of Frugogo energy drinks. Beyond it a concrete passage almost featureless except for staff notices all entitled GO FRUGO! led past the staffroom to the toilets. As she pushed open the door marked FEMALE, Mishel turned on Hugh. 'Why are you following us now?'

'I have to go as well.'

'Not in here you don't,' she said while Tamara retorted 'That's right, away from us.'

As they stalked into FEMALE he hurried past to MALE. Opposite the door a concrete wall sported oval urinals, out of sight from the corridor, while the wall at right angles was occupied by cubicles green-eyed with VACANT signs. The urinals faced a row of sinks beneath a mirror, and Hugh glimpsed his reflection as he crossed the room. That must be why he had to overcome an impression that someone was there with him or at any rate uncomfortably close, unless it was his awareness that the girls were next door. He couldn't hear them, and surely they couldn't overhear his trickling in the porcelain. The fluorescent lights hummed as if trying to display nonchalance on his behalf. He zipped up his flies, although he felt nervous enough for the action to seem premature, and headed for the sinks. He saw his reflection turn to face him, and at once he had no idea which way either of them had turned.

He was straight ahead, but that was no help. The exit was to the left or right, whichever contained most of the maddeningly monotonous hum, although how could that be true in the mirror as well? He could see the door twice, and he only wished that were twice as helpful. He snatched his hands back from a gush of aggressively hot water and sidled alongside his distressed reflection to rub them under the snout of the hand dryer. The machine was still exhaling without having stopped for breath when he heard the girls emerge into the corridor. At once, in a panic that felt as if a hole had opened under his guts, he realised that only the girls' banter had prevented him from grasping that unless he'd followed them into the staff quarters he wouldn't have known which way to go.

He lurched towards their voices and into the corridor. Mishel emitted more of a gasp than he quite believed was genuine, and Tamara said 'Don't bother trying to scare us.'

'Nobody needs to be scared,' Hugh did his utmost to believe.

'Why are you wandering after us now?' Mishel demanded.

'I have to go to work too, haven't I?'

So long as he stayed behind them they would lead him to his section next to theirs. They emerged among the bottled drinks, where a younger man whom Hugh couldn't have named without reading his badge was restocking the shelves. If Justin had left Hugh in charge of them he mightn't be at such a loss. Were the girls trying to lose him? Was this another of their sly games? As he dodged shoppers and their equally sluggish trolleys Tamara veered into a side aisle, Mishel into another. He nearly cried out to them to stop, but he mustn't betray his condition. He struggled past two double-parked trolleys and dashed after Mishel, who turned on him. 'What do you think you're playing at, Hugh Lucas?' she said loud enough for customers to hear.

'Nothing.' Since this seemed feebly defensive, he tried retorting 'I was going to ask you that. Can't we just walk along like workmates?'

'You know what, I think you're a bit sick in the head.'

'More than a bit,' Tamara said, having arrived at his back.

He had to deny it before he was out of another job. As he twisted around to keep both girls in view, however, he saw what he'd been in too much of a hurry to notice: he was faced by shelves of feminine necessities that couldn't have been any more intimate. His face blazed, and he would have fled if he'd known which way to turn. A straggle of schoolchildren appeared behind Tamara, visibly attracted by the prospect of an argument, and Hugh was about to retreat when Justin blocked the other end of the aisle. 'What on earth are you doing there?' he said well before reaching Hugh.

'I was with them.'

'You were no such thing,' Tamara declared.

'He was harassing us again.'

'You keep doing it to me,' Hugh complained. 'You've got me so I can't think.'

Justin glanced at each of the girls in turn before waving Hugh away with a regal gesture that smelled of the latest deodorant. 'Get where you belong and be quick about it. I'll be having a word with you later.'

As Hugh blundered past Tamara he had an oppressive sense that someone was delighting in his situation, which was why he couldn't help blurting 'Aren't you supposed to be at school?'.

'They're here at the invitation of your manager.'

This information was provided by an at least middle-aged woman as severe as her grey suit. Too late Hugh noticed that the children had clipboards, though nobody was writing on them. 'Thinking of getting a job here when you grow up?' he blustered, which was less than placatory, since he was gazing at the teacher while he struggled to remember which way he ought to turn. The ranks upon ranks of merchandise seemed to be arranged with no logic he could grasp, and he couldn't see the sign for his section, never mind the aisles themselves. In desperation he swerved away from Justin as the supervisor caught up with him. He'd taken several paces before Justin said 'Where are you gadding off to now?'

Hugh spun around and marched in the opposite direction. Justin waited for him to be well past and then said 'Not that way either. Having a joke? I don't see anybody laughing.'

Somebody was, however silently. Hugh felt almost suffocated by their secret glee. When he heard a stifled giggle he rounded on it and saw a boy covering his mouth. He and two companions were skulking at the back of the school group and up, Hugh was sure, to no good. In a moment he realised – the clearest thought in his mind, the only clear one – that they already had been. 'I know you,' he warned them. 'You were on the bus.'

More than one of them wanted to be told 'Who says?'

'You know you were. You know I know.'

This suggested he was clinging to the only knowledge he had, and he was about to remind them what else he knew when the teacher addressed Justin. 'Excuse me, is this the way you usually treat your visitors?'

'It isn't, and it can stop right now. What are you waiting for, Hugh?'

Hugh felt as if the secret glee were pinning him to the spot, surrounding him with his aggravated confusion. 'They were smoking,' he informed the teacher. 'Not just smoking smoking either.'

'We never, Hugh,' the boy with the giggle said.

'William,' the teacher said, but then, more reprovingly to Hugh 'Excuse me, if you have something to say –'

'Cannabis.'

'I beg your pardon?'

She might almost have taken him to be offering, given her tone. 'That's what they were smoking,' Hugh insisted.

'And may I ask how you're so sure?'

'Yes,' Justin said quite as heavily. 'I'd like to know that too.'

'Oh, come on. You'd both have been able to tell. Everyone can these days.'

'I most certainly can't, and I hope none of you can.' Having been rewarded by various demonstrations of innocence from her charges, the teacher stared hard at Hugh. 'I'm afraid,' she said, 'I think there's only one way anyone would know.'

'Which way?' Hugh pleaded, inflaming his panic. 'What are you trying to say about me?'

'He's a druggie,' someone whispered.

'I'm nothing of the sort. Who said that? Too scared to own up? Can't you keep your children under control? Isn't that your job?'

'That's it,' Justin said. 'Enough.'

'I'm not standing here to have people tell lies about me.'

'That's right, you aren't. You're not here.' Before this had finished exacerbating Hugh's disorientation Justin said 'You're suspended. Go home.'

'Will he be able to find his way?' the teacher said, and Hugh saw too late that his section was beyond the aisle at her back.

'He'll have to. We can't spare anyone to go with him,' Justin said while continuing to face Hugh. 'You'll be hearing from us. Better stop whatever you've been doing to yourself and sort yourself out unless you want to end up playing round with litter on the moors.'

Hugh might have searched for a retort to this, except that he could see the moors across the car park outside the window beyond the checkout desk at the far end of the aisle behind Tamara and Mishel. They were all in a straight line ahead, and once he was in the open he would be able to see the bus stop. He strode forwards like a robot with a rudimentary brain, hardly aware of the girls as they dodged aside. He blundered past the tills and followed a parade of laden trolleys out of the supermarket. The bus stop was almost as good as ahead between the parked cars, and he made for it at once, hoping that the relative openness would lift at least some of the confusion from his mind. Once he was home he would be free to think of ways to help Ellen if he could – and yet for a moment too fleeting to grasp, the ambition seemed so mistaken it was nightmarish.

FIFTEEN

At first Rory thought it was the deepest sleep he'd ever had – so deep that it seemed he might never wake up. His eyelids were gummed shut with such thoroughness that he couldn't tell how dark it was around him. When he tried to blink they didn't begin to respond. He lifted his hands to his face, however little he could feel them. His fingertips must have reached his eyes, despite the absence of sensation. He pushed at the lids, and plucked at them, and clawed at them to no avail. His eyes weren't gummed shut at all; they'd grown shut. They were covered by a senseless mass of flesh.

He cried out. He must have, even if he couldn't hear a sound. He felt as though he were struggling to raise a scream beyond the surface of the inert lump he'd become. He had only the vaguest impression of scrabbling at his face – perhaps just the knowledge that he must be doing so. He gaped like a dying fish as he screamed again and again. At last he seemed to hear the faintest whimper, so feeble that he scarcely recognised his own voice. He dragged in a breath and screamed once more and crawled up the lifeline of the pathetic noise into wakefulness.

His face was buried in the pillow, and the quilt was draped over his ears. His fingers were digging into the mattress. The awkwardness of the position surely explained why his body had relinquished many of its usual routine sensations. When he moved his limbs, regaining any sense of them took rather longer than it should. At least he was able to unstick his eyelids and identify that the bedroom was bright enough for late morning, which his boyhood clock – one of the very few items he'd taken from the house in Huddersfield – confirmed it was. Although its large circular face was crowned with bells, he hadn't heard the alarm several hours ago. He reached for the glass of water on the floor beside the mattress and canted his head up to take a drink. Surely he needn't be concerned that he could scarcely taste the water, even if it would ordinarily have been more of an event on his palate. He planted the blurred glass on the vague floor and blinked his vision clearer as he located his phone on the board pierced by a knothole that snagged one groping fingertip. He held the mobile above his face while he fumbled for the button until the display lit up, accompanied by an unexpectedly muted electronic fanfare. Within the last hour he'd missed a call from Hugh.

Rory levered himself into a sitting position, splaying his legs across the floor, which felt no more immediately solid than the pillow under his fist. He succeeded in regaining more sensation by dealing the wall a good thump with his shoulders to prop himself up. Perhaps the lingering dullness had slowed his mind down, because as he thumbed the key to retrieve Hugh's call he remembered that he'd had a version of the nightmare once before, when Charlotte's sleepwalk had wakened him. Hadn't he dreamed he was in a house but unable even to judge whether it was dark? The memory seemed less important than discovering that Hugh had left no message, or if he had, it was wholly inaudible.

'Don't mess me about,' Rory grumbled and poked the key to call Hugh. Straining his ears eventually rewarded him with his brother's voice – just Hugh's name inserted in the Frugone answering message. 'Don't just ring and keep your gob shut,' Rory protested. 'I've got enough problems. Call me back.'

He held the mobile in his fist while he kicked off the quilt and made for the bathroom. Once his belated ablutions were behind him he tramped still naked to the kitchen. While the coffee percolated he gazed out of the window at the unforthcoming view of green hills slotted into a straightforwardly cloudless sky. The first taste of coffee enlivened him somewhat, or the jab of caffeine did. If Hugh wanted to speak to him, he'd had ample time to ring back.

Should he have called Ellen or Charlotte instead? Rory thought he would feel better for a few sharp words with Charlotte about Ellen. Within three simulations of a bell she said 'Rory. You're a surprise.'

'I try.'

'You don't have to with your family. What's up? Not that anything needs to be.'

'Has Hugh been in touch?'

'Not for a little while. Today, do you mean? Not even this week.'

'He rang this morning and didn't say why and now I can't get him.'

'I expect it won't be too important then, would you say?'

'I wouldn't, nothing like. You mean because he isn't?'

'Not at all. I'd never say that, and I'm sure I've never given that impression. If anyone – I haven't, that's all.'

'You're making out I have.'

'I should think you're how a lot of brothers are.'

'One of a mob, you reckon.'

'You're a bit of a hedgehog today, aren't you, Rory? Are you worried about something?'

'Can't you speak up? That's not helping.'

'How's this? I'm in the office, you understand.'

'If you want rid of me just shout.'

'I don't. I asked you what was wrong, if something is. Why do you think Hugh would have called?'

'I know why he should have.'

'Do enlighten me.'

'About Ellen.'

'Why, what's wrong with her?' Charlotte said urgently enough for him to resent it on Hugh's behalf. 'What have you heard?'

'Stuff you mightn't want us to. We know how you're messing with her book.'

'I wouldn't put it that way, and I don't believe Ellen would. She's turning out to be quite the pro.'

'Maybe that means something different where I live.'

'As far as I'm concerned it means professional.'

'I wouldn't know.' When this was met by a silence even more muffled than her voice kept growing, Rory said 'I wouldn't, are you saying?'

'I wouldn't, no. I'm sorry if you've somehow run away with the notion I think I'm better than you. I don't believe I've ever given that impression.'

She was giving it now, Rory thought; her language and her tone were. 'Anyway,' she said, 'I should be getting back to work. How's yours?'

'I'm working on an idea,' he retorted, and at once it ceased to be a lie. 'I'll say ta-ta. Hugh may be trying to call.'

'Let's hope,' Charlotte said and left Rory with silence, which was just what he seemed to need. It felt like the seed of a project based on his dream. Only one visitor at a time would be admitted to the installation, a lightless room. The visitor would have to don a face-mask and earplugs and padded gloves and other special clothing – anything that would muffle their sensations. Or could this be done less cumbersomely? In any case cameras would monitor visitors while they explored the room as much as they dared. It would be entirely empty and no doubt a good deal smaller than they imagined, since the experience was about stimulating the imagination – indeed, letting it loose to perform. *Nothing and Nobody* seemed to be the ideal title, not least because it felt capable of describing Rory himself. It was close to reviving his nightmare, and he decided to leave developing it further until he'd dealt with his very probably needless anxiety about his uncommunicative little brother. He took a tasteless gulp of coffee as he called Hugh's number, but the only answer was the message with Hugh's voice almost lost in it. 'Still me. Still waiting. If you've got owt to say, for buggery's sake get it said,' Rory urged and moved up the list to Ellen's number.

He was doing his best not to lose patience by the time she interrupted the distant bell. 'Rory? Yes, it's me.'

'No need to sound ashamed of it.'

'If you say so.'

'I bloody do, and you ought. Has anyone been saying different?'

'I suppose not,' Ellen admitted, and with even less conviction 'Not that I've heard.'

'That'll be because they haven't been.' When he didn't hear agreement Rory demanded 'Has Charlotte been making you feel bad about yourself?'

'Charlotte,' Ellen said with an approximation of a laugh. 'Why would she want to do that?'

'Doesn't want to doesn't mean she hasn't, the way she's been getting you out of shape. Sounds like she's treating your book like she owns it just because she paid for it. Watch out or there'll be nothing of you left. You won't recognise yourself.'

She was silent for so long that even Rory wondered if he'd said too much until she spoke. 'They haven't paid me yet.'

'Then they're treating you like you're their slave and you shouldn't bloody let them.'

'Oh, Rory, I truly don't think so,' Ellen said, more in the manner of her old self. 'Charlotte says it's how publishers have to work. I think she's helping me find out there's more to me as well.'

He might have been persuaded by her enthusiasm if he hadn't caught a laugh, so odd that he didn't recognise her voice. Rather than acknowledge it he said 'Have you heard from Hugh?'

'What about?'

'I don't know what you talk about.' This sounded ridiculously jealous, and Rory tried to amend it by adding 'Maybe your next book.'

'I haven't heard from him for days, and it wasn't about that. What are you trying to get at now?'

Rory could see no way to avoid saying 'He thought where you could make it happen.'

'So have I.'

For no reason Rory could define he was reluctant to ask 'Where's that?'

He was assuming she preferred not to discuss it until the book was written, unless her answer had been inaudible, when she said 'Thurstaston.'

'That's weird. It's his as well.' Rory refrained from mentioning that it was also his own but said 'He was going to look it up and tell you what he found.'

'Do you know what he did?'

Her voice had grown so faint that Rory couldn't judge whether it was urgent or wary or both. 'I don't,' he said.

He shouldn't mention Thurstaston Mound or Arthur Pendemon in case his brother would. Just the thought of doing so seemed capable of shutting him inside himself, blanking his vision and filling his ears with an utter hush, but he heard Ellen say 'I went there.'

'Any use?'

Presumably she answered him. As he strained his throbbing ears he managed to distinguish some kind of mutter. He wouldn't have said it was Ellen except for knowing it had to be. 'I didn't get that,' he complained. 'Say it again.'

The response was so incomprehensible that he could have imagined it was mocking him. He shut his eyes in case that helped him concentrate his hearing, but it felt like cutting off another sense. He widened them until they stung and gazed at the blank sky. 'Can you hear me?' he said. 'Something's up with someone's phone, it sounds like. Tell me another time.'

Had she gone? Rory pressed the mobile hard against his ear. Surely her phone was the problem, because he was able to hear his brother, or at least the message with Hugh's voice embedded in it. 'Me again. Where are you? Lost your phone?' Rory said without raising an answer. He'd had enough of waiting. It would be Hugh's fault if Rory disturbed him at work.

'We're your Frugo superstore at Huddersfield. Competing to be cheapest. This is Doreen serving you. How can I help you today?'

Rory had already tried to interrupt, but there was no stopping the formula. 'Can I speak to Hugh Lucas?'

'Who wants him, please?'

'I'm his brother.'

'Hold for a moment, please,' she instructed Rory and gave way to Vivaldi performed on an instrument centuries younger than the composer. After a number of seasonal bars and two assurances that Rory's call was important to someone, Doreen said 'Putting you through.'

As soon as the acoustic fell away, not down a hole but into the body of the supermarket, he said 'Hugh.'

'It's not, no. Wouldn't be.'

'He'll be here in a moment,' another girl called. 'Is that the can man?'

'I'll ask him. Tamara wants to know –'

'I'm Rory Lucas.'

'Says it's him. Doesn't sound that mad.'

'Ask him if he's after any models.'

'Tamara –'

'I heard,' Rory said with the impatience he'd been reserving for Hugh. 'Are you offering?'

'He's asking if we're offering.'

'Tell him there's plenty of his kind on the shelves.'

'Maybe we can give him a bulk deal. There's plenty of your kind –'

'I'll do without your bulk, thanks all the same.'

'What's up, Mishel? What did he say?'

'You don't want to know. Skitting how we look and he can't even see us. Can't see anything worth seeing if you ask me. He's as rude as his brother,' Mishel said and directed her voice at the phone. 'If you've got anything else to say you won't be saying it to us.'

He could hardly wait to begin speaking until he heard his brother take the phone. 'Christ, are they the sort of twats you have to work with? I thought it was just that wanker that got himself promoted over you. Don't let anybody tell you you haven't got it hard. I wouldn't be able to keep my gob shut if I had to put up with the likes of them as well as whatever you said he was called, Dustbin, it ought to be. Sounds like waste all right. A load of crap that thinks it's better than the rest of you.'

'Who do you think you're talking to?'

Rory shut his eyes and had to open them at once. 'I wouldn't know. Who?'

'I won't use the words you've been using.'

'Hugh doesn't either, so don't take it out on him.'

'What's he saying, Justin?' Rory heard one of the girls enquire with something like concern.

'Back to work, ladies, please. This isn't for your ears.' To Rory the supervisor said 'I take it your brother has been claiming he's been victimised.'

'He's said nowt about it. Doesn't mean he hasn't been. I'm warning you not to, that's all. Anyway, why am I talking to you? I asked for him.'

'I'm assuming you aren't very close.'

'You do a bloody sight too much assuming, pal,' Rory said, all the angrier for feeling that the accusation was related to the truth. 'What's your reason if you've got one?'

'If you were you'd know not to ring here for him.'

'I know we're not meant to ring him at work. I just want a quick word to see if anything's up with him.'

'Plenty, I'd say, but you can't do it here.'

'Why not? Spit it out, for Christ's sake.'

'I'll terminate this call if there is any more abusive language.' When Rory squeezed his eyes shut in an attempt to keep his lips that way, Justin said 'He was sent home yesterday until further notice. It looks very much as if he's been doing something to his brain. I don't know who's responsible or who he thinks he has to impress.'

Rory widened his eyes once he was sure he would say only 'What's he been doing?'

'Behaving completely inappropriately for a Frugo employee. I'm not interested in what other people may get up to, but it won't do for anyone who wants to hold down a real job.'

Rory succeeded in maintaining restraint for Hugh's sake. 'You've not told me what he did yet.'

'I'm afraid I can't discuss it with you. I wouldn't want my employers to be sued for alleged slander. Some people seem happy to claim payment however they can. Of course I'm not referring to anyone specific.' As Rory tried to visualise the supervisor's fat smug face Justin said 'I take it you'll be visiting your brother. I hope you'll devote your efforts to helping him in any way you can.'

'I don't need you to tell me that,' Rory declared and rang off before he could say anything else. As long as the job was Hugh's choice he shouldn't jeopardise it any further. His fury grew as he listened yet again to the message, and he could scarcely wait for it to finish droning so that he could say 'Can't you answer, for Christ's bloody sake? I know you're not at work. It's me. It's your brother. Whatever's up, you can talk to me.'

His ignorance of the situation felt like a lump of nothingness at the centre of his brain, and capable of blotting out his thoughts. Suppose Hugh was indeed unable to answer? From the little Justin had implied, Rory suspected that Hugh might have given way beneath the accumulated pressures of the job or, to judge by Rory's solitary experience with them, of his workmates. When teaching had almost broken him down he hadn't wanted to admit it or even to speak to his family for weeks. Charlotte had sent him encouragement, Ellen had kept assuring him how much they all cared about him and would look after him, but Rory believed it had been his own roughness that had dragged Hugh out of the dark lonely pit he'd become. That sort of conversation, more like a monologue, was best conducted face to face, and Rory was already dressing. He shoved his feet into a pair of trainers that were muddy from the moors and hurried down the corridor to slam the door behind him.

The lift was a grey box for eight people, seven of them represented by space. Without its control panel and the midget door to the emergency phone it would have been entirely featureless. Well before it descended twelve floors Rory found the sight of little more than nothingness unwelcome. His mind must be narrowed down to worrying about his brother, because when he stepped out of the tower block the car park and the queues of vehicles on the main road seemed flattened by the sunlight, insufficiently present. He rubbed his eyes and blinked stickily as he headed for the van.

How hot was the interior? As he drove to the road he lowered the window, but wasn't sure if that made any difference. A Volvo almost blinded him with its high beams to indicate that it was making way for him. The traffic was reduced to pacing the pedestrians by roadworks that had occupied a lane. Rory closed the window, even though he couldn't smell the gathering fumes, and laid his mobile on the seat beside him as the traffic halted ahead.

A lorry that blocked most of his forward view crawled a yard before stopping with a muted flare of brake lights – grimy, they must be. Its next effort covered half the distance, and the eventual one after that even less. When Rory saw a gap alongside he swerved into it, only just ahead of a Rover, which flashed a blank patch into his eyes. Presumably its horn wasn't working, but the driver compensated with a vigorous mime. Now the traffic in the inner lane was overtaking Rory, and the length of the lorry kept him out, forging forwards beside him but never far enough to let him dodge behind. His fists were clenched so fiercely on the wheel that he'd ceased to feel them. A Peugeot in front of him surged ahead several yards, but not enough to overtake the lorry so that Rory might be able to. His frustration seemed to swell behind his eyes, clogging his senses, and for too many seconds he imagined he was hearing his own voice only in his head. 'Ring ring. Ring ring,' he said, or rather the phone did.

The speed of the traffic gave him time to glance at the display. Hugh was calling at last, and Rory was about to speak to him when the Peugeot advanced another few yards. The headlights of the Rover glared at once. He switched the mobile to loudspeaker mode and drove forwards, blinking his smudged eyes so fiercely that it felt like nervousness. 'You can hear me, can you?' he demanded.

'I think so.'

'Of course you bloody can or you wouldn't be answering.' Rory tilted his head towards the phone as he braked to a halt, and felt as if he were shouting down a well to his brother. 'How long does it take to return a call?'

'I couldn't find it.'

'Which?'

'This.' As Rory lost patience with being unable to see what was meant, Hugh said 'My phone.'

'All right, no panic. We're talking now. What's up?'

'I just told you.'

If that was enough to distress Hugh so much, worse must be wrong with him. 'Well, you've found it now,' Rory said. 'Hang onto it till I get there and keep talking if you want.'

'Not just the phone.'

'Christ, you're in a bad way, aren't you?' Rory said in case a dose of bluff humour might help. 'What else, then?'

'Everything.'

'Buggeration, that's a lot,' Rory said, though he suspected his attempts to buck Hugh up were falling short. 'Eh, don't you try to tell me what to do. I'll go where I want when it suits me.'

'Who's there? Who are you speaking to?'

'Just some twat in a flash car that thinks nobody's good enough to get in his way.' As the Peugeot had drawn alongside the cab of the lorry, the Rover had instantly glared in response. 'I'm on the road,' Rory said. 'I'll be with you when I can, but don't panic if I'm a while. It's a nightmare here.'

The Peugeot sprinted ahead of the lorry, but not as far as the length of his van. 'What did you say?' Hugh seemed less than anxious to learn.

Was his voice growing faint with emotion? 'Driving right now, it's a nightmare,' Rory said and closed the gap.

'What kind?'

'The kind that gets on your nerves.' In case this sounded like an accusation Rory said 'It's just a figure of speech.'

'It isn't. I'm in one now.'

The Peugeot gathered speed as the lorry did, and Rory saw that the roadworks had come to an end, opening the outer lane on the approach to a large busy roundabout. 'I'm out of mine,' he said. 'I should be with you very soon.'

'Are you certain?'

The Rover veered into the third lane, and Rory bade it a mute but expressive good riddance, which failed to revive much sensation in his hand as he returned it to the wheel. 'I don't know what'd stop me,' he said.

'I didn't mean that.'

The Rover sped onto the roundabout, and the lorry and the Peugeot were at the edge when Rory saw a gap in the circling traffic large enough to admit both the car ahead and the van. 'Let's leave it till I see you,' he said.

'Just answer me one thing first.'

The lorry and the Peugeot braved the roundabout, and Rory floored the accelerator. He needed the first exit, for which he was in the correct lane, but the lorry wasn't taking that route. As it blocked the exit at length Hugh said not quite faintly enough to be inaudible 'Nightmares.'

'Right, them.' Rory was going to have to circumnavigate the entire crowded roundabout. He would have welcomed a break from Hugh's commentary, but as he set about overtaking the lorry in the midst of the headlong traffic he was provoked to add 'What about them?'

'Have you started remembering any? Because –'

For a heartbeat Rory managed to believe that only the mobile had failed, and then he realised that he couldn't hear the vehicles all around him or even the van. At least he was more or less able to see, despite a blur unpleasantly suggestive of the notion that his eyeballs had grown an extra skin. He tried to blink them clear as he accelerated desperately past the next exit. At the second blink his vision was extinguished like an image on a television that had been switched off.

He heard himself cry out, a distant feeble almost formless wail that he remembered uttering in an attempt to waken from a nightmare. It didn't work. He no longer knew how he was driving the van, since he was unable to feel the controls. He only knew that he was trapped inside it, as vulnerable as a mollusc in a fragile shell. If he wouldn't be able to feel what happened to him, this was the opposite of reassuring: it felt like his ultimate dread. He was nothing but a helpless consciousness enclosed in an insensate mass. Nothing and nobody, he just had time to think before he was.

SIXTEEN

'Have you started remembering any? Because I have. Only I'm not just remembering,' Hugh pleaded before Rory switched his mobile off. Hugh couldn't blame him. However desperate he'd been to talk about his plight and explain why he hadn't returned Rory's calls, he shouldn't have rung his brother while he was driving. He pressed the mobile against his right ear to confirm there was silence, which meant that Rory would be concentrating on the road. Had he really heard a cry just now, the sort of almost powerless sound he uttered whenever he was struggling to waken from a bad dream? It could hardly have been Rory; it must have been himself. Disturbing though it was to be unsure of his own voice, he supposed this further expressed his helplessness – and then he gasped. He was so preoccupied with how remote the cry of panic had seemed that he'd overlooked something far more immediate. He knew he was holding the phone to his right ear.

Quite a time passed before he was able to risk moving it away. He was terrified of losing the faculty he'd somehow regained. Eventually he laid the mobile on its back between his hands, which he flattened on the old stained wooden table where he and Rory had spent boyhood mealtimes with their parents, and gazed around the kitchen. For hours that felt like the beginning of eternity the room and the rest of the house had become appallingly unfamiliar, harder to find his way through than a maze many times the size of the building, in which every recognisable object seemed to mock his confusion. Now he grasped that the door to the small back garden was to the right of the unrelieved pane of glass above the metal sink ahead of him, while the door to the hall was on his left. He made himself turn his chair around with a protracted stuttering screech of its legs on the linoleum. There were the cupboards and the laminated working surface, but far more important, with his back to the sink and cooker and refrigerator and the garden that was mostly occupied by a pair of rusty swings standing knee-deep in weeds, he had no problem with understanding that the hall door was now to his right, the opposite of the door to the garden. How had he recaptured his sense of direction? He could only assume that talking about his condition, no matter how perfunctorily, had done the trick. His mental interlude must have been the result of all his confrontations with Justin and Tamara and Mishel, and perhaps it came of indulging his imagination too. That was best left to the creative members of the family, and for the moment he didn't even want to think about the situation at work; he wanted to celebrate the return of the sense that he'd taken so much for granted. Pocketing the mobile, he made for the hall.

Apart from Rory's portraits – Hugh and their cousins gazing ahead in frozen anticipation – there wasn't a great deal to it, since it was halved on the right by stairs. To the left the lounge recalled his and Rory's boyhoods: the old squat television with its dusty almost square screen did, and the video recorder piled with tapes so often used that their labels were palimpsests of his and Rory's handwriting and their parents' too, and the bookcase not overfull of books that Hugh had learned from his father to buy in charity shops and library sales. Just the free books Charlotte used to send her cousins before the publishers warned staff that complimentary copies should be given only to the press were new. At the top of the stairs the bathroom announced itself with a flush that never quite stopped trickling, while his and Rory's old rooms were more or less ahead and the largest, once the parental bedroom, was now Hugh's. All the doors were open, as he'd flung them during his panicky quest for his sense of direction; otherwise the diminutive hall – big enough for him, he always thought – would have been much dimmer. He turned right along it into his room.

He'd left most of the relics of his boyhood – ramshackle scale models displaying too much glue, Scottish comic annuals, a poster for an AIDS benefit concert by Hindi rappers Jihadn't in Manchester (one of his very few demonstrations of adolescent rebellion, which had his parents wondering for at least a year and very possibly still if he was gay) – in his original bedroom. The one he occupied now retained much of his parents' bedroom furniture, wardrobes and a dressing-table too rickety to move. His single bed was newer, and so were the posters for Rory's exhibitions, and the bookcase piled with material Hugh had read and written while training as a teacher. They could rouse his guilt over the career he'd abandoned because of his inability to cope, not to mention his failure to share the house, no doubt because he was impossible to live with – but just now he felt guiltier for crossing to the window and pushing the musty faded curtains wider to gaze along the deserted street. He was starting to regret having troubled his brother.

Perhaps trying to contact him had even aggravated Hugh's state, or Rory's absence from the phone had, so that Hugh had ended his first call without a word. He'd fled to the toilet, only to be unable to find his way back for longer than the most protracted nightmare, despite hearing the *Sesame Street* theme so often that it might have been taunting him. He mustn't risk putting the phone down again, although the need to keep it on him threatened to revive his terror of losing his way. All at once it seemed crucial to know what he absolutely mustn't do, but he was nowhere near identifying it when the mobile came to life.

As he wondered whether to apologise to Rory he saw Ellen's number. It only intensified his sense of some action it was vital to avoid. Surely that couldn't be answering the phone, though he almost dropped it from nervousness. 'Are you busy?' Ellen said. 'Can you talk?'

He mustn't burden her with his problems at the supermarket; she sounded tense enough. 'I'm not at work just now,' he said.

'Not even for me?'

She might be trying to sound innocent if not coquettish, but it made Hugh uneasy. 'How do you mean?'

'Rory says you've been finding things out for me. He called before.'

In the midst of his mounting anxiety Hugh felt betrayed. 'Why?' he complained.

'I wasn't completely clear about that. Something was wrong with his phone, I think. He kept not being able to hear me, but he was asking if you'd been in touch.'

Hugh saw this might have been his fault for neglecting to leave a message. 'What did he say I've been doing?' he was impatient to learn.

After a pause that struck Hugh as surely unintentionally cruel, Ellen said 'Looking into Thurstaston.'

If her tone seemed oddly guarded, Hugh hadn't time to analyse it. 'I told him not to tell.'

'Why, Hugh?'

Even this sounded nervous, unless he was mistaking his state for hers. As he stared out of the window he had to make an effort to identify which direction Rory would arrive from. 'He'd no right, that's all,' he said.

'You mustn't blame him. Please don't fall out with him over that or anything else for that matter.'

'I expect you'll have done all the research you want, though.'

'I don't know.' In the same odd tone she said 'What have you found?'

'I told you how it hasn't changed, where we spent the night.' This made the situation sound more intimate than he could expect her to like, and he tried to leave the remark behind. 'Maybe something could be holding it like that,' he blurted.

'Holding.'

'From inside. Something that lives there.' He did his best to laugh at his presumption or her wary echo as he added 'In your book, I mean, obviously.'

'Obviously.'

Was she teasing him? She didn't seem to be enjoying it. 'Maybe you ought to have a look yourself if you haven't,' he said.

For some reason this silenced her and seemed capable of doing the same to him, or perhaps he was confused by a sudden notion that he mustn't turn around. 'I can tell you what to look for,' he tried saying.

'What?'

He could almost have imagined that she didn't want to hear. 'Some weird name,' he said.

'Don't say you've forgotten it, Hugh.'

Her laugh sounded dutiful yet not wholly unrelated to hysteria as he twisted around to glare at the room. Of course it was deserted all the way to the door, which led to the landing and the empty rooms and the unoccupied stairs that descended to the rest of the unpeopled house. 'I wouldn't when you might need it,' he assured Ellen. 'Look up Pendemon. Arthur Pendemon.'

'Who?'

He was starting to wish that his answers wouldn't lead to further questions; he felt as if he would never find his way out of the tangle of them. He turned back to the window, outside which the street led in two directions, the one no longer than the building and the far more extensive other, which ought to produce Rory any moment now. 'He lived there, whoever he was when he was at home,' he said.

'Where?'

'At the top where we all climbed up. It says that's the site of his house.'

Hugh was distracted by a sight beyond the window, more so once he realised it wasn't beyond. A mass of cloud as black as the depths of a pit had crept above the houses opposite to blot out the sun and display his dim reflection on the glass. He was dismayed to find he was grimacing, and glad that Ellen couldn't see – and then he began to distinguish the room behind him. It was darker than his image, and at first he could only make out the vague shapes of furniture. Why did he feel unwillingly compelled to search the reflection? He'd started to wonder what was keeping Ellen quiet by the time he located an object he didn't recognise – a more or less oval shape so dark as to be featureless, but identifiable by its outline as a head. Someone was behind him.

He spun around so fast that the mobile almost flew out of his grasp. A figure imitated him, even mocking the desperate grab his other hand made at the phone, and as he recognised the presence he was able to laugh – indeed, less able to stop. 'What's funny?' Ellen's tiny voice cried between his hands. 'What's wrong?'

'I thought someone was here. It was just the mirror,' Hugh said gradually more steadily as his mirth trailed off. 'Rory will be soon. Here, I mean.'

'Had I better let you go?' Just as reluctantly Ellen added 'Unless you've got something else for me.'

'I would have but the computer at the library went silly.' He was painfully aware how feeble this must seem, and as he faced the window again he said 'What have you turned up, then?'

'Do you mind if I don't talk about it just now?'

Hugh didn't. Indeed, he'd regretted the question before it had finished leaving his mouth, because it seemed bound up with the disquiet that his glimpse in the window had planted in his mind. The clouds had bared the sun, erasing the image of the room, leaving him unable to confirm that he'd seen the reflection of the mirror on the wardrobe and within it his own head. Since it would have been a back view, he couldn't have glimpsed anything like a face, never mind one that appeared to be peering out of its own darkness – soil in the eye-sockets, perhaps, and deep within it the shrunken vicious glint of buried eyes. If this was how having an imagination felt, he was glad he wasn't Ellen. 'Don't till you want to,' he said. 'I know writers aren't supposed to talk about their writing till it's done.'

'That's what you think it's about, is it, Hugh?'

Was he presuming by attempting not to? As he searched for any comment it would be safe to utter, Ellen said 'I'm sorry. I don't meant to be nasty to you.'

'You can if it helps.'

'It doesn't,' she said, but added 'Thanks for going to all that trouble for me.'

'I'd have done more if I wasn't stopped.'

'Stopped.'

The tone of her echo no longer tempted him to laugh. 'By their old computer,' he said.

'Oh yes, you did say.'

What was troubling her? Was she working too hard? Hugh made a last attempt to be of use. 'Are you taking a day off now and then?'

'For what, Hugh? Sitting inside myself? Having a good look at myself?' Ellen let out such a disgusted sound that he assumed she was more than impatient with any suggestion of indolence. 'I need to lose myself in my writing if I can,' she said.

'I expect that's what writers have to do, but couldn't you take a day off and still be sort of working?'

'How?'

Was a trace of the reflection confusing his view of the street? He was unable quite to grasp either while saying 'You could go and look at Thurstaston and see if it brings anything into your head.' When she kept her thoughts about this to herself, her silence made him babble 'It's close enough for an afternoon out, isn't it? You're the closest of anyone.'

He wasn't sure what she whispered then: surely not that she wished otherwise. 'I'm the next,' he blurted. 'I could come with you if you wanted.'

As soon as the offer stumbled out of his mouth he knew how mistaken it was. He might have imagined that the utterance had robbed him of the ability to put it into practice. He couldn't go with Ellen or indeed with anyone just now. So long as he faced the window he would know which way his brother had to come, but if he turned around he would lose that sense and everything that depended on it. He was striving to ignore any hint of a reflection on the glass when Ellen said 'I don't think that would be a good idea either.'

The longer they kept talking, the more desperate he might grow to admit his state. He mustn't trouble her with it, especially since he would be telling his brother about it very soon. At least Rory had a reason to come after all. 'I'd better let you go, then,' Hugh said. 'Good luck with your books.'

'Speak soon,' Ellen said as if she could think of no other response.

Hugh switched off her call and held the mobile in his hand, whichever of them wasn't gripping the windowsill. Though the sky had grown too clear to back any reflection, he wasn't going to turn so much as an inch. No face was peering out of the darkness it had brought. Nobody was creeping closer, as silent as the depths of the earth, to wait for him to look. None of this could help Ellen or have anything to do with her, and so he should put it behind him, though he would have preferred a different choice of words. He wasn't a writer and shouldn't try to think like one. He should concentrate on the street. Rory would arrive that way, the long way, the one that took longest but certainly not much longer. Long before Hugh was unable not to glance over his shoulder he would be rewarded by the sight of Rory's van, and then – he was so sure of it that he didn't need to speak the hope aloud, to hear how empty the room and the house were except for himself – everything would begin to be just as familiar.

SEVENTEEN

'Anyway, I should be getting back to work. How's yours?'

'I'm working on an idea. I'll say ta-ta. Hugh may be trying to call.'

'Let's hope so,' Charlotte said and looked up from nesting her mobile behind a pile of opening chapters accompanied by letters, most of them addressed to her by name and some of them spelled right, to find Glen loitering within earshot. He took her glance as an invitation to sidle behind her desk, perhaps so as only to murmur 'Problem?'

'I couldn't say.'

'Anything I should know about? Anything connected with us?'

She hoped he meant the pronoun to stand for the publishers. The sooner she satisfied him, the sooner he might leave her to feel a little less boxed in. 'Family matters,' she said.

'They can be the worst. I get the feeling maybe these aren't, no?'

'More like a problem in communication. Families have those.'

'You bet. Remind me to tell you about a bunch of mine

sometime. So you don't think it's anything to put our author off her work for us.'

'I was just saying she's shaping up to be a professional.'

'That's what I like to hear. I guess she must have too.'

'I imagine she might, but I wasn't talking to her. It was another of my creative cousins.'

'Sounds like my kind of family. Who's this one?'

'He's an artist.'

'Professional? Can we use him?'

It was partly Charlotte's sense of being trapped in the meagre space behind her desk, not to mention underground and under observation, that made her retort 'I don't think he'd be your sort of professional.'

'Hey, don't be so sure you know what I'm about.'

Charlotte glanced over the top of the box that contained her desk, but none of their colleagues appeared to be listening. Perhaps they were too intent on keeping their jobs under the new regime, unless eavesdropping on a disagreement might help. 'Forgive me,' she murmured, 'I didn't mean –'

'It's OK, I'm not blaming you.' Glen pushed a heap of bound American proofs towards Charlotte, clearing a corner of her desk to sit on. 'Just because I have to focus on what our bosses want,' he said low and aimed it down at her, 'all that means is leaving other stuff at home. It doesn't mean I stop appreciating what else matters.'

Above his head the aura of concentrated light around a fluorescent tube exhibited how low the concrete ceiling was – had always been. 'So who's your artist?' Glen said. 'What's his claim to fame?'

'Rory Lucas. I won't be offended if you haven't heard of him.'

'Wasn't he the guy who made the slide show of a bunch of famous paintings that you had to watch with all the random noises and bits of music?'

'*Extra Sense*,' Charlotte said, doing her best to hide her surprise. 'You heard about it, then.'

'More than heard. Went to see it when it was at the Tottenham Gallery. I liked the way the soundtrack changed how the pictures felt to you. And then I hung around to watch other people reacting. That was fun too.'

'I'm sorry I didn't see you. I went a few times.'

'Yeah, well, I was there. We missed each other.'

Charlotte hadn't intended to suggest otherwise, but before she could say so Glen said 'Anyway, I'm with you about him.'

'Well, good. I'm glad.'

Glen frowned for the duration of a blink. 'I'm saying I believe you're right, he's not for us. He wouldn't sell.'

Did he suspect her of doubting he'd visited the exhibition? Would the truth have made any difference? He was already saying 'OK, let's try and nail your other cousin down.'

'Have you had a chance to read her chapters yet?'

'Read them a couple of times. Once with dinner and once in bed.' He paused as if inviting a response before adding 'I think they work pretty well.'

'Well enough for us to make an offer?'

'Once you've worked your magic on them. And listen, don't let anyone tell you editing can't be just as creative as writing a book.'

'So we'll make an offer when . . .'

'Have we had her proposal for the next book?'

'She's working on it. She's found a setting for it.'

'Anywhere famous?'

'Maybe it will be by the time we're finished with it,' Charlotte said and couldn't understand why she was wary of saying 'Thurstaston.'

'Where's that? Why did she pick it, do you know?'

'It's on the coast looking out to the Irish Sea past Wales. We spent a night there with our other cousins the last time we camped out.'

'There'll need to be more to it. You're making it sound like a book for kids and a pretty old-fashioned one too.'

'I'm sure Ellen will invent something. She's done a lot of that already, after all.'

'Better make sure. No time like now.'

Even once he headed for his desk and she had room to move the heap of proofs aside, Charlotte still felt shut in. She had to glance behind her to check that the wall wasn't as close as the sense she had of a presence looming at her back. The darkness in the corner to her left was a shadow, not soil seeping through the plaster. It was absurd to delay speaking to Ellen, and she lifted her desk phone. As she began to wonder if the ringing wouldn't end until it snagged Ellen's automatic message, Ellen said 'Charlotte.'

'Just me. Not a reason to sound like that, I hope.'

'If you say so.' With no discernible lessening of nervousness Ellen said 'Had we better talk about Rory?'

'Why, what's the matter with him?'

'Nothing if you say not.'

'I don't know why I'd say anything was.'

'I thought he'd been, I suppose we'd have to call it *interfering* a bit over my book. I hope he didn't annoy you. I didn't tell him to, say anything, I mean.'

'He was just being Rory. We all know how he can be. He didn't do any harm. Your book's just between us,' Charlotte said, then had to append 'And the publishers, of course.'

'All right, no more Rory.' After at least a second's silence, which Charlotte found close to ritualistic, Ellen said in her original tone 'What about them?'

'We just need a little more from you.'

'I can send some more chapters over the weekend. That's all I'm doing now, the work you asked me to.'

'Well, I hope that's not your entire life.' Charlotte had the oppressive notion that in order to live her image of a writer Ellen had become a literary hermit locked away with her book. Another silence made her add 'We're waiting for an outline of your next one, and we think . . .'

'Go on. Whatever it is, you'll help me deal with it, won't you?'

Ellen's voice dwindled as Charlotte glanced over her shoulder again. Of course the slanting mass of shadow in the corner hadn't grown, and it was even less likely to have become more solid. It was certainly incapable of concealing a watcher. Nobody was spying on her from where the corner met the floor, and she needn't glare at the dark niche to convince herself. Once she began to feel she was putting off answering Ellen she turned back to the phone in a rage at her irrationality. 'All it is,' she said, 'the place you told me you wanted to use, we'd like there to be a reason for using it.'

'Thurstaston.'

Why did people keep saying the name? It was beginning to resemble some kind of invocation. 'I know you chose it because we were all there,' Charlotte said, 'but that won't be enough for your book.'

'I'd like to talk to you about that night.'

'Not now.' As she hastened to say this Charlotte had to wonder which of them was more on edge. She wasn't going to look behind her, but the view ahead was bad enough. She'd never realised how much the office brought to mind an underground bunker or an air-raid shelter that might collapse with a direct hit, the walls caving in beneath the weight of countless tons of earth. She tried to fend off these fancies by adding 'Unless it's for your book.'

'I don't know if it is.'

'Better leave it for now, then.' Charlotte wished it felt like more of a relief to ask 'Have you thought of anything that could be?'

'Hugh may have.'

'Sorry, what's this to do with him?'

'He wants to help. Between ourselves I think he's a bit sweet on me. Mind you, he hasn't seen me since we all met, and I'm sure –' Ellen trailed off or interrupted herself with a surge of determination. 'I do appreciate you all rallying around my book,' she said.

Perhaps Charlotte felt as if Rory and now Hugh were threatening her professional relationship with Ellen, although why should that work on her nerves so much? Somehow Ellen's remark seemed to aggravate the sense of earth pressing against the walls, staining the lights dim, creeping closer and livelier at Charlotte's back. 'So what's Hugh's contribution?' Charlotte had to ask.

'He says where we slept out that night, it's where someone used to live.'

'And how does that fit in?'

'I think he must have told me because it sounds like a magical name.' After a breath that Charlotte found unnecessarily hard to take, Ellen said 'Arthur Pendemon.'

It appeared to have power. Charlotte saw three of her colleagues stand up and retreat at once. In a moment she realised they were vacating their desks for the weekend. Rather than lending the basement a little more space, the exodus made her feel abandoned in a cell that was far too airless and not nearly light enough. She was absolutely not about to look behind her, even when two more people left their desks. Her job required her to stay on the phone and ask 'What do we know about him?'

'That's all Hugh did, I think. I haven't looked yet.'

Charlotte could perfectly well search for the name while talking to Ellen, and she made to transfer the receiver to her left hand. It had to be the shadow of her movement that fell across the computer screen; nobody had reared up out of the darkness at her back. Her colleagues would have noticed, however few of them remained. She raised the phone again as Ellen said 'Do you remember seeing anything?'

Charlotte found she had no great wish to learn 'Such as what?'

'Maybe we all slept where his house was, except I didn't notice any bits of it, did you?'

'That's my dream.'

'I don't understand. Why would you want that?'

'I didn't. Anything but. I mean it was – Glen, oh thanks.'

He'd veered to her desk on his way to the lift to return Ellen's chapters, dog-eared now. 'Monday,' he mouthed and left Charlotte with a brief squeeze of her upheld wrist, so that for a second she thought he meant to take the phone. She couldn't help wishing he had. The conversation had begun to feel like a trap into which she and Ellen were leading each other with no sense of its limits, let alone of a way to escape. 'What are you saying about him?' Ellen urged.

'Nothing. I'm saying I dreamed I had to go down under where there used to be a house.'

She felt as if the nightmare were poised to continue. The cellars might consist of rooms barely large enough for her to stand upright or move her arms away from her sides. The one to which she was led down unlit steps treacherous with soil, and then narrow sloping passages so lightless that her eyes felt caked with earth, would press her head and shoulders low with its cold stone roof. Even before the cell shut with a dull thick slam that resounded into the underground distance, she would feel like a crippled child. For an endless moment she scarcely knew she was hearing a voice. 'Anyone there?' it said or finished by saying.

Charlotte glared around the office, which was almost deserted. 'I still am.'

'No,' Ellen said and seemed to wish she could leave it at that. 'I asked was there anyone with you in your dream.'

Why had Charlotte thought the room was only almost deserted? Nobody was visible in front of her. Everyone else had sufficient intelligence to leave while there was air to breathe, before the walls collapsed inwards as their age proved unequal to the weight of earth. Meanwhile Ellen's question had revived the sight of eyes no longer buried, blinking away earth to peer gleefully up at Charlotte. 'This isn't getting us anywhere,' she said more sharply than Ellen deserved. 'We'll have to cut it short. They're locking up.'

Having felt desperate enough to invent this as a reason, she was irrationally afraid that it might prove to be true – that she could somehow be imprisoned in the subterranean room all weekend. 'See what you can find out,' she said and struggled to believe that her next breath didn't taste of earth. 'The sooner we've got your synopsis the better, all right? And if you need to call me don't hesitate.'

She would never have expected to be so briskly professional with Ellen. Perhaps her tone was why Ellen didn't answer, instead giving way to a silence that felt not just deep but dark until Charlotte cut it off. She shut down the computer before leaning left to retrieve her bag. A dark shape, vague but eager, swelled out of the corner in response – her own shadow. She grabbed the canvas bag and shoved Ellen's chapters into it, followed by three sets of bound proofs. She was already on her feet, and didn't spare the restlessly shadowy area behind her desk another glance. All the movements that she was unable to avoid glimpsing under desks as she hurried out of the basement room had to be her shadows. No wonder they seemed to be imitating her as they kept pace.

She wasn't anxious to use the lift, even if she would have such space as it offered all to herself. She almost ran along the corridor narrowed by lockers to the stairs. Such was her haste to reach the street that the door was creeping shut on its inexorable metal arm before she was fully aware that the staircase was unlit. Someone must be working on the lights; she heard activity above her – it couldn't be below her – in the dark. Shouldn't the electrician be using a flashlight? Presumably the scraping, like nails on the concrete, showed that he was applying some tool to the problem. She thought of asking how long it would take to fix, and had opened her mouth when she realised that the clawlike sound was approaching out of the dark as the wedge of light around her dwindled to nothingness. Barely in time she blocked the door and dodged into the corridor. She would use a lift after all.

One was waiting behind its doors. It hadn't finished opening when she darted in and jabbed the button to send it upwards. As the doors faltered and set about meeting again, a Ram editor emerged from the Women's and sprinted for the lift. She'd shoved her handbag between the doors when a fellow editor called for her to wait. 'Sorry,' she said to Charlotte and withdrew.

'Sorry,' Charlotte responded, having automatically retreated into a corner, and lurched forwards. She'd said it without thinking, but to whom? She hadn't backed into anyone tall and thin, let alone taller than she was and considerably thinner. The dry jagged sound beneath the nonchalant hum of the lift was too faint to define; it certainly wasn't the clicking of teeth bared in a delighted grimace or already far too bare. Nevertheless she twisted around to see that she was utterly alone, unless someone had sneaked behind her as she moved. The sight of the lift was oppressive enough, the windowless grey cage little wider than her outstretched arms and so indefinitely lit that she couldn't tell how many shadows were sharing the space.

As soon as it lumbered to a halt she dragged the doors apart, bruising her fingers, and ran across the unguarded lobby. The crowd outside on New Oxford Street made her feel hemmed in, particularly at her back. If a smell of earth seemed to linger in her nostrils, it must be as imaginary as it had been in the first place. A bus to Bethnal Green and beyond was approaching, but before she could risk a dash across the road she saw that it was too full to stop. She wanted to be home, up on the roof. Hugging her stuffed bag as if it were an emblem of her ability to function, she struggled through the crowd to Tottenham Court Road.

The stairs to the Underground were so packed with commuters that she took a firmer grip on her bag, though the gesture helped the crowd to pin her arms against her sides. Whoever was immediately above her seemed anxious to travel, but did he really need to press against her back? She could imagine he was eager for his dinner – he felt famished to the bone. He was forcing her downwards step by helpless step, but nobody would notice, since she appeared to be acting just like them. As she reached the circular concourse at the foot of the stairs she opened her mouth to release some kind of noise and swung around. There was nobody in sight who resembled the person she'd sensed behind her. Everyone looked well-fed and entirely unaware of her, and she couldn't be sure that she'd turned to face a loitering smell of earth.

She was heading for the Central Line when she faltered at the ticket barrier. The relentless escalator would carry her down to a platform almost as overloaded as the train was bound to be. All at once she couldn't live with being borne into the subterranean dark amid a press of bodies and increasingly less air. Before she could step aside someone shoved her forwards – a businessman intent on finishing a mobile call. As she fought her way up to street level, against a descent of commuters so implacable it seemed as mindless as earth collapsing into a pit, she kept having to suppress the notion that a hand was about to seize her by the shoulder or the neck.

At last she stumbled out beneath the sky, which was too distant and too overcast to offer much relief from the pressure of the crowd, and battled along Oxford Street to the stop ahead of the one opposite the publishers. She was just in time to catch a bus, although she would have said it was full even before several passengers joined her in the aisle. As it made its ponderous halting journey to Bethnal Green, her view out of the windows was restricted to a parade of shops and bars supporting older architecture on their backs, a spectacle occasionally varied by a glimpse down a side street of a church or some other venerable building. The view made her feel all the more shut in, as though the windows were no better than antique panoramas exhibiting an artificial progress. Once she was off the bus she would breathe more freely. Had somebody behind her been gardening? That might also explain why they were so thin.

As soon as the bus reached Bethnal Green Road she left it, three stops short of hers. It sailed away before she could identify the passenger who'd stood so close. The pavements were crowded with homecomers, and even though the traders were packing up their stalls of clothes and discs and jewellery and groceries, the route still felt constricted. Charlotte took a side street that bordered a park, which accommodated several haphazard games of football and more supine forms of recreation. As she crossed the park she hesitated only once, distracted by the twitching of an elongated shadow beside her. It belonged to a young tree that must have shifted in a breeze she hadn't noticed. The tree was far too slim for anyone to have sidled from behind it or to be using it for cover.

An alley between gentrified four-storey tenements led from a gate in the railings to the pavement opposite her flat. She unlocked the door at the top of the steps and tramped up the stone stairs. Even the passage that enclosed them as they climbed from balcony to balcony felt unappealingly narrow just now. Without pausing to dump her bag in her second-floor flat she continued up to the roof.

She dropped the bag on the faded sunlounger flanked by potted plants – Susie's from the top floor – and leaned on the wall beside the communal barbecue shrouded in plastic. A train whined along the viaduct parallel to Whitechapel Road, beyond which an airliner as bright as a sunlit knife was sinking above the Thames towards Heathrow. Charlotte raised her face to the tattered sky and had taken several increasingly deep breaths when her mobile rang.

She recognised the number, though she had only ever used it to say that her train to Vivaldi was delayed. She thought it best to put on a voice as professional as it was amiable. 'Glen?' she said with a hint of surprise.

'Sure. Sorry if I'm calling when it's not appropriate, but I don't know if you need to hear the news.'

Whatever she might have expected of him, it wasn't this, especially his wariness that sounded close to nervous. 'I don't either,' she said.

'I guess that means you haven't. OK. Sorry.' His pause might have been meant to express further sympathy before he added 'I'm afraid it's about your cousin.'

'Oh, Glen, come on. Not more afterthoughts about her book,' Charlotte blurted, and then his silence gave her time to hold her suddenly tense breath.

EIGHTEEN

She had to research Thurstaston, otherwise she would be letting her family down – Charlotte, who believed she was worth publishing, and Hugh, who'd already done some of the work for her, and even Rory, who had tried in his abrasive way to help. She didn't need to think about the mirror in the cliff, even though it must have been stuck among roots in a burrow, not held in the remains of a hand. Or perhaps she could think of it if she rendered it manageable by working it into her next book. After all, the first one seemed to be letting her come to terms with the injustice she'd suffered at the tribunal; indeed, her new chapters were rendering the memory remote. Perhaps Carlotta or Hugo or Roy could find a magic mirror buried on the common or hidden in a cave by a sorcerer, and why not Arthur Pendemon, if he was as wizardly as his name suggested? Each of them would look into the mirror and see the dream they most wished for, although what would Helen visualise? Presumably her old folk in miraculously rude health, except that as Ellen tried to hold onto the idea it was ousted by the thought of confronting an altogether less welcome reflection, not an old woman but somebody who didn't even have age as an excuse for her mass of pallid bloated spongy flesh, which managed to be both puffy and sagging, a feat unworthy of applause. This wasn't a memory, it had just been a glimpse too brief to be trusted. She mustn't let it reach her nerves again. She dismissed from the screen the chapter she'd started to reread to see if any of it was worth preserving. As soon as the jittering cursor lodged on the Frugonet icon she clicked the slippery mouse.

She'd had enough of her blurred reflection. Across the street a girl was baring almost the whole of her slim bronzed self in a minute bikini on a second-floor balcony. Ellen considered stepping onto hers to catch a little of the late-afternoon sun, and imagined herself as one of a pair of figures in an old-fashioned clock; if she emerged the other girl would have to leave her lounger and retreat into her niche. Equally, as long as the slim girl was out there could be no place for – Ellen left her musings at that, because the computer had brought her the Internet. Once it responded to her password – rohtua, which had started making her feel backward when she'd learned she had to rewrite her book but which no longer did – she typed 'Arthur Pendemon' in the search box.

She'd hardly clicked the mouse when the screen filled with pallor. It was displaying a page of search results, the first of which looked promising: *Arthur Pendemon's Dwelling at Thurstaston Mound*. The next listing included a quotation:

> . . . Arthur Pendemon, who sounds like he fancied himself as some sort of demonic economist . . .

She must have leaned towards the monitor, because her ill-defined reflection appeared to swell up. She recoiled – sat back, rather – and clenched her clammy fist on the mouse to bring up the site.

It was called Mumbo Jumbjoe, which was also the pseudonym of its apparently solitary writer. A sidebar listed topics: *Flying Sauce*, *Pyramid Selling Ancient Egyptian Style*, *Happy Crappy Mediums*, *Where to Shove a Bent Spoon and Other Useless Tricks*, *Aliens Stole Their Brains* . . . The page on which

Ellen had landed was entitled *Vic and Ed's Ectoplasmic Extravaganza*, and she saw why soon enough.

> Blame the Victorians and a few Edwardians while you're at it. Eras of scientific advance my arse. Maybe they were, but they go to show too many people that ought to know better can't cope with too much reason and get desperate to believe in something else, anything you can't prove. What's changed, eh? You'd think humanity couldn't live without magic. Back then it was everywhere a lot of people looked. You couldn't walk down your garden without tripping over a fairy, and even Conan Doyle ended up thinking they were real. Pity he didn't have Sherlock Holmes to sort him out, because he got taken in by the spiritualists after his wife died. Freud ought to have gone into why their victims needed to see lots of white stuff coming out of someone . . .

This startled a laugh out of Ellen, one that felt guilty and surreptitious. She'd begun to dislike the tone of the site so much that she might almost have been sharing someone else's resentment. She propped her chin on her fist, at least one of which yielded more than she appreciated, and scrolled down.

> Doyle was just the best-known writer to get into the occult. William Butler Yeats, horror writers like Stoker and Machen and Blackwood, Sax Rohmer that thought up Fu Manchu – they all joined the Order of the Golden Dawn, Victorian England's cult sensation. So did the Astronomer Royal (just the Scots one) and the President of the Royal Academy (no Scot him) and Oscar Wilde's wife (bugger her). The Order didn't order Baldy Crowley, but he was the magician that got all the publicity, and maybe he gave away what it was all about deep down. One thing was having magical duels. Baldy challenged the founder to one, and a couple of magic men who'd gone up north had a real old witchy rumpus. Step forward Arthur Pendemon, who sounds like he fancied himself as some sort of demonic economist, and Peter Grace . . .

Ellen pushed herself to her feet and leaned forwards to drag up the sash of the window. Perhaps the cloying smell that reminded her of digging in the earth was outside the building, because her action seemed not to affect it. Of course, someone must be gardening. As the girl on the balcony raised a slim arm to acknowledge her, Ellen retreated behind her desk. She passed a hand over her moist forehead and wiped it on her old baggy trousers before closing her fingers over the mouse.

> The story goes Pendemon thought Grace was calling up too many spirits and devils and the rest of that lot when he wanted to use them himself. Seems like even demons get tired and want a night off now and then. You'd think these two masters of the occult might have learned to share and be good little boys, but Grace told Pendemon if he wanted any of the powers Grace was supposed to have made slaves out of he could fight him for them. He must have thought his were bigger and nastier, but Pendemon had a trick under his pointy hat if it wasn't up his robe. 'All flesh incubates the dark,' he's meant to have said, and 'At the core of every soul horror waits to gnaw forth' and 'The mass of men are vessels of dread for the thaumaturge to draw upon.' In English that means he thought he could use anybody handy to send Grace something as horrible as horrible gets. Anyone who wandered near Pendemon's house . . .

What use was this to Ellen's book? She let go of the glistening plastic lump and raised her ponderous hand to dab her infirm forehead. She was lowering her hand to wipe it when it faltered in front of her nose, that pallid excrescence that appeared to have split in half to trouble both inner edges of her vision. With a good deal of reluctance she brought the hand closer. Was it the source of the underlying smell? She wasn't sure, though her hand was certainly as moist as an imperfectly squeezed sponge. She let the flabby appendage flop on the desk, only to wonder which she found less appealing – the hand or the prospect of reading the rest of the text. Couldn't she look at Pendemon's house instead? Even that would involve wielding her fat etiolated sweaty hand. It and the insidious smell, which she was increasingly unable to believe had any source besides her own dank self, had begun to sicken her. She was staring at the hand as if this might render it no longer part of her, except that the rest was at least as bad, when her mobile wriggled against her padded hip before emitting its protracted note.

She saw her hand jerk nervously, and tried not to think that she saw it wobble like a jellyfish stranded on the beach of the desk. She fumbled the mobile out of her pocket and poked a key with a blundering thumb as she lifted her hand almost close enough to touch her pulpy cheek. 'Ellen?' Hugh said.

'I'm afraid so.' She hoped he hadn't caught that – she didn't want to have to explain – and so she added 'Are you checking up on me?'

'Why, do I need to? What's wrong?'

'I meant are you checking to see if I've found out anything about the person you mentioned who used to live where we were talking about.'

What had happened to her language? She was sidling around the subject without understanding why. As she gazed at the screen she was close to fancying that the information below the edge was about to inch into view – that it was determined not to stay buried. Hugh didn't help by mumbling 'Have you?'

Ellen had the odd impression that he would prefer not to know, unless he hoped for a negative answer. A faint tremor rose through the lines on the monitor, as if the text were about to take on more life. As she reached to quell it with a fat hand at the end of an arm that was surely not as plump, she was suddenly afraid that her pudgy clutch would dislodge the lurking words from their den. She closed her eyes while she admitted 'I'm just starting.'

'Leave it alone for a minute, can you?'

Ellen risked slitting her eyes and saw that the upper half of the rest of the sentence had crept into view.

. . . would have the worst

she couldn't avoid glimpsing before she clicked the mouse to close the page. She wanted to blame Hugh for her nervousness, and wished she didn't have to ask 'Why?'

'It wasn't what I rang about. It's Rory.'

'Has he got you acting as his secretary now? Go on then, put him on.'

She was so concerned to shut down the computer, if only since it was a distraction, that she didn't immediately notice Hugh's pause. 'I can't,' he said.

'Don't tell me he wants you to do his talking for him as well.' As the screen turned black, exhibiting her pale blob of a face, Ellen raised her voice in case she could be overheard. 'He's good enough at talking to my editors about me when I didn't ask him to. Is he sorry now he did? He ought to tell me to, well, he can't to my face, but he ought to tell me himself.'

'It isn't that,' Hugh protested in something like anguish. 'I said I'd tell you about him.'

'When did you say that?'

'When I spoke to Charlotte.'

Ellen couldn't help growing resentful, however prematurely. 'You were speaking to her about . . .'

'What've we been talking about? My brother. Why are you making this harder for me?'

'I'm sure I wasn't aware that I was.'

'Ellen, I'm sorry. It's not your fault, it's mine.' Hugh swallowed hard enough to be audible and said 'I phoned him when he was coming to see me and he was in a crash.'

Hugh couldn't feel guiltier than Ellen immediately did for having assumed the subject was her book. She stared in renewed loathing at her blurred pallid swollen face and wondered how much it was puffed up with self-absorption. She saw a hole open in it as she set about asking 'How bad?'

'Bad.'

The hole closed, and she felt her thickened lips quiver like gelatin as they rubbed together. They parted with an unpleasant sticky sound as a preamble to saying 'Just tell me, Hugh.'

'He's not dead.'

Eventually she had to ask 'What is he?'

'Unconscious. Maybe in a coma.'

Ellen unstuck her lips again, and so did the oversized blob. 'Apart from that . . .'

'I don't know. I haven't been yet. I've only just rung the hospital.'

'When will you be going?'

'Soon as I can. Charlotte's coming tomorrow.'

From his tone Ellen could have assumed the events were directly connected. 'She's staying over,' he added on the way to blurting 'You can too if you like.'

Why should a family reunion make Ellen apprehensive? She could only blame Hugh's feelings about her, but she would have to cope with those for Rory's sake. 'I'll see you then,' she said. 'I'll ring to say what time. Are you meeting people at the station?'

'I might have to stay here. Get a cab if you don't fancy walking up.'

'Which way is it? How far?'

Hugh was silent long enough that she thought he was preparing to say more than 'You're best getting a cab.'

How could he have experienced a vision of her plodding uphill to his house, the noisome sweaty mass of her quaking from head to foot with every step? As she struggled to expel it from her mind she managed to say 'Try not to blame yourself, all right? Rory needn't have answered while he was driving. He ought to have switched his phone off.'

'I shouldn't have asked him to come.'

'Don't brood, Hugh. We'll all be together again soon,' Ellen said, which ended the call, or silence did.

Staring at her undefinable reflection didn't help her take her own advice, but she wasn't anxious to return to Mumbo Jumbjoe or visit any of the other sites. She pushed her chair back and stood up, and the girl on the balcony turned her head. She'd donned sunglasses, which obscured whether she was gazing at Ellen with sympathy far too close to dismay if not bordering on revulsion. All at once Ellen felt sick and headed for the bathroom.

Rory's portraits flanked her as she hurried down the hall. She could have thought her own painted eyes were foreseeing her present state and concealing their distress. She shoved the bathroom door open, and then she recoiled. One glimpse in the mirror, not even of her entire shape, was enough. She grabbed her portrait from its hook and carried it in front of her face to the mirror. It was almost exactly as wide as the protruding plastic frame, and so tall that she couldn't see her reflection over it once she slammed it into place. She hadn't glimpsed herself again, let alone anybody else. Nobody a good deal more than sufficiently thin to hide behind her had dodged out of sight, as she confirmed by twisting her head around so hard her neck ached. Perhaps she wasn't going to be sick after all, though she felt worse than queasy as her distended hands splashed cold water on her clammy face. She might have to deal with worse than nausea. When she recalled the veiled gaze of the girl on the balcony, she wondered how she would be able to bear stepping outside the door.

NINETEEN

'Is Charlotte in there?' Catching sight of her at the back of the lift, Glen waved a handful of papers. 'Pass these to her,' he said and called 'They're for your cousin.' Someone in the front rank that was pressing everybody else towards the walls accepted the documents, and as the doors struggled together against the mass of bodies Glen's attention drifted left of Charlotte. His eyes widened, and he reached out as if he wished he could rescue her from the crowd. Then the doors shut, though only just, and the cage packed with bodies set about ascending, so sluggishly that she could have imagined it was being dragged down and in danger of sinking into the earth. People were relaying the papers to her over their shoulders, since there wasn't space for them to turn around. Were there three pages or four? As they arrived beside her she saw they were bordered in black. She was about to take them when the person whose bones were digging into her left side did, and she noticed that his hand was covered more with soil than flesh.

She couldn't retreat even an inch. She could only watch as he transferred the papers to his other shrivelled hand so as to grasp her face and twist it towards him. When her eyes strained to look away he released her and gestured at the doors, scattering earth like black dandruff on the shoulders of the woman in front of him. The lift shuddered to a halt and the doors staggered apart. For a breath, if she had been able to draw one, Charlotte thought only darkness was waiting beyond them. Then earth piled in, flinging everyone helplessly together on the way to filling her eyes and nose and mouth. Her companion seemed quite at home in it, because his fingers wriggled wormlike through it to fasten on her hand and pull her deeper into the suffocating dark.

She fought to cry out, but her mouth was gagged with earth. She strove to free herself from the scrawny clutch, but she was pinioned by bodies that had ceased to move and the one that should have. She tried to suck in a breath, but it consisted of earth too. Was she dreaming out of utter desperation that she'd managed to produce a sound? It was feeble and flattened, muffled by distance or worse. Nevertheless it seemed to travel past the blackness, and she put all her dwindling energy into repeating it. This time it succeeded in wakening her, and she threw out her hand to rid it of the sensation of being held. It collided with a barrier in front of her at considerably less than arm's length.

There was nothing like that so near her bed, and certainly no wall. She wasn't in her flat; she wasn't even on the roof. She'd thought spending the night on the padded sunlounger would rid her of the sense of being shut in before she had to travel to Hugh's – her four rooms had never seemed so oppressively small and dim, or even slightly until last night – but she hadn't slept much. She'd kept being wakened by a smell of earth and having to remind herself that it belonged to the plant-pots by the lounger. Each time she'd opened her eyes the night sky had looked far too close, a black lid above her face. Once it had grown lighter she'd managed to doze fitfully, and then it had been time to get ready to leave. Nothing had relieved the claustrophobia that felt as if her surroundings were smaller than her head: not showering in the glass cell of the bathroom cubicle rendered nearly opaque by steam, nor walking down the narrow street overshadowed by tenements to the main road that might have seemed wider without the traders' stalls and the crowds around them, nor the bus crammed with shoppers, nor the multitude of Saturday commuters at Kings Cross. As for the train to Yorkshire, it consisted of just two carriages for a journey of over two hours. Her seat and the one in front trapped her in a space so restricted that she had to slant her knees towards the window in order to press them together. She was further pinned by the side of the carriage and by her neighbour in the aisle seat, who must have been startled by Charlotte's nightmare cry. Charlotte opened her aching eyes and turned to make some apology, but the seat was unoccupied.

It was the only empty one in sight. When had her skinny neighbour deserted it? As soon as she was seated Charlotte had closed her eyes in an attempt to ignore the lack of space, and so she hadn't observed her seatmate, she had only felt the gaunt shape settle next to her. They must have been so eager to descend that they'd advanced into the foremost carriage as a station closed around the train. It was Leeds, where Charlotte had to change.

None of the disembarking passengers looked particularly thin, but locating her next train was surely more important. As she hurried to the nearest monitor a faint quake rose through the display, bone-white letters on a background black as earth. A train to Huddersfield was leaving platform thirteen in three minutes. Charlotte sprinted up an escalator towards the expansively arched roof and along a wide corridor with a view across the city to the moors. Despite the spaciousness, she felt as if her nightmare were still cramping her mind as she dashed down a second escalator to her train.

Was she the solitary passenger? The nearest carriage was deserted. Half the seats faced forwards, to be confronted across the midpoint of the carriage by their twins. Charlotte sat there to take advantage of the space between the halves, although it rather made her feel as if she were facing an unseen audience instead of just her overnight bag. She was regaining her breath and wondering why her brief sprint should have made it hard to breathe when the train jerked forwards.

A guard came calling for tickets, to little if any effect elsewhere on the train, and then Charlotte was alone. Trees and hedges blotted out the sky before the train was engulfed by a tunnel – no, just a bridge no more extended than the nervous breath she took. Several bridges that felt like threats of carrying her underground preceded the first station, where the train opened its doors for nobody visible and emitted a string of beeps as shrill as an alarm to indicate they were closing. As fields partly overcome by suburbs spread out on both sides, Charlotte did her best to concentrate on the sky. Was she apprehensive about seeing Rory? She couldn't understand why else the journey was making her so tense. The train halted at another station, and as it shrilled she was tempted to make for the doors. Of course they were too distant, and her nervousness was unforgivably irrational. Or perhaps she was right to take the sound as a warning, because the train had barely left the station when it plunged into the dark.

The tunnel shut her in with the rows of empty yet unfriendly seats and the vista of their equivalent beyond the doorways that kept rocking out of alignment between the carriages. The further rows appeared to be squeezed together like the segments of an accordion robbed of air. Why did she need to imagine that anybody sitting there would have to be unnaturally thin? The blackened hand that twitched between the seats as if responding to her thought must be the reflection of a crack in the wall of the tunnel, just a small crack, not an indication that the place was unsafe. The wall was rushing past almost as close to the side of the carriage as she was, with a muffled roar that made her ears feel boxed in. Perhaps a wider passage would have been unable to support the weight of the earth under which it was buried. She was far too capable of sensing all that weight, which felt poised to squeeze any possibility of breathing out of her. How long might the tunnel be? It had walled her up for over a minute, enough time for her to lose count of her nervously shallow breaths, but there was no sign of daylight, nothing ahead except seats thrashing back and forth like sleepers unable to escape a nightmare. Why had she let herself be taken on this helpless ride? If Rory was in a coma he wouldn't even know that Hugh and his cousins were there. The thought made her feel spied upon, grubby with guilt at having had it. She was too far into her journey to turn back from visiting the hospital. She could bear the rest of the tunnel, even if its walls seemed to be blackening the light that spilled from the carriage, absorbing it as a preamble to draining the light inside. The tunnel wasn't about to cave in, crushing the train like a tin can, shattering the windows, packing the carriages with earth and debris. The notion would have been easier to shake off if it hadn't felt underlain with secret glee, as if somebody were wishing it on Charlotte, anticipating it with wicked delight. She gave in to glancing over the back of her seat, but the others were owning up to no presence. As she faced forwards again a lanky shape leaped into view beyond the lurching doors. Its scrawny outstretched limbs were branches. It was a bush at the side of the track, and it was sunlit. The train had escaped from the tunnel.

She had been underground for less than three minutes, but she felt as if they or their stifling confinement hadn't released her – felt surrounded by a darkness all the more claustrophobic for its invisibility. When fields beneath a sky piled with shades of grey began to flank the carriage, the openness seemed ready to immure her in another tunnel. Whenever the train slowed, her breath did too. It was only halting at a series of small towns as yellow as sand, some of them dominated by factories. Each time it announced its departure with the shrill alarm, she dug her fingertips into the upholstery to resist fleeing to the doors. All this appropriated most of half an hour until Huddersfield raised lofty chimneys beside the track and gathered an industrial estate around it, corrugated metal buildings that resembled the outsize houses of a gentrified shanty town. In another minute Charlotte was able to liberate herself from the train.

She didn't want to be shut in a taxi. Hugh's number rang as she came in sight of a low huddle of them outside the station, and she loitered beside them as the simulated bell continued to ring. She was wondering if he'd gone out, though surely he would have taken his mobile with him, when he gasped 'Charlotte.'

'Are you at home?'

'Where else would I be?'

The question sounded embittered or worse, not at all like Hugh, but she thought it best to pretend she hadn't noticed. 'I'm at the station. How do I get to you?'

'Aren't there any cabs?'

'More than enough, but I'd sooner walk.'

'A cab's quicker. It won't cost much.'

'Is Ellen there?'

'No.' With equal bewilderment Hugh said 'Why?'

'Then there's no rush, is there? I thought we were all going to the hospital together.' At once she felt sufficiently guilty to add 'Or has there been a change? Is Rory conscious?'

'He wasn't an hour ago. He hasn't been yet.'

'But you've seen him. How is he otherwise?'

'I don't know. I've been waiting for you two like you said.'

'Since yesterday?'

'He wouldn't care either way, would he? He wouldn't have known I was there.'

She heard dismay bordering on desperation. She oughtn't to make him feel worse about his brother. 'Let's talk about it when we're together,' she said. 'Which way are you from here?'

'Empire Street.'

'I know the address, Hugh.' She didn't understand why he'd taken several seconds to prepare to say it. 'I'm asking how I get there,' she said.

'Up the hill.'

Charlotte assumed this referred to the road that climbed past a small factory, dilapidated but not defunct. 'I see it, and then?'

'Is something up with your phone?'

'Not that I'm hearing. I go up the hill, and then . . .'

'So it's me.'

'Your phone? It'll just be a crossed –' Charlotte said, having grown aware of another voice in her ear. Before she could identify its few muddy words or distinguish more than how pleased it seemed to be with itself, the line went dead.

She was almost irritated enough to call Hugh back. Instead she went to the last taxi in the queue. How could just stooping to the vehicle make her feel shut in? Even asking for directions did, though the driver was almost maternally anxious to help. So did climbing the steep road towards a blackened sky that looked pregnant with a storm and all the lower for it, and following the road across a bridge around which the air was thick with the fumes and the rumble of four lanes of traffic beneath, and tramping along a protracted stretch walled on one side by a factory while trees above a wall overhung the other. At least the route wasn't crowded; indeed, there was never anyone behind her whenever she failed to resist the temptation to glance back. She felt especially ridiculous for doing so as a narrow side street brought her to her cousin's house.

It was the near end of the terrace that formed the right side of Empire Street. Clothes of all colours drooped on lines in front gardens as small as the sandstone houses. Hugh's had no clothes-line, just an abundance of weeds bordering the cramped mossy path and raising their ragged heads from its cracks. Charlotte was hauling the unhinged gate aside when a plump woman in a sari stepped out of the next house. 'How is Mr Lucas?' she said. 'Have you seen him?'

'Not yet. We're going soon.'

'Where are you going, please?'

'To the hospital.'

'Please forgive me. I did not know this. Could you say that Mrs Devi was asking about him?'

'I will,' Charlotte said and wished she didn't have to add 'If he knows we're there.'

Mrs Devi lifted stubby hands beside her face as though to shape her mouth rounder. 'What has happened to him?'

'He was in some kind of accident on his way here.'

'He was run over? I forever tell the children –'

'No, in his van.'

Mrs Devi looked as confused as Charlotte had begun to grow. 'He is a driver? Where does he keep it?'

'Sorry,' Charlotte said and would rather not have gone on. 'Who are we talking about?'

'Mr Lucas,' Mrs Devi said, vigorously waggling her fingers at Hugh's house. 'Are you not familiar with him?'

'He's my cousin. Are you trying to tell me something's wrong with him?'

'He has not been to work for nearly three days now.'

'You get time off even if you work for Frugo. I expect he'll have taken some because of our cousin, the one who's in hospital, that's to say his brother.'

'He has not been out at all.'

Charlotte peered at Hugh's house, but the faded scaly front

door remained shut, and her voice hadn't brought him to any of the windows, which were slated with reflections of clouds. She tried to conceal her unease as she said 'I'll let him know you were asking.'

'If he ever needs his neighbour he knows where I am,' Mrs Devi said and withdrew into her house.

Charlotte felt watched but could see no observer. As she advanced up the path she had the impression that the house wasn't growing as it should. Of course this was an illusion, but she could almost have imagined that the house was shrinking to shut her in, like a cottage in an unpleasant fairy tale. She spent some energy in fending off the idea as she thumbed the grimy plastic bellpush.

The electronic tolling sounded blurred by dust or age. When it brought no response, Charlotte rang again and levered the knocker up and down above the equally rusty letterbox. The reluctant clanking was followed by a protracted rattle and a thud. Though it sounded like the springing of a trap, it was the sash of an upstairs window. Hugh leaned out, only to stare both ways along the street. 'I'm here,' Charlotte called.

As his eyes met hers she saw they looked hollow and sleepless, presumably from worrying about his brother. 'Are you coming to let me in?' she eventually had to ask.

She was waiting for his footsteps on the stairs when he reappeared at the window. 'Can you?' he said.

He jerked a fist over the sill, so violently that he might have been trying to punch someone invisible in the face. By the time Charlotte grasped his intention he'd dropped the key beside the path. As she retrieved it she smelled earth, but she wasn't taking that as any kind of omen. She twisted the key in the stiff lock and pushed the door wide.

The interior smelled stale, too nearly airless. At the end of a narrow hall halved by stairs and watched over by copies of Rory's family portraits, she saw and heard a tap release a dull flat drip into a metal sink. As she closed the front door the hall with its drab brownish wallpaper took on more gloom. She was expecting Hugh to appear at the top of the stairs by the time she reached them, but she couldn't even hear him moving. 'Are you all right?' she called.

'I'm still here.'

The tap emitted another drip, and she wondered how long he'd left it that way. She made for the kitchen, past a room where a dusty television squatted near a bookcase rather less than full of Cougar books and shabbier volumes. A gentle turn sufficed to quell the drips, and she was returning to the hall when she faltered. It couldn't really have narrowed. Perhaps that was an effect of the gathering darkness, which seemed capable of transforming the space beneath the stairs into a den. Of course nobody was crouching there, and so she oughtn't to have sounded nervous as she called 'Aren't you ever coming down?'

'You come up first.'

If his tone had betrayed any enjoyment, Hugh might almost have been proposing a game. Charlotte hurried past the earthy shadows under the stairs and grabbed the banister. At the top she was faced with a rudimentary landing beneath a low roof. A faint glistening trail wandered back and forth over the faded brown carpet, starting in the room from which she heard the spring-like trickle of a presumably unstoppable flush. The track, reminiscent of a snail's but surely too large, also led in and out of the front bedroom. She couldn't help hesitating before she pushed the door open and ventured into the room.

Hugh was standing with his back to her beyond the single bed and facing the window. The end of the plain pale quilt near the foot of the bed was grubby with marks, from which she deduced that he'd been lying down with his shoes on. As she stepped forwards she kicked an object on the floor – a plastic cap that belonged to the can of shaving foam in Hugh's hand. She had trouble believing she'd identified the source of the trail that led from the bathroom to him. 'What on earth have you been doing?' she said. 'Why have you made such a mess?'

'It's my house.'

'Nobody's saying it isn't,' Charlotte told him, though there was little in the shabby room to demonstrate his ownership – just some discarded clothes on a chair. 'People are worried about you, that's all. Mrs Devi was saying you haven't been to work for days. You'll have taken them off because of Rory, won't you?'

'Who?'

Charlotte's attempt to laugh only shook her voice. 'Rory. Your brother.'

'I know who my brother is. I asked who else you said.'

'Mrs Devi. The lady from next door.'

'First I've heard she's called that. I didn't know you'd be checking up on me.'

'How long are we going to talk like this? Can't you look at me?'

He only shrugged – left shoulder, then the right, and again as if trying to establish which was which. Oughtn't she to go to him? She'd taken a step, watching her feet to avoid the trail on the carpet, before she realised he was moving, so tentatively that she could almost have concluded he was having to remember how to turn. His wary gaze found hers at last, only to fall to the can in his hand. Much of his face reddened as he lurched to grab the cap beside his feet and jam it onto the container, which he dropped on the bed. Having waited for an explanation or even for him to look at her again, Charlotte said 'All right, I won't ask.'

'Don't.'

That hadn't worked the way she'd hoped it would. As his gaze sought her face he held out a hand. She could almost have thought he was pleading mutely to be led from the room until she realised he must want his key back. When she planted it in his hand his fingers twitched as if they were eager to close around more than the key. The room was threatening to feel as small and dark as the inside of her skull. 'Aren't you going to offer me a drink?' she said.

His face grew yet more mottled. 'I'd have to go out.'

'You've nothing to drink in the house?'

'Not the kind you're after. Are you feeling bad?'

'No,' she said and more truthfully 'I'm feeling thirsty. We're talking tea here, Hugh.'

'I've got that. I'm some use.'

'I'm sure nobody would say you weren't.' When his eyes remained guarded, little better than blank, Charlotte said 'I expect it's in the kitchen, is it?'

'It will be.'

Even this didn't move him until she made with some impatience for the stairs. As she reached the landing she felt his breath on her neck. At least it was Hugh, not some imaginary pursuer, but she said 'No need to get so close.'

'Sorry,' he gasped, which tousled her hair.

'I'll follow you down. I'm just going to the private room.'

She didn't glance back as she shut the door. The overcast sky blackened the window, which was already on the way to opaque with a rash of glass pimples. A greyish shower curtain sagging from immovable plastic hooks helped confine her in the token space between the bath and the opposite wall, where its reflection in the mirror failed to add even a pretence of spaciousness. The trickle of the cistern behind her might have been mocking her own activity, but she hadn't finished when she realised she had yet to hear Hugh go downstairs. Was he listening like a sly jailer outside the door? The room seemed shrunken by darkness, and the light cord was out of reach. She rose to her feet as soon as she could, because she felt watched too. What was twitching the shower curtain aside to peer around it? Her own hasty movement had stirred it, and the shrivelled clawlike hand consisted of wrinkles in the plastic. It was enough to put her in a fury at her rampant imagination, and when she stalked out of the room the sight of her cousin loitering in his bedroom doorway made her angrier still. 'What do you think you're doing now?' she demanded.

His face was reddening again, a process that her question accelerated. 'Waiting for you,' he mumbled.

'Don't you think I can find my way around your little house? I wouldn't mind if it was twice the size.'

She oughtn't to seem to be denigrating where he'd chosen to live, but he had to be the reason why she was on edge. She felt worse than guilty for wishing Ellen would arrive so that she wasn't alone with him. 'Come on, let's make that tea,' she said.

The instant she planted a foot on the top stair he came after her. 'Not so close,' she had to warn him again, and kept hold of the banister. Gaining the hall would have been a relief if it had been wider. She was heading for the at least slightly roomier kitchen before she noticed he had frozen three steps up. 'What's –' she cried as she turned to see what in the front room was appalling him. He was gazing across it and through the window, and in a moment she saw the figure outside the house.

TWENTY

As Ellen plodded into the station concourse a voice as large as the building finished an announcement, and she heard a tuneless humming behind her, which rose as if she'd aggravated its impatience. Nevertheless it was being emitted by an invalid tricycle, not its rider, who called 'Can you mind out, love? I can't see round you.'

She might have fled without looking at him, to a different exit and home – she'd already had children turning to stare at her once they'd sat ahead of her on the bus across Southport – but she mustn't care about anything more than Rory. As she moved aside the tricycle droned past her, laden with a pensioner whose pink scalp peeked through his grey hair and who bulged on both sides of the seat, not least his tweedy buttocks. At once he halted, blocking her progress. 'I still can't make it out,' he complained. 'When's the next train to Manchester?'

'In just a few minutes, and I'd like to be on it if you don't mind.'

'Can't stop you if there's room.'

She felt as though he were putting into words the image that had haunted her for days and equally sleepless nights, and so her retort was more of a plea. 'What do you mean?'

'The same as I say, love. It's an old-fashioned habit of mine.'

As the tricycle cruised forwards its humming grew more laboured. Perhaps Ellen should have saved her breath as she did her best to overtake, but a remnant of her old profession made her say 'You ought to have that serviced. It's under too much strain.'

His large already purplish face shook as he poked it up at her. 'What's it to you?'

'I'm only advising you. I used to care for people like you.'

'Given up now, have you?' he said and slitted his overflowing eyes as if to keep a thought in. 'Hold on a tick. Weren't you in the paper?'

She only had to run for the train, if her legs were up to running. She was stumbling away when he said 'It was you plain enough. No wonder you didn't want to show your face.'

The tricycle hummed alongside her, sounding unbearably smug, and she turned on him in the hope that some of the scattered commuters might come to her defence. 'Why shouldn't I?'

'Good God, woman, don't grimace at me. You're ugly enough.'

It must be a standard insult of his, Ellen tried to believe – perhaps one he'd levelled at any wife or wives he had – but it didn't tell her anything she didn't already know. Nobody was going to intervene on her behalf, since they could see the truth of his remark, if they could bear to look. Indeed, she had a sense that one of the spectators was delighting in her experience. Their glee seemed to pace her as she trudged ahead of the old man, her eyes so swollen that they felt like insomnia rendered solid, her lips too engorged to utter another word.

The first carriage on the train had a space for wheelchairs and the like at its near end. Ellen dumped her wheeled case in the luggage alcove of the only other carriage and plumped herself onto the closest pair of unoccupied seats. She was wearing her most voluminous clothes, but she couldn't tell whether they were clinging to her because they were no longer large enough or with her inelegant sweat. As the train filled up, more than one person thought better of sitting next to her. She was beginning to dread that someone might have to – that she would be trapped with their reaction or their attempts to conceal it all the way to Manchester – when the train jerked forwards.

She felt the vibration travel upwards from her feet, a quivering that passed through every inch of flesh. As she moved uneasily the seat seemed to yield too much, unless she did. She lifted a ponderous arm to open the meagre slat of the window, which brought her upper regions a humid breeze, although it also intensified the earthy stench that had become her companion, no doubt a symptom of her state. She was so enclosed in bloated flesh that she couldn't judge how hot she was. Whenever a shadow moulded itself to her she could have taken it for moisture welling up from her body. She tried gazing out of the window, but the headlong countryside occasionally halted by stations was eager to parade the sight of her face bulging like a fungus under bridges or being dragged like a fallen moon – an object as rotund and blotchy and porous – over fields and townscapes. Sometimes the spectacle compelled her to touch her face, but she was unable to determine how swollen if not rotten it might be – no less than her groping fingers. If she rested her hands in her lap she couldn't avoid noticing how much they resembled stranded sea creatures, bloated and pallid and ready to grow more discoloured. In the end she had to settle for staring at the back of the next seat, although it made her feel caged, like an exhibit but one so unsightly that spectators couldn't bear to look. She would be with her family soon, and surely they could stand whatever she'd become or at least show her a modicum of sympathy. The prospect went some way towards sustaining her as far as Manchester, and the thought of Rory did. In one sense he must be in worse shape than her.

The train wobbled to a halt at Manchester, and then she did. She kept her seat while the carriage emptied, not least because nearly everyone who passed her stared at her, unless they glanced at her and quickly looked away. She remained seated even once she was alone in the carriage; she didn't want another confrontation with the tricycling pensioner. Or was she alone? Perhaps if she peered into the dark under the seats she would find she wasn't quite. She would do nothing of the sort; she might be missing the next train to Huddersfield. She stumped along the aisle to grab her luggage and lower herself from the train.

The tricyclist was blocking the way off the platform while he lectured the ticket collector about facilities for invalids. Neither man immediately acknowledged Ellen. 'Excuse me,' she said to the collector, 'could you ask –'

'Just because I'm in a chair doesn't mean I can't talk.'

'I'm aware of that. So could –'

'See, there's people like her that don't think us cripples ought to be heard. We're just in their way, that's what they think.'

Ellen was growing hotter with frustration, which made her feel heavier still. 'Well, if you don't mind my saying so –'

'I do mind. We're not meant to have feelings, you see,' the old man informed the collector. 'At least there's some that still care about us. She got fired from her job for mistreating the likes of me.'

She might have tried to refute this if the collector hadn't said 'Do you two know each other?'

'I know all I want to know about her, thanks very much.'

'You don't know anything about me.' Despite feeling like a child in an outsize body, Ellen couldn't resist adding 'And I'd rather not know anything about you.'

'See, she admits it. That's how much she cares about cripples, and they were supposed to be her job.'

Ellen had a sense of helplessly performing a script for someone else's amusement or worse. 'I always cared for my patients, however disabled they were.'

'You can see how much, can't you? She won't even face me. Maybe she thinks I'm nothing to look at, but –'

'I don't care how you look,' Ellen said and stared at him. 'It isn't how people are on the outside, it's inside that counts.'

'And you're as bad one way as you are the other. Don't go putting on your nasty face again. I told you, there's no need to make yourself worse.' As Ellen's cumbersome lips shifted he said 'Just dry up, you ugly woman.'

She thought the collector was coming to her defence until he said 'Can you both go through now, please? There's another train in.'

She must have deserved everything, then, since he apparently thought so. As the tricycle moved off with a satisfied hum she brandished her ticket at the collector, though her distended fingers came close to dropping it on the ledge of the booth and letting it lie. She dragged her case and herself across the concourse to the departures monitor and saw that the next train to Huddersfield left in ten minutes. Having shown her ticket to another official, who looked unimpressed by it or her, she blundered into the nearest carriage on the train.

Despite its size, the train was nowhere near full by the time it left the station. Ellen couldn't blame the handful of commuters for wanting to avoid her, especially once she saw her blurred face slithering sluglike across the inside of a bridge. It was as dim as some bedroom item rendered monstrous by a nightmare that refused to dissipate. She closed her bloated eyes and clasped her hands tight in her lap against the temptation to finger her face. They felt like clammy lumps of tripe resting on more of the same, and in general refusing to see only aggravated her sense of herself as just a hulk of loathsome meat. Now and then sunlight flooded over her, unless it was some exudation of her own, which reminded her of the old man's advice. She wished she could indeed dry up and wither too. Writers might be meant to use their own experiences, but she was afraid she'd passed the limit. Her imagination felt crushed by her body, reduced to a sense of the misshapen mass of flesh.

At last the train wavered to a stop in Huddersfield. Once she heard she was alone, unless someone was silently watching her, she opened her eyes and heaved her deformed bulk towards the platform. Perhaps the ticket collector had seen her coming, because he took her ticket without looking at her. She trudged out to a taxi rank, where she felt her midriff swell like an inflated tyre as she bent to the window of the first vehicle. She was sure the driver barely managed not to shrink away, but she wasn't going to subject him to her presence in the car. As soon as she'd obtained directions to Empire Street she stepped back.

The beginning of the route was steeply uphill. The dark sky looked laden with moisture, if no more so than Ellen felt. A bridge over the ring road seemed to coat her with noise and grimy fumes before the route led between a factory and a wall overhung by trees. When she plodded into the shade of the foliage it seemed to leave her moister. Most of the few people she encountered were on the opposite side of the road, and all were by the time she came abreast of them. Were they glancing hastily away from her or from somebody behind her? Surely she was bad enough. If there appeared to be a scrawny shadow on the pavement when she turned her burden of a head, it must be an elongated stain. The clumps of outstretched spindly objects at the ends of two thin twisted branches of the main discolouration couldn't drag her back or down or chase her off.

Beyond the factory a side street led past a copse to Hugh's house. An unpainted gate slouched in the entrance to his garden, more like a scrap of wilderness. However shabby the building was, it looked like a haven to her. Whatever had befallen her, surely Hugh and Charlotte would understand. She was suddenly so desperate to see her family that she grew afraid of being prevented somehow as she and her thunderous luggage made for the house. She had almost reached the gate when she saw Hugh.

He was on the stairs, framed by the window and the doorway of the front room, and seemed paralysed with shock. There was no question that she was the cause of his distress. In a moment Charlotte peered across the room at her and cried out, unless she was too appalled to make a sound. Ellen couldn't run, but she and her case lumbered away as fast as they could. The front door must have opened, because this time she heard Charlotte, whose question only spurred her onwards. 'Oh, Ellen, what have you done to yourself?'

TWENTY-ONE

That couldn't be Ellen, Hugh tried to believe. It mustn't be. Perhaps his thoughts were visible, because she retreated, dragging her wheeled suitcase or using it as support. As soon as she disappeared from the double frame of the doorway and the window he had no idea which way she'd gone. The banister gave a pained creak before he realised how hard he was clutching it. As he managed to relax his grip in case the rail came loose from the uprights, Charlotte ran to open the front door. 'Oh, Ellen,' Hugh heard her cry, 'what have you done to yourself?'

They could have been his words, and he shouldn't let her speak for him. He was too prone to behave as if Rory and their cousins were more capable of just about anything than he was. If he couldn't help Ellen, he was no use whatsoever. He swung towards the sound of Charlotte's footsteps dulled by moss. The hall was straight ahead, and so was the path. He was able to keep Charlotte in sight all the way to joining her outside the gate.

Ellen was heading doggedly towards a clump of trees as if

she planned to take cover among them. 'Ellen, don't,' Charlotte called and ran after her. 'Ellen.'

'Where are you going, Ellen? Come in the house.'

The ominous rumble of her luggage faltered to a halt, and then she did. She didn't turn, and even in the silence her voice was barely audible. 'Don't you want your neighbours to see me, Hugh?'

'I always would.' He only mouthed this, from embarrassment more than doubled by Charlotte's presence. Aloud he said 'We don't want them seeing us arguing, do we?'

'There's nothing to argue about. I saw you both.'

'What did you see?' Hugh felt so guilty that he imagined it might help to protest 'We weren't doing anything.'

'Oh, Hugh, don't start any of that now. I saw what you both think of me.'

'It was a shock, that's all,' Charlotte was determined to assure her. 'Come on, let's go inside so we can talk properly.'

'About what? It won't do any good.'

'I'm certain it will, aren't you, Hugh? And more to the point, Ellen will.'

She was facing Ellen by now, and he had to. As he moved to stand in front of Ellen he saw her lips shift as if they were trying to recall how they used to feel. 'Tell me how,' she said without inviting.

'By going to see Rory,' Charlotte said. 'We're all here for him, remember.'

'I don't think he'd like to find this at the end of his bed.'

'I'm sure he'll appreciate it when we've come all this way to see him. You aren't planning to waste the journey, Ellen. What sense would that make? Suppose we had to tell him?'

Ellen pressed her lips together, squeezing them paler still. Hugh was afraid that she meant to leave without further discussion, and dismay made him clumsier than ever. 'Maybe he won't know,' he no sooner thought than said.

Ellen forced her lips apart with her tongue before it appeared to flinch from them. 'You mean he'll be safe from having to look at me.'

'No, I mean maybe he's waiting for us all to bring him back to himself. Maybe we're the only ones that can.'

It was Hugh's latest if not last attempt to wield his imagination. Though he thought it sounded more desperate than persuasive, it delayed Ellen long enough for Charlotte to say 'Hugh could be right. We won't be able to live with ourselves if we don't find out, will we?'

'Don't go off without us. We need you.'

The towing handle of her case had sunk into its sockets, but Ellen pulled it up. Hugh thought his blundering had driven her away until she trundled the luggage around in a reluctant arc and to some extent followed it. 'Take me in if you want to,' she only just audibly said.

Since he was managing to look at her without betraying his distress, he could surely restrain it if he touched her. He took hold of whichever arm wasn't involved with the suitcase, and his guts shrank as if he'd been punched in the stomach. The arm felt frail as an old woman's, and he was unable to judge how much of the handful consisted of cloth, how much of skin emptied of flesh. The long-sleeved blouse was as baggy as the trousers it went some way towards covering up, and he didn't know whether he'd taken it for a nightdress only because the clothes looked as if she'd slept in them. He tried not to look at her starved loosened face beneath the clump of unkempt maddened hair. He thought he'd concealed his reaction, but as he took a pace towards the house Charlotte said 'You bring the bag, Hugh.'

Ellen produced a version of a laugh. 'He is.'

'Oh, Ellen, don't be silly. You're just playing with words now.'

'Or they're playing with me,' Ellen said, which fell short of being a joke.

Hugh relinquished her arm, only to wonder if she would think he'd recoiled. Might she have been so involved in her writing that she hadn't had time to eat or had forgotten to? Perhaps other writers looked as strange – perhaps it came with the job – but he was dismayed to watch Charlotte lead her away as Ellen must have escorted people she cared for. He didn't move until Charlotte glanced back, presumably to see why she couldn't hear the trundling luggage. He grabbed the handle and hurried after them in a panic that his sense of where they were might desert him once they vanished into the house.

Charlotte hesitated outside as the small case bumped and wobbled along the path. 'Go in, Ellen,' she urged and turned to murmur 'Have you got much to eat at home?'

'Nothing for me,' Ellen said at once.

'You can have a snack at least before we go to the hospital. When did you eat last? What did you have?'

'More than I should have.'

'I've used up nearly everything I bought at work,' Hugh was unhappy to have to admit. 'I've got some bread, I think. We could have toast or bread and milk.'

'Don't treat me like an invalid,' Ellen warned them and took refuge in the hall.

Charlotte had to make some kind of effort to follow. Hugh lifted the luggage over the doorstep, and as he wheeled it to join the case she'd left at the foot of the stairs he thought he knew why she'd been reluctant to enter. In the street he'd been unable to locate the source of all the scents – several front gardens, he'd assumed – but now it was apparent that Ellen was doused in perfume, and not just one. Perhaps he should have restrained his bewilderment, but it was too quick for him. 'What's happened to you?' he cried.

Both women swung around to stare at him, and he could have concluded that they'd both taken the question personally. He might have felt compelled to answer if Ellen hadn't said 'You aren't saying you can't see.'

'No, I mean why?' At once he had the anguished notion that she'd hoped he would deny her state. 'Is it being out of work?' he babbled. 'I mean, you aren't, of course, you're writing. Is that it, the writing, the stress? Or Rory, is it him?'

His cousins gazed at him for at least a mute second after he ran out of suggestions. 'Oh, Hugh, we love you,' said Ellen. 'Don't ever change.'

Of course he had, but he mustn't bring up his problem if he could keep it to himself; she and Charlotte had enough to worry about. Ellen's words had come close to a phrase he wouldn't have dared to admit yearning to hear from her, but he couldn't take advantage of that now. 'Thanks,' he said. 'Really, thanks. So which –'

'One of those, I expect. All of them if you like.'

stayed in his room until Charlotte headed for the bath-m, and on emerging she'd discovered him outside. Had she ;ed him lurking out there? Certainly her impression that ieone unseen was uncomfortably near had rendered the fined space yet more claustrophobic. She could only assume : Hugh didn't want to be left alone with his anxiety, for :n now as well as for his brother. 'I expect it's like you were ing yesterday,' she murmured. 'She's under a lot of stress.'

Iow much of it was Charlotte's doing? She might blame n and the new regime at the publishers, but this hardly olved her of responsibility. She didn't need Hugh to remind by pleading 'What can we do?'

Leave her alone for a while if that's what she wants. Maybe ing Rory will help.'

How thoughtless was that? Hugh seemed less than suaded. He was silent while he brought four piebald slices toast on a cracked plate to the bare stained table, and oduced a battered carton of Frugerine from the battered rigerator, and lifted the plump ragged cover from the clay pot to fill two mugs, after which the kitchen grew oppres-e with his and Charlotte's painfully polite crunching. Last ;ht's Indian meal, which Hugh had arranged to have deliv-:d even though the takeaway was only in the next street, d soon turned wordless too, and afterwards the cousins had plied themselves to trying to enjoy a string of comedy shows television. Charlotte had kept wondering if she alone could ar an unpleasant snicker as dry as an insect's stridulation aid the mirth of the various studio audiences. The sound had lowed her to bed, inside her skull at any rate, along with ;ense of so much left unspoken that it had felt more like a esence in the dark. Whenever she'd managed to doze she d wakened either afraid to learn where she might be or nvinced that the pent-up darkness was more crowded than e'd left it. Once if not more often she'd heard a model aero-ane suspended on threads stir as if fingers – no less flimsy d jerry-built, she'd thought for some reason – were toying th it in preparation for doing so to her. The prospect of :ntioning this made the kitchen seem smaller and darker, as she were in danger of reviving the night. She finished her

'Then what do you think you should –'

'That's all now, Hugh. No more or I'm leaving. Like Charlotte said, we're here for Rory, not for me. Show us where we're sleeping.'

Charlotte was giving him a private frown, presumably for leaving her no chance to question Ellen. 'Upstairs,' he mumbled.

'We'll find our own way, shall we?' said Charlotte.

'I shouldn't think it takes much finding,' Ellen said.

He could have imagined they were making light of his condition, but surely he'd managed to hide it. While he was able to follow them he knew which way to go. 'I'll bring the cases,' he said.

Ellen was first up the stairs, fast enough to suggest she was seeking a refuge. As Hugh brought up the rear with a case Charlotte said in some haste 'That's Hugh's room.'

He thought she was trying to head her cousin off from being troubled by its state. Ellen pushed the next door open, only to wonder 'Isn't this?'

It was more like a museum of his boyhood. As Ellen gazed wistfully at the misshapen scale models and puerile books, Charlotte said 'It's all his house.'

Hugh could have taken this as a rebuke for forcing Rory out, and did. If he'd still been living here, Rory wouldn't be in hospital. Ellen opened the third door, beyond which there was hardly any furniture except an infirm wardrobe and a single bed, not even a mirror. 'This'll do for me,' she said at once.

Charlotte gazed around the landing as if she wished it were larger or less shadowy, and Hugh came close to wondering if one shadow too many was lurking in a corner. He wheeled the dwarfish case ahead of her into his old room and had to assume she wanted him to emerge before she went in. She made him feel like a jailer for lingering outside, but he was growing nervous of letting his cousins out of his sight in case they were his only means of orientation. In a moment she said 'Wasn't there some talk of a cup of tea? You'd like one, wouldn't you, Ellen?'

Was she trying to send him downstairs so that he wouldn't inhibit any female conversation? 'I'd better phone the hospital,' he countered. 'We need to find out when we can go.'

As the number rang Charlotte came to the doorway, and he

heard the bed creak in Rory's old room. The switchboard operator transferred the call to the ward, and as the bed amplified Ellen's restlessness Hugh wondered unhappily if his brother could move even that much. Charlotte was raising her eyebrows at him by the time the ward sister spoke. 'Intensive Care.'

'How's Rory Lucas? It's his brother.'

'The same as when you called this morning, Mr Lucas, and this afternoon. No change, but that's no worse.'

'I've got our cousins here now. When can we come and see him?'

'We're having a few problems on the ward just at the moment,' the sister said, and Hugh was disconcerted to overhear a laugh that sounded anything but pleasant, not merely muffled but clogged. He could only suppose it was somewhere other than the ward, since she didn't react to it, instead saying 'Do you mind if I put you off for a while?'

'If you've got to. Till when?'

'Tomorrow would be best.'

'It won't make any difference to him, or will it?'

'Not at the minute, sadly, I'm afraid. I'll contact you if there's any significant development.'

'Thanks. That's kind,' Hugh said, but as soon as he pocketed the mobile he thought he'd been too eager to accommodate her – worse, that he was glad to have a reason to delay travelling all the labyrinthine way to Leeds. 'The ward's shut to visitors till tomorrow,' he announced, and Ellen let out a groan that vibrated her bed. He had to dodge as Charlotte darted out of her room. 'I'll make it,' she informed him, at which point he grasped that she was thinking of the tea, not proposing to escape from the house. He might have been grateful if he hadn't needed to choose which cousin to stay with, which direction to take. As he hurried downstairs, terrified of losing sight of Charlotte, he began to dread that the reunion would turn into the longest night of his life.

TWENTY-TWO

As the smell of breakfast drifted through the h
tramped out of the bathroom. 'None for me.'

'It's only toast,' Charlotte called up the stairs. 'Th
is.'

'I know that. I said none, thanks.'

'You ought to have something,' Hugh protested be
back to the grill more hastily than Charlotte unde

'I did last night.'

'You didn't have much,' Charlotte said.

'I had all I wanted. Don't start another argumen
be going to the hospital.'

'You wouldn't not see Rory,' Hugh cried, twis
as if she'd unbalanced him.

'Then don't either of you make me. I'll stay u
it's time to leave,' Ellen declared and shut herself i

Charlotte would have expected her to spend l
bathroom. In a moment Hugh voiced her own feeli
audibly. 'What's wrong with her?'

She might have asked the same about him. T

toast as fast as she civilly could in order to call 'I think we're ready, Ellen.'

The narrow hall flattened her voice, reminding her of the size of the house – the lack of it, rather. 'I'll be down,' Ellen responded but wasn't while Hugh picked up the plates and looked uncertain where to put them. Was he really so incapable or just taking advantage now that there were women in the house? Charlotte seized the plates and bore them together with the synthetically buttery knife to the sink, which at least gave her a view of the meagre back yard and its outgrown swings. Once she'd washed up she made for the hall with Hugh at her heels. Ellen was descending the stairs, pausing if not resting on each step. She was wearing the same clothes again or still – unnecessarily capacious trousers and a nightdress, if not a blouse that resembled one too much for anybody else's comfort. 'Aren't you going to get changed?' Charlotte had to ask for fear that Hugh would say worse.

'I don't think Rory's going to mind, do you?'

'I hope he might, if you see what I mean. Maybe you should –'

'I've nothing to change into.'

Charlotte could only wonder what Ellen's case was full of – perfume bottles, to judge by the scents of her, which were close to suffocating in the narrow hall. 'Would you like something of mine?'

'You're kind, but it wouldn't be any good.' As Charlotte parted her lips Ellen said 'I've told you I won't have an argument. If you want me with you at the hospital, let's be on our way.'

She was almost at the front door when Hugh said 'Hang on, I'll phone a taxi.'

As Ellen hesitated the gloomy perfumed hall seemed to shrink. Charlotte pushed past her to drag the front door open. 'Good heavens, we can walk that little distance,' she said. 'It'll do us good.'

Ellen frowned as if she suspected some kind of gibe, then held up her hands. Presumably they signalled resignation before she glanced askance at them and jerked them away from her face. 'I expect it won't make any difference,' she said. 'Lead the way then, Hugh.'

'You two go out. I've got to lock up.'

This simply meant pulling the door shut with one hand through the letterbox. He kept hold of it as though it or something beyond it had seized his fingers, a notion so unwelcome that it drove Ellen to a feeble joke. 'The house won't fall down without you, Hugh.'

As the women left the narrow path he dashed after them. Ellen was staring about as if, all too understandably, she hoped not to be seen. Perhaps someone was observing the cousins from one of the houses; certainly Charlotte felt spied upon. Nobody was skulking behind the trees at the junction, although as she hurried past without sparing them a glance she heard an unseen magpie utter its sniggering call. Of course the bird was the shape, pale as bone where it wasn't black as earth, that she thought she glimpsed among the tree-trunks.

Hugh stayed just behind his cousins as they turned along the road towards the station, although the pavement was broad enough for the three to walk abreast. Perhaps he was leaving room well in advance for an approaching Muslim woman, veiled and so thoroughly robed in black that only her eyes and hands were visible. Ellen watched her pass and turned her head to keep the woman in sight until Hugh muttered 'What's wrong?'

'That should be me.'

'You mustn't say that. You've nothing to be ashamed of. You're the same, same person you've always been.'

Charlotte thought this was increasingly less accurate, but wasn't it also the case with her and Hugh? She might have suggested as much if Ellen hadn't said 'I'm sorry, now I'm starting arguments. Forget I spoke.'

Charlotte doubted he could do this any more than she was able to. Perhaps his attempts kept him silent as far as the bridge over the ring road. As they stepped onto it he raised his voice. 'Watch out for the troll.'

'Why are you saying that?' Ellen presumably wanted to know.

'Our dad used to,' he said so awkwardly that Charlotte didn't need to look back to know his face had turned red.

As the polluted uproar from below closed around them, Charlotte found little to enjoy in the notion of a presence waiting under the bridge to snatch her and her cousins into blackness.

Of course it couldn't be so dark above the ring road, and she wasn't going to imagine that descending the hill brought the party closer to any such presence. The interior of the station wasn't dark, even if a huge voice that sounded blurred by dirt seemed to bring the walls and the roof of the booking hall inwards. As Charlotte made for the nearest ticket window Ellen said 'Buy mine and I'll pay you.'

'I will as well,' Hugh said at once.

Charlotte felt like the solitary adult in charge of an outing, at least until she led her cousins past the unstaffed barrier onto the train. Hugh seemed uncertain where to sit in the deserted carriage, and ready to move yet again once the women were seated. Ellen looked uncomfortable wherever she rested her gaze, on her cousins or her lap or the empty aisle, and Charlotte was oppressed by her behaviour and Hugh's, not to mention Ellen's overpowering perfumes. There was worse to come, she remembered as the train cruised forwards: there was the tunnel. Every shadow that flooded the carriage was a reminder, every bridge felt capable of growing longer than its dark should last. She rummaged in her mind for a topic of conversation, the more neutral the better. 'Will you have to take a holiday, Hugh?'

'Where?' His own question seemed to confuse him. 'When?' he tried instead.

'Now, I was thinking.'

'I wouldn't call this much of a holiday.'

The left side of his mouth betrayed that he was straining at a joke. Ellen took it seriously enough to shake her head in agreement, then raised her hands just short of holding it still. 'I meant time off from work,' Charlotte said.

'For Rory,' Ellen appeared to think he needed to be told.

'I know what for.' Hugh stared out at a small station that was dragging the train to a halt. He might have been waiting until the door alarm cued his next line. 'They sent me home,' he said.

'Because of Rory? That was kind of them, wasn't it, Charlotte? It's good to know there are still some employers who –'

'Because of me.'

As fields carried off the small town Charlotte felt trapped between the unwashed windows, and Hugh seemed to see nothing on either side to encourage him. 'You'd have been upset, would you?' Ellen offered him. 'I'm sure they understood. We all were, but he's your brother.'

'He wasn't hurt then. I was no use, that's all.'

'Of course you are. You're all sorts of use. Who said you weren't?'

'Me. Didn't you hear me?'

'If it's only you that thinks it,' Charlotte said, 'we certainly don't, and I'll bet –'

'There are plenty, and one's all it takes.'

Charlotte had a sense of buried glee, but how could it be Hugh's or anybody's there? The blackened underside of a bridge filled the window beyond him, giving way to a dazzle of sunlight that rendered the glass more opaque. 'You shouldn't let people . . .' Ellen said and seemed to regret having spoken.

'It's not just people.'

Charlotte felt as if Ellen were leaving her to put a question neither of them wanted to ask. 'What, then?'

'It's Frugo. I can't find my way round now it's bigger, and it's affected me. You know it has.'

It was certainly blotching his face. 'Don't let it get on top of you,' she said. 'Go back as soon as you can and do . . . what do you think, Ellen?'

'See if you can find your way and if you can't there must be people who can help.'

'They aren't like you. Not many people care like you do.' His gaze dodged back and forth, perhaps in search of a way for him not to admit 'I've been suspended. I had a row with my supervisor and someone else as well.'

'They haven't fired you yet, though,' Charlotte said.

'They will, for misconduct. No point arguing. You know how that goes, Ellen.'

'Even if she does you should at least –'

Charlotte couldn't help starting as her mobile went off. She silenced it, wishing that she hadn't used the We Go Frugo jingle as her new ringtone for a joke, only for the displayed number to aggravate her tension. 'Yes, Glen.'

'Is this a bad time?'

'I've had better.'

'Gee, I'm sorry. Should I leave this till you want to call me back?'

'If we need to talk it may as well be now.'

'We aren't likely to be cut off, are we? You sound shut in.'

She yearned to deny it as another bridge engulfed the carriage and was swept away by sunlight that emphasised the thickness of the muddy window. 'Say what you have to say, Glen,' she urged.

'How's your cousin?'

'Not conscious yet, the last we heard. We're on our way to see him.'

'Ellen's with you, right? The reason I'm calling is mainly for her. Maybe I should speak to her in person.'

As Charlotte held out the phone Ellen said 'Doesn't it work so we can both hear?'

'Do you want me to go away?' Hugh said, though he seemed to be pleading for the reverse.

'I meant you as well,' Ellen said without taking the mobile. 'You're involved too.'

Charlotte looked away from his colourful reaction and poked the hands-free button. 'Glen? Can you hear me?'

'Pretty well,' he said a little fuzzily but loud enough to be comprehensible above the muffled thunder of the wheels. 'Are we in a meeting?'

'Ellen would prefer it if you don't mind.'

'Whatever's best for our author. Good to speak to you at last, Ellen. Let's hope we'll have a reason to get together and celebrate soon.'

She seemed not to know where to put her hands – nowhere near her face and not in her lap. Splaying her fingers on the upholstery on either side of her, she leaned forwards. 'You weren't calling to say we have.'

'Working on it. How's the new book coming?'

'I'm a bit distracted at the moment,' Ellen said, and her lips worked as if searching for a shape.

'I figured you might be. That's why I thought I'd help. I had some spare time, so I looked into the place you came up with. Thurstaston.'

Ellen pressed her lips fat and then sucked them inwards, so

that Charlotte might have felt compelled to speak if Hugh hadn't. 'What did you find?'

Glen's voice grew louder but less clear. 'Who's that?'

'Only Hugh,' Hugh said. 'Their cousin.'

'Hi, Hugh. Sorry, I thought I heard someone else. I guess they were up on the street. Couldn't have been down here.'

Charlotte didn't care to be reminded that his apartment was below street level. 'So you said you looked where again?'

'The net. That's my Saturday night, a man and his computer.' Was he listening for her reaction? He paused before adding 'I found a bunch of stuff about a guy who lived there that maybe you could work up somehow, Ellen. Thurstaston Mound, he lived at. Well, more than lived.'

The carriage shook. The train was braking for a station, but the shudder or Glen's last remark was enough to send Ellen's hands towards her face. Perhaps they were intended to suppress a question. Charlotte wasn't eager to ask it, however much their muteness felt like an unacknowledged presence. She could have imagined this was why Hugh blurted 'You mean Pendemon.'

Darkness engulfed the carriage. It was the shadow of the station, and the door alarm began to shrill. Nobody visible was boarding – nobody at all – but Glen said 'What did somebody set off?'

'It's just the doors,' Charlotte told him.

'You're getting out of what is it, a train?'

'Not getting out,' she had to say.

The beeping addressed her a second time, and then the train crept forwards. As sunlight and a ghost of mud coated the window afresh Glen said 'Sounds like you know about him.'

'I looked him up,' Ellen said. 'I didn't read it all.'

'What did you read?'

'Wouldn't it be easier to email her the link?' Charlotte said as Ellen failed to speak.

'I could do that, except when's it going to reach her?'

'Not till I get home. I don't know when that'll be.'

'I'm the same,' said Charlotte. 'I mean, I've got no access here.'

'Hey, don't sound so pleased about it. How about the guy who isn't speaking?'

Hugh's gaze darted about as if he wondered where the person referred to might be, and then he worked on producing a laugh. 'I haven't even got a computer.'

'You must like living in the past. Maybe I should read some of this in case you want to think about it, Ellen.'

'That couldn't have been his real name, could it?'

'Pendemon? I'd say not. The guy who runs this site has some fun with that, well, with the whole thing. Seems like he doesn't believe in any kind of magic.'

Charlotte sensed that Ellen had been seeking some kind of reassurance, but Hugh had a question for Glen. 'Do you?'

'If it pays you bet I do.'

'Is he Mumbo someone,' Ellen said, 'your man with no beliefs?'

'Jumbjoe, that's his byline. Maybe he's not the sceptic he wants us all to think or he wouldn't write so much about it. You're right, he figures Pendemon's a fake name. Nothing to do with penning demons either.'

Did Glen mean to lighten the mood? He seemed to have achieved the opposite. The air trapped by the unopenable windows felt heavy with resentment thick as earth, stale as old breath. 'I thought it was trying to sound like Pendragon,' Hugh said.

'Pen means head, doesn't it?' said Ellen.

'Head demon, huh? I don't think he got that job. Let's see what you don't know.'

Charlotte had a thought she was far from relishing. 'We'll be coming to a tunnel soon.'

'I'd better make this fast, then. Did you see he got into a fight with another magician, Ellen?'

'Something Grace, wasn't it?'

'Amazing,' Hugh said and looked painfully out of place.

'You got it, Ellen. Peter Grace. I don't believe in that name either.'

Charlotte thought the rush of the train had grown hollow ahead, but the tunnel didn't appear. Perhaps the sound suggestive of the gaping of a pit had been on the loudspeaker, although it didn't affect Glen's voice when he asked 'Did you see what your guy tried to send Grace?'

'I don't know. I didn't get that far.'

Ellen's hands began to writhe on either side of her face as if to ward the information off. Charlotte leaned across the phone on the seat to stroke her cousin's arm, but Ellen snatched it out of reach as Charlotte said 'Glen, I think you'd better –'

'He collected nightmares.'

Charlotte felt as if a pit were indeed yawning beneath her, even if it had yet to swallow Glen's voice. She straightened up hastily, only to fear that Ellen might think she'd recoiled from her. By this time Hugh seemed to feel nervously driven to ask 'How?'

'This isn't a site that'll give you his method. It does quote things he's meant to have said.'

'I saw some of those,' Ellen intervened.

Charlotte thought she might be trying to hush Glen, but he retorted 'At the core of all men is darkness and terror?'

'Something like that.'

'These are what he's supposed to have told his followers, not that he ever had too many of those. They all ran off when he tried to use them,' Glen said. 'The essence of each man is the infant he once was, at the mercy of the dark?'

'No,' Ellen said forcefully enough to be denying the idea.

'The hidden child shall serve the adept, and its terror shall become its weapon?'

'No.'

'The husk shall return to the world and carry on its mundane mummery, having yielded up its substance to the sorcerer?'

Ellen's lips were opening yet again, plumply audible before she spoke, when Hugh demanded 'What's all that meant to mean?'

'Like I said, he collected people's nightmares. I'm not saying I believe it any more than this site does. You don't have to either, Ellen. Just use it if you can.'

She'd closed her mouth by now, though her lips were continuing to shift. 'What's kind of interesting,' Glen said, 'is he's supposed to have made a couple of mistakes.'

'What?' Hugh said with an urgency Charlotte found disconcerting.

'That last quote I gave you sounds as if he thought he took the nightmares out of people, doesn't it? Or maybe he didn't care. The people he's supposed to have lured to his house, they went away with nightmares some of them didn't even know they had. Of course that could just have been they were scared of the place because they knew his reputation.'

Hugh's gaze was dodging about so wildly it looked helpless, and Ellen seemed equally uncertain where to rest her wriggling fingers. As for Charlotte, she'd grown too breathless to speak, and so Hugh asked the question. 'What was the other mistake?'

'I guess he thought nobody could get at his own nightmares. You could say he did it to himself by being so obsessed with other people's, or maybe it makes for a better story if Grace turns Pendemon's own nightmare on him after one of his followers joined up with Grace and told him what it was. Or it could just have been a coincidence, but that's not the kind of book your cousin's writing.'

Again it was Hugh's question that broke the stale constricted breathless silence. 'What was?'

'He was scared of being buried alive,' Glen said before a rush of blackness engulfed his voice. The train had entered the tunnel at last. For an instant Charlotte was glad that it had quieted him, and then she seemed to taste the dark that clogged her mouth and stole her breath.

TWENTY-THREE

As Ellen saw blackness racing towards her she had time to hope that it would blot her out. Extinguishing the lights would do, but it only closed around the train, displaying her on either side. Even if she stared resolutely ahead she was still aware of the loathsome bloated pallid shapes that flanked her like guards conducting her to some inevitable fate. She saw Charlotte grab the mobile and switch off the silenced call before shutting her eyes tight, while Hugh made it plain that he had no idea where to look. It had been kind of them to pretend they could bear the sight of Ellen, and she couldn't blame them for giving up. Charlotte ought to be proud of Ellen's developing vocabulary, of the number of words she had found for herself: bulky, bulging, puffy, inflated, pasty, revolting, disgusting, foul, fetid, noisome, emetic, vomitive . . . She was going down the list that filled her head when Hugh spoke, barely audible above the hollow uproar of the train. 'Is it him?'

Charlotte raised her head as if to search but kept her eyes shut, presumably for fear of glimpsing Ellen. 'Is who what?'

'Pendemon,' Hugh mumbled and turned his gaze away from

the window beside her, only to find the view across the aisle as unwelcome. 'Has he done something?'

Ellen's fingers writhed, not just because she could scarcely bear how they felt whenever they rubbed flabbily together. She was remembering the buried object that she'd taken for a bunch of twisted roots until it had seemed to grope for her hand. 'Can we leave him alone for now?'

'You think he has,' Hugh said with a kind of dismayed eagerness.

'I didn't say that and I'm not thinking it either. What are you trying to prove, Hugh?'

'Maybe just that I'm worth listening to.'

'You know you are. When has anybody ever said you weren't?'

'Let's talk, then,' Charlotte muttered. 'We need to.'

The train clattered at length through the dark before Hugh said 'Do you remember what we talked about last time we were there?'

By leaving Thurstaston unnamed he rendered the memory of the twisted object that had stirred under the earth more ominous, and Charlotte didn't help by saying 'Remind us.'

'We were saying what we dreamed the night we slept there.'

Ellen hadn't mentioned her dream, and didn't want to recall it now, even if it was no worse than her present state. 'I don't see anything unusual about that,' Charlotte said, shutting her eyes tighter. 'Everyone dreams.'

'Yes, but how many dreams do you remember all these years later? Was it just that one?'

'It still is.'

'Then mustn't that mean it wasn't an ordinary dream?'

'It was pretty ordinary,' Charlotte said, and Ellen wondered if this was meant to fend off the memory. 'I wouldn't make any great claims for it.'

'What was it, though?'

'Just some kind of cellar. I was going to be pulled down into it if I hadn't woken up.'

'Anything else you remember? Where –'

'I'd rather not discuss it here.' Charlotte's eyelids trembled as though she were equally nervous of keeping them closed or opening them. 'Or maybe anywhere,' she admitted, mostly to herself.

'Sorry, I should've realised.' Hugh's gaze dodged about so wildly that it might have been searching for an intruder before fastening on Ellen. 'What about you?'

Did his scrutiny explain why she felt spied upon, her every word analysed in case it went too far? She couldn't resist glancing around, but nobody appeared to be lurking behind any of the seats; the darkness had brought nothing dreadful into the carriage except her reflections. She understood Hugh's question all too well, which was why she retreated from giving the answer. 'I should have,' she tried telling him instead.

'No, I mean did you dream something? What did you dream?'

'I'm going to be like Charlotte,' Ellen said, wishing that she were. For an instant she'd glimpsed an underground room that surrounded her with her hideous self. 'I want to save it,' she said, only to find this didn't reassure her at all.

'I thought we wanted to talk.'

'Nobody's preventing you,' Charlotte said, how encouragingly Ellen couldn't judge.

'You already know what I dreamed.'

Charlotte's mouth opened and closed as if she were struggling to breathe, unless she was reluctant to speak. With her eyes closed she might almost have been trying to talk in her sleep. Eventually she said 'Tell us again.'

'I couldn't find my way, and now I can't.' More resentfully than Ellen had ever heard him sound he added 'I said once.'

'You don't need a nightmare to explain that,' Charlotte protested. 'Life's enough of one too much of the time.'

'Not this much.'

Charlotte lowered her head and folded her arms hard. If she hadn't spoken Ellen might have had to ask 'What do you mean?'

'Not this much of a nightmare.' Hugh faltered, and Ellen tried not to think he was letting the darkness or something in it creep closer. 'All right, I didn't tell you everything,' he mumbled. 'I can't find my way anywhere at all.'

'Oh, Hugh.' With a visible effort Charlotte opened her eyes to peer at him. 'There's no need to go looking for a nightmare to explain it, surely,' she said. 'Didn't it start with all your stress at work?'

'Maybe that was part of it.'

Ellen felt dismayingly unable to help, as incompetent as the tribunal's verdict had made her feel. 'You need to see a doctor,' she urged.

'I couldn't find my way there either.'

His attempt at a laugh was too perfunctory to invite an echo, but Ellen imagined she'd heard one, muffled by the buried thunder of the train. 'We –' she began and then was afraid to promise. 'Someone will take you,' she said.

'You're forgetting about Rory.'

'I mean after we've visited. Or no, I'm being stupid. You could see a doctor at the hospital.'

'No, I'm saying you're forgetting what he dreamed.'

Charlotte closed her eyes as though to exclude the remark. 'What has that to do with anything?'

'It was about not being able to see, wasn't it? And now he can't. Don't you think an artist's nightmare has to be losing all his senses?'

Charlotte turned her face to him without opening her eyes. 'I'm sorry, Hugh, but I think Ellen was spot on.'

Ellen didn't understand this any more than Hugh appeared to. 'What are you saying I did?'

'You said he was trying to prove something. This isn't the time or the place, Hugh. We never said you had no imagination, so don't work so hard at convincing us you have. It's getting out of hand and not in the best of taste.'

'You're just upset about Rory, aren't you?' Ellen told him in the hope that would stop his gaze from jerking back and forth. 'You want to find something to blame besides yourself. Don't blame yourself and then you won't need to do this.'

Had she embarrassed him into silence? She was looking away from him, which showed her the door at the end of the aisle twitching as if someone hidden in the dark between the carriages were about to put in an appearance, when he said 'What's wrong with her?'

Ellen didn't know if she was being referred to or addressed. A sidelong glance at Charlotte offered her no clue, nor did Hugh's agitated gaze, even when he raised his hands on either side of it like blinkers. Charlotte took it on herself to answer, almost inaudibly. 'I'm claustrophobic.'

Hugh kept his hands up to direct his gaze at her, although the pose was beginning to put Ellen in mind of someone under threat. 'Since when?' he said.

'Hugh,' Ellen objected. 'Now you're going too far in the other direction.'

His fingers bent clawlike towards his eyes. 'How am I?'

'We aren't saying don't use your imagination at all.' She nodded at Charlotte, which made her face feel even more repulsively unstable, and leaned towards him to whisper 'Since we've been in here, of course.'

She sensed that he was struggling not to recoil from her, and so she straightened up before she'd finished speaking. His gaze left her at once, darting along the aisle. 'I didn't get that,' he complained and shut his eyes.

Ellen didn't need to be reminded yet again how unbearable he and Charlotte must find the sight of her. Perhaps he also disliked the restive jerking of the door as much as she did. She couldn't touch him to persuade him to look at her, she could only speak up. 'Since we came in the tunnel.'

'How long have we been in it?'

'I'm not looking,' Charlotte breathed. 'I can't say.'

'How long have we been talking? It feels like, I don't know –'

Charlotte cried out. It wasn't much of a cry; it was the kind of enfeebled wordless protest she might have uttered in her sleep while fighting to break out of a nightmare. Nevertheless it appeared to bring a response. The door at the end of the carriage slid swiftly yet noiselessly wide, and a thin blackened shape that might have been scaly or in some sense ragged sprang into the carriage.

It dodged behind the nearest seat, dropping low as it vanished, and Ellen threw her hands out to clutch at her companions. Barely in time not to subject them to her touch, she realised what she'd seen. The door hadn't opened. Only sunlight had prised the darkness wide, incidentally throwing the shadow of some object that had passed before Ellen could locate it. Although the sounds of the train had grown more spacious, they and the light seemed to fall short of Charlotte's awareness; she might still have been shut in a dream. At least Hugh's eyes were open, even if he looked less than reassured by the choice of views. 'We're out,' Ellen said, hoping this might release Charlotte from her panic – and then she wondered whether, in some sense she preferred not to grasp, they were nothing of the kind.

TWENTY-FOUR

Charlotte was first off the train. Before a signboard had identified Leeds Station she'd crouched forwards like an athlete impatient to begin a race. She stood at the door all the way along the platform and only just waited for the alarm to acknowledge that the train had stopped. Hugh watched her jab the button and dart onto the platform. He would have dashed to keep up except for Ellen, who hesitated as a thin figure, mostly covered in black and otherwise alarmingly pale, appeared outside the window. Although he was only a teenager, his approach seemed to startle Charlotte. 'Come on, you two,' she said without owning up to nervousness. 'Bring each other.'

He couldn't advance until Ellen did, or he might be lost. As soon as she took a few reluctant steps he was at her heels. When she looked back he was afraid she would tell him to overtake her, but she was peering beyond him as if she fancied someone else wanted to pass, not a pleasant fancy to judge by the expression on her starved slack face. Twisting around showed him the aisle was deserted, and once he grasped which way to turn he saw Charlotte losing patience with his and Ellen's antics. 'Nearly there,' she urged.

He felt she was blaming him for the delay – blaming him for having imagined too much aloud. If it had all been his imagination, why didn't she climb aboard to help instead of directing operations from the safety of the platform? She watched Ellen until her cousin ventured forwards, glancing both ways as she left the cover the train provided. Hugh stayed close while an escalator raised them all to a walkway considerably more than wide enough for them to progress abreast, where Charlotte looked over her shoulder to see why he wasn't beside her and Ellen. Was she about to tell him to keep up? Even if he was the youngest, he wasn't going to be treated like a child, and he couldn't help demanding 'Why did you make that noise, then?'

The question appeared to render Ellen nervous of the muddle of sounds beneath the vast arch of the roof. 'What did you hear?'

'I don't mean now. In the, you know where.' He felt inconsiderate for being forced to add 'The tunnel.'

Charlotte frowned at a queue of commuters within earshot at a cash dispenser. 'Not here, Hugh.'

'Where, then?'

'Preferably nowhere,' she said and stepped on a downward escalator.

As he followed his cousins Ellen's mass of perfume struck him in the face, and he retreated a metal step. Her uneasy question had heightened his awareness of the noises of the station, so that he heard somebody without very much to them scuttling after him. He clutched at the unstable rubber banister as he swung around to see that the escalator above him was empty. Some object must have caught between the treads, but it was no longer audible, never mind visible. 'Careful you don't fall,' Ellen told him.

Had her attention been drawn by the sound? He had no chance to ask as they descended, and by the time they reached the ticket barriers it seemed too late and too trivial. Beyond was a vaulted hall full of benches and echoes. 'How far is it to the hospital, do we know?' Charlotte said.

'The taxi will,' said Hugh.

'Maybe it's close enough to walk to. We could see if there are any clothes shops on the way.'

'We don't want to waste time getting to Rory,' Ellen objected. 'We aren't here to shop.'

Charlotte visibly thought better of responding. Hugh would have supported her if she'd suggested Ellen ought to buy something else to wear, but he couldn't raise the subject, especially while he was distracted by an echo surely too thin to be actual footsteps behind him. At least they fell short of pursuing him out of the station to a taxi rank, where Charlotte was asking 'Could we go to the hospital?'

The maternally plump driver looked sympathetically at Ellen. 'Which one, love?'

'We're visiting our cousin,' Ellen said, not without resentment. 'He was in an accident.'

Hugh felt provoked to establish that Rory was his brother, but said only 'He's in a coma.'

'You'll want the General,' the driver said, still gazing at Ellen.

Hugh could have said so at the outset if he hadn't hung back, and wondered whether Ellen was rounding on him because of it. Perhaps she was taking a sly revenge by enquiring 'Which way do you want to go, Hugh?'

'How do I know?'

Her starved face sagged at his tone. 'I mean which way do you want to sit.'

'Sorry. I thought –' He made to touch her arm until he sensed how little she would welcome that. 'Can I face the way we're going?' he said and felt childish.

'I will too if nobody minds.'

'I don't,' Charlotte said.

She stepped back while Hugh followed Ellen into the vehicle, and then she seemed to reconsider ducking under the low roof. Hugh was expecting her to propose to walk by the time she took a loud deep breath and climbed in to sit opposite him. 'Is that everyone?' the driver said.

Charlotte twisted around to stare at her. 'Who else is there going to be?'

'I thought there was someone behind you.'

Hugh felt as if the interior had grown smaller and darker,

unless he was sharing Charlotte's discomfort. 'That was me,' he said in the hope that it would end the misunderstanding and let him feel less nervous, but everyone gazed at him – even the driver, using her mirror – as if he had no idea where he was. 'If you say so,' the driver said and sent the taxi up a ramp.

As a green light released the vehicle into the traffic she lowered her window. In a few hundred yards the taxi veered into a cross street and then another, by which point Hugh had already lost the way back to the station. A shadow flexed its thin limbs on the seat beside Charlotte – only a shadow. It wasn't plucking at the sleeve of her black Cougar T-shirt to make her and her cousins look; that was just a breeze through the driver's window. In a moment Hugh realised why the driver had left it open, and was afraid Ellen would think even less of herself. His gaze dodged about in search of any subject he could mention and lit upon a passing Chinese restaurant. 'That looks like a good place to eat,' he said wildly.

'Do you want to know the best restaurants?' the driver said.

'We might, mightn't we, Ellen?'

'I can't speak for you.' She inched away from him as if she had to manoeuvre a ponderous burden. 'And you shouldn't for me,' she said.

'Don't be like that with us. We're your cousins. I was only trying –'

To his further dismay, it was Charlotte who interrupted. 'Not in here.'

Did she mean because of the space or because of the driver? Surely the woman at the wheel couldn't be delighted by their struggles to communicate – she didn't look the type – but nobody else was to be seen. 'Shall I tell you when we come to them?' she said.

'I'd really rather you didn't,' said Ellen.

Hugh was afraid this might provoke the driver to turn hostile if not personal. 'I shouldn't think any of us will want to eat till we've seen how Rory is,' he said.

He was tempted to inform the driver that his brother was an artist, but suppose that let her identify him from the news and she detested his work? Hugh didn't want to be responsible for any more awkwardness, and so he joined in the silence, although it made Rory into yet another subject nobody was anxious to mention. He was reduced to wondering where it was safe to look: not at the streets challenging him to grasp the route, nor at Ellen as he sensed her shrinking away from him or herself, nor at Charlotte's determination to keep her eyes wide as if closing them might plunge her into a nightmare, unless she was struggling to cope with one she could see. The driver couldn't be watching all or indeed any of this – she was intent on the road – and yet Hugh felt somebody was, and revelling in Hugh's plight as well. Were his cousins suffering the same experience? He couldn't refer to it while the driver might hear, but he was barely able to contain it until the taxi executed yet another turn that brought them to the hospital. At least this gave him an excuse to speak. 'I'll pay,' he said at once.

His cousins climbed out while he handed the driver a ten-pound note, and Ellen was shutting her door when she stiffened. Apparently the sight of Hugh with a hand through the aperture in the security grille didn't appeal to her. The driver was reaching for change, but he had a sudden notion that somebody else was about to clutch at his hand. He snatched it away and backed out of the taxi, thumping his skull on the underside of the roof, to accept the change through the driver's window. He was afraid his cousins might ask why he'd behaved like that, but they only insisted on giving him money before Ellen said 'Let's find him.'

'He's in Intensive Care,' Hugh said, which felt for a moment like knowing where to go. He dogged his cousins past a gathering of smokers, more than one of whom gave Ellen a concerned look, and through the entrance to the lobby, where a receptionist directed them to the first floor. Not too far, Hugh thought, and the lift was just around a corner, whichever way that led. The large featureless grey box took its time over closing, and he fancied that Charlotte was urging it to get the process over with while Ellen hoped nobody would join them. As the doors came within an inch of meeting he imagined that somebody was about to squeeze between them without pushing them further apart. Or might that happen when the lift reached the first floor? He felt as if it were weighed down by several kinds of apprehension. Certainly it was in no hurry to arrive, and he thought he wasn't alone in tensing when it did.

The corridor was deserted, and led straight to Rory's ward in the direction Charlotte and Ellen took. Hugh tried not to be distracted by the entrances they passed – operating theatres, children's cardiac, children's intensive care – although he felt as though he were avoiding the possibility that someone might be lurking in one of the side passages. Somebody thin rose up to meet his cousins as they pushed open the doors to the ward they needed, but she was the sister in charge, and she'd only stood up behind her desk. 'We're here for Rory Lucas,' Charlotte said.

'Have you come far?'

Hugh was reflecting that her accent had made her sound fatter on the phone as Charlotte told her 'London.'

'You may as well all go in.'

Hugh couldn't help feeling this seemed ominous. 'How is he?'

'Comfortable. No change since you called. It was you, wasn't it?' When he assumed it must have been she said 'Furthest on the left.'

He was grateful to have his cousins to lead him past sleeper after sleeper fitted with tubes. He tried not to glance at them, though this felt like ignoring an intruder. Most of them were unattended and presumably unaware of it. Worse, Rory was equally unaware he was the opposite.

He was lying on his back, his head slightly raised by a pillow as if this might lift his awareness. Various tubes led to and from him, but Hugh wished he could feel more encouraged to see little sign of injury, not even plaster. Rory's expression was utterly blank, and Hugh had the distressing idea that the tubes were draining his personality, reducing him to an inert mass indistinguishable from the contents of the other beds. He didn't stir when Ellen made to hold one of his hands as Charlotte clasped the other. Hugh busied himself with bringing them chairs and fetching a third one, after which there appeared to be nothing to do beyond feeling guilty and useless. Smiling sympathetically across the aisle at a woman seated by an even older man's bed soon lost any meaning, and he'd thought of something to ask a nurse well before she came to write on Rory's clipboard. 'What was wrong yesterday?' he enquired of her. 'Why couldn't we visit him?'

The brawny girl nibbled her pinkish lower lip as she glanced along the ward, and Hugh thought she'd heard someone come in until he realised she was checking that the sister was on the phone. 'We had a bit of excitement with one of Rory's friends,' she murmured, 'didn't we, Rory?'

Ellen had ventured to take his hand at last. She turned up her free one and then hid it beside the bed. 'Are you saying someone came to see him?'

'Not till you all did. Are you glad they have, Rory?' When this produced no visible response the nurse said 'Another patient got a bit lively, that's all.'

Charlotte crouched restlessly forwards in the gap between Rory's bed and his insensible neighbour's. 'I assume it had to be more than a bit for us not to be allowed to come.'

'Sister didn't want any more of a panic.' The nurse turned her head an inch towards the peremptory clatter of the phone returning to its stand. 'I shouldn't think Rory minded waiting, did you, Rory? Your family's here now,' she said and retreated down the ward.

Was it her professional opinion that addressing Rory might revive him, or had she been trying to encourage the visitors? Hugh's face grew hot at the thought of talking to the absence that was his brother, especially in front of an audience that didn't consist only of their cousins. Nevertheless he was about to move his chair away from the foot of the bed, once he decided which of his cousins might find his closeness least unwelcome, when he heard a whisper at his back. 'It was him.'

At first Hugh was afraid to turn, and even when he did he couldn't tell which way he had. It confronted him with the old lady opposite, who was still grasping her husband's limp fingers, and with the question he had to ask. 'Who?'

'My Jack here.' She lifted his hand as if that helped her identify him and then let it subside. 'He was the one who was making the fuss,' she said.

'That's good, is it? Mustn't it mean he was conscious?'

'Not of his old Annie. The way he carried on it was more like he was having a bad dream and couldn't wake up.'

Hugh heard restlessness behind him. He couldn't look around, instead demanding 'Did you hear that?'

'What?' Ellen said with none of his nervous triumph.

'What this lady said.'

'Call me Annie, do.'

'We're all capable of hearing, Hugh. Nobody's lost their wits.' Rather less sharply Charlotte added 'Did your husband actually say anything, Annie?'

'He did that. Said there was someone on the screen that shouldn't be.'

This seemed remote enough for Hugh to experience some fleeting relief. 'In a cinema, you mean?'

'I wish he'd been dreaming about all the times he took me when we were courting. We used to go to the pictures twice a week and he always bought me flowers as well. I sometimes dream about that when I'm going off to sleep.' Annie's eyes grew unfocused and moist before she appeared to remember the question. 'It wasn't any picture-house,' she said. 'You'd have thought he was on about the screen around your Rory's bed.'

Hugh tried to recapture his sense of triumph but was closer to regretting his insistence. 'What did he say about it?' Ellen asked somewhere behind him.

'We couldn't make half of it out, me and the nurses. They're a credit to the hospital, let me promise you. Your Rory's in the best hands.' Hugh was afraid she'd lost her conversational way again, and was on the edge of having to prompt her when she said 'He kept saying they were hiding behind the screen. On the floor, it sounded like, or maybe they went under the bed.'

Hugh had to ask the question. 'Who?'

'Nobody they'd let in a hospital. Some man that was all bones and so dirty he left marks on the screen. Jack thought he was a big spider at first, he was going so fast, or maybe it was how he was going.'

Hugh heard movement behind him again as Charlotte said 'You seem to have understood quite a lot. Was that the half?'

It was clear to Hugh that she was inviting no more, but at the end of some visible musing Annie said 'One thing that was funny – well, you mightn't have thought it was. No, I don't think you would have.'

With enough impatience for all three of Rory's visitors Charlotte said 'What wasn't funny?'

'It was just they were doing something for your Rory and the screen really was round his bed.'

'But you didn't see anything,' Hugh urged.

'Do you know, he got me so I almost thought I did.' Perhaps Hugh's expression made her add 'Don't fret, it was just a shadow. Nobody's that thin.'

Hugh was trying to decide whether he could risk looking behind him when Annie patted her husband's hand before levering herself to her feet. 'Will you keep an eye out for him while I go to the littlest room?'

'For your husband,' Charlotte said.

'There's nobody else for me to care about.'

This silenced Rory's visitors until Annie left the ward, but as soon as the doors met with a gentle thud Hugh said 'It was him.'

'I don't know why you sound so pleased about it,' Charlotte said.

'I'm not,' Hugh said and was provoked to turn to her. 'You know what I meant.'

'Perhaps I don't want to know.'

'You do, don't you, Ellen?' When she only held up her hands and lowered them as they strayed within her vision Hugh said 'Know, I mean, not want. I don't want either.'

'Then try not being so obsessed with it,' said Charlotte.

'That won't make it go away, will it?'

As he saw that they ought to be discussing how this could be achieved Charlotte said 'What are you imagining now? What sense does it make?'

Hugh felt his face grow blotchy, and was about to protest that it wasn't up to him alone to interpret the situation when he realised 'He stopped us coming last night, didn't he?'

'And the point would be . . .'

'Maybe he doesn't like us all to be together. Maybe he doesn't want us talking about him.'

'Rory can't, Hugh,' Ellen said as if addressing a patient.

'Maybe he's going to be able to now we're here. Maybe that's what he, not Rory, we all know who we're talking about, maybe that's what he's afraid of.'

'Ellen was talking about Rory.'

This felt like several rebukes compressed into one, but Hugh might have kept at his subject if he hadn't heard the ward doors bump discreetly open. Apparently both of his cousins welcomed the excuse to look away from him. 'Thanks,' Annie murmured as she returned to her husband's bedside. 'Sorry for going on about being thin. I didn't mean anyone here.'

Ellen's gaze fell inwards and did its best to hide. Before Hugh could revive his subject, if that was advisable within Annie's hearing, the doors emitted another polite thud and let in a tall pale figure. The pallor belonged mostly to a white coat, though the doctor's hair was on its way to matching. He frowned afresh at each patient he visited, scribbling observations on a clipboard, and gave Rory what Hugh hoped was a deft examination. Charlotte was opening her mouth to speak to him, since he'd acknowledged the visitors with no more than a single nod, when Annie said 'Excuse me, doctor, could I have a word?'

'Please,' he said and indicated the exit with the clipboard.

As he marched away as if impelled by his bent head with Annie in pursuit Hugh blurted 'Shouldn't we talk to him?'

'We're going to,' Charlotte said and sprang to her feet as though escaping from a trap.

'We'd better not all go crowding round him,' Ellen said. 'Just you go, Charlotte, and you can tell us what he says.'

Charlotte hurried down the ward but stopped short of the doors, the twin windows of which framed Annie's inaudible conversation with the doctor. As whichever door Annie was beyond let her reappear in full while Charlotte dodged past the other, Hugh said urgently 'What do you think while she's not here?'

Ellen gazed along Rory's immobile body at him for so many seconds that Hugh wondered if he had spoken too low. He was about to repeat the question when she said 'I can't see how talking about it will help. It might even do the opposite.'

'You mean you believe me?' This heartened him so much it left thought behind. 'We've got to persuade Charlotte,' he said.

'No we haven't. Maybe if we don't keep talking about it it'll go away,' Ellen said under most of her breath.

'Don't mind me,' Annie called across the aisle. 'I'm not listening.'

This made Hugh feel as if someone besides Ellen were, but

he had to ask 'Wouldn't Rory want us to do anything we have to that'll help him?'

'I'm sure he would, only he can't know what that is.'

'But suppose we have to –' Hugh sucked in the opposite of a gasp, which left him briefly speechless. 'Did you see that?' he cried.

Ellen shook her head vigorously and seemed dismayed by the sensation. 'What now, Hugh?'

'His hand moved. His other hand.'

'I didn't see.'

'They do,' Annie contributed, if that was the word. 'It means they're still in there somewhere.'

'Has Rory that you've seen?' Hugh enquired, however impolitely with his back turned.

'Not that I've noticed, and I've been keeping an eye.'

'Ellen, I think I made him.'

He gazed at Rory's hand in the hope it might respond – just the twitch of a finger would do. 'I wish we could,' said Ellen.

'We can. I did, that's what I'm saying. Didn't you see, Annie?'

'To tell you the honest truth, I didn't.'

Hugh blundered to the seat Charlotte had vacated. He closed his hands around Rory's and then relinquished it, not merely because it felt limp as tripe and yet unnaturally warm, perhaps with sunlight through the window overlooking the bed, but in case he might appear to be manipulating it. 'You can hear us, can't you, Rory?' he said and found he didn't know how loud to speak, which left him uncertain where his voice might reach. 'Do you know what you want us to do?'

That was stupidly ambitious; the blazing of Hugh's face told him as much. Even urging Rory to signal yes and no with a finger, as he would in any number of films, might be. 'You know what we were talking about, don't you?' Hugh nevertheless insisted. 'Did he do this to you?'

No doubt someone was digging below the ajar window, and a breeze had brought the smell of earth in. 'Don't, Hugh,' Ellen said.

'Don't what?' Hugh retorted, fiercely for him. 'He doesn't seem to mind.'

'He isn't going to, is he?' Ellen's face worked as if she hardly knew how to shape it, and she sat forwards to lower her voice further still. 'You're just upsetting yourself and me as well. We both know the crash did this.'

'Yes, but what made him crash?'

As she gazed sadly at him Hugh was afraid that Rory would agree with her by indicating him with a finger. His brother didn't stir, however. Might a more explicit question rouse him? Hugh was searching for one that wouldn't sound like an attempt to displace his own guilt when the ward doors crept open. Their slowness unnerved him even once he saw they were admitting Charlotte.

He set about vacating her chair, but she waved him down. 'I'll sit at the end for a change.'

Ellen barely waited for her to finish. 'What did the doctor say?'

'Physically Rory isn't in a bad way at all. Not even any broken bones. The van's a wreck but his belt saved him.'

'You're making it sound as if that's bad somehow.'

'Of course that isn't, but –' Charlotte sat on the edge of the chair in the aisle. 'They've given him scans and everything else they do,' she said, 'and the doctor says they're going to change the treatment if there's no improvement soon.'

'I expect that's all they can do, isn't it?'

'It may be, but that's not my point. I couldn't get him to come right out and say it, but I don't think they know why Rory's in a coma. He couldn't tell me any reason at all.'

Hugh opened his mouth. He closed it at once – dismayingly, to no effect. The sound that was scraping his nerves continued with scarcely a break. While it was a cry he might very well have uttered, he'd last heard it from Charlotte in the tunnel. This time the powerless desperate almost shapeless plea was struggling from between Rory's slack lips. It took perhaps a minute to subside without rousing him, and then he was as inactive as before. Hugh waited until Ellen and Charlotte looked at each other and eventually, quite possibly reluctantly, at him. 'Do you believe me now?' he said.

TWENTY-FIVE

As soon as the doors clumped shut behind Annie on her hasty way to lunch Hugh said 'What do you think's happening to you, Ellen?'

He wanted her to admit to living in a nightmare, Charlotte guessed. Her own instinct was to hope for an interruption – hope that Rory might cry out again and bring back the staff, not that their prolonged examination had identified any change – but the hope was so irrational that she would have been ashamed to betray it. 'Hugh,' she protested instead.

'We've got to talk. We mustn't let anything stop us. You have to see that now.'

Charlotte wondered if he imagined he was exhorting Rory as well as both his cousins. His face was red with the effort or embarrassment of attempting to take the lead. 'Depends what you want to talk about,' Ellen told him.

'I said.'

'Hugh, you know we love you, but you aren't too good at understanding women. Sometimes we just need to be left alone.'

His face grew more thoroughly suffused as he searched for

somewhere to look, and Charlotte had to intervene. 'Not if we need help,' she said.

'You know we'll help you in any way we can, Charlotte,' Ellen said.

'That's right, we should help one another, but we can't if we don't know what's wrong.'

'I shouldn't think either of you is in any doubt about me.'

'I can't speak for Hugh, but I am. Honestly, Ellen, what's happened to you? If it's stress and I'm responsible, I'll take as much of it off you as I possibly can. Just tell me how.'

'That isn't what needs taking off me, and nobody can except me.'

'I'm not sure I understand that. In fact I'm sure I don't.'

'Oh, Charlotte, for heaven's sake. You're getting as bad as Hugh.'

'I'd say that was as good.'

'Sorry, Hugh. I'm sure Charlotte's right and it must be stress. What else would you expect just now?'

Ellen swung her free hand towards Rory before letting it drop out of sight, and Hugh held onto his brother as he turned to Charlotte. 'She can't have got like this since then, can she?'

'You're forgetting I lost my job.'

'So did I, but I'm still eating. Why won't you?'

As Ellen sprang to her feet a haphazard bouquet of perfumes filled and seemed to shrink the space around the bed. If any of this had stirred Rory it would have been worthwhile, Charlotte thought, but he was as inactive as a statue. 'They used to say you had to be cruel to be kind, Hugh,' Ellen declared, 'but you're being kind to be cruel.'

'I don't mean to be.' Hugh struggled to hold her with his gaze as he said 'I just don't see why you have to do this to yourself.'

'Oh, Hugh.' Ellen stretched her arms wide, less like a preamble to an embrace than as if to ensure none could occur. 'Take a good look and say what you're seeing,' she said. 'Don't dare to be kind, that's all.'

'I'm seeing you. The same person you've always been.'

'Inside, you mean. Maybe I'm the same person, but not the same thing.'

'You aren't a thing.'

'I know how you feel about me, but don't bother any longer. That's what I am.'

As Charlotte caught up with Ellen's first comment and felt absurdly unobservant not to have realised, Hugh turned his dismayed gaze on her, which she saw Ellen take as evidence that he couldn't stand any more of the sight of her. 'Can't you talk to her?' he pleaded.

'Ellen, you tell us. How are you expecting us to say you look?'

'Obese. Gross. Lumpish. Doughy. Pasty. Mammoth. Gargantuan. Cumbersome. Hippopotamish or whatever word there is. I haven't finished.' Ellen held out her hands as if they were objects she was disgusted to have picked up. 'Then there's putrid,' she said, 'and foul and rotten and tainted and septic and festering. Are you proud of me? I'll make a writer yet with all these words. And as for the smell –'

'Stop it, Ellen. You're just indulging yourself now.' As Charlotte saw Hugh's eyes flicker wildly in their sockets she felt as if she'd been delegated to calm her cousins down, although who could be calmer than Rory? 'Let's stay with how you started,' she said. 'You aren't overweight, you're very much the opposite. You weren't the last time we all met, and you haven't had time to put it on since.'

'Listen to her, Ellen. She's telling you the truth.'

'I've said before I'm glad we're so close, but you're both trying too hard. I know what I am.'

'All right then,' Charlotte said and stood up. 'Come and show me.'

Hugh didn't quite clutch at his brother's unresponsive hand. 'Where are you going?'

'Not far. We shouldn't be long. Let's hurry, Ellen. Stay there, Hugh.'

For a moment Ellen looked too concerned about him to leave him, and then she tramped like a mime of defiance to join Charlotte. As Charlotte hurried down the ward, which felt significantly narrower with the two of them abreast, she heard Hugh murmuring to Rory. 'Mum and dad don't know about you yet, that's why they're not here. They'll be down below us, all the way down. On their outback holiday they always wanted, but it means I can't get in touch.'

The ward doors cut off his monologue, and Ellen said 'Maybe we should leave them together for a while.'

'As long as you like,' Charlotte said and turned along the corridor.

It wasn't nearly spacious enough – with its lack of windows, it underlined the remoteness of escaping from the hospital – but it was ample compared with the Ladies'. She had to lead Ellen into the room, which was narrowed by cubicles and additionally cramped by a pair of sinks. Only the mirrors above the sinks were important, except that Ellen jerked up a hand to block the view until she'd turned her back on them. 'Why were you so anxious to bring me in here?' she said.

'Just to look at us.'

'You aren't asking me to get undressed. You wouldn't care for that any more than I would, believe me.' When Charlotte shook her head and did her best to seem amused by the first suggestion, Ellen said 'Then why in here?'

'Because we can see us together. Just have a look.'

As Charlotte faced the mirrors she was confronted by Ellen's stubborn back. 'I've seen all I want to of myself,' Ellen said.

'Please, Ellen. See yourself with me.'

Ellen twisted around, her eyes wide enough to be parodying madness, but didn't stop until she was facing away from the mirrors again. In the instant during which she braved her reflection her hands wavered towards her eyes before sagging by her sides. 'All right, now I have. Can we go?'

'What did you see, Ellen?'

'You putting on a good show. Nearly managing not to look as if you'd rather not be standing next to this. Nice try at a smile but you couldn't quite keep it up.'

'If anything about you is making me unhappy it's the thought of you starving yourself for no reason at all.'

'You aren't going to convince me, Charlotte. I've seen how people look at me that don't need to pretend, look at me and say things they don't care if I hear, even people I used to care for. When I was at my appeal –'

She fell silent as a nurse blinked at the sight of the cousins facing opposite ways. 'Everything all right?' the newcomer said.

'Would you say anything wasn't?' Charlotte risked asking.

The nurse gave Ellen a longer look on her way to a cubicle. 'Needs feeding up,' she said.

Ellen barely waited to emerge into the corridor. 'She must have heard you going on at me, that's all.'

'Why would she lie about your health even if she did hear? She's a nurse.' When Ellen looked determined to remain unpersuaded Charlotte said 'Shall we ask a nutritionist? There ought to be one in the hospital.'

'Don't go to any more trouble on my behalf.' Ellen gave in to a secret smile, or at least her mouth winced. 'If I'm supposed to be deluded, what about you? What was all that fuss in the tunnel about? Are you blaming Glen for that as well?'

'Maybe what he said.'

Hugh was murmuring to Rory and clasping his hand as though it were a lifeline for at least one of them. Charlotte pushed the door open, and as she followed Ellen she abandoned caution. 'I'll say I was having a nightmare if you will,' she said.

'And us,' said Hugh. 'Now we're agreed, let's really talk.'

'All right, we're having nightmares. Let's deal with them like adults.'

'We have been, haven't we? We've been helping each other with what's wrong with us. If we hadn't we'd never have got here for my brother.'

'We did,' Charlotte agreed, taking her seat at the foot of the bed, 'and do you know what else is important?'

'What?' Hugh said, not entirely eagerly.

'We started before we heard from Glen. We don't need anything he said to explain what's happening to us.'

'You mean you're going to,' said Ellen.

'I think I know what it is in my case. I'm feeling closed in by all the changes I'm surrounded by at work.'

'Sounds simple,' Hugh admitted.

'And you're confused by all the ones at yours. And Ellen, don't you feel we're trying to change your image and maybe secretly you think it's for the worse? As for Rory, he was in an accident. I don't see why we have to look further than that.'

'You said the doctor had to,' Hugh objected.

'I suppose I was really saying they haven't sorted out the

coma yet. That doesn't mean they haven't got the treatment right. Perhaps they have.'

This sounded feeble if not desperate, even to Charlotte. She felt as though she were trying to explain away not just his condition but with it Rory himself. She mightn't have been totally surprised if he'd risen up or at least made some sign of protest, but it was Ellen who responded. 'I'm sorry, Charlotte, but you're wrong.'

'You didn't speak to the doctor.'

'I wasn't thinking of him.'

Had a cloud settled over the sun? It couldn't have drawn the walls inwards. Ellen extended her hands and snatched them out of sight while Hugh's gaze ranged back and forth as if he'd lost control of it. He seemed about to utter the unspoken question when he stumbled to his feet and whirled around to glare out of the window. 'Who's down there?'

Apparently nobody was, or nobody that he could see. In a few moments he turned around as though groping for a direction and, having located the chair, dropped into it. 'He doesn't like us talking about him,' he muttered, and Charlotte saw the bed shudder.

Hugh had bumped it, she told herself. Certainly his brother gave no unequivocal sign of having heard the remark, let alone understood it. 'What makes you say that?' Ellen said just as low.

'We'd just started talking about that night at Thurstaston when Rory had his crash,' Hugh said as if he could hardly bear to realise. 'And I don't know about anyone else, but I've been getting worse since we talked about coming here, never mind while we've been doing it. It's like he doesn't want us all together in case we figure out too much about him.'

Before Charlotte could speak Ellen said close to inaudibly 'Have you seen him?'

'I don't know.'

'Have you, Charlotte?'

'What do you think? How is any of this going to help? Don't kick the bed or whatever you're doing, Hugh. That won't either.'

'I'm not.'

Perhaps she hadn't glimpsed a momentary tremor, and she was about to apologise when Ellen said 'I have.'

'Oh, Ellen, how can you –'

'More than seen. I think I've touched him. I didn't tell you I went back to Thurstaston.'

She was speaking so quietly it might have been out of misplaced respect – not, Charlotte thought, for anyone's intelligence. 'What happened?' Hugh whispered.

'He's in the cliff. He made me put my hand in. He nearly got hold of me. Don't make me remember any more.'

'He's already got hold of us, though.'

Charlotte felt as if her head were a lightless cell with no room for her spirit to stand up, part of a prison that her cousins had erected with their muttering. They'd shut her in with their gullibility, and she was all the more resentful when Hugh said 'Can't you feel it now?'

'What do you want me to feel?'

'He's talking to everyone, Charlotte. It isn't just about you.'

Ellen's stare suggested that her face – indeed, her whole body – was somewhere she was desperate not to be. Hugh's eyes jittered in their sockets as though nothing they showed him were capable of reassuring him. He and Ellen were aggravating their own problems, Charlotte thought, and so would she unless she told them so. She was taking a breath when Rory spoke.

At least, the sound had ambitions to be a word. It was certainly the best he could achieve along the lines of a refusal or a denial. It was feebler than his previous cry, not loud enough to bring any of the hospital staff. Hugh and Ellen might have imagined that he was sinking deeper into a nightmare, so deep that it swallowed most of his plea, but wasn't it equally likely that he was protesting about the arguments around him? 'It's getting worse for him as well,' Hugh said. 'We've got to do something while there's time.'

Ellen seemed reluctant, though by no means as much as Charlotte, to ask 'What?'

'We can talk about that on the way. We have to go back.'

His gaze strayed towards footsteps approaching down the ward. Charlotte hoped they belonged to a nurse or someone more authoritative who might intervene somehow, but it was Annie. 'Going somewhere nice?' she said.

TWENTY-SIX

Ellen felt less alone for having admitted the truth about Thurstaston until Hugh whispered 'Everyone else should stay here. I'll go.'

'Rory doesn't have much choice, Hugh,' Charlotte said.

'I know that,' Hugh muttered as if reproving her for a tasteless joke. 'That's why I'm going. I mean you two.'

'So you can't be as bad as you think you are.'

'I don't follow.'

'That's all you seem to have been doing lately.'

'Why are you being like this, Charlotte?' Ellen gripped her toadstool knees through the inadequate concealment of her trousers to keep her detestable hands from invading her vision. 'How do you think it can help?'

'I'm simply saying if Hugh's able to go all that way by himself he can't very well be as disoriented as I've been imagining he is.'

'You sound as if you want him to be.'

Charlotte hunched her shoulders as if clenching her body around her thoughts. Perhaps she was miming her awareness of Annie at her back, since she said almost inaudibly 'If we're going to argue, let's do it outside.'

'Why do we have to at all?' Hugh said as low. 'That's what he wants.'

Charlotte stared at him and opened her mouth, then twisted around on her chair. 'Annie, could you call us if there's any change? We just want to step into the corridor for a few minutes.'

'You go and have your conference. That's what families are for.' Annie patted her husband's unresponsive hand, perhaps in memory of a discussion or many of them. 'Your Rory's safe with me,' she said.

Hugh glanced nervously out of the window as he stood up once his cousins had. Ellen saw Annie watching her with a mixture of concern and encouragement that she might have directed at a patient who had risen from one of the beds. She trudged after Charlotte with Hugh at her heels, but Charlotte stopped short of the exit and swung around. 'You know what we should do while we have the chance.'

'Sounds like you're going to tell us,' Hugh said rather than invited.

Charlotte turned to the sister behind the desk. 'I wonder if there's anyone we could consult? I've developed a bad case of claustrophobia. Hugh's sense of direction has gone haywire, hasn't it, Hugh, and . . .'

Ellen heard the words flinch from describing her. If even Charlotte couldn't find any for her, Ellen's state must be worse than she knew. Sheer professionalism let the sister hide her revulsion as she gazed at Ellen while telling Charlotte 'We should have people you can see.'

'Can we now?' Hugh said.

'You'd have to make appointments, I'm afraid.'

'How soon?' As he grew red-faced with impatience or with embarrassment at sounding childish, he added 'I mean how soon will they be for?'

'I couldn't speak for our consultants, but –'

'Today?'

'No, not today. I shouldn't think this week.'

'That's no use. It's too late.'

'Well, I'm very sorry,' the sister said, perhaps unaware that he'd addressed the complaint to Charlotte.

Charlotte left it until she'd bustled him out of the ward as if dealing with an impolite child. Once the doors shut behind Ellen as well Charlotte said 'I come back to what I was saying. You can't be as bad as you've been making us worry you are if you can do without medical help.'

'If it's only a nightmare I ought to be able to live with it, shouldn't I? I'll have to for Rory's sake.'

As Ellen realised she didn't agree with him or Charlotte, Hugh managed to direct his gaze at her. 'Not just his,' he said.

'You can't use us as an excuse,' Charlotte said, 'if you won't tell us what you're proposing to do.'

'I wouldn't say he was making excuses, Charlotte.'

'All right then, reason, though I don't think that particularly fits either. Maybe I will if you tell us, Hugh.'

'We don't want you going off by yourself without a plan,' Ellen said, 'and no idea what you may be facing.'

'I'll find him and dig him out if you tell me where. He won't like that. I bet he doesn't like the light, in fact I know he won't.'

'Hugh,' Charlotte said as though she wanted to compete with Ellen at gentleness. 'A few minutes ago you were acting as if you thought someone was outside the window. I'm assuming that was supposed to be the same person.'

Hugh's gaze veered left and right along the corridor. He might have been searching for the person referred to, if not a way to escape the interrogation, as he said 'I wish we were in one of your books and things would be simpler.'

'Books aren't as simple as all that. You should try writing one sometime,' Ellen said and felt ashamed of turning on him. 'Anyway, no need to get confused. Take my word, he's in the cliff. If he seems to be anywhere else as well that'll just be part of the nightmare.'

'So at least now you're accepting things aren't real,' Charlotte said. 'You tell her, Hugh.'

'We're all living in our nightmares,' Hugh said, struggling to keep his gaze on Ellen. 'Is that what you mean?'

'I'm asking you to tell her whether she needs to starve herself.'

'Of course you don't, Ellen.' Hugh's eyes grew moist if no more stable. 'You mustn't,' he pleaded. 'Look at you.'

Ellen found her lips difficult to operate, proof that they were as thick as they felt. 'I'd rather not,' she succeeded in pronouncing.

'We are,' Charlotte assured her, 'and what do we see? Tell her, Hugh. This is a lot more important than going off.'

His eyes had lost their way again. Ellen watched him drag his gaze back to her as he said 'You're thin enough. You're too thin. Don't be any more.'

'He's right, Ellen. You must see that,' Charlotte said, but then she looked away from Ellen. 'What's the matter with her?'

Ellen thought this meant her until she realised Charlotte was peering into the ward. Annie was beckoning while she leaned sideways towards Rory's bed and turned her eyes to it. Charlotte shoved the doors apart and hurried down the room. 'What's wrong, Annie?'

'I don't know if it's wrong,' Annie said and returned her free hand to clasping her husband's. 'I thought I heard him say something.'

'Who did?' Hugh called, his breath fluttering on the nape of Ellen's neck.

'Your Rory. Who else would it have been?'

Ellen rubbed her moist neck and snatched her hand away from rediscovering how spongy her flesh was. 'What did he say?'

'He doesn't look like he said anything, does he? Maybe I dozed off for a minute and dreamed it. I truly thought I heard him, but I haven't been getting much sleep.'

Ellen sought refuge in the space between the beds. Rory appeared not to have shifted, and his hand didn't stir when she made herself reach for it. At least he didn't flinch from her touch, but she kept her gaze on Annie while Hugh insisted 'What did you think he said?'

'I thought he was asking for something,' Annie said, only to shake her head.

Charlotte was sitting sideways on her chair as if she were a mediator. With sufficient patience for all three of them she prompted 'And that would have been . . .'

'Something to write with. I thought it was because he couldn't talk.'

'It's harder to write,' Hugh objected.

'He mightn't realise, might he? I don't know what else he'd have meant by a pen.'

Ellen felt Hugh's stare fasten on her. As she met it he spoke for at least the two of them. 'What exactly do you think he said?'

'I'm not sure exactly. I don't suppose he would have been. Something about a pen, that's all I could make out.' More obstinately than Ellen thought was called for Annie added 'If I did.'

'Something pen, you're saying he said.'

'That's about it,' Annie said and then fingered her lips as if to check that they were working properly. 'Half a tick, though. Maybe it was more like pen something. It wouldn't have been pendulum, would it? That doesn't seem to make sense.'

'It doesn't,' Charlotte told her cousins in particular.

'How about demand? I suppose that would mean he was wanting it.'

'He's wanting all right,' Hugh said and stumbled to his feet. 'I've got to be going. I need to be there well before dark.'

Charlotte crouched over the end of the bed as if a weight had pressed her skull down. 'Suppose you aren't?'

'I will be. I've plenty of time still,' he said and lurched at the aisle.

Ellen imagined him losing his way, wandering desperately as the night caught up with him. She squeezed Rory's hand before levering her sluggish body, her slug of a body, off the chair. 'You're going to need me, Hugh.'

'I'll be best off by myself,' he hissed, concealing his words from Annie with his left hand. 'You don't want to see.'

'I've seen once,' Ellen murmured, only to grasp that he was referring to whatever he might have to do. 'I'll need to show you where. You'll stay here, won't you, Charlotte?'

'Someone certainly has to,' Charlotte said but seemed inclined to follow them, presumably to dissuade them. 'You're actually going to do this,' she said under her breath.

'That's right,' Hugh said and strode with a little less conviction towards the doors. He held the left one open for Ellen, so that she almost failed to notice he was uncertain which way to go. At least the corridor was empty, but she would be visible to spectators soon enough. It was just the start of the journey, and already she was dreading what she and Hugh might encounter on the way, never mind at the end. As the doors met with a discreet thump like the surreptitious fall of a lid, she heard Annie summarise the sudden exodus. 'Was it something I said?'

TWENTY-SEVEN

The express was more than an hour out of Leeds, and flanked by suburbs as bad as identical, when Hugh ceased to be able to silence his doubts. 'This is wrong.'

Ellen opened her eyes as if they were sluggish with gum. 'Don't say you're having second thoughts after we've been to all this trouble.'

Perhaps she was thinking of the farce outside the hospital, where he had looked the wrong way for the first three taxis she'd elected him to hail. Or she might be remembering how his disorientation and her loathing of spectators had almost made them miss the train once she'd succeeded in ushering him through the crowd to buy tickets. He'd spent most of the journey gazing at her, largely so that the views from the train wouldn't snatch away any lingering sense of direction, but could she think he was striving to convince her that she didn't revolt him? Of course she didn't, though he had to stifle his dismay at the sight of the frail undernourished sufferer she'd become in case she mistook it for disgust. 'I'm not,' he said, and when her depleted face worked as if she wished she could slough it 'You aren't, are you?'

'I'm not my cousin, Hugh.'

'Charlotte, you mean.' Since she wasn't there he risked saying 'I wouldn't want you to be.'

'We shouldn't put her down. She's done a lot for me.'

Beyond Ellen heads swayed gently with the motion of the train, and Hugh had to tell himself that none of them was shaking in mockery of his remark, let alone too thin to be decently alive. If anyone like that was behind him, surely Ellen would have noticed, but in a sense it was the lack of intrusion that bothered him. 'Is it hard for you, doing this?' he said.

'No harder than it's been for you, I should think.'

'That's what I was getting at. That's what's wrong.'

'You're saying you'd like me to feel worse.'

'You know I wouldn't like it. I'm asking if you do.'

'Well, you're certainly making it happen,' Ellen said with a kind of anguished triumph.

Hugh stretched out his hands, only for her gaze to weigh them down until they sank to his knees. 'I don't mean to, but –'

'Just leave well alone, Hugh.' Ellen's lips worked on their shape before she gave in to adding 'Except well isn't the word.'

'It will be,' Hugh said and advanced his hands again. 'I promise.'

A hint of affection not entirely divorced from amusement glimmered in her eyes. 'What are you trying to promise me, Hugh?'

'To stop what's happening to you. What you think is happening. What he's making you think.'

Each variation seemed less able to reach her. Perhaps they were driving her further inside her head – and then Hugh realised that his hands were hovering as if he couldn't bear to touch her. Before he had time to be inhibited by his clumsiness, he took hold of her arms. The sleeves of her crumpled garment yielded even more than he was afraid they would, and his innards quailed as he felt how gaunt her arms had grown, but he held her as she did her best to draw back. 'Don't, Hugh,' she said low and unevenly. 'Especially not here.'

'Why not here?' His head was filling with a mass of stale perfume and the drunken rocking of the carriage, but he didn't let go. 'What don't you want people to see?'

'You can't still need to ask that. You aren't so lacking in imagination.'

'I don't mind if they all look. They're welcome to see how much I care about you.' Though his face was growing more uncomfortably hot than any childhood fever, and he seemed to be clinging to her so that his hands wouldn't betray his awkwardness, none of this could silence him. 'I'm not doing this just for Rory,' he blundered onwards. 'It's mostly for you.'

'If you say so, but you're hurting me.'

He was about to take this as a simple rebuff when he grasped that he might be bruising her starved arms. He released them so hastily that he wondered if he seemed eager to be done with touching her. As he patted them to compensate, a jerk of the train flung him back on his seat. 'That wasn't me,' he protested. 'It was the driver.'

'You're a good person, Hugh. We all know you are.'

He felt as if she'd placed him at a distance far greater than the gap between the seats, and so he could only return to his dogged subject. 'Do you understand what I was trying to say now at least?'

'Are we back at that again? Can't we find our way away from it and leave it alone?'

Though her choice of words seemed thoughtless, Hugh managed to say only 'Don't you think someone else is?'

'I've no idea what you're asking me to think.'

'I don't want to say too much.'

'You are, though. It just isn't making a great deal of sense.'

Hugh leaned forwards, gripping the edge of the seat to reassure Ellen that he wasn't about to grab her. 'Suppose talking about you know who brings him?' he said barely louder than the monologue of the wheels.

'Too many people around, Hugh.'

He was behaving irrationally in at least one way: it surely couldn't matter how quietly or otherwise he spoke. He sat back, to Ellen's visible relief, before saying 'Now we're on our way you know where to do you know what, shouldn't he be trying to make things worse for us?'

Hugh had begun to wonder if she found his language childish by the time she said 'Perhaps he's distracted by us splitting up.'

'Leaving the others at the hospital, you mean.' When she confirmed this with a solitary nod Hugh said 'But he made us all have nightmares when we weren't together.'

'Maybe it takes more of an effort to keep them up.'

'Suppose it's to make us think he doesn't care if we find him?'

'I think you were right before. We ought to stop talking about it. Let's concentrate on getting there and seeing what can be done.'

This made Hugh more aware of the purpose of their journey than he wanted to anticipate. Perhaps Ellen sensed his disquiet, because she said 'Think of Rory if it helps.'

It almost did, but only for a moment. 'Maybe he's there,' Hugh blurted. 'Him.'

'I thought we said that's just a kind of nightmare.'

'He could be busy doing something to Rory. Suppose that's why we're being left alone?'

'I expect Charlotte would call us if there were any developments.'

'We should have asked her to.' Hugh dragged his mobile from whichever pocket it was in. 'I want to be sure,' he felt defiant for saying.

He'd begun to wonder if some event at the hospital was distracting Charlotte by the time she said 'Where have you got to?'

He could have done without her turn of phrase. 'We're on the train,' he said.

'I thought you'd have to be. Any problem?'

'Not here, well, not more than we've been having. How about there?'

'Just the same as when you left.' Before Hugh could decide whether this contained any accusation Charlotte said 'Sorry, I should have thought. I didn't notice.'

'What didn't you? What's wrong?'

'Quiet a moment, Hugh. You're right, absolutely. It's going off. I'll take it out if I need to.' Closer to the phone she said 'We aren't meant to use mobiles in here. There's a sign at the entrance, apparently.'

'We just wondered how Rory's getting on. Will you let us know if there's any change?'

'So long as I can reach you.'

'Why shouldn't you be able to?'

'You'll have to go underground, won't you? Sorry,' she added, not addressing him. 'I have to go now, Hugh.'

'All right, maybe we'll talk again.'

As he wished he hadn't made the prospect sound uncertain Ellen said 'Hold on. Tell her hold on.'

'Ellen wants a word.'

'She'll have to wait until I go outside.'

Ellen tugged one of her hands from beneath her and inched it forwards, then shoved it back into hiding. 'Doesn't she want to speak to me?'

'Of course she does. She just can't in the hospital. She's going where she can.'

Ellen's gaze was sinking inwards by the time her mobile came to life. It sang O at length and eventually arrived at *klahoma*, the final vowel of which she thumbed off. 'Charlotte?' she said. 'You'll want to be part of this, Hugh.'

She switched on the loudspeaker and laid the phone next to her before sitting on her hand again. 'I was thinking, we never called Glen back.'

'It sounded as if he'd finished to me, but I can give you his number.'

'Do you think it might be better if you rang him? He won't know mine, so he mightn't answer it. You could always tell him it's for my book. I just thought we should find out if he had anything else to say about, you know, why he rang before.'

Charlotte sighed or made hard work of a breath. 'I'll see if there's anything to get out of him. It can be my excuse to stay out here for a few minutes.'

With that she was gone as though the impatient clawlike clicking of the wheels had surged to drag her down. Ellen's hand crept out to finger a key and retreated into hiding. Hugh levelled an encouraging gaze at her, even once his eyes began to smart with the prolongation of the task. She might have been holding herself rigid in anticipation of the call, but the motion of the train assailed her with the occasional shiver. When the phone began to sing its tinny O she jabbed a key and snatched her hand back. At first Hugh thought she'd broken the connection in her haste, and then he heard a voice, muffled enough to be buried. 'You need to put the loudspeaker on again,' he said and activated it for her.

'Glen isn't answering, you two. I've left a message for him to call one of us.'

'You aren't waiting outside till he does,' Hugh protested.

'I'm not, that's right. I'm going to Rory in a minute. In fact, make that now.'

The clamour of an ambulance had begun to overwhelm her voice. Hugh had the disorienting impression that the artificial wail was rising from beneath the carriage or even from underground. It grew muddily blurred as it filled the loudspeaker, and then it sank into silence, but not before drawing a bony hand into sight behind Ellen's head.

Hugh didn't know whether he was more dismayed by it or by how Ellen might react when she noticed it. He was panicking over where to look when Charlotte said 'If anyone needs to call me I'll have the phone on mute.'

'Thanks, Charlotte,' Ellen said. 'We'll know you're there.'

'Good luck then. Be careful,' Charlotte added and might have been searching for less of a cliché as the owner of the hand peered between the seats. She was a pensioner whose reddish hair and bony face looked faded as an early photograph. 'Would you care to turn that down?' she said. 'We don't all want to hear your business.'

'Goodbye, Charlotte,' Hugh called, possibly in time for her to hear. 'Gone now,' he told the pensioner. 'Is it all right if we talk?' This sent her back into her seat, but her intrusion felt too much like an omen of a worse one, and left Hugh with such a sense of being spied upon that he was afraid of making some disastrous mistake out of nervousness. 'Let's talk,' he appealed to Ellen. 'It doesn't matter what about. Anything except, anything else at all.'

TWENTY-EIGHT

By the time they came to change trains Ellen felt as if she and Hugh were reverting to childhood. They'd been reduced to playing a word game, competing to produce the longest word by adding a letter at each turn. Go, god, goad, gonad . . . Hugh had won that round and quite a few others by creating a plural while Ellen did her best not to resent his nervous triumph; she was supposed to be the writer, after all. She had even let him finish off the list of be and bee and beer and beery with begery, though she'd hoped his tentative lopsided smile had shown he meant it as a joke. Once they'd agreed they could rearrange letters the rounds had gone on longer, in some cases almost long enough she forgot why they were playing. At least the contest was preferable to I Spy, their solitary game of which had reminded them that neither liked to look towards the windows, not to mention around the carriage in search of anything hidden. I, in, inn, nine, linen, linnet . . . She'd baulked at letting Hugh turn this into entitle, though he'd seemed proud to have finally lit on the word. Now it was a question of how precarious an item he would find to stack on top of me and men and mean and meant and mental. She might have pointed at her mouth to suggest aliment if that wouldn't have risked touching her rubbery lips with a spongy finger. 'Mentaly,' Hugh said at last with some defiance.

'You win,' Ellen said and shut the lids of the moist bags of liquid that were her eyes, because the high walls of a railway cutting had conjured two reflections of her out of the dark.

When the train coasted to a halt she didn't open her eyes. She wasn't going to be tricked into glimpsing her reflection, even by the stench of clay and worse that drifted into her nostrils, presumably from herself. The train lumbered to a second halt, and Hugh murmured 'Liverpool.' Only the notion that she might force him to touch her and pretend again that he could bear it made her look.

Under an outsize clock magnifying ten to three in the afternoon the station concourse was crowded, but everyone seemed too preoccupied to notice Ellen, unless they'd seen her and weren't anxious to repeat the experience. Hugh poked a button to summon a lift to take him and Ellen underground. As the doors opened, a small broad square-faced man topped with a handful of parallel strands of grey hair limped towards them, brandishing a Cougar bestseller, *Just Be You*. He followed the cousins into the lift and then retreated, waving the paperback as if miming a vigorous farewell, though Ellen knew he was fending off her appearance and her stench. 'Forgot something. You go on,' he said and stepped back.

Hugh's attempts to keep a reassuring gaze on her made her say 'Don't waste your time on me, Hugh. We both saw that.'

'We heard him too, didn't we? He had to go back for something.'

'He didn't fool me, so don't try. He was being polite, like you.'

'Maybe he was claustrophobic. It says it's for eight people but they'd have to be squashed in.'

Rather than demand whether he had in mind the amount of space that clammy misshapen Ellen was occupying, she said 'No, it was me.'

'Maybe you're right, but not the way you think. You've put

on too much.' Hugh's gaze jittered but didn't veer away. 'It's even getting to me in here,' he said.

His honesty was less welcome than she must have been determined to believe. As the lift crawled downwards she felt as if they were being dragged into the earth. 'So you've agreed with me all the time,' she told him.

'I haven't, Ellen. What do you think I said?'

'You tell me. Go on, make yourself clearer.'

Patches of his face had begun to look raw, the way his brain might feel for all she knew. 'Too much . . .' he repeated, waving his hands as if to send away the remainder of the phrase.

'Finish it off. One more word.'

'Smelly.'

While she had invited directness, she couldn't have imagined he would be so cruel. The doors drew back, revealing a tiled corridor that led to the underground platform. A thin shrill echo mocked her as she said 'We don't need anyone to make me feel worse. You're doing fine.'

'I don't understand,' Hugh pleaded as he chased her out of the lift. 'What am I meant to have done?'

Ellen thought she glimpsed her reflection in the white tiles on both sides, a pallid writhing like the antics of a massive grub. Hugh's presence at her heels was quite as unappealing. 'Don't you know what you're saying?' she enquired, not even over her shoulder. 'Haven't you any sense of that either?'

'I said . . .' She heard his footsteps pause as his voice did, but she wasn't waiting for him. 'Smelly,' he said and hurried after her. 'That's what you used to call perfumes.'

It was true, but how could she be sure that he hadn't been inadvertently accurate? She trudged to the end of the corridor and along the platform to the nearest trio of mud-brown plastic seats embedded in the wall. 'Just leave me alone for a while,' she said, and when his eyes began to flicker with panic 'Sit by me but don't say anything till I want you to.'

He left a seat between them when she took the furthest. She couldn't tell whether he was respecting her wishes or simply loath to sit closer. A board above the platform announced that their train to West Kirby was due in four minutes. The digit yellow as a warning on a traffic light twitched and diminished, and Ellen was reflecting that it was also the colour of cowardice – of her apprehension about the journey – when a figure emerged from the tiled corridor. It was the man with the book.

He must have caught the lift as soon as it returned to ground level. He hadn't even bothered to pretend that his imaginary errand had delayed him. Perhaps he'd hoped Ellen would have departed. He aborted his expression as he noticed her and trotted hastily past. 'Don't,' Ellen muttered as Hugh opened his mouth. Beyond the man another board subtracted a minute, and she heard the rumble of the train.

She could have thought the boards were taunting her and Hugh. At best they felt like an extension of her mind, determined to postpone the outcome of the journey. The train slowed as it wormed into the light, naming West Kirby in yellow letters that scuttled across a strip above the driver's window. Hugh jumped up as if he felt the need to demonstrate eagerness, then seemed at a loss until Ellen wobbled to her feet. As they boarded the train, so did the man with the book.

At least he stayed out of their carriage, which meant they had it to themselves. Ellen sat facing away from the driver and the man. She preferred not to watch the train burrow into the tunnel – it was a little too reminiscent of groping inside the cliff – but instead she felt darkness advancing at her back. The train raced under the river to Birkenhead, and had stopped at two more stations when the doors between the carriages rattled open to admit the man with the book.

Ellen tried to ignore him, especially for fear of alerting Hugh. He seemed disagreeably fascinated by the progress of the dark outside the window, unless he was doing his utmost to disregard Ellen's reflection. The man behind him apparently felt required to explain the change of carriages, however. 'Smokers,' he complained.

Hugh twisted around to catch him wrinkling his nose and waving the book like a fan. 'Hugh,' Ellen warned, but too late: he'd grabbed the back of the seat to swing himself into the aisle as he demanded 'Why were you doing that again?'

The man shut the door and squatted on the seat to its left, planting the book on his lap. 'I'm sorry?'

'Never mind being sorry. Just tell this lady why you didn't get in the lift.'

'I don't want to hear it, Hugh.'

'She doesn't want to hear.'

'She does really, and I do. What was wrong with it? You can say. We need you to.'

'I said I dropped something and had to go back.'

'You said you forgot it before.'

'Forgot it or dropped it. Same thing.'

'No it isn't. We know about words,' Hugh said and jabbed a finger at the book. 'She specially does. She's going to be published by them.'

'Is that right?'

While Ellen wasn't certain that the question was addressed to her or indeed to anyone, she said 'I hope so. Hugh –'

'First time I've met a writer. I suppose you have to be different from the rest of us.'

'Better, you mean,' Hugh said. 'So what did you drop?'

The man's face had begun to compete with his for overall redness. If Ellen were writing the scene she might have described this as the colour of a pair of traffic lights warning her to stop. Meanwhile the man was saying 'What do you care?'

'I care a lot,' said Hugh, not quite turning towards Ellen, who would have responded that he cared too much about her – that he was as helplessly trapped by it as he was making her feel. 'We don't think you left anything behind,' he said. 'We think you just didn't want to get in.'

The man's gaze strayed towards Ellen and retreated, no more hastily than she could blame him for. 'Think what you like,' he said.

'It isn't what we like, it's the truth.' Hugh clutched at the seat across the aisle with his free hand, though the carriage was steady enough. 'Why couldn't you get in?' he insisted. 'And don't say you're claustrophobic. We know someone who is.'

'Too much disinfectant.'

Hugh shook his head or swivelled it from side to side. 'Too much . . .'

'They must have sprayed in there to cover something up. I'm surprised you could breathe.'

'Then how did you manage to come down in it?' Hugh enquired in a kind of unwilling triumph.

As Ellen saw the man's lips stiffen she succeeded in parting her own. 'You're right,' she told him, and the reflections that were wadded against the windows mouthed it. 'There was something that ought to be covered up.' When Hugh gave her a defiantly unhappy look she said 'Sit down before you forget where we're going.'

Her cruelty silenced him, though for some seconds he appeared not to know how to resume his place. She couldn't help by touching him, but she was at the very edge of her patience by the time he abandoned his handholds and shuffled to face her before subsiding opposite. The small squat man had already failed to lose himself in his book, which he laid on the seat next to him. Ellen stared at Hugh hard enough to keep him quiet – almost hard enough to distract her from the grotesque reflections squashed against the windows by the dark. She was peripherally aware that the small man alighted at the last of the underground stations, even if she didn't glimpse him as the train moved off. His departure seemed not to have left the carriage as empty as it ought to be, an impression that worked on her nerves until she realised 'He didn't take his book.'

'Shall I get it for you?'

'Just stay there, Hugh.'

He wasn't ready to abandon his compulsion to help. 'About him, you know, I was only trying –'

'And could you stay quiet as well? You've said considerably more than enough for a while.' When he made to speak she added 'Otherwise I'll be telling you where to go and leaving you to it.'

She wondered if he might take this less as a threat than as an opportunity to protect her, but some aspect of it hushed him. He gazed at her as if he didn't know where else to look, which left her feeling trapped inside her flesh, peering out of the blurred mass of her face. The onslaught of sunlight as the carriage emerged from the tunnel was some distraction, though it aggravated her clamminess – and then she noticed something else. 'It's gone,' she said.

Hugh's gaze seemed focused on reminding her that he was

forbidden to speak, and so she lurched past him. 'His book,' she said, not having found it on the seat or on the floor. 'It was there.'

'I wouldn't know. You said I had to sit.'

Ellen felt as if, having intensified her sense of her condition, the man had snatched away the possibility of a Cougar book. The train had halted at a station for nobody visible to board before Hugh said 'Maybe he's showing us what he can do.'

'What do you mean?'

'Maybe there wasn't a man at all.'

Was this a desperate attempt at reassurance? It simply left her feeling more unsure of herself. If she concentrated on the horizon, where the edge of the slate of the sea cut into a heavy black sky, she could imagine that the train was scarcely moving. There were very few stations to go, and soon the train swung away from the water, and there were none at all.

A man with a rucksack over his left shoulder stepped back as she dumped herself on the platform, and she almost believed he was only making way for her and Hugh. She stumped past the unstaffed booth and the end of the platform into the little booking hall, where she turned on Hugh. 'Where are you proposing to get your spade?'

'I must have been thinking we could borrow one from the house. There'll be a shop, won't there?' he came close to pleading. 'Let's ask.'

A solitary taxi was at rest outside the station. Once Ellen made for it he succeeded in reaching the driver's window. 'Excuse me, do you know where we can buy a, gardening equipment, sort of thing?'

The large tattooed man inclined his shaven pate in a lazy sidelong nod. 'Should be some in the next road.'

'Can you take us?'

'It's not that far,' the driver protested, then glanced askance at Ellen. 'Are you going on anywhere?'

She felt referred to rather than addressed, and left Hugh to say 'You could wait and take us to Thurstaston.'

'Helping the rangers, are you?'

'I expect so,' Hugh was sufficiently thrown to tell him. 'I'll sit in front, shall I, Ellen? You can have the back.'

At least this let her sit as far from the driver as she could. Nevertheless he lowered his window all the way as he started the engine, and didn't ask whether she minded the breeze that fluttered her old nightdress, peeling it away from her moist flesh only to paste it more uncomfortably still. He turned left off the main road and immediately left again, which brought them in less than a minute to a hardware store next to a wine bar. 'Do we both need to go in?' Hugh said.

'I take it you're asking me to.'

'I'll give you the money if you can.'

She wondered if the driver thought this sounded like a bribe; it felt absurdly like one. 'Don't go digging in your pocket,' she said. 'We're both out of work.'

As she struggled out of the taxi she was confronted by spades, four of them hovering in the gloom beyond the shop window. They were hanging from hooks on the wall, and the shop was darkened by an advancing mass of cloud. There was a spade for her and for each of her cousins, but what was that supposed to mean? She ought to bury her imagination for a while, and did her best to fancy that the bell above the door was indicating she could.

The comfortably plump woman in trousers and an overall behind the small counter might have been dressed for gardening. 'Brought the dark with you,' she said and sniffed. 'Needing help?'

Ellen gathered that the woman was eager to see the last of her, and why. 'Just a spade,' she said and was nervous enough to add 'For the garden.'

At once she was intensely aware why she was buying the item. Perhaps the banality of the transaction made its purpose real for her. A smell of earth that no amount of perfume could disguise clogged her nostrils, challenging her to breathe. If she fled the shop she would be letting her cousins down, and Hugh would feel compelled to find his way in. She plodded to the wall, shaking the resonant floorboards, to clutch at the biggest spade – the one, she couldn't help thinking, that might be most use as a weapon. She almost wrenched the hook loose in her haste to lift the spade off. She laid a twenty-pound note on the counter when the woman failed to take it, and that was where the woman placed her change. 'Would you like a bag?' she said.

As Ellen wondered if it might be advisable to hide the implement until she and Hugh were on the beach, the woman produced a plastic bag that would barely cover its head. 'Never mind,' Ellen said and bore the spade out of the shop.

The bell drew attention to it, and so did the taxi driver. 'Here's the digger,' he said. Hugh glanced so unsteadily at her that she thought he too might be fully aware at last of their undertaking. 'May as well keep it with you,' the driver said as she headed for the boot.

When the car swung away from the kerb the thin object lurched towards Ellen, tapping her on the shoulder with its handle. She grasped it by the shaft to keep it off, though this entailed too much awareness of the deformed hand at the end of her misshapen arm. Meanwhile the taxi found a different route to the main road and then set about climbing a hill. Soon the last houses were left behind, and the car was dwarfed by sandstone banks whose colour anticipated the thick brown of the cliff. Although the taxi was speeding uphill it was so enclosed that Ellen felt as if it were plunging into the earth.

It gained the summit of the road at last and swerved right at a crossroads towards the underside of the sky. 'Is this the way?' Hugh blurted.

For a moment this made Ellen as nervously distrustful as he sounded. 'This is it all right,' she said, hoping this reassured him more than it managed for her.

The road did indeed end on the brink of the cliff. To the left a solitary triangular kite was drooping its tail against the charred sky above the common beyond a centre for visitors to the nature trail; to the right a path led down to the beach. Hugh fumbled out money and paid the driver while Ellen supported her weight on the spade, having clambered forth. As the taxi performed an impatient three-point turn and sped inland, Hugh said 'Who's that? What's he want?'

The spade scraped across the tarmac as Ellen twisted around to see a figure turning its back in a gap in the hedge where a path led to the visitor centre. She'd failed to notice him when she left the taxi. He wore a grey anorak with the hood up and greenish rubber boots over equally muddy trousers, and was carrying a spade. 'Up here if you're helping with the path,' he said.

His voice was so muffled by the hood that Ellen had to strain to be anything like certain she was hearing him. The anorak was fatter than the humid afternoon warranted, and a good deal bulkier than him, to judge by the bony outlines of his legs. 'That's all right. We'll follow,' she called to send him on his way.

'No we won't,' Hugh whispered, and even lower 'Don't speak to him.'

Ellen peered after the figure as it shuffled along the path. The anorak was stained so variously grey that patches reminded her of lichen, not least by their texture. 'Why not?' she murmured.

'He's –' Hugh relinquished whispering and said at the top of his voice 'He's not there.'

The man was out of sight beyond the hedge now. His spade rose above it at some distance, long enough to beckon, scattering lumps of earth. 'Don't be silly, Hugh,' Ellen said, but when his eyes began to dodge from side to side she tramped to the gap in the hedge. The common was deserted under the blackening sky; even the kite had vanished. Were there traces of footprints on the path until the hedge around the visitor centre concealed it? They didn't look shod; indeed, they struck her as somehow even barer. 'Just come on,' she told Hugh and made for the path to the beach. She oughtn't to have spoken so sharply, but her nerves were to blame. She was beginning to wonder what else might intervene to prevent her and Hugh from reaching their goal.

TWENTY-NINE

When Hugh dug the spade into the base of the cliff, a handful of clay trickled down at him. Ellen glanced nervously upwards, but nobody was visible against the sky, although it was almost black enough to hide a watcher. 'Go on,' she urged, sounding muffled by the gloom. He planted one foot on the metal blade and leaned all his weight on it, heaving out a lump of earth as big as a man's head, which came so readily that someone might have been pushing it. Hugh stumbled backwards and, having flung away the spadeful, thrust the blade into the gaping cavity. Before he could exert his weight the mass of earth above him quivered as if it or its tenant were shaking off slumber. The next moment a bulk taller and broader than a house collapsed towards him.

'Watch out,' Ellen wasted time in crying as she made to drag him back. The sound of her approach only distracted him. He swung around to shove her out of danger – swung around the wrong way. His gaze and his frantic movements failed to coincide in search of her as the wall of earth slid towards them so lethargically it might have been relishing its deliberateness.

Charlotte couldn't cry out, she could only dash to grab him and Ellen, to haul them clear if there was time. She had nothing to say that would help, and in any case she needed to devote her breath to sprinting faster. But her mouth was open, and it filled with mud as she and her cousins were buried deep in earth.

It blinded her and stuffed her nostrils as soon as she was desperate enough to try to draw a breath. It pinioned her, arms helplessly outstretched, and she was as incapable of movement as a statue. Nevertheless a hand found hers, and she wondered which of her cousins had somehow managed to reach out until she realised that the fingers consisted of very little more than bones. As she struggled to fend off their clasp she grew aware of another unwelcome companion – a large insect that was attempting to crawl over her breast, buzzing silently with the effort. This was one outrage too many, and Charlotte attempted to project her distress into a cry that barely penetrated her clogged ears, if indeed she wasn't imagining she had uttered it. She put her entire self into the next suffocated protest. Enfeebled though it was, it succeeded in emerging from the dark, because it brought a response. 'Are you all right, dear?'

This made no difference to the insect, which continued to nuzzle her breast. She opened her eyes to find she was still holding a hand. The fingers weren't so bony, and surely not as limp as death. They were Rory's, and the breath on her neck was an earthy draught from the open window. As she reassured herself that his hand was too warm to be other than living, Annie spoke from her post by the opposite bed. 'I was letting you have your nap. You have to take them when you can in here.'

The silenced mobile finished vibrating as Charlotte took it out of her pocket. 'Was that what was disturbing you?' Annie said. 'I should think they're a nuisance, those things. I wouldn't want anyone being able to get me wherever I am.'

Charlotte's eyes were muddy with sleep, and she had to blink hard before she could make out the displayed number. It was Hugh's. 'Could you keep an eye again?' she said. 'I just need to step outside for a few minutes.'

'Everyone's deserting us,' Annie informed or at least said to her husband, and reminded Charlotte 'You never did say where your family ran off to.'

'That's what I'm going to be hearing about, I hope.'

'All right, you can tell me all about it when you come back.'

Was she establishing this as her reward for watching over Rory? Charlotte left her a faintly promissory smile and hurried down the ward. The corridor seemed narrower than ever, except where side passages made room for shadows, more of those than she had time to identify. She dashed to the lifts and sent herself forwards as soon as one parted its doors. She was tempted to return Hugh's call at once, because she found the ponderous descent even more suffocating than the lack of windows. She managed to resist until she was out of the lift and past the reception desk, only for a mass of cigarette smoke that was loitering outside the main door to catch her breath. She hadn't finished coughing by the time she walked a few yards while raising Hugh's number. It rang several times, and then there was silence that she tried not to fill with a cough. As she spluttered instead Hugh demanded 'What is it?'

'Nothing as long as you're both all right.' When this earned no response she had to ask 'Are you?'

'Same as you saw. How about you? You sound as if you can't breathe.'

'Of course I can,' Charlotte more or less declared until a cough completed her last word. As she retreated from the smokers and the fumes of a tarrying taxi she said 'Why did you call?'

'Just wondered if you'd anything to tell us.'

'I don't think so.' While she felt ashamed of having fallen asleep on watch, surely Annie would have alerted her to any change. 'He's as you left him,' she said.

'No, I mean did your editor call, that's to say Ellen's.'

'Not a sound.' This resembled a warning more than Charlotte liked, and made her wonder 'Where are you?'

'Pretty well there.'

'You're really going to do whatever you're planning to do, then.'

'Unless you've got any better ideas.'

'I think you've left me behind this time. If you're going through with it,' she felt forced to add, 'go all the way.'

'That's a promise.'

It seemed more like a threat if not worse. She heard Ellen

ask a question, which prompted her to say 'Does Ellen want to speak to me?'

'Do you want a word?'

'Just tell her to look after Rory.'

'She says –'

'I heard,' Charlotte said, though she barely had. Ellen sounded too remote, no doubt because she and the phone were in the open, together with a harsh uneven breath of wind. Her request could easily seem ominous, and Charlotte felt the need to add 'We'll all –'

'That's right. Anyway, time we got on. We'll have plenty of chance to talk later.'

'Go on,' she said, 'good luck,' by which time Hugh had gone, leaving her the impression of calling into a hole. She took a breath that was a kind of suffocation, since she held it while she hurried past a queue of cars and a sampling of three generations of smokers. She expelled it at last and was taking another, which felt parched by the hospital and pinched small by a tinge of disinfectant as well as constricted by the lobby and the visitors who were close to filling it, when the phone twitched in her hand.

She swung around and dodged through the crowd, which couldn't really be arranging itself to block her escape. 'Nowt to be afraid of, love,' a woman told her or a granddaughter.

'Plenty of room,' said a man on two sticks, perhaps to justify not moving aside. Charlotte found a gap not too far from him and ran into the open air, or at least what passed for it beyond the exit. She let out a gasp to make way for a less stale breath and used some of that to say 'Yes, Glen.'

'Hi. It's me sure enough,' he said as if he thought her overly abrupt. 'How's the invalid?'

'They say he's comfortable. It's the kind of thing they say. I suppose he is if the word's even relevant. I don't know and I don't know if he does.'

'I'm sure you're doing –'

'All I can. Don't say it, Glen. It won't make me feel any better, and certainly not him.'

She was as thrown by her outburst as she imagined Glen must be. As she glanced around to see that nobody had eavesdropped he said 'Anyway, you wanted me.'

'We did. Me and Ellen,' Charlotte said and felt bound to add 'And Hugh.'

'You aren't going to tell me he's helping her write as well.'

'He just likes to be involved when he can be,' said Charlotte, wishing she had given herself time to think. 'We're all one family.'

'So there's how many listening?'

'Just me,' Charlotte said and at once felt overheard.

'Gee, what's happened to your family?'

'They –' She couldn't explain to him or invent a story either. 'I'm outside,' she said.

'What brought you out? You weren't waiting for me?'

She feared being trapped into lie after lie, but her answer stayed all too close to the truth. 'I wanted some air.'

'Can't ever get enough of that. So what else did you need?'

Reassurance would have been welcome, but she couldn't ask for that without betraying far too much. 'We wondered if you'd been going to tell us anything else.'

'When I ended up talking to myself, you mean? I thought you'd had enough of me.'

'We'd gone underground,' she said, and hastily 'So what did you say that we didn't hear?'

'Remind me where I'd got to.'

'You were saying –' This brought the tunnel all the more to mind, but she had to go on. 'You'd just told us what he was afraid of.'

'Your cousin's guy. Well, he was.'

Charlotte would have preferred not to have to ask 'He was what?'

'Buried there under some kind of mound.'

She wasn't sure if this or her confusion made her brain feel dark and cramped. 'Where, do you know?'

'Where his house was.'

Presumably almost a hundred years of erosion had flattened the mound. 'Was that all?' Charlotte asked or hoped.

'All I can think of right now, except you could tell her good luck from me.'

He meant with the book, Charlotte had to remember. 'Thanks, Glen,' she said to end the call, which seemed to have been no earthly use. She silenced the mobile and turned to the hospital. The prospect seemed more oppressive than ever, and she could think of at least one reason. While she waited for one of her cousins to call, she would have to think where to tell Annie they'd gone.

THIRTY

'What did she say?'

Ellen kept the question in her eyes as she watched Hugh end the call. Beyond her the steps leading to the beach were unequal slabs of sand edged with stained yellowish strips of wood that put him in mind of exposed bones. 'She says go on,' he said.

'And what do you say, Hugh?'

'I say go as well,' he said and stowed the mobile in his pocket.

'Then let's,' Ellen said as if she wanted to believe they were playing a game, and set about descending to the beach.

She grimaced at her legs more than once, perhaps holding them responsible for the irregular strides she had to take. The spade clanked against the edges of the steps as Hugh followed her. By now the entire late-afternoon sky was as good as black with the possibility of a storm. It appeared to jerk lower, giving way beneath its burden, with every step Hugh took. It had already cleared the beach of any visible human audience to his and Ellen's behaviour. Across the river, which had retreated several hundred yards from the cliff, it was reducing the summits of the skyline of Welsh mountains to shadows of themselves. The only signs of life were dozens of thin-legged birds that scurried along the water's edge to peck at the glistening sand. They were too remote to bother about Ellen or Hugh as he joined her on the beach. When she didn't move or speak but only gazed towards the mountains as if she hoped for a glimpse of the sun, Hugh had to ask 'Anything wrong?'

'Rather than everything, you mean?' Without relinquishing the distant view Ellen said 'Maybe my imagination isn't up to this. I can't get it round what we're going to do.'

'We don't need to imagine, we just have to do it. We've got to go back to where you brought us for a walk, yes?'

'When you all got the exercise I needed.'

Hugh lifted the spade towards the blackened sea beyond the river. 'It's that way then, isn't it?'

'That's right,' Ellen said, looking at last.

'It's right and it's right,' Hugh declared, and then doubt overtook him. If he'd regained at least some of his sense of direction, why had it been restored? He could easily feel that the nightmare was biding its time before overwhelming him with worse. This prompted him to wonder 'What are you feeling like now?'

'No better for being asked.'

However clumsy the question had been, he couldn't improve on it. Leading the way would draw her attention to his improved state, and he loitered until she became impatient with his reluctance. He suspected that she was battling some of her own as she set off along the beach.

As he trudged to keep pace with her, their goal seemed to stir in its sleep, or its surroundings did. A quivering advanced from the horizon through the vast black slab of mud that was the sea. Several small boats at anchor near the river's mouth squashed their reflections flat and then were pushed up by them, a sight that put Hugh in mind of lids being raised from beneath. Clumps of grass began to twitch as if the buried heads of which they were the muddy greenish scalps were about to rise from hiding, a prospect at which the seabirds appeared to take fright, soaring in an elongated flock like a cautionary arrow along the shoreline. The next wind brought swathes of sand whispering along the beach, hissing in the grass and constantly changing their outstretched shapes as if each unstable flattened mass were attempting to form a secret sign before dissipating among the furrows etched by the tide. The mats of shrubs that patched the cliff face rattled like restless skeletons, while the bushes at the edge of the common nodded together, only to straighten up as eagerly as any audience. Hugh tried not to let them make him feel watched and anticipated, and of course the presence he heard stirring in the rusty hulk of an abandoned boat at the foot of the cliff was composed of wind and sand. He'd grown so concerned to separate the landscape from his uneasy perception of it that he didn't realise he had strayed ahead until Ellen called 'Where do you think you're going, Hugh?'

'Wherever you are,' he promised and saw that she'd halted by the path they'd all climbed to the common. 'Is he up there?' he said almost too low to be heard.

Ellen's mouth seemed reluctant to let out her voice, even though she was standing well away from the cliff. 'There,' she murmured and snatched her hand back.

She'd pointed at a hole in the cliff, a few inches lower than her head. In the midst of his apprehension Hugh wondered whether it had been in the photograph he'd found on the Internet. Otherwise the stretch of cliff was unchanged, and he didn't like to think what else the power behind this might be able to do. Ellen ducked to glance in and immediately recoiled, pushing at the air with both hands and then gripping them behind her. 'There,' she said again, and more loudly 'Hugh –'

He lifted the spade like the weapon it could certainly become and tramped fast towards the cavity. It was big enough to stick his head in, not that he intended to, which meant it was equally capable of producing a head. As he came within arm's length – only his own arm, he hoped – the hole, which was too close to perfectly circular for his liking, emitted a wordless moan and a trickle of earth. Hugh faltered until he realised these must be caused by the wind. In any case, if the worst the hole could bring forth was the kind of noise an old-fashioned ghost might have emitted, how much courage did he need? He'd used hardly any yet, and it should be nowhere near running out. He dug the spade into the sand and leaned on the handle while he crouched to peer into the hole, and a face peered out at him.

Darkness seemed to close not just around his vision but over him, and to hold him as fast as earth. He couldn't lift the spade or use it to thrust himself backwards – and then his helpless immobility gave him time to see the truth. The face in the depths of the burrow bared its teeth as Hugh grinned before straightening up. 'It's all right,' he told Ellen. 'That's not him.'

'What isn't?'

Perhaps she hadn't glimpsed the item. 'It's glass,' Hugh said, letting go of the spade to reach in.

'Don't,' Ellen cried, but his fingertips had bumped into a thin bare object – a bone? No, it was a handle, and he strained his arm further, pressing the side of his face against the clammy surface of the cliff. He must have snagged the handle, because it tilted into his grasp, so that he was able to ease his find out of the burrow. 'See,' he said, 'it was just a mirror.'

The oval glass was about the size of a baby's face, and set in black wood. Clay stained the glass and the handle, which was banded with marks that might have been left by thin fingers. As Hugh rubbed the mirror clean with the back of his hand it showed him the black sky. Indeed, the image was dark enough for midnight, and flaws in the glass made the sky appear to be sprinkled with unblinking stars. 'Ellen,' he said. 'Look.'

She did, but not at him, and still less at the mirror. She crouched to glare at the cliff and shrugged, unless it was a shudder. 'He isn't there,' she muttered.

'I told you he wasn't.' Though Hugh hadn't quite, he felt entitled to the claim. He would have moved his prize into her line of vision if he hadn't been engrossed. The space between the points of light was infinitely black, but was one of them more than a point? As he squinted and lifted the mirror towards his eyes he could imagine that the spark in the depths was composed of flecks of light. He couldn't look away, but beckoned to Ellen, murmuring 'Come and –'

'Don't you understand what that means?'

'I don't understand what this does.' As he brought the mirror within inches of his face he saw that the distant mass of pale light was a nebula if not a galaxy. How much of this was an illusion? The blackness within the glass appeared to have begun an endless fall, and Hugh felt on the brink of one, as if the egg-shaped glow at the centre of the mirror were eager for his company. The impression made him blurt 'Maybe you –'

'He's got out, Hugh.'

Hugh supposed he ought to feel as disturbed as Ellen sounded, but not yet – not until he identified the appearance in the mirror. Perhaps it was shaped less like an egg than like an eye. 'He left this, didn't he?'

'We don't want it. We don't want anything to do with it. Drop it, Hugh. Get rid of it. It's just an old mirror.'

Hugh tilted it towards his face. To his surprise, however nervous, he couldn't see himself. He seemed unable to see anything except the ill-defined shape of an eye – more like a simile or a substitute for one, all that his mind was able to encompass – in the midst of infinite darkness. It must be an eye, since it was widening as if to help him comprehend its essence. 'It's more than that,' he insisted, because it seemed crucial that Ellen should see – so important that he managed to relinquish the sight in order to hold the mirror out to her. 'Really, look.'

She turned her eyes away, but not fast enough. Her face convulsed so violently that he might have imagined it was desperate to take a different form, any form. When she grabbed the mirror he thought she meant to risk another glance, and then he saw her plan. 'Ell –' was as much as he had time to protest before she flung the mirror past him to smash on a rock.

'What have you done?' he cried and stumbled to retrieve the mirror, which was lying face down on the rock. When he picked it up no glass was left behind, and he thought it might not be broken after all. As he turned it towards him, however, the mirror gave way, though it seemed less to shatter than to ripple like dark water into which an object had just sunk. He even thought he saw glittering blackness spill out of the frame to glisten for an instant on the sand. 'Look at it now,' he complained and swung around, brandishing the empty frame. Then it dropped from his hand, although he didn't hear it fall. There was no sign of Ellen anywhere on the beach.

THIRTY-ONE

It wasn't a rubber mask, grotesque enough to give children nightmares and sufficiently rotten to disgust anyone. The eyes were part of its discoloured substance, which quivered like a misshapen lump of jelly as if to prove it was alive, however little it deserved to be. It was Ellen's face, one glimpse of which was enough to make her hurl the mirror away. 'What have you done?' Hugh cried.

He cared more about his find than he did about her. She couldn't blame him, even for turning his back as if he'd been waiting for an excuse to finish enduring the sight of her. How might he look when he had to face her again? Which would be worse – unconcealed revulsion or another instalment of his pretence that she wasn't as hideous as he'd just betrayed she was? She didn't think she could bear either. She floundered away as fast as her swollen legs would work and stumbled behind a vertical ridge of the cliff.

It was prominent enough to hide her bulk, but how long would Hugh be fooled? She felt pathetically childish, like both an inept competitor at hide and seek and an outcast sent to stand in a corner. She could see nothing but brownish clay, a section of which was faintly stained by an almost formless blotch, her shadow. Her nostrils were growing clogged with the smell of moist clay or of herself. If only the night of which the sky was a promise would fall and render her invisible! She heard Hugh utter some remark, so muffled that he seemed not to care if she heard, and then he called her name.

While she didn't press her face into the clay, she hunched her shoulders as if this might somehow make her less apparent, a kind of magic only a child would believe. Hugh's next shout was more worried and more distant, and she was afraid he might lose his way without her, except how could he on a beach? He didn't, because in a few seconds she heard him behind her. 'There you are,' he said.

She inched into her dark corner and felt as if she were speaking to the clay. 'Can't you just let me be?'

'What are you being?'

'You tell me, Hugh. Go on, the truth.'

'A worm.'

Perhaps after all she hadn't wanted so much truth. 'Well, thank you,' she complained.

'You're welcome.' After quite a pause Hugh added 'In a manner of speaking, I mean. That's what you look like, what I said.'

It seemed that his refusal to see how she'd changed had been her last defence. 'Well then,' she said bitterly, 'take a good look.'

'I am.'

'Can't you stop?' Ellen pleaded, not just about looking. 'Don't you understand anything?'

'I'll stop if you stop being a worm.'

This was too much, and she twisted around to confront him. 'How do you suggest I do that?'

'You have now. You looked as if you wanted to crawl inside the cliff.'

Was he secretly amused by her reaction or by his own wit? If she'd persuaded him at last to be less wary of her feelings, she wished she hadn't tried so hard. 'Maybe I did,' she said.

'Don't crawl in yet. You're meant to be helping.'

'Remind me how.'

'You can make sure nobody comes along while I'm digging.'

'Have you forgotten what I told you?' Ellen said as that fear came flooding back. 'He's got out.'

'Unless he's gone further in.'

At once she was aware of the cliff at her back. She imagined hands sprouting from the clay to drag her close to whatever face might burst forth. As she lurched away from it, Hugh recoiled an extravagant step. 'What's wrong?' she was shocked into asking.

'Nothing really. Come to think, that's exactly what we need.'

'I don't understand you.'

'You can do that if anyone wanders along. Chase them away. Scare them off.'

'You think I'm that bad.'

'I just want you to feel you're some use.'

He could have been offering her an illusion to distract her from her state, though she wasn't far from feeling he no longer cared whether he convinced her. If he'd had enough of her at last, she could only blame herself. All these thoughts gave way to panic as he took hold of the spade, which was standing to attention in the sand. 'If he can move about,' she whispered, 'how do we know what he'll do?'

'That's what we're here to find out, isn't it?' When she met this with silence Hugh said 'Or do you want to leave Rory how he is?'

'There's no need to be so aggressive. It isn't like you.'

'Maybe it is. Maybe I've got to change as well.' Before Ellen could decide how this referred to her, Hugh stalked away to brandish the spade at the hole in the cliff. 'Are you in there, Pendy?' he shouted. 'Going to show yourself?'

The hole and the clay around it seemed to shiver, and Ellen prayed that only her vision had. 'Hugh,' she cried, 'you shouldn't –'

'Then we'll have to come and find you,' he declared and rammed the spade into the cliff.

The burrow gaped in protest or an equally silent warning. It grew more than twice as wide when he dug out a spadeful of clay in which a thin object was writhing – not a crumbling finger, a worm scaly with earth. Hugh turned as if the loaded spade were the needle of a compass. 'Don't come any closer,' he told Ellen.

'Why not?'

'You don't want to end up looking like a pile of mud.'

He flung the contents of the spade away, spattering the beach. He must have had this sort of careless action in mind, but how insensitive was his task going to make him? As he drove the spade into the cliff again she didn't know whether she was more afraid of seeing deeper into the hole or of having no chance to from where she stood. Hugh swung around with the spade heaped high, and she saw a dark mass drop out of the cliff behind him. It was only a lump of the roof of the burrow, and she managed to keep her cry behind a grimace. Nevertheless once he'd slung the spadeful in the general direction of the aloof river and frowned at the collapsed section of earth he said 'Go a bit further.'

'What are you asking me to do?'

'I'm saying go away. You're putting me off.'

'How am I, Hugh?'

'I don't want to have to keep looking at you.'

Ellen forced her puffy lips to work. 'I can't blame you, but tell me why not at least.'

'Because it's wasting time,' Hugh said with the remains of patience. 'But if I don't I might throw something at you.'

Why couldn't he aim the spadefuls away from her? His sense of direction must have deserted him again, unless he was afraid it would. Ellen did her best not to feel rejected as she trudged backwards several yards, apparently not far enough to erode Hugh's frown. The next pile of earth he threw across the beach fell short of her and to her left, apart from a clod that exploded sufficiently close to scatter particles over her feet. 'You're no use there,' he said.

'Can't I do anything right?'

'Feeling sorry for yourself isn't going to help either. You might just as well be a pile of mud.'

'All right, let's have your advice how I can improve myself.'

'Don't be sarcy or I won't. Just because I'm not as good as you doesn't mean I'm never worth listening to.' He stared at her as though it demanded an effort and said 'You can't see from where you are.'

'Is there something? What –'

'You can't see if anyone's coming along up above.' More disdainfully than she would ever have expected of him Hugh said 'You need to be up there.'

She ought to have known this without being told. It showed how thoroughly she was absorbed in her own flesh, which was infecting her mind with sluggishness. As she lumbered to the foot of the path she saw that the entrance to the burrow was wide enough for a thin person to crawl forth. Despite this it was darker than ever, perhaps because the sky was, so that she had to squint in an attempt to be sure that the clay at the back wasn't shifting furtively. 'Aren't you going?' Hugh urged.

His wearily impatient gaze sent her plodding upwards. Every stretch of the zigzag track brought her above the hole in the cliff. It occurred to her that the higher she climbed, the greater the weight of the clay she was tramping on, rendering it heavier. If Hugh's digging had undermined it, suppose she was the factor that made it collapse? She glanced down from a bend in the path as he unloaded the spade across an immoderate extent of beach. He looked up to discover why she was hesitating, and for an instant if not longer – it felt as protracted as the worst nightmare – she saw his unconcealed disgust at the sight of her. She must be even more revolting when viewed from below. He didn't have the grace to blush as he neutralised his expression and said 'Anything up?'

Even if she had been able to part her swollen lips she couldn't have answered him. When she floundered along the path it was mostly in a desperate bid to leave his revulsion behind. With each laborious step she seemed to feel her legs bulge from supporting their unsavoury burden. She tried to forget herself in her surroundings, although the blackened sky towards which she was climbing felt like more weight she was unable to avoid. She couldn't tell whether the wind was raising the smell of the cliff or of her clammy self. She clambered over the treacherous edge at last and might have fled across the common if Hugh hadn't immediately shouted 'Anyone?'

The expanse of restless grass was deserted all the way to the distant hedges that enclosed its landward sides. 'No,' Ellen said. The wind made short work of her answer, and she leaned over to call 'Nobody.'

'Tell me the moment there's somebody.'

'You too,' Ellen immediately regretted having said.

Either Hugh couldn't bear to look at her or dismay at her remark kept his head down, unless he was bent on making sure there were no signs of life within the burrow. He ducked into it, and she heard a dull thud almost too muffled to be audible but unpleasantly reminiscent of a tentative heartbeat. It was the impact of the spade, and in a few seconds another heap of clay was strewn across the beach. The hole must be dauntingly wide and deep by now, since Hugh barely reappeared in the course of the action. The next soft thump was still more muted, and only clay emerged. By craning over the edge, Ellen was just able to distinguish another buried thud, but how audible would any warning be to him? While the beach remained empty, the weather mightn't daunt walkers much longer; a strip of light had begun to glare beneath the lid of the sky across the river. She could almost have imagined that Hugh's digging had magicked the entire landscape open. She was gazing at the horizon, where the cloud was lifting in the direction of the beach, when she heard voices across the common. Two women in orange anoraks and tugged by large russet dogs had appeared at a gap in the hedge.

'Hugh.' When this brought no response she leaned out so precariously that she was afraid her weight would overbalance her. 'People,' she cried.

A wind did its best to return this to her mouth. She had to repeat it before Hugh followed the latest evacuation of clay out of the tunnel. 'Where?' he demanded.

'Up here. Coming this way.'

'Get rid of them. I'm seeing more in here.'

He vanished into the tunnel without giving her time to reply, and she turned to see the foremost woman stooping to release her dog from its leash. Ellen imagined the animal racing unchecked across the common and down the path to join Hugh. It might dig faster than he could, not to say unstoppably, and what would happen once the woman followed it? 'Excuse me,' Ellen protested, which had no effect. 'Don't,' she shouted and tramped across the grass, waving her blurred blobs of hands on either side of her face.

The woman who had yet to emerge from the gap in the hedge spoke to her friend, who peered towards Ellen and to some extent straightened up. 'Can we help you?' she rather less offered than said.

'Don't come this way,' Ellen cried. 'Don't let your dogs.'

'We're allowed to let the dogs off here.'

'Not down the cliff. It isn't safe.'

She was dismayed to be reminded how that might apply to Hugh. The sounds of the spade were inaudible now. The women shaded their eyes as harsh light spilled from beneath the cloud. 'We can't hear you,' said the woman who had nearly unleashed the dog.

'Not safe,' Ellen came close to screaming, and floundered after her massive shadow as it flopped towards her audience. 'Not safe.'

'What isn't?'

'The path. It's gone.'

'Still can't hear you.'

'You heard me just before.' Ellen had begun to feel that her voice was as feeble as a cry in a nightmare. Was only the wind stealing it? The unquiet grass fluttered the outline of her shadow as if it were preparing to grow more misshapen. 'No path,' she cried with all her breath.

'Where isn't there?' the woman enquired, stooping to her impatient dog.

'To the beach. You can't go that way to the beach.'

Ellen was about to claim to be helping the rangers in case this lent her credibility when the woman shaded her eyes once more. She stiffened and then stood up fully, yanking at the leash. Whatever had changed her mind affected her friend too. Without speaking, both women retreated, dragging their dogs through the gap in the hedge.

They must have seen Ellen clearly at last. Her hideousness was some use after all. She turned to trudge back to her post and was instantly blind. The cloud had lifted above the sun, which was all the more dazzling because of the blackness. Ellen shielded her eyes and kept them lowered so as not to see her hand in any detail. 'They're gone,' she called as she reached the edge of the cliff.

Hugh didn't respond, surely only because the wind had borne her voice away from him. She was about to lean over when she heard a dog bark. She swung around, but it wasn't as close as the wind must have made it seem. It wasn't on the common. Just her shadow was, and the shadow of the hand that was about to take her arm.

'Hugh, are you trying to scare –' None of this had even left her mouth as she turned to confront him. The sun glared around him, blotting out his face and appearing to char his silhouette thin – altogether too thin. She was able to cling to the notion that it was Hugh until the figure darted forwards, its skin flapping in the wind, to demonstrate with its embrace how skeletal it was. It might have been whispering a parody of affection in her ear, unless that was simply the wind in its gaping face. Certainly the hiss grew sharper as her captor drove her backwards. Its spidery weight shouldn't have overwhelmed her, but terror did. Perhaps it took away her sight as well, or perhaps that was the sun.

THIRTY-TWO

'Look at it now,' Hugh protested and swung around, brandishing the shattered mirror, but there was nobody to accuse of the damage. He was alone on the beach.

The cliff seemed to loom over him as the landscape borrowed blackness from the sky, unless his vision was growing as dark as a tunnel. He was scarcely aware that the mirror had slipped from his fingers. If he didn't hear it fall, no doubt that could be blamed on the amplified pounding of his heart, which was pumping his face hot as shame. He'd driven Ellen away by not caring how sensitive she'd become about herself. He'd been so determined to make her look in the mirror that he'd neglected to consider how threatening she might find it. 'Ellen, I'm sorry,' he called, but the wind was as good as a gag. At least she couldn't have gone far while his back was turned, however little she might like him to find her. The only concealment within hundreds of yards was a vertical ridge of the cliff just a few paces away, and now he noticed a trail of marks in the sand. At first he hadn't realised they were footprints because they were so partial, but they led from beside him to the far side of the ridge. 'There you are,' he said and followed them.

He thought he was answered, but not as he might have expected. He heard a stuttering hiss like a thin surreptitious giggle behind the ridge, and had to assume it betrayed how nervous he'd made Ellen. 'I'm sorry,' he murmured. 'You mustn't hide from me.' How desperate was she to do so? Hugh could have imagined there was only space in the niche for someone much thinner than even Ellen had grown. 'I didn't mean –' he said as he stepped forwards, but there was no reason to continue. Nobody was behind the ridge.

As Hugh stared at the expanse of clay he heard the shrill sound again. It was an intermittent whisper of sand that was trickling over the edge of the cliff. Ellen couldn't have gone up there unobserved, but she'd had as little time to hide anywhere else. All the same, he had lost her or – perhaps worse still – had overlooked her. It left him feeling unutterably lost himself.

'Ellen,' he cried and heard the mocking whisper of the sand. Another shout that left his throat raw started bones rattling restlessly together, unless it was the wind clattering the branches of shrubs on the cliff. A supine shape reared up at the water's edge and split into airborne fragments – a flock of birds. A distant form threw itself flat in the water and went under, crushed by the fishing boat of which it was the reflection. A thin silhouette was standing in wait for Hugh when he moved away from the ridge. It was the spade, and its having remained where he'd left it suggested that it might be the solitary fixed point he could rely on. He dashed to it and clutched the handle with both hands. 'Ellen,' he yelled.

Suppose his shouts were driving her away? She could well have had time to dodge out of sight while he'd been wandering under the delusion that he could find his way again. Could she have taken refuge in the abandoned hulk of a boat? Surely she didn't loathe him so much that she would lie among the rubble, but wasn't it more a question of how much she loathed herself? He was clinging to the spade while he craned on tiptoe in an attempt to see into the boat before he risked making for it when the rudiments of a body sprang up beside him.

He nearly lost his grip on the spade, not to mention any

sense of where he was, in the moment it took him to realise that the faceless shape was his shadow on the cliff. The sun had prised up the lid of black cloud above Wales, spilling light across the beach. It seemed to delineate movement near the water. Not just the pools left behind by the tide but every trace of moisture on the sand had grown as blinding as the exposure of the sun, so that Hugh had to slit his eyes in order to distinguish the blurred silhouette at the river's edge.

It could only be Ellen, even if he didn't understand how he'd overlooked her. The loss of perception was so close to unforgivable that his face blazed with more than sunlight. As the outline of the silhouette began to flutter, he was afraid she was shivering until he realised that her clothes must be flapping around her thin form. The spectacle of her standing alone, surrounded by trembling clumps of grass on the beach as harshly bright as scraped tin, distressed him so much that he could barely speak. He let go of the spade and cupped whichever hand it was by that side of his mouth. 'Ellen, come back. It can't be safe.'

Although she didn't turn, she must have heard him, because she took a pace away from him. How treacherous might the sand be if it was as wet as the light made it appear? He snatched his other hand off the spade and was about to yell more of a warning when he grasped that the mere sound of his voice might be intolerable to her just now. Instead he padded as fast as he stealthily could across the beach.

The route was even less direct than it looked. The sand around the numerous pools exuded water just as deep if he strayed too close. Rocks that promised to act as stepping-stones across expanses of mud proved to be lumps of it into which his feet sank. More than one narrow elongated stretch of water pretended to be shallow enough to walk through until he was nearly at the margin, and then he had to tramp the entire length of the obstacle, because all the points where he thought he could jump across turned out to be too wide. Whenever he was diverted away from Ellen he had to keep glancing back for reassurance that she hadn't disappeared again. She seemed not to have stirred, and he would have liked to think she was waiting for him. He was still unable to distinguish her as more than a bony sketch against the intensifying sunlight. How could the wind be fluttering the outline of her head? Of course, it was her hair.

The shoreline was by no means as close as the perspective made it seem. In any case the dazzle that had settled on the beach, collecting in the furrows of the sand as well as permeating every scrap of water, rendered his vision nearly useless. He almost trod in the next extensive pool until he saw how wide and deep it was. The detour would take him hundreds of yards further from Ellen, and he seemed no closer than he had been five minutes ago. He was growing desperate to speak to her, to persuade her to come back – and then, blushing at his stupidity, he understood that he didn't need to shout. He dug out his mobile and keyed her number.

There was no immediate response, and he wondered if the cliff was blocking the signal. The display showed a call in progress, however. A wind blundered into his ears, so that he was barely able to distinguish Ellen's ringtone, which sounded like a shapeless cry. For a moment he assumed the wind was also why it sounded more remote than Ellen appeared to be. Then the wind subsided, and the twitching clumps of grass did, and there was no question how distant her phone was. Not only that: it was behind him.

Ellen must have dropped it in her haste to flee. Hugh saw her realise as he did. At least, the figure turned sideways towards him and the sound. Its profile was alarmingly unstable with the fluttering of hair blurred by the light on the river. Then the light finished jittering as the wind dropped, and Hugh was able to make out the profile, such as it was. The head was as hairless as a skull. The material that had kept flapping was all that remained of the face.

Hugh was staring in paralysed fascination as the entire outline of the silhouette recommenced flickering with the wind when Ellen's ringtone ceased, having completed its word and the next few jolly bars. He clutched his phone to his ear and had begun to gabble a warning that was almost incoherent with panic before he heard the automatic message. 'Stay where you are,' he could hardly wait to plead. 'Call me and say where you've gone.'

Was the silhouetted figure listening? Except for the instability that outlined its bony shape, it hadn't moved. It might have been waiting for him to stray within range – and suddenly Hugh realised how easy it had been made for him to come this far, particularly given the state of the beach. He'd been too grateful for his sense of direction to suspect why it had been returned to him. How long would it stay with him if he retreated? The only way to find out was by turning his back on the figure at the shoreline. He thrust the uncommunicative mobile into a hip pocket and had to remind himself how far away the figure was before he could face the cliff.

He was dismayed to see how far away it was – considerably farther than the river's edge. His extended shadow slanted towards it, petering out at a pool that drowned the shadow of his head. The spade was standing guard in front of the hole in the cliff, some distance upriver. The route to it was a maze of water and glistening sand that the lurid light rendered indistinguishable from mud. Which path had he originally taken? He was so far from identifying it that he could easily conclude there wasn't one. A pace in the direction of the spade sent his shadow forwards, and he was terrified that it would be joined by a companion. He twisted around, shading his eyes. The shoreline and the beach along it were deserted.

At once he sensed a presence at his back. He even thought he heard the surreptitious flapping of its ragged skin. As he spun around so wildly that he almost sprawled into a patch of mud, a black shape jerked out its hands. It was his shadow, but had the figure at the shoreline cast one? In any case it might be thin enough to hide behind him without betraying its position. He imagined whirling helplessly in a desperate attempt to locate his tormentor while it continued to dodge out of sight, his gleeful partner in a nightmare dance that would snatch away the last of his sense of direction. Could the apparition on the shoreline have been designed to lure him away from his only weapon, or from Ellen, or both? Perhaps the panic that was close to shutting down his mind was meant to keep him where he was. With an inarticulate cry that might have expressed rage or determination if the wind hadn't stifled it, he dashed towards the cliff.

He could barely see his footing, but this drove him heedlessly onwards. He slithered over mud, flailing his arms as his shadow mocked his efforts not to topple headlong. He waded through pools that filled his shoes with water and pasted his trousers to his shins. He stepped on rocks that gave beneath his weight, revealing they were lumps of mud that hung onto his feet and relinquished them with a sound like the smacking of satisfied lips. All this appeared to bring him no closer to the spade or the cliff, which shone beneath the black sky as though it and its bristling grassy scalp had just been dug up. Whenever he was tempted to detour around an obstacle, he imagined turning aside to find the ruin of a face at his shoulder. Even when he reached dry sand his feet sank into it, so that running felt like floundering in slow motion through a medium that ought not to have existed outside a dream. Only the sight of the spade, and the impression of a pursuer that was delighted to bide its time until it chose to seize him, kept him struggling onwards as if he could catch up with his faltering breath. His shadow parodied his labours and taunted him with how much closer it was to his goal. It was on the far side of a pool through which he had to splash; it was supine on a stretch of mud that didn't yield beneath it, instead waiting to give way underfoot; it was pretending that an extensive brownish slab was as solid as a rock. At last it touched the expanse of dryish sand on the far side of which the spade was printing a T on the cliff. Hugh's shadow lurched for it, and as he followed, the hole in the cliff gaped to remind him that its tenant was elsewhere. He grabbed the handle and swung around, wielding the tool like a scythe. Nobody was behind him, or behind him, or behind him.

Then where was the figure he'd seen? Had it followed Ellen, wherever she was? Hugh clung to the spade and faced the mouth of the river as he groped for his mobile. He was using the wrong hand for whichever pocket it was, but he was afraid to let go of the weapon, if indeed the spade could function as one. He only just managed to extract the phone without dropping it, and then he had to key Ellen's number wrong-handed. He brought the mobile to that side of his face and heard his call arrive. He lowered the phone and strained his ears, to no effect beyond tuning in the sound of his unnerved heartbeat.

He could hear the shrivelled ringing of the mobile in his hand, but there was no sign of Ellen's ringtone.

The hole in the cliff emitted a derisive whisper, and he couldn't be sure it was soil shifting in the wind. Ellen's mechanical message came to an end as he pressed the phone against his ear. 'Call me back,' he pleaded. 'I need to know where you are. You could be in danger. I'm not just saying that. Don't stay away. We need to be together.'

He'd run out of words. No one who could be any use to a writer would have, but he hadn't time to bemoan his inadequacy. He terminated the call and thumbed through the list to Charlotte's name. She wasn't replying either. She must be inside the hospital, but her unresponsiveness aggravated his panic. 'I've lost her. I've lost Ellen,' he confessed, but how did that help? 'Call her when you get this,' he tried urging. 'Tell her she's got to call me. Call me if you speak to her. Call me anyway. Somebody call me.'

His words were letting him down again before deserting him. He had an unhappy sense that they were playing tricks on him. How long might he have to wait to hear from Charlotte? At the very least until she made her way out of the hospital and listened to his message and contacted Ellen or gave up the attempt. He shouldn't leave her to try to raise Ellen. He redialled Ellen's number and lifted the phone, and then he snatched it away from his face. Her mobile was singing, faint with distance but increasingly unmistakable, somewhere above him.

Did this mean she was coming back? Hugh opened his mouth to shout, but the risk of scaring her off silenced him. He shoved the mobile into his nearest pocket and sprinted to the path. As he began to scramble upwards her ringtone fell silent. He hoped she might call to discover what he'd wanted, but his phone stayed mute. He climbed faster than he'd ever climbed in his life, digging the spade into the path for extra speed. It couldn't have taken him much longer than a minute to reach the top and crane his head above the edge of the cliff. Nevertheless the common was deserted.

Hugh levered himself onto it with the spade and leaned on the handle as he took out his mobile again. He jabbed the redial key, and in just a few seconds he had his answer, somewhere ahead. The crescendo and its conclusion weren't as distant as they'd seemed; up here they were more obviously muffled. He advanced a tentative step, and another faltering one, and then he was hurrying across the common, almost blind with the light on the grass and with panic that his shadow mimed by brandishing its spade. Ellen's phone wasn't in the distance. It was under the earth.

THIRTY-THREE

Charlotte thought she had nodded off for only a moment again, but this time it wasn't a jerk of her head that roused her. Her eyes wavered open to see that Rory's were still dormant. Though the whole of him was as inert as his flaccid hand in her determined grasp, she was sure there had been movement. She glanced across the aisle at Annie, who leaned sideways on her chair while keeping hold of her husband's fingers. 'Is he back?' she whispered.

Hairs stirred at the nape of Charlotte's neck, and she was hardly reassured by recognising that a breath had troubled them. It must be a breeze through the window under which she was sitting, which let her feel marginally less enclosed whenever she remembered it was ajar, but she couldn't help peering over her shoulder to make certain the gap was unoccupied. 'Who?' Annie had left her anxious to know, or at any rate anxious.

Annie's laugh wasn't quite as sure of itself as she wanted it to sound. 'Why, who do you think?'

'I've no idea,' Charlotte said, hoping she hadn't. 'That's why I'm asking.'

'Who else could it be but your Rory?' Having issued the rebuke, Annie said 'It's all right, you've just woke up.'

Charlotte felt as if she hadn't entirely once she realised she should ask 'Why were you saying he's back?'

'I was only asking. It looked like he woke you. I couldn't see what else would.'

Charlotte thought the conversation had grown uncontrolled as a dream – perhaps not a nightmare, but little more bearable. 'Do you mean you saw him move?'

'No, I saw you.'

'It wasn't just me.'

As Charlotte finished speaking, the truth caught up with her. She laid Rory's hand down and took out her mobile to see that she had indeed missed a call. 'It's never that devil of a thing again,' Annie said.

'It is.' Charlotte stayed polite while adding 'Would you mind if I step out and deal with it?'

'It's not up to me to mind.'

'If you mean Rory, I don't think he will.'

'We can't say, can we? Nobody's really sure if they know we're here, our men. Maybe we're all that's keeping them here.'

Charlotte squeezed Rory's unresponsive hand for encouragement – his or her own – and stood up. 'I definitely need to take this call,' she said. 'I won't be any longer than I have to be.'

'I expect he'll understand. You've still got a job.'

Charlotte let the misunderstanding explain her haste in making for the corridor. Her anxiety for her cousins was almost enough to blot out any other. She hurried to the lifts, where a nurse beside a patient on a trolley stopped a pair of doors from closing. Charlotte immediately regretted sidling in, because the trolley seemed to take up far more space than was reasonable. She tried to breathe evenly as the doors crawled together and the occupant of the trolley raised his sketchily grey-haired head to speak. 'Who's in here?'

'Just a lady who's having a ride with us, Jonah.'

'I know there's a girl.' The man's loose wrinkled face worked as if his dissatisfaction were a weight he was unable to dislodge from it. 'Aren't we moving?' he complained.

'Just as fast as we can.'

Charlotte was afraid this might mean not at all. The man's head fell back, and his watery eyes rolled in their sockets as if searching for an intruder or some assurance that the lift wasn't stuck. Perhaps he was sensing her nervousness, but his unease was aggravating hers, so that she imagined their fears nourishing each other while the lift stayed buried between floors and the air grew unbreathably stale. Since the trolley blocked her access to the controls, she was on the point of asking the nurse to give the button another push when the lift shuddered like a troubled sleeper and settled into place before, with a considerable show of reluctance, it set about parting its doors. As Charlotte hauled them wide and launched herself between them, she heard the man protest 'Who's in here?'

If there had indeed been an intruder she was ashamed to hope she'd left it beyond the doors, but she did. Too much of a crowd surrounded her in the reception area and in the smoky open air for her to look at every face. She was busy retrieving the missed call, which began to address her as she did her best to emerge from an oppressively insubstantial medium composed of the murmur of the loiterers outside the hospital. 'I've lost her,' Hugh confessed, or rather had. 'I've lost Ellen. Call her when you get this. Tell her she's got to call me. Call me if you speak to her. Call me anyway. Somebody call me.'

He sounded reduced to a nightmare. How could Ellen have left him in that state or indeed at all? For the duration of several unnecessarily conscious breaths Charlotte couldn't think which of them she ought to phone first. Replying to Hugh's call would be easier, and only a sense that she ought to have news about Ellen made her key that number instead. Since Ellen was presumably not answering his calls, had the cousins fallen out somehow? Not necessarily, because she didn't respond to Charlotte either. When the pretence of a bell ceased at last, it had only roused the answering service.

'Ellen, why aren't you answering anyone? You've got me worried. Why aren't you with Hugh? We don't want you splitting up. We don't need this on top of everything else. I've had to come out of the hospital again to call you. I'm going to wait here for a few minutes, but I don't want to be away from Rory any longer than I absolutely have to be. Please let me know what's going on. Please call.'

She was beginning to sound far too much like Hugh's message, overwhelmed by an excess of words. Having to speak to someone who wasn't even a version of Ellen or indeed real had brought her close to babbling. Until she shut up, Ellen wouldn't be able to reply, and so Charlotte ended the call. She stood with the inert mobile in her hand while black shapes multiplied next to her – taxis full of visitors to the hospital. The gathering blackness reminded her of nightfall, although that was hours away. Her mobile didn't ring, and didn't ring, and didn't ring. She bore its silence for a little longer than she thought she could, and then she gave in to calling Hugh. His phone rang as long as Ellen's had and spoke to Charlotte in exactly the same automatic voice.

She could have imagined that she was the victim of a trick – that somebody who had answered both her calls was putting on the bright efficient female voice. Perhaps the truth was worse: perhaps Charlotte had missed her chance to speak to Hugh. 'Hugh, I'm sorry,' she said. 'I should have called you back. I was waiting to hear from Ellen. Have you yet? Call me anyway. I'll try and stay out here until you do. Don't leave me worrying. Let's talk and decide what's to be done.'

She was losing control of her words again, as though they were being sucked into a black hole. If they were being swallowed by deadness, why were his and Ellen's phones dead? There must be a signal at Thurstaston for Hugh to have made the call. Ellen might have switched off her mobile so that he couldn't reach her, whyever she was behaving that way, but it made no sense for him to have turned off his. Could the batteries have failed in both? It seemed far too conveniently inconvenient. Charlotte paced back and forth alongside the taxis, only to have to assure the foremost driver that she wasn't looking for a ride. When his replacement made the same assumption Charlotte felt as if they were urging her not to loiter. 'Aren't you there yet? Where are you?' she said uselessly twice to the same artificial voice, and then she knew that wasn't enough.

If she called the police, what could she tell them? Certainly not just that she was unable to raise her cousins, but how could she explain that she was concerned because of their intentions?

Suppose she managed to persuade the police to search, what might they catch her cousins doing if they found them? Of course she was presuming that the disinterment was taking place, if it hadn't already happened, whereas she could be sure of nothing of the kind. She only knew that Hugh and Ellen weren't receiving her calls, and she'd had enough of herself and her doubts. What if she and her cousins were being prevented from contacting one another?

As soon as she thought it she knew she had been resisting the notion. However credulous it was, could she dismiss it when that might be at her cousins' expense? She stared at her silent mobile and then at the taxis before marching towards the hospital. She was willing the phone to ring, but as she reached the lobby she had to mute it. She dodged around a queue of visitors at the reception desk and sprinted into a waiting lift. 'Who's in here?' a voice enquired as the doors shut, but surely that was just an echo in her head. Her fears for Hugh and Ellen outweighed any other panic, so that she was able to ignore the lack of windows in the lift and in the corridor.

A nurse was writing on the clipboard at the end of Rory's bed. 'Any change?' Charlotte was more than anxious to discover.

'He hasn't missed you.' That was Annie, and the nurse said 'Nothing yet.'

'I've been called away urgently. Can I leave you my number in case anything happens?'

'Give it in at the desk. We'll do our best to keep you posted.'

Suppose Charlotte became as unreachable as her cousins? Perhaps it wouldn't need to be like that; perhaps she would hear from one or both of them before she ventured too far. She advanced to give Rory's hand a squeeze that felt like leaving him for worse than the unknown. As she turned away Annie met her eyes. She looked as though she had a less than favourable question, but all she said was 'I'll be here.'

Charlotte remembered her saying 'Maybe we're all that's keeping them here.' That might be true, but as she'd meant it or the opposite? Perhaps if Charlotte didn't act he might stay there until he died. That was one more fear to drive her away from him. 'I will be,' she promised and managed not to add 'I hope.'

THIRTY-FOUR

'I will be.'

'So will I,' Rory said, but only inside his skull. He couldn't judge how long ago he'd last heard Charlotte speak, let alone when somebody else had made the remark to which she'd responded. At some point this person had also said 'He hasn't missed you.' Perhaps he hadn't, but he was doing so now, assuming that Charlotte and Ellen and Hugh were no longer with him. He needed to communicate how he felt, if he was capable of feeling anything any more. Weren't his thoughts a kind of feeling? Wishing that his cousins and his brother hadn't left him was, and surely that ought to bring him to the surface of himself. Only he had no idea where that might be, especially now that he was surrounded by silence, wadded in it like a sculpture packed in a box and just as unable to move. He ought to have struggled towards Charlotte's voice, but now it was too late.

It needn't be. If he'd managed to hear, however increasingly hard it was to distinguish this from the memory of a dream, his senses hadn't entirely deserted him. Were any others waiting to be noticed? Not his vision, since he couldn't even tell whether he was seeing an uncoloured void or an equally featureless dark. He couldn't imagine what there would be to taste, and there seemed to be nothing to smell. As for touch, he appeared to have forgotten how that worked. He had no idea where his hands might be, and that went for the rest of him. He couldn't even identify which part of him was being teased if not taunted by a persistent draught, which also had to mean he was alone, because surely any visitor would have closed the door or window on his behalf.

He had no means of measuring how long he lay inert within the thought before its implications overtook him. He couldn't be wholly senseless if he was feeling a draught. It was on the upper surface of an extension of him somewhere in the middle distance. It was on the back of his hand, beyond an arm that felt dully pierced by a needle at the tip of a tube that rested on it. Could he raise the hand to his eyes or open them to find it? Before he knew it he did both.

He was lying under a white slab almost as wide as his vision. It was the ceiling of a large long room – a hospital ward. To his left a window open at the top was letting in a breeze. To his right was a line of beds, each occupied by a supine sheeted figure. They were matched across an aisle, and directly opposite him was a solitary seated visitor. Now he recalled Charlotte saying she'd received some kind of urgent message, but had Hugh and Ellen also been called away? He was starting to recapture an impression that they had recently been at his bedside. 'Where is everyone?' he wondered aloud.

The loudness of his voice surprised him and startled the woman, who cried 'Oh, he's back.'

For a moment Rory was afraid to learn whom she was addressing. If she meant to alert the staff, it didn't work. Perhaps it was a proclamation to anyone who might be interested, but her entire audience seemed as unimpressed as the patient whose hand she was holding. 'How long was I gone?' Rory said.

'Only a couple of days, dear. I expect my Jack and the rest of them would call it just a nap. How has it left you feeling?'

Rory flexed his limbs, which hadn't lost too much strength. 'Alive,' he said.

'That's all you should expect, I always say. Then anything else is a bonus.'

This struck Rory as less a thought than a substitute for one, but his renewed senses welcomed even that. 'Weren't my family here?' he said.

'They're one right enough.'

'Yes, but I'm asking when did they go.'

'Your brother and the very thin girl only stayed for a bit, and then they had –'

'Which thin girl?'

'What was her name again?' Presumably the woman wasn't really waiting for her husband to answer, because she told him 'Ellen, that was what.'

'I wouldn't call her thin,' Rory objected.

'You mustn't have seen her for a while.'

He tried to remember how long it had been, but the memory of losing his senses as he drove around the roundabout was in the way. He was disconcerted to realise how careless he'd just been in testing his limbs. Why weren't they broken? He'd ended up no worse than bruised and stiff. Perhaps, as was said to be the case with drunks, his state had protected him from serious injury. For the moment it seemed more important to discover 'What did they have to do?'

'Did you all go to a camp somewhere?'

This made Rory feel as if the past had crept up behind him. 'Not recently, no.'

'Well, that's where they've gone.'

'What for?'

'They weren't telling us, were they, Jack? They went off and you wouldn't know who was looking after which.'

Rory heard his questions growing aggressive but was too uneasy to rein them in. 'How do you mean?'

'Him carrying on like he didn't know which way to turn and her not wanting anybody seeing her, which you can understand.'

Rory didn't, which left him still more anxious. Hugh had been losing his way when Rory was robbed of his senses, and now or at the same time Ellen had fallen distressingly ill. 'Why would they go all that way if they're like that?' he demanded. 'Forget I spoke. You said you don't know.'

'No, I said they never let on. The other girl did.'

He managed to cling to his patience and ask 'What did she say?'

'Did you leave something there when you were sleeping out?'

'Not that I know of.' That meant no until his words caught up with him. 'Such as what?' he was compelled to add.

'Something you buried by the sound of it.'

'I've never buried anything.'

'Maybe it was one of them that did. I just got the feeling you were mixed up with it somehow.' She appeared to be giving Rory a last chance to explain before she said a shade defiantly 'All I know is they were off to dig it up and it seemed like it was for your sake.'

Rory felt as if she were arousing memories he didn't realise he had. The first time his senses had come close to shutting down, he had been researching Thurstaston. He'd found a reference to someone called Pendemon, and had he overheard Hugh and their cousins discussing the owner of the name? 'They should all have had a bit more faith if you want my opinion,' the woman said.

Rory wasn't sure he did, but heard himself say 'All?'

The woman leaned forwards as if to keep a confidence from her husband. 'I'd lay money the other girl went off there too. Maybe she didn't think they were up to it by themselves, the way they both were. They should have trusted things would come out right, shouldn't they? It's my belief they will if they're meant to. You're the proof.'

While Rory didn't care to be reduced to this, he stayed quiet as the woman said 'Funny that you can't think what they're after if it's supposed to bring you back. Anyway, they're the ones need bringing back now, aren't they?'

At once Rory knew she was right, but not in the way she imagined. Whatever Hugh and their cousins had set out to do for his benefit, it wasn't just unnecessary now; it felt more dangerous than his mind could encompass. He had to call them back. 'Where are my things?' he said.

'Nurse will have to show you.' His urgency seemed to alarm the old woman, who clutched her husband's hand with both of hers as she called 'Nurse.'

'You'll know where they're keeping people's stuff, won't you? Just tell me where.'

'I don't know where they can have got to.' This apparently referred to the staff, because she added 'They ought to look at you if you're thinking of getting up.'

'I just want my mobile.'

'Are you stuck with one of those as well? You can't use them in here.'

'Then I'll have to outside.' Rory had another thought and slid open the drawer of the bedside table, which was so rudimentary it was colourless. The drawer did indeed contain a key with a blurred number inked on a plastic tag, which he used to indicate the metal lockers at the far end of the ward. 'I won't tell anyone you said,' he assured her. 'It's all locked up in there, yes?'

'You oughtn't to be walking when there's nobody to see to you. You don't know how you'll be.'

'Let's find out.' Rory hoped to encourage her by including her, but it simply made her more nervous. He withdrew the needle from his arm and laid the tube on the bedside table before groping under the sheet, where he found a reason to be grateful that his sensations were still understated. He took some time and care over disencumbering his penis from a tube, which he hung over a metal stand, where it emitted a single unstoppable drip. In shuffling his feet one at a time to the edge of the bed he pulled the sheet from beneath the mattress. Planting his hands on the bed, he levered himself more or less steadily into a sitting position, which bunched the sheet in his lap. 'You mightn't want to watch this,' he advised.

'Don't you worry about that, love. You won't be showing me anything I haven't seen on my Jack.'

Rory found this flirtatious and equally uncomfortably maternal. Perhaps she only meant how he was dressed, which was bad enough. He was wearing an abbreviated gown that tied none too closely at the back, so that it would have exposed his buttocks if they weren't done up in a plastic pad, all of which left him feeling worse than infantile. He poked his feet over the brink of the mattress and lowered them to the floor, then stared at the woman as he wobbled off the bed. He meant to make her look away, but she gazed at him with additional concern. Resting one hand on the windowsill, he wavered to his feet. Perhaps he'd managed to deflect more than her attention, because she vanished.

So did the room and his body into utter nothingness. Only the realisation that it contained some kind of light prevented it from extinguishing his mind as well. He was about to devote any strength to producing a nightmare cry when he became aware of his hand on the windowsill. He hadn't reverted to insensibility after all. He'd just stood up too quickly, and the insight seemed to restore his senses. The blankness retreated to the limit of his vision and beyond, exposing the sight of the ward full of beds and the woman watching him more solicitously than ever. 'You aren't well, are you?' she seemed almost to hope.

'Never better,' Rory declared and took several increasingly confident steps to the end of the bed.

She looked as if she weren't entirely convinced he was walking. Her husband and the occupants of the other beds were demonstrating how out of the common it was. Rory wasn't about to let anyone steal his confidence, not least because he had a sudden unappealing notion that someone would be glad to. As he padded down the aisle between the sheeted bodies he had to fend off the idea that their insensibility was capable of drawing him in. He hurried to the farthest of the lockers opposite an unoccupied desk and slid his key into the lock.

His mobile was resting on top of a pile of his clothes. The thought of venturing outside in his present outfit to phone resembled a bad dream. He grabbed the mobile and his clothes and shut the locker before shouldering the doors aside and dodging into the corridor. It was deserted, which only made him feel more like an escaping prisoner. Nobody could stop him, or was there someone who could? Was he forgetting a name it was dangerous to forget or else to remember? Hugging his belongings, he followed the overhead signs to the nearest Men.

The room beyond the terse word was deserted too. Above the sinks a mirror multiplied the white tiles of the walls, so that Rory felt surrounded by a relentless absence of colour. He was suddenly afraid of not seeing his reflection. He made himself step forwards, and in a moment saw a ridiculously costumed apparition with his face. He took refuge in the nearest cubicle, where he planted his clothes on top of the low cistern before fumbling to undo the gown and tear off the degrading pad. In no time he was dressed, socks and shoes too. He stuffed the pad into a bin and left the gown hanging in the cubicle as he returned to the corridor.

Nobody could see the escaped patient now. He was just another visitor. He hurried to the lifts, the nearest of which opened at once to his summons as if it were as impatient as he was. It certainly seemed eager to box him in with its dull flat grey doors and walls and floor and ceiling. The greyness struck him as less a colour than a substitute for one, and as much of a threat to close his senses down as the white tiles had been. He stared at the numbers above the doors and tried to grasp what colour the illuminated digits were. Perhaps the attempt to determine it helped him retain his senses, but he hadn't identified the tint of the lacklustre 1 by the time the doors released him.

The lobby was scattered with visitors and staff, who presumably saw as little of him as he did of them. As he emerged from the building his mind appeared to lighten to match the sky. So long as it didn't grow as blank, he thought, and switched his mobile on. He took several unnecessary moments to decide on calling Charlotte. Wherever she was, he assumed it must be out of reach, because she was represented by an automatic message. As he listened for Hugh and then for Ellen, his concentration felt dangerously close to blotting out his surroundings. Worse still, it seemed to have blotted out his family. All three were as silent as packed earth.

THIRTY-FIVE

As Charlotte stepped on the escalator at Liverpool Lime Street she became afraid that she would miss a call. Retrieving the mobile from her handbag, she triggered the display. While the stairs bore her downwards she was able to watch the signal dwindling as if, like her, it were being dragged into the earth. It vanished as the stair beneath her feet, sending her off the escalator. She had yet to hear from Hugh or Ellen in response to her increasingly terse messages. The destination boards at either end of the underground platform promised a train to West Kirby in two minutes, which meant that for at least another ten she would have no chance to hear.

She dropped the mobile in her bag, where it nestled against the flashlight she'd bought in an Indian store near the station. Whichever way she looked along the sparsely populated platform she was confronted by a tunnel shrunk around darkness, but for hours she'd been unable to distinguish her claustrophobia from her anxiety about her cousins, if indeed that hadn't overwhelmed any other feelings. In the taxi from the hospital, and then on the train out of Leeds, she'd kept hoping that a call from Hugh or Ellen would let her go back to watch over Rory. She ought to contact the police; she couldn't contact the police. The two imperatives persisted in switching back and forth inside her skull, even more insistently now that she was unable to make a call.

Before long a train with WEST KIRBY luminously emblazoned on its brow rose out of the left-hand tunnel. More people than Charlotte had time to identify boarded as she did. Her section of the carriage was unoccupied but flanked by onrushing blackness. She seemed to be able to live with this; perhaps she was growing resigned to her condition. She was more troubled to be met by darkness when the train emerged from the tunnel on the far side of the river.

Her phone showed that nobody had tried to call while she was underground. She hoped Hugh or Ellen had thought to bring a flashlight, although would they have expected their task to take so long? Of course she didn't know that it had. Attempting to raise her cousins yet again wouldn't help them or her nerves. Streetlamps alongside the railway drove back the dark, which only made her worry how much light her cousins had and what it might be illuminating. Houses flocked by, curtained windows glowing, and she thought of families at dinner or in front of televisions while her cousins were caught up in their secret task. At least the darkness should conceal them from observers, unless the flashlight attracted attention. This was one more oscillation of alternatives to add to the clamour inside her skull.

When the train came to the end of its stations the mobile was still playing dumb. Despite a belated impression that she hadn't been the last passenger, Charlotte was alone in stepping onto the platform. There was nobody to collect her ticket, and not a single taxi outside the small station. She was retreating in search of some advertisement for a local firm when blackness swelled out of the night as a taxi pulled away from a more or less Mediterranean restaurant. She had to mime desperation, not that it involved any pretence, before the driver swerved across the road and jettisoned the sluggish firework of a cigarette. 'How far are you going?' he said.

Perhaps he was ready to go home. Certainly his large roundish mottled face looked as if a lie-down might return more of its shape. 'Thurstaston,' she told him.

'What's there?'

'I will be.'

'Shake a leg, then.'

From the frown that swelled the ridges of his brows she could have taken him to be advising her to walk to Thurstaston. As she ducked under the low roof, to be greeted by a dim bulb that illuminated a No Smoking sign, he said 'By yourself?'

She couldn't help slamming the door as if to keep out a pursuer. 'As you see,' she said, though she'd renewed the darkness.

He emitted a snort that might have been derisive or an attempt to unblock his nostrils. 'Meeting someone,' he said.

It sounded ominously unlike a question. The taxi had left the station behind by the time she grasped that he was explaining what he'd previously asked. 'I hope so,' she said, which seemed wilfully pessimistic. 'I'm sure I will.'

The taxi sped out of reach of the lights along the main road and accelerated uphill between banks of rock that shored up the black sky. They blinkered Charlotte's vision, so that she was striving to concentrate on the lit patch of road the night was paying out when the driver enquired 'Which way?'

She was wondering nervously what could have stolen his sense of the unquestionable direction when she realised that he was anticipating the crossroads. 'Down to the cliff,' she said.

'Night walker.'

She assumed he meant her rather than anyone he glimpsed as the taxi emerged from the cutting and swung right at the junction. The side road unbent to reveal the distant Welsh coast, an elongated fallen constellation dying to the orange of a mass of embers. It was pinched progressively smaller by the hedges bordering the road, and sank into the dark before the taxi veered into a lane beside the unlit hulk of a café. 'This you?' the driver said.

'It's fine, thanks.'

Two stumpy tubes of amber light in metal cages guarded the entrances to paths off the lane. Otherwise it and the car park to which it led were deserted. As Charlotte took out her purse the driver flashed his headlamps several times and then blared his horn at length before leaving the beams raised high. 'Where are they?' he was determined to learn.

'I'll find them.'

'They ought to be finding you.' All at once he sounded so paternal that Charlotte was afraid he might lock her in for her own supposed safety. She'd caught hold of the door handle when he slid his window down to shout 'Anybody there?'

This provoked a response – a protracted clattering giggle as dry as a skull. Before it trailed off Charlotte identified it as the complaint of a restless magpie. 'They won't be here,' she said, as angry with her own nerves as with the driver. 'I have to walk.'

'You ought to be met when it's dark like this.'

She heard a threat instead of the rebuke he intended. If she tarried much longer, the metal cell might start to seem like a refuge. She peeled a note off the stained scrawny wad in her purse and handed it to the driver. 'All yours,' she said when he made to give her change as she clambered out of the taxi.

'Just take a bit of care. You never know who's about at night,' he said and lingered until she ventured onto a lit stretch of path. 'Hope they're waiting for you,' he said and executed a U-turn so leisurely that he might have been deciding to halt again. Instead he drove to the road and, with a last red-eyed glare of the brakes, was gone.

The glow of the caged light fell short of the track onto which the path led. The murmur of the taxi dwindled beyond hearing as Charlotte stepped onto the track, and then there was only the wind in the hedges. They scraped thorns together as she turned right towards a bridge, on the far side of which the track continued to resemble the floor of a tunnel narrowing into invisibility. Its walls were trees growing close together and embedded like vines in the roof of the sky. Her footsteps grew shrill and encountered company under the bridge, but only hers emerged, unless the others had become so thin that they were less than whispers. Of course nobody was at her back. She managed not to glance over her shoulder more than twice and to derive some slight comfort from the raw lamps on a road alongside a caravan park behind the trees to her left, although the place was so silent that any tenants might have been holding their collective breath.

Soon the lamps ended and the trees gave way to bushes, opening out the sky. It felt as if the walls had thickened while lowering the roof, and left the track just as dimly indistinct. The need to strain her eyes distracted her from feeling too closed in, and she wanted to conserve the flashlight beam. She almost wandered past the entrance to the common in the dark.

A sign nailed to a post on the overgrown verge had disoriented her, because she couldn't recall having seen it before. She leaned close to it and squinted hard, but still had to use the flashlight. The tip of the wooden pointer had rotted away, leaving a gap like a dead reptile's lichened mouth. Many of the letters had sloughed off where they weren't obscured by moss, so that she was barely able to distinguish even ASTON OUND, which might have been a phrase too occult for her to understand. She swung the flashlight beam away to illuminate the way through the gap in the hedge. As soon as she stepped onto the path across the common she switched off the beam.

She oughtn't to have peered so closely at the lit sign. A blurred pale patch clung to her vision, obscuring the route. A wind hissed through the blackened grass to meet her, and she was also greeted by a muted tolling of bells, which it took her some moments to recognise as the hollow clangour of ropes against the masts of boats. A rise in the faint narrow path showed her the nervously restless lights of Wales, and as she glimpsed a thin shape silhouetted against them on the far side of the common, a mass of blackness clattered up from a clump of bushes at her side. Its cry was louder and harsher than hers. It flew away cawing to add its blackness to a treetop, and Charlotte tried to steady the flashlight beam as she turned it on the silhouette near the edge of the cliff. At first the light seemed too attenuated to define it, especially given her imperfect vision. She had to advance several reluctant paces before she was sure of the object. It was a spade stuck upright in the earth.

She had no doubt who'd left it there. 'Hugh,' she called. 'Ellen.' This appeared to earn her a derisive response, but only from the treetop. She was no longer willing to brave the unlit dark, and followed the unbalanced dance of the flashlight beam along the ragged path. Hundreds of yards away from the spade, she saw that it was guarding a hole in the earth.

Was it a grave? It looked regular enough – and then she remembered her dream. For several breaths the memory – the pebbles that proved to be eyes, the face rising out of the soil that coated it – felt capable of robbing her of movement. She couldn't abandon her cousins, wherever they were, and so she stalked along the shaky path across the dim common and managed to grasp both the spade and her handbag while she poked the flashlight beam into the rectangular darkness. It was far too reminiscent of her dream, yet quite different. Beyond the hole left by a trapdoor that lay open on the grass, an iron ladder scaly with rust led down into a cellar.

It must be all that remained of Pendemon's house. No, there was a further rectangular opening in the bare wooden floor. By leaning forwards she was able to distinguish a ladder that depended from it, and beyond that, stairs leading downwards. Although they were dim, she had a notion that something was wrong with them, and she thought the same about the trapdoor. She trained the flashlight on it until she realised that she could just see the ground through it. At once she felt as if the common had collapsed beneath her, precipitating her into the unknown. Pendemon's house had vanished, but not in the way she'd assumed. The trapdoor was a grimy skylight, and the carpeted stairs led down into the house itself.

THIRTY-SIX

Black and white. Sky, hospital. Black sky, white hospital. Rory was so concerned to ensure his senses were intact, since the silence of the mobile against his ear felt as if his hearing had shut down, that the reason for the colour of the sky didn't immediately occur to him. He almost grabbed a man who was walking away from a taxi. 'What time is it?' he demanded, having realised that his watch must have been destroyed in the crash.

'Nearly eight. Just coming up.'

Rory found the additional phrase redundant, not to mention unwelcome in some way he hadn't time to grasp. The thought that Hugh and their cousins were out somewhere in the night on his behalf with no means of communication dismayed him. Why couldn't he have regained consciousness before any of them left? They weren't even all together. His lurch after the vacated taxi only seemed to send it faster onto the main road. No other taxis were in sight, and he saw that he oughtn't to leave people wondering what had become of him. He turned almost fast enough to leave his vision behind and hurried back into the hospital.

While visitors were loitering in the reception area, they didn't appear to be queuing. Rory dodged around them and waited for the receptionist to notice him – waited several heartbeats before blurting 'Excuse me.'

She still didn't look at him. 'Which ward do you want?'

'None of them. I've been.'

Even when she peered at him she seemed hardly to be seeing him. 'Aren't you visiting? Didn't you just come in?'

'I had an accident. I'm discharging myself.'

'From where?'

'Whichever your ward is where you stick tubes in folk.'

'Intensive Care?'

He'd snagged her attention at last, rather more of it than he needed. 'That'll be it,' he said as if he were unconscious of her frown. 'Can you tell them I'm fine and I've gone?'

'You mustn't leave your bed till someone's seen you.'

'I can, look. I've got to be somewhere else.'

Her expression had vanished as though it had never existed, and he hoped her objections had too. 'What's your name?' she said.

'Lucas. Rory Lucas.'

She hadn't reacted when he heard a murmur at his back. 'Isn't he the feller that was in the smash-up?'

'The one built a hill out of rubbish, you mean.'

'It wasn't a hill,' Rory muttered.

'Right enough, a mound.'

'Not one of those either,' Rory said louder and turned to confront the man, but no face owned up to having spoken. He swung around again to find that the receptionist had changed sex – at least, had moved aside for a broader-shouldered colleague. 'What seems to be the trouble, Mr Lucas?' the replacement said.

'None that I know of. You can see I'm fit to leave.'

'Better let a doctor be the judge.'

'Look, I know how I feel. If there's any problem I'll be back.'

As Rory took a sidelong pace towards the exit the man mirrored him. 'I can see myself out,' Rory said, turning to the doors.

He must have moved too hastily. At once he was surrounded

by nothing, not even colour. He felt as though he were floating inert in the midst of a void. He couldn't let anyone observe his condition, and so he stumbled forwards in the hope this would lend him balance. He was just aware of blundering inside a segment of the revolving doors, which someone must be pushing. Suppose he tottered all the way around only to flounder blindly back into the hospital? As soon as he felt a shift of the air on his face he staggered towards it. He must be in the open, because he could smell cigarette smoke. As if the detail had returned all his senses to him, the blindness set about seeping towards the edge of his vision. There were no taxis on the forecourt of the hospital, and so he headed for the main road.

He was wary of moving too fast now. He could imagine that senselessness was lying in wait for him. He was yards short of the road when a taxi swung onto the forecourt and coasted towards the hospital entrance. He had to retrace practically all the steps he'd taken outside to be in a position to board once the passenger made way for him. He couldn't help peering into the lobby to make sure nobody had pursued him, and perhaps this was why the driver said 'Have they let you out, then?'

'Can we go to the station?' Rory slammed the door and, having sat back, clipped the seat belt into its slot. When the driver only squinted in the mirror Rory had to demand 'How do you mean?'

'You got your release.'

Rory fancied he was being asked to produce some kind of document until he saw that the driver was being facetious. 'I was visiting,' he said.

'Is that a fact.'

Insisting that it was might make Rory sound too determined to convince his questioner. 'Can we get going now?' he urged instead.

'When they've got this woman and her chair in unless you want us running them down.'

Rory was dismayed to realise that he hadn't noticed the large car ahead, into which a man was helping an invalid while a second man stowed a folded wheelchair in the boot. Surely Rory's senses weren't deserting him again; surely he was just preoccupied with leaving the hospital behind. He stared at the entrance to reassure himself that none of the emerging crowd was after him, and so he failed to observe the departure of the other car. He was sagging with relief as the taxi left the forecourt when the driver said 'How are they getting on?'

'I wish I knew,' Rory almost said despite knowing that the man didn't have Hugh or Ellen or Charlotte in mind. 'Well enough,' he hoped.

The taxi was among white buildings now – so white that he could have thought the world was being drained of colour. 'What's wrong?' the driver said.

'Nothing whatsoever. I'll be fine.'

A frown narrowed the driver's eyes as if to fit them better into the strip of mirror. 'With them.'

'Oh, I see,' Rory said and tried to judge a laugh. 'Nothing too bad.'

'Something must be or they wouldn't be kept in.'

Rory nodded, careless of how much agreement that implied if it saved him from further discussion, but it felt like a threat of subsiding into unconsciousness. It seemed to have silenced the driver until the man said 'Parent, is it?'

'Neither of them. They're away having a good time.'

'Wife.'

'I've not got any of those.'

'Give us a hint at least. Man or a woman?'

Rory wondered how determined the fellow might be to turn the situation into a game. He would have advised him politely or otherwise to desist if the man weren't providing a stimulus without which Rory felt in danger of losing awareness. The fear was enough to make him blurt 'Both.'

'That's bad, that. Same problem?'

Rory seemed to have left himself no answer except 'Yes.'

'Something that's making the rounds, is it?'

'Nothing like that. Don't worry, I can't pass it on to you,' Rory said as the taxi swerved into another onslaught of whiteness.

'What, then? Not a secret, is it?'

'I can't say.'

'You're never telling me the hospital don't know.'

'That's the truth,' Rory said, only to reflect that he didn't know much. Rather than give in to calling Hugh or their cousins again – rather than risk hearing the same voice take their place – he shut his eyes. 'I don't want to talk about it any more,' he said.

'You shouldn't let them put you off. They've got to know something, it's their job. You ought to go back and make them speak up.' Perhaps the driver saw how much this troubled Rory, but his pause seemed little more than momentary. 'Here you are,' he said.

Rory was afraid he'd been returned to the hospital, but he was almost as disconcerted to see the railway station. How long had he been unconscious of his surroundings? Presumably as long as the driver's pause had actually lasted. 'You sure this is where you think you ought to be?' the driver said.

'It's where I want.' As Rory focused on the digital display beyond the complications of the grille he was unnecessarily reminded of a bedside monitor in a hospital. He slipped a fiver through the gap beneath the grille and looked back from the pavement to find the driver watching him with such concern that it seemed to menace Rory with inertia. 'I was visiting,' he repeated and willed himself to leave it all behind, to move, to turn.

The sky was black, the interior ahead of him white. The black taxi had brought him to the station, not the hospital. However incomprehensible the giant voice that filled the tiled booking hall might sound, that must be the fault of the address system rather than of Rory's senses. Nevertheless he took care not to outdistance them by dodging too fast through the crowd to the nearest available ticket window. 'Where can we get you?' the clerk said.

He tried not to be thrown by how pensionable she looked. 'Thurstaston,' he said.

'Not here, pet.'

'I'm not expecting it to be. It's where I have to go.'

'I'm telling you you can't do that from where you are.'

'Of course you can. I can, I mean. I've done it.' Rory's panicky frustration must be affecting his eyes, since the window appeared to be growing opaque, veiling the clerk's face. The patch of blindness shrank as he managed to grasp his mistake. 'Sorry, it was the nearest station,' he said and manufactured a laugh. 'West Kirby. I know you've heard of there.'

He would have been surer if he'd been able to distinguish her expression. Her face drifted into focus as she told him the price. 'Going now?' she said, and he wished he could without lingering over the transaction. Once her skinny fingers had stretched through the aperture under the window to hand over his tickets and token change he made for the destination board.

A train would be leaving for Liverpool in less than fifteen minutes. At least he could stop worrying about his unsteadiness once he was seated. Perhaps he might doze, except that the prospect of losing consciousness revived his panic. He bought a flimsy plastic cup of coffee at a refreshment counter. A girl in a white overall reminiscent of a hospital uniform shut the steam in the cup with a lid. This must have made the hot drink safe, because he forgot about holding it as he showed his ticket at the booth.

The train straight ahead was his. Every door was open, but he walked to the farthest to save time at his destination, however much it felt like trying to leave a pursuer behind. He remembered to plant the cup on the rudimentary table before he sat down. He was about to lift the lid when it occurred to him to phone again before the train moved off. He groped for the mobile and poked at Hugh's number and lifted the faraway bell to his ear.

The ringing ceased at last, to be succeeded by silence that felt as if a listener were holding his breath. When the belated voice spoke Rory found it worse than artificial. He could have fancied it was eager to abandon all pretence, to reveal the identity beneath the bright mechanical repetition. 'Call me. Don't leave me wondering,' he said with at least as much desperation as impatience and tried Ellen, to be met by the same silence and eventually the same message, which seemed to have grown hollower, as if it were emerging from deep in a hole. He could only reiterate his plea and call Charlotte. This time the silence and its companion voice, beneath which lurked an echo like a muffled mocking imitation by another speaker, made Rory feel close to being dragged into the depths, and so did his own repeated appeal. It was beginning to resemble a ritual whose purpose he didn't understand and might prefer not to, but he was unable to bring any other words to mind. Indeed, he had reverted to pleading 'Don't leave me –' yet again before he fumbled to shut off the call.

He let the phone drop on the upholstery and stared around him. Commuters were boarding trains on either side of him, tugging their shadows after them. Shouldn't this be sufficiently vivid to anchor Rory's senses even if the artificial light reduced the trains to monochrome? Perhaps the unreality of his calls had affected him, because he could easily have taken the windows for screens on which he was projecting images. He was stretching out a hand to touch the glass when the train jerked forwards, having shuddered like a dreamer struggling to leave a nightmare behind.

Had it spilled his coffee? As he made to dodge the threat of being scalded he saw that the dribble had only formed a ring around the base of the cup. It was too pale to stain the table. It lingered like an obscure symbol as he moved the cup, but in a moment he couldn't see where it had been. Perhaps the girl at the counter had put too little coffee in the cup, because Rory wasn't sure whether he was tasting it or simply how he thought it should taste. At least it wasn't as hot as he'd anticipated; indeed, he could imagine that he felt it growing colder in his hand. He took a gulp and was almost sure he tasted coffee, however faintly. When another mouthful proved no more conclusive he planted the cup on top of its lid so as to concentrate on the view from the train.

The streets sailing past the windows were threaded with headlamps brighter than the generalised amber glow that blotted out the sky. He tried not to feel that the glow was muffling the cityscape, although in the distance it looked thick as orange paint, smudging the shapes of buildings. Or was fog doing that? He wouldn't have expected to encounter any at this time of year; it made him feel as if he'd been unconscious longer than he knew. Straining his eyes seemed to attract the indistinctness, which drained substance from a line of houses he'd thought were clearly defined. As he tried to make sense of this he realised that he couldn't hear the train.

He was devoting his energy to seeing, that was all. He peered at the interior of the carriage until his impressions seeped back, the upholstery yielding beneath his weight, the wheels clicking like the needles of a knitter at a bedside. How much of his brain did it take to hold onto these details? When he reached for the cup he couldn't judge how hot it was, even by tipping the drink into his mouth. He downed it before he was able to taste it, and he was trying to believe that he had swallowed a drink when he grew aware that the windows had turned blank.

Surely it was just that his perceptions had fallen short of them, but that was bad enough. Once he put down the cup at which he'd been staring he was able to recapture the sight of the city steeped in ochre. As it fled past the windows he couldn't help reflecting that it was the colour of light about to die – the colour of the death of colour. Had the fog advanced, if it was fog, or was his peripheral vision shrinking? When he glared across the city he saw that another layer of buildings had lost all its features, while beyond it he could distinguish nothing at all. The train had fallen so silent that it might have been denying its existence, so that he was suddenly afraid of being too intent on the view to hear his mobile if it rang. While he didn't want any of his senses to falter, he needed to be certain that Hugh and their cousins could reach him. Suppose he had already missed a call?

The busy clicking reappeared as he groped over the upholstery, and the carriage established its presence around him. Having located the mobile, he clenched his fist on it as he saw that there had indeed been a call. He couldn't read the number, which resembled digits less than random blackened scratches, as if somebody had tried to claw their way up through the miniature screen. Rory jabbed the key to ring the number back and clapped the mobile to his ear. A bell that sounded shrivelled by distance had barely repeated its note before it seemed to recede into silence. 'Who's there?' Rory said or shouted, he couldn't judge which.

In a moment he had an answer of sorts, though the voice was so muffled or so remote that it might as well have been buried. He couldn't make out any of the trinity of syllables, let alone the identity of the speaker. 'What did you say?' he demanded, which brought a repetition of the answer. It was just as incomprehensible, but perhaps distance wasn't the problem; perhaps the voice was whispering close to his ear.

'Speak up,' Rory urged and strained to grasp the response. It seemed to be playing at remoteness again, and as he strove to hear he felt as if he were being drawn into whatever depths it might inhabit. No doubt the narrowing of his vision aggravated the effect. He was so anxious to identify the name he kept being told that he only belatedly noticed how much of the city had vanished.

He stared in dismay through the window beside him and then across the aisle. He could see no more than a few hundred yards in either direction, and even the visible buildings looked perfunctory, little more than outlines nobody had bothered to fill in. Behind them there appeared to be nothingness, not so much as a hint of the sky. As he peered past them, desperate to make out whatever was there, another lurid line of buildings was erased. He turned his reluctant head to see a street merge with the advancing blankness on the far side of the carriage. Was he merely observing it, or attracting it somehow? He was distracted by the slowing of the train. Presumably the fog, or a medium that improved on fog, was closing in ahead as well, but he was suddenly afraid that it was designed to halt the train – to prevent him from finding Hugh or Ellen or Charlotte.

That was worse than stupid. He was letting his thoughts trap him in his skull. The train had reached a station, that was all. Admittedly so had the surrounding blankness. As the walls of the suburban station blocked his view of the city he saw the opaque medium creeping up a ramp towards the platform. He couldn't discern even a hint of the city beyond the enclosed ramp, but at least someone was approaching up the slope. As the carriage passed it Rory saw a man emerge from the blank mass that filled the lower half of the passage. The man's face did not, however.

Rory just had time to see that nothingness was trailing the figure up the tunnel before the entrance coasted out of sight, by no means far enough. The next moment the train stopped, and all the doors sprang open as though welcoming the traveller. As Rory's head lolled against the upholstery he saw the figure stalk fast out of the passage. It was little more than a ragged silhouette, scrawny and blackened. If he'd been capable of gratitude Rory would have felt glad of his inability to distinguish much above its neck, where the jagged outline suggested a collapsed cavity rather than a face. Nevertheless the figure was advancing at speed, and so was the vast absence at its back. Rory's fists clenched, or did their shaky best to do so, reminding him that he was still clutching the phone. Was it attracting the intruder? Perhaps, because at last he heard the name that the whisper had been repeating. It belonged to the figure that leapt into the carriage and so, he thought too late, did the all-encompassing blur that followed. As he saw his companion clearly at last, he was almost glad when the nothingness claimed him.

THIRTY-SEVEN

As Charlotte backed away from the impossible aperture in the earth, a mass of blackness reared up in pursuit. It was a shadow dragged out of the depths by the flashlight beam, but she couldn't be reassured while she was so aware of walking over a roof. She was still gripping the handle of the spade, and as her retreat pulled it out of the earth, the unsteadily illuminated patch of ground around the skylight and the entire dim common stirred as if the buried house were preparing to slough its concealment. She mustn't think she'd roused the house or anything within it. All she was seeing was wind in the grass, but the knowledge didn't help much. She could hardly think for yearning to be off the hidden roof and as far as an uninterrupted run would take her from the house.

She believed at last, which made her realise how desperately she'd been hoping not to have to do so. The possibility of different explanations for her cousins' states and her own had fled as she wished she could. So the house was indeed beneath Thurstaston Mound, but not in the sense they'd assumed. Had the mound collapsed simply from erosion, or could it have been somehow encouraged to collapse? Certainly it appeared to have trapped the occupant of the house in his own worst nightmare. Charlotte had no doubt that he'd been buried along with the house.

The idea was enough to send her several paces backwards. What had she imagined she could do here? For that matter, what had Hugh and Ellen done? She ought to try to locate them, but the prospect of calling out so close to the open skylight didn't appeal to her. Using her mobile was a problem too, even once she'd dealt with the spade by leaning it against her rather than risk digging it into the earth that covered the roof. She hung her bag on the handle and trained the flashlight beam on the hole in the ground, and then she peered at the mobile to key the call one-handed. All at once she was afraid to hear Hugh's or Ellen's ringtone in the depths below the skylight, and she re-called the hospital instead.

'Putting you through,' the receptionist said as the edges of the hole grew restless. In a few seconds Charlotte heard not just her own unquiet heart but the sister on the ward. 'Sorry to bother you,' Charlotte said, which seemed grotesquely remote from her situation. 'I was wondering if there's been any change with Rory Lucas.'

'Rory Lucas?' Presumably the sister was questioning a nurse, but the audible reply came from Annie, who called 'He's not moved since she left him.'

'Nothing yet, I'm afraid. We've got your number, haven't we?'

'You have, thanks,' Charlotte said, already envisaging a situation where she might prefer it not to ring. She ended the call, and her finger wavered over the keys until she became furiously impatient with herself. She jabbed the key to display the list of names and selected Hugh's. A breathless silence followed, and a heartbeat, and then an imitation bell began to shrill in her ear. Her heart had time to thump again before the call belatedly triggered the theme from *Sesame Street*. While it was muffled, she couldn't doubt that it was somewhere beneath her.

She felt as if she wouldn't be able to move until it was answered, and quite possibly not then. It might depend who spoke. As the jolly theme jingled on, it sounded increasingly like a mockery of childhood. The melody fell silent halfway through a jaunty rising phrase, and a voice spoke in Charlotte's ear.

She had to take a disoriented moment to recognise why it wasn't audible beyond the skylight as well. It was the automated message, responding from somewhere that seemed hardly to exist. 'Hugh, are you there?' Charlotte pleaded. 'Can you hear me? Answer me, Hugh.'

Nobody did. She terminated the call and managed not to yield to the temptation to repeat some or all of the words at the top of her voice. She brought up the list again and thumbed Ellen's number. 'Be somewhere up here,' she prayed under her breath. She hadn't finished whispering when the title song from *Oklahoma* commenced its crescendo in the depths of the house.

Like Hugh's tune, it sounded several floors deep. The protracted cry suggested an attempt to rise above a nightmare. When it arrived at the rest of the verse, Charlotte was assailed by an image of Ellen prancing helplessly at the behest of the music in the dark. Ellen might be too frail or too distressed to offer much resistance. The unwelcome fancy made Charlotte shout her cousin's name before the song was cut off by the familiar message. 'What are you both doing down there?' she could hardly wait to plead. 'Can't either of you answer?'

The question seemed to grow more ominous as it left her mouth. 'Someone speak to me,' she called loud enough to be heard without the phone, an appeal that raised nobody as far as she could tell. She dropped the mobile in her bag and clenched her fist on the handle of the spade. She knew where she had to go now if she could.

The mouth of the house worked, eager to swallow her, as the grass around the hole trembled in the wind while the flashlight beam magnified her nervousness. She did her best to lose her temper with that and to hold onto her anger as she followed the shivering beam to the hole, which was far too reminiscent of an open grave. The resemblance wasn't entirely dispelled when the beam plunged into the dark.

It crept across the floorboards and spilled over the brink of the trapdoor to grow dimmer on the stairs. 'Hugh,' Charlotte called down. 'Ellen.' She didn't know whether she was more afraid to find out why they didn't answer or to descend into the house. She succeeded in recapturing some of her anger as she clung to the spade, which she wasn't about to leave behind when it was the nearest thing she had to a weapon. She lowered it through the skylight at arm's length and let it fall with a thud that resounded through more levels of the house than she could judge. Without going after it she wouldn't have a weapon. She slipped the strap of her bag over her shoulder and nestled the bag under her arm, and turned to set foot on the ladder.

Beyond the cliff and the foreshortened river the Welsh coast glittered as if to communicate a message she had neither the time nor the ability to decipher. Perhaps it was simply reminding her how much light she was leaving behind. Under her foot the topmost rung felt treacherous with rust. She mustn't take these as excuses not to proceed, and a flare of anger was enough to send her onto the next crumbling rung and the ones beneath, taking her up to her waist in the lightless house. The flashlight beam shrank from the edge of the cliff as she groped for the next rung with a foot, and she was aware of the gaping space beneath her and closing in at her back. She gripped the highest rung with her free hand, and as scales of rust scraped together under her fingers she brought the flashlight to waist level. Darkness flooded across the common, blotching her vision, so that when the flashlight beam jerked downwards with her uncertain descent she wasn't sure how many shadows were fluttering around her among the rafters. She planted both feet on a rung and closed her fist on another while she aimed the light at the floor. The beam wobbled across the boards until it encountered a shape that had been lying low. The light seemed to rouse the thin twisted limbs as the object glared at her with its solitary orb.

It was a telescope. Either its stand had collapsed or, to judge by its position, it had been toppled from blocking the trapdoor. Suppose it had been dislodged from beneath? Charlotte clutched at the ladder and swung the light around the space under the roof. Shadows started out of the corners and sank back, but apart from the telescope and the spade and a scattering of earth, the attic was bare. Nevertheless she was feeling more than reluctant to step down into it, never mind the rest of the house, when she heard a noise beyond the trapdoor.

Despite its faintness, she couldn't mistake it. It was a groan, and although it was muffled by distance or some other cause, she recognised the voice. 'Ellen,' she called, scrambling so hastily down the ladder that the shadows of the rafters appeared to collapse the roof. She must be too concerned for Ellen to have time for claustrophobia, but she retrieved the spade in a bid to feel less vulnerable on her way to the trapdoor. 'Ellen,' she called down into the house.

There was no reply, and no movement apart from the uncontrollable roving of the flashlight beam, which had found the second ladder. It was wedged between the frame of the trapdoor and the verge of the stairs, and looked all the more precarious for the unstable light. Other than the stairs that led down from a landing to an enclosed windowless bend, nothing else met her eye. How many of her burdens was she going to cart through the house? She transferred the mobile to a hip pocket and dropped her handbag through the opening, followed by the spade. She was certainly announcing her presence, but what might it sound like? 'Ellen, it's me,' she felt forced to call as she turned to descend the ladder.

It wasn't just the sight of the telescope that halted her, although for a moment she thought it was crawling with insects. They were symbols etched on the barrel. The wavering beam had lent them movement, and she shouldn't linger to examine them. She was more concerned with the tracks that led from the trapdoor, tracing how the heavy telescope had been dragged or shoved across the loft to clear the way down. Ellen must have shifted it, but if she'd managed that in her condition, how desperate had she been to hide? The thought sent Charlotte downwards as fast as she dared clamber, into the house that smelled oppressively of earth.

The wooden ladder wasn't staggering towards the edge of the stairs. She couldn't really feel the movement – at least, not as much as the antics of the flashlight beam encouraged her to see. All the same, the vibrations came close to paralysing her until she sprinted down the last few rungs to sidle none too confidently onto the floor. She was glad to let go of the ladder, which had felt surreptitiously moist, but the carpet yielded like soft earth, as if the floor it covered were no more solid. That wasn't as unsettling as the sight ahead.

She was facing a bedroom. The door was wide open, framing the dim bulk of a capacious four-poster bed. She grabbed the spade before she sent the flashlight beam into the room. A dark ill-defined shape scrambled backwards across the discoloured quilt and obese greyish pillows to its lair beneath the sagging canopy, but it was just the shadow of the humped bedclothes. Although they were rumpled enough to be outlining worse than uneasy sleep, the bed was empty. None of this was why she found it hard to breathe. With the heavy velvet curtains open, as they were now, the occupant of the bed would have seen a panorama of the Welsh coast and mountains beyond the large window, but the view consisted of brownish clay packed against the glass.

She felt as if her claustrophobia were poised to engulf her. Indeed, she didn't understand why it was holding back. Glancing up in search of reassurance, she saw a fitful star beyond the portion of skylight visible through the trapdoor. What else had she glimpsed? She lifted the flashlight and was managing to ignore the blackness that rushed at her out of the bedroom when she saw the marks around the trapdoor.

They were scratches. However old they were, age hadn't faded their desperation. The small dull oval object lodged in the deepest scratch might very well be a fingernail. Only its shadow made it appear to be trying to work free of the ceiling. Charlotte was drawing a breath to prove she still could when it almost blotted out another sound. It was Ellen, distressed beyond words.

Was she further down the house or in one of the rooms off the landing? There was another open door to Charlotte's right and two of them shut at her back. 'Ellen,' she repeated.

At first she wasn't sure that the response was a word, if it was even a response. She was so anxious to locate it, still more when she failed, that she only belatedly recognised it. 'No,' Ellen had said – groaned, rather.

Did she want to keep Charlotte away or to deny her own identity? 'Yes, I'm here,' Charlotte told her. 'I've come to help.

Don't make me wander about in here. Say where you are. And where's Hugh?'

She was talking so much in the hope of provoking an answer, but she hushed for fear of covering one up. There was no sound other than the abortive flattened echo of her voice in the open rooms and down the staircase. 'Ellen,' she persisted as she crossed the spongy carpet to the second room.

It was crowded with objects standing still in the dark. She saw the shadows of their heads first, swelling across the carpet towards another buried window. They were orreries, six of them, and it took her some moments to realise why there needed to be more than one: they didn't represent the familiar solar system. Two of the stars orbited by planets were so black that the flashlight seemed unable to illuminate them, while another was encircled by nothing more than jagged fragments of itself. Quite a few of the planets were misshapen to a degree that Charlotte could hardly believe was cosmically possible. The orrery closest to the window suggested not just a diagram of a planetary system but, in the relationships of its thirteen globes and less globular bodies, some larger and more ominous meaning. She imagined the owner of the house gazing from the window at night or through the telescope until he discerned all these vagaries of the universe, and then she had the disconcerting notion that he'd constructed them as a means of sending forth the visions they portrayed. 'Ellen,' she urged, struggling to disengage her mind from the thoughts that had invaded it, and sent the flashlight beam around the room. There was nowhere for Ellen to hide among the sluggish dance of shadows, and she hadn't made another sound. Charlotte swung around to stride across the landing and, before her apprehension could prevent her, grasped the icy scalloped brass doorknob to open the third room.

It was empty, which should have been all that she needed to see. Nevertheless as her gaze was drawn to the circle of marks on the floor, the flashlight beam sank away from the heavy black curtains that covered the window. The circle encompassed perhaps half the square floor, and she suspected that its centre was precisely at the midpoint of the square. It consisted of symbols and ideograms that looked unnervingly alive, as if besides trembling on the edge of growing comprehensible they only awaited a signal to start crawling after one another. Indeed, the restless light seemed capable of rousing them. They were carved out of the floorboards, whereas the marks that filled the circle were less defined, though not too faint to suggest a series of frantic attempts to escape. Charlotte was forming the impression that the prisoner had been large and very leggy; in fact, she could think that it had been scrabbling at the limits of its prison with an unnecessary number of legs. Was the circle entirely deserted? Was that a stain on the floor in the middle, or a small dark lump? Perhaps it wasn't even as small as it had seemed at first glance, but her uncertainty about its size might be due to the tendrils it was extending across the boards. Surely only the movement of the light made it appear to flex them – and then she wondered if her own attention could be letting it take shape. The thought was enough to drive her out of the room with a slam of the door. 'Ellen,' she repeated to no avail, and so she had to twist the greenish brass knob to push the next door wide.

The room was almost as bare as its neighbour. A single item occupied the carpetless floor in front of the secretively curtained window. Until she succeeded in steadying the flashlight Charlotte took it for a cage; it had bars on all sides and across the top. As their shadowy antics subsided she began to distinguish what the bars enclosed: a pillow, a small tangled blanket incongruously printed with fairies emerging from flowers, a contorted shape under the blanket. Just the upper portion of the withered head was visible, which was more than enough. The eyes peering at her across the pillow were far too large. Even if they were empty sockets they were twice the size they ought to be in proportion with the small head, and wasn't there movement in their depths? Perhaps only the light was troubling their shrunken contents; perhaps shadows were making the shrivelled form appear to be struggling feebly to raise its head and writhe out from under the blanket. All the same, Charlotte backed out of that room faster still and ensured the door was shut tight, however unlikely it seemed that anything could escape the cage that was a cot.

Had its tenant been bred for some arcane purpose? Its deformity seemed too extreme to be accidental. She refrained from thinking how it might have been used or intended to be; there was enough to dread in the prospect of exploring further. 'Ellen,' she appealed. Any sound from her cousin might have helped her feel less alone, but she heard none.

She was retrieving her handbag from beside the ladder when she realised that she didn't want to be encumbered on the stairs, the corner of which was entirely too blind. Her anger at having to leave the bag lent her the courage to venture downwards. As she reached the bend she lifted the spade like an axe, but below her were only more stairs. They or the carpet brown as clay yielded underfoot as she paced down to the middle floor.

It contained another four rooms. Those that would have faced the river and Wales were open. Clay appeared to press itself more heavily against the window of the first room as the flashlight beam glared on the panes. Otherwise the room was walled with bookshelves, and piles of old books squatted on the floor, while a fat tome sprawled open on a reading stand in front of a leathery chair at the window. Charlotte might have fancied that the reader was about to return, and neither the impression nor the illustration on the left-hand page – a diabolically gleeful face whose eyes weren't opening so much as forming out of the pallid flesh – encouraged her to linger once she'd seen that Ellen could be nowhere in the room.

There was more sense of a presence in the adjoining room. A desk that looked too bulky to have been carried upstairs stood in front of the window. Another black chair, its leather sagging like senile flesh, was turned half to the doorway as if its occupant had heard Charlotte and leaped to ambush her. She made herself step forwards to check that Ellen wasn't hiding out of sight from the doorway. There were only shelves as tall as the ceiling. They and the ones on the other walls were heaped with papers inscribed, she guessed from the one that was pricking up its corners on the desk, in a spidery introverted hand. Even more than its neighbour, the room smelled of old paper as well as damp earth, so thickly that she choked. The clay at the window was reminding her how much deeper she was buried. 'Ellen,' she called, which didn't save her from having to open the door opposite. At once she was blinded by the light shone into her eyes by the figure in the room.

Instinctively she raised the flashlight and her weapon, and so did the imitator. She had to let the beam sink to be mimicked, by which time she'd identified her own reflection. What about the crowds of dimmer silhouettes brandishing feebler lights on either side? They were Charlotte too. All four walls of the room were mirrors, and she suspected that the back of the door was one, which would turn the entire room into a mirror once it was shut. She had the sudden terrible notion that Ellen was cowering in a corner, trapped by her aversion to seeing herself. Charlotte had to take several increasingly reluctant paces forwards to be certain Ellen wasn't there. It wasn't just that the multiplied dazzle made it hard to see; her first step had revealed that the floor and ceiling were also mirrors. Advancing into the room felt like setting out across a void peopled with a multitude of reproductions of herself, and she thought the inventor might have imagined he was creating a universe in his own image. Or was there more to it? Although she'd halted, she seemed to glimpse movement that couldn't be wholly ascribed to the nervous swaying of the countless lights. In the black distance beyond her most minuscule images, had something grown restless? She could imagine that it was attracted by the light or by her arrival. It appeared to be taking vast dark shape in the process of closing around her from every side, as if she were already in its mouth or paw or some monstrously unidentifiable part of it. All at once she was terrified that the door was about to shut behind her, rendering the void complete. Wasn't it inching towards its frame? Even if this was an illusion produced by the wavering of all the lights, she headed for the doorway so fast that she almost slipped on the glass floor and fell into the arms of her inverted self. The swollen carpet gave her back some equilibrium, and she slammed the door with such force that she might have hoped to hear the mirrors shatter. Before the episode could discourage her from proceeding, she hurried to the next room and shoved the door wide.

Her first impression was that the room was packed with soil, but the flashlight showed that the darkness wasn't quite so solid, although sufficiently thick to absorb much of the beam. The light grew dimmer as it crossed the threshold and petered out towards the middle of the room. The thought that Ellen could be submerged in the depths of the blackness was so dismaying that Charlotte was hardly aware of leaning through the doorway. 'Ellen,' she shouted as if her voice had to penetrate the medium that filled the room.

In a moment, as she swung the flashlight beam from side to side in an attempt to illuminate the limits of the room, she felt the blackness settle on her face and hands. Even though it was less substantial than cobwebs laden with soot, those were the sensations it resembled, and it was as cold as water too deep for the sun to reach. These weren't the only reasons why Charlotte almost dropped the flashlight and the spade. She'd heard Ellen moan, but not in the room. Otherwise she would have been unable to judge whether Ellen was lost in the blackness, which was absorbing the flashlight beam so fast that it had shrunk to the length of her arm.

The medium seemed greedy to engulf not just the light but her. She slashed at it with the spade while she backed out of the room, and almost let the spade slip out of her grasp as she clutched at the doorknob. Having dragged the door shut, which took more effort than she'd used to open it, she dashed for the stairs. Her retreat was so instinctive that she'd reached the next bend before she remembered why she was descending. 'Ellen, I'm coming,' she promised.

While her cousin didn't answer, perhaps noises did. They were beyond the stairs and the shakily illuminated section of the ground-floor hall the staircase framed. Although they were barely audible, whether by intention or because there was so little to them, they were footsteps. They sounded disconcertingly uncertain of themselves, but they were approaching. In a moment Charlotte felt less sure of this, though she couldn't judge whether they had turned aside or were employing more stealth. 'Ellen?' she hoped aloud.

The footsteps halted, and she imagined someone waiting for her just around the corner in the dark. She was no longer convinced it was Ellen, not least because an aspect of the house had at last become apparent to her: she hadn't seen a single light or even a fitting for one. Who could have lived in so much darkness? Who still could? Ellen was somewhere below, and

Charlotte ran down the last flight of stairs to have done with any other confrontation. As she left them she jerked the flashlight up as if the beam rather than the spade were her defence.

The hall was deserted except for shadows that fled in all directions to lurk wherever there was concealment. Of the six doors leading off the hall, the broad front entrance seized her attention first, if only because the thought of opening it to let in a landslide reminded her how thoroughly she was buried. The door under the stairs must belong to a cellar, which she very much hoped she wouldn't have to enter; the whole house felt far too reminiscent of a basement, and smelled like one too. Instead she made for the closer of the open doors, the one at the front of the building. As the light found it she saw that it wasn't simply open; it was held that way by the mass that filled the doorway if not the entire room.

Perhaps the room had been a conservatory, unless some kind of underground growth had broken through the window. The tangle of vegetation was so convoluted that its elements were beyond separating. She could easily imagine that different varieties of withered leaves and shrivelled flowers were sprouting from the same plant. Had the owner of the house tried to create a new species for some purpose? Whatever had grown in the room was dead now, possibly of uncontrolled luxuriance, and no insects were swarming in the mass of sunless pullulation, just shadows. At least she could be certain Ellen wasn't in the room. She wished she could have closed it before crossing the hall to the other open room.

It was just a room, she did her best to think as the light ranged around it, but its very emptiness seemed ominous. It was so bare that it didn't even have a window, let alone a carpet, and she was unable to determine the colour of the walls. She only had to lean through the doorway in case Ellen was hiding just inside, and she didn't know why she should hope so fervently that Ellen wasn't. 'Ellen,' she called, though it felt more like a prayer. Having heard no answer, she ducked into the room.

The shapeless hulk that lurched at her was yet more darkness, brought down from the ceiling by the movement of the light. That wasn't why she gasped with all her breath. She saw at once that Ellen was elsewhere, but the instant gave whatever was in the room the chance to touch her. Her skin began to crawl as if insects were hatching under her clothes, or perhaps not even as if, since she felt the twitching of feelers and the fumbling of many legs. Instinctively she knew that these were the least of the delights the room had in store. Now that she'd been seized she could only stumble forwards to discover what else was waiting, and she wasn't surprised to hear Ellen groaning on her behalf.

But it wasn't on her behalf, because it was in another room. Ellen was still alone and in distress. The thought jerked Charlotte's head up, back into the hall. If the sensation of being infested didn't entirely vanish, at least it felt like someone else's nightmare that was trying to invade her. It had to be less important than her cousin, and she managed to leave it behind as she hurried to the room beyond the entrance to the cellar. Surely Ellen needn't be down there. Surely Charlotte would find her by opening the next door.

It led to a dining-room. Paintings that she preferred not to examine, having glimpsed that they were portraits or self-portraits of a gaunt man with unpleasantly prominent eyes, watched over both sides of a long black wooden table, at the far end of which stood a solitary chair. Someone was sitting on it or, more accurately, perched. Charlotte sucked in a breath that emerged as a word while the flashlight beam steadied. 'Ellen.'

She was lying face down at the table, arms outstretched, hands splayed on the wood. She didn't stir in response to Charlotte's voice, and only a feeble movement of her blouse proved she was breathing. None of the portraits widened their eyes to watch Charlotte venture along the room; that was just an effect of the light, which caught the unnaturally rounded eyes and made them glisten like ice. 'It's me, Ellen. I'm here now,' Charlotte said and, having propped the spade against the table well within reach, took her cousin's right hand.

At least, she tried. It was pressed flat against the wood. If anything, Ellen flattened it harder, and Charlotte was afraid that her cousin was doing the same to her face, as if she wanted to erase it and all sense of herself. Charlotte opened her mouth, but the sound she uttered was wordless and by no means comforting. A portrait had thrust its head forwards to peer at them.

All of its companions on the left-hand wall appeared to widen their bulging whitish eyes in glee as Charlotte swung the beam towards them, so wildly that the flashlight almost flew out of her hand. She'd grabbed the spade before she realised that the frame out of which the face had peered was lower on the wall than the portraits to either side. In another moment she saw it was a service hatch. Beyond it were a kitchen and a revival of the footsteps she'd heard from the stairs. As she made herself advance around the table and past Ellen to look through the hatch, a dark bulk crept out of hiding behind a massive iron kitchen range while the light glared back from a window walled up with clay. A figure was wandering around another table attended by a single chair. He was dodging back and forth as if led by his frantic shadow. 'Hugh,' Charlotte said.

He didn't react, and she had to wait until he strayed towards the hatch again before she could see his face. It looked pinched around a desperate obsession. His eyes were fixed beyond recognising her, perhaps even beyond sensing anyone was there. Perhaps he was conscious only of the light that was showing him his way or rather demonstrating that he couldn't find it – and then another thought appalled Charlotte. How had he and Ellen found their way down the lightless house? There was no sign of a flashlight except for hers.

They must have been shown the route or led through it, and she couldn't doubt who their guide had been. 'Where is he?' she blurted.

Hugh might not have heard. He didn't falter in his wandering, which had begun to remind her of the kind of mechanical toy that recoiled whenever it encountered an obstacle. She repeated the question to Ellen, hardly expecting an answer. When her cousin stayed prone and mute Charlotte saw she was as locked into her obsession as Hugh. They were out of her reach, and she'd spoken in a last pitiful attempt to make contact. She already knew the answer.

As she turned towards the hall she saw the light leave her

cousins behind and heard Hugh's footsteps falter to a stop. At least he mightn't injure himself in the dark where she was abandoning him and Ellen. While that distressed her, she was afraid she would be facing much worse. 'This is for you,' she told them and realised she was talking to herself. She walked almost steadily out of the room and didn't break her stride until she was at the cellar. Taking hold of the doorknob, which looked and felt fungoid with verdigris, she eased the door open.

Darkness wobbled away from the flashlight beam, not far enough. As she leaned forwards the beam illuminated steps that led down into a room perhaps half as extensive as a floor of the house. The floor and walls were composed of bare brick, but had she glimpsed something that distracted her from any claustrophobia? Had there been the faintest glow through the gaps between the steps – a glow that had made them look coated with lichen? The appearance had vanished, and she couldn't revive it however she moved the beam. Perhaps it would become visible again if she were to switch the flashlight off, but the mere thought had her struggling to breathe. The cellar was sufficiently daunting, and she had to recall the state in which she'd left her cousins before she was able to set foot on the top step.

Possibly the steps were overgrown even if she couldn't see it. They felt slimy, so that she clutched at the single banister and nearly lost her grip on the spade as the shadows in the corners of the basement performed a gleeful dance. Was there a better way to support herself? Planting the spade on the next step, she leaned on it as her foot joined it. The steps no longer felt slippery, and she wondered if the impression could somehow have been produced to deter intruders. The idea scarcely had a chance to form, because stepping down resembled sinking into thin chill mud.

No, despite the lack of substance, it felt worse. Even shining the light on the steps couldn't dispel the sense of treading in an essence of darkness, of an utter absence of illumination rendered tangible. It was just a trick to ward off trespassers, she did her best to think. It had seized her imagination but not her body, even if she shivered from head to foot as she took another step down, helped by the spade. An ordinary cellar was bound to be cold, and how much colder would it be under an entire buried house? She was managing to tame the latest shiver with that argument when she began to distinguish exactly where the steps led.

The floor wasn't as bare as it had looked from the hall. It was inscribed with signs, an arc of them that lay closer to the walls than to the steps. As she trained the flashlight on the characters, releasing formless shadows from the corners of the room, Charlotte saw that they formed rather more than a semicircle; indeed, it seemed very possible that they encircled the steps. Perhaps the years had faded them, unless they were meant to be nearly invisible. They were easy to mistake for a ring of black lichen, the negative image of a fairy ring in a field, until they fastened on the imagination, when their nature became more evident if not entirely clear. If they were runes, they could well be depicting a pack of misshapen creatures, their jaws gaping in terror of the pursuit or to close on their prey ahead of them, unless both meanings were intended. Charlotte thought of nightmares that grew worse in order to devour their victims, and her skin crawled with the memory of infestation. That was just a nightmare, not even her own, but suppose it was only a hint of the horrors that might be lying in wait? As if to confirm her fear, she heard Ellen groan like someone desperate to wake.

She was expressing her own plight, not suggesting that Charlotte was in someone else's nightmare. Her voice sounded more muffled, so that Charlotte imagined Ellen's face crushed against the wood, while Hugh was no longer able to move for disorientation if not for the darkness in which she'd left him. Nobody except Charlotte could release them. 'I'm going,' she promised, perhaps too low to be heard by anyone outside the cellar, and took the deepest breath she could. Although it tasted subterranean, she vowed to make it last until she was standing in the cellar. It was the nearest she seemed able to come to a prayer.

The flashlight beam swayed, spilling across the bricks. Each step she descended showed her more of the characters whose meaning and purpose she might very well prefer not to learn. She felt as if they were closing around her like a noose. Was it only because of their undefined threat that she gripped the flashlight harder, and the spade? She was growing fearful that as she lowered the spade for support it would be snatched through a gap between the steps. She tried not to let it make a sound as it encountered each step, but her timidity aggravated her nervousness, and the light was already betraying her presence. She slammed the blade against the wood, and once more. Then it struck bricks with a clang that resounded like some kind of bell in her ears as she leaned on the spade and set foot on the floor of the cellar.

A shiver climbed her body and seemed to lodge deep in her brain. It was only the chill of the bricks, she tried to think, although they felt not quite solid enough, as if they might give way beneath her. When she turned to peer past the steps the light danced so wildly that she could have fancied it was as anxious to escape the noose of runes as she was struggling not to feel. They did indeed form an endless chain, though the tottering shadow of the steps obscured a few. The shadow disguised something against the back wall – a crouched shape to which it was surely lending movement. Charlotte dodged around the steps, no less desperate than afraid to see, and the shadow lurched away, exposing the shape.

Her first impression was that it resembled a dead spider – long dead – and she tried to find it as unthreatening, despite its size. It looked not merely withered but drawn into itself. Its arms were hugging its raised knees, its fleshless head buried among all its scrawny limbs, as if it had been trying to rescind its own birth. What had it been so frantic to hide from? She needn't wonder so long as it had been rendered immobile. Surely it was just a husk, and the last of its lingering influence had seized on her and her cousins only because they'd spent too long above its house or slept there. It was so decayed that she couldn't judge whether the discoloured material through which its bones showed was all that remained of its skin or of its clothes or both. A few blows with the spade ought to scatter it and any remnants of its powers beyond reconstitution, and Charlotte did her best to feel encouraged by the incongruous pathetic spectacle of socks drooping on the shrivelled ankles. Or were they the remains of blackened rotten skin? Either ought to mean that the former owner of the house was incapable of any action. Charlotte stepped forwards, lifting the spade, only to realise that she would need both hands to wield it. She was making to leave the circle and place the flashlight on the floor outside it – she was attempting to decide which to do first, because it seemed somehow important – when she heard movement above her in the hall.

She was able to hope it was one of her cousins – Hugh, since she recognised the footsteps as a man's. Perhaps they were so heavy and deliberate because he was relearning how to find his way. She managed to believe this until the newcomer blocked the doorway and began to descend the steps, so deliberately that it seemed not so much careful as gloating. He didn't bother to hold onto the banister with the hand that wasn't flourishing a knife half the length of Charlotte's arm.

He was dressed in hobnailed boots and a butcher's apron: nothing else. His arms and legs and torso were grotesquely muscular beneath a thick simian pelt, which was as black as his ropes of greasy hair. His tread sounded like blows of a hatchet on the trembling steps. Charlotte was striving not to panic but to think whether she should stand her ground and defend herself or try to elude him until she could flee up the steps – she was attempting to overcome the shudder that had reawakened in her brain, shaking her thoughts apart – when he turned away from the steps, and she saw his face.

It was swollen and purple with many veins. Its width made his cracked eyeballs look even smaller. It bore a clown's wide fixed idiotic grin, and the thick lips and malformed nose were drooling. As the man stalked towards her, raising the knife, the hem of the striped apron rose in sympathy, hoisted by an erection sprouting from a bed of matted hair. Charlotte jerked the flashlight up in the hope that it would blind him. While it made his eyes redder still, he didn't falter. The light showed her that his pelt was swarming with parasites, and it revealed another aspect of him. He'd forgotten to bring his shadow, or his creator had overlooked the need.

Either detail might have proved too much for Charlotte. He was an amalgam of nightmares, an overload of them. The fears that constituted him – collected, she thought, in the dreadful bare room overhead – were reduced to nothing but themselves, far less than the victims who'd been forced to suffer them. They had no personality, no substance. They were no better than stale horror stories hollow with clichés, mechanical devices void of any function other than to terrorise. They had nothing to do with Charlotte; how could they have been dredged from her own mind? 'Unbelievable,' she protested in a voice that barely shook, and stepped out of the circle. The instant both her feet were outside, the figure vanished like a bubble that had been pretending it was flesh.

She gazed at the floor where it had stood or seemed to stand, and listened to her heartbeat insisting that she was in more of a panic than she could afford to acknowledge. The bricks within the circle looked even barer for the disappearance – bare enough to be assuring her that the house had finished playing tricks. Perhaps whatever power it had accumulated was spent, having done its worst. The shape that was cowering behind the steps hadn't altered its position; if it appeared to have moved, that was only because the light had.

Charlotte made to lay down the flashlight, and blackness dropped towards her as silently as a spider. It felt as if the ceiling had sagged, and she could do without inviting any threat of claustrophobia. On the floor the flashlight would bring down too much darkness without providing sufficient illumination, she saw now. It would be best left on a step, and she was about to return to the circle when she heard another movement somewhere in the house.

It was a scurrying or scuttling, which suggested rats if not a creature excessively provided with legs. Though her heartbeat was rehearsing her panic again, Charlotte was determined not to be impressed by another vanishing trick. The menace seemed banal, a conjurer's cheapest illusion, too uninspired to be magical. 'No imagination,' she tried to scoff, 'don't put yourself to any trouble' – and then she recognised the sound. The intruder wasn't animal or insect. Earth was trickling into the house.

As she strained her ears to reach beyond the pounding of her heart she was able to locate the sound. It was at the top of the building. Earth must be falling through the skylight, because she heard it strike the attic floor on the way to becoming more muffled as it spilled onto the carpet below. It wasn't simply trickling, it was piling into the house as if somebody were shovelling it in. Its fall didn't quite cover up another noise – a series of creaks that grew louder and more numerous. Was a floor about to collapse? The noise seemed too shrill to be wooden. Just as Charlotte identified the sound of glass under pressure, the highest windows gave way with a clangour that was followed by the thunder of earth filling the rooms. It hadn't lessened when the windows on the middle floor began to creak.

This was too much, Charlotte wanted to believe: not just the windows caving in but the amount of earth that was falling through the skylight. It wasn't her nightmare, it was a version of the terror that had turned upon the occupant of the house. It must have driven him into the cellar once he'd abandoned clawing at the trapdoor to the attic. 'It's all yours,' she cried over the uproar, of which perhaps only her heartbeat was real. The cowering figure shivered, or its shadow did as the beam of the flashlight enacted her nervousness. The movement suggested that the light was capable of threatening the figure, quelling any last remnants of its power. She thrust the beam at the shrivelled crown of the head, and the bony shape reared up to its full height to knock the flashlight out of her hand.

She thought jaws were gaping wide until she saw the entire face was. The beam just had time to exhibit this, and how the denizen of the cellar was beginning to stoop as if to mock her height or to bring its lack of a face level with her eyes, before the flashlight hit the wall. It emitted a flicker that seemed almost taunting and then died for good.

Perhaps the utter darkness was even worse than being buried. It clung like soil to her eyes and seemed to fill her nostrils. Certainly the smell of burial did – thick clay and a staler odour. The sounds of weakened glass and falling earth had ceased as if they'd never been, only to isolate the sound of shuffling in the dark. She'd backed towards the flashlight, but how far? The advance of the footsteps seemed too rapid, not nearly blind enough. She wanted to believe this was yet another trick, but no mere nightmare could have dislodged the flashlight from her grasp. She would never be able to find it before the occupant of the cellar found her, and in any case there was little chance that she could make it work. She would have thrust out the spade to defend herself, but suppose the enlivened remains snatched it from her? She was retreating further when she realised that she didn't even know which way: back into the circle, perhaps. She didn't know why this should aggravate her dread, unless it was stressing her blind disorientation – and then she remembered that she still had light, however meagre. She was almost too terrified to keep hold of the spade with just her right hand while she groped in her hip pocket. She heard the bony shuffling close in on her before she managed to catch hold of her mobile. As she dragged it out, it emitted a pallid glow. Dim though this was, it didn't need to reach far. Her pursuer was within arm's length.

It raised its tattered scrawny arms and ducked its collapsed head towards her face. This was almost enough to send her backwards, which would indeed drive her into the circle. A last flare of instinct made her dodge towards the wall. The figure shuffled swiftly after her, dropping into a crouch from which it might spring on her, throwing her to the floor, where it would begin by lowering its jagged hollow absence of a face towards her. Was this a nightmare it was sending her? She sensed dreadful glee at the prospect of unimaginably worse, and her loathing made her lash out. She hardly knew what she'd done until she felt the spade hack through bone or gristle and saw a shoe and its withered contents left behind.

The lopsided figure hobbled at her with blind determination. When she drove the spade through the other ankle, reducing her pursuer to her own height, it kept coming on its stumps. As it jerked out its shrivelled hands to grapple with the spade she jabbed at its ribs with all her strength, splintering them. The instant it toppled backwards she was on it, tramping on the blade to sever the arms. As the torso struggled like a segment of a worm to elude her, she smashed the skull like a hatched egg. Too much of the body continued to move, not only because of the wild antics of the dim light, even after she'd leaned all her weight on the spade to chop the crawling fragments smaller.

In the end it was disgust with the process that made her give up. As she turned towards the steps she heard a restless scrabbling at the bricks. Surely she'd done as much as she could by herself. 'Ellen,' she called in a voice that hardly seemed capable of escaping the cellar. 'Hugh.' She'd retrieved the flashlight, but it didn't work. Only the muffled glow of the phone lit her way as she stepped into the circle, and the steps weren't visible at all.

EPILOGUE

'Have you finished your new one yet, Ellen?'

'I might have if I hadn't had to come to London.'

'Hey, no panic. Take the time you need. Just don't kill him off at the end. You don't want to keep a good magician down.'

'He wasn't good.'

'I don't think Glen meant it that way, Hugh.'

'You got it. Good as in marketable. From what you sent me I'd say he's your best character. Don't waste him, especially not now.'

'He wasn't just a character.'

'He's mine now, I suppose, Hugh. I can do what I like with him.'

'Which could mean a lot of money if you keep him alive for a series.'

'Why especially now, Glen?'

'I just heard about a television series they're making. Matter of fact, it's the guys who own us. Frugo are getting into movies for the big screen and the small one too.'

'Some of us.'

'Sorry, Rory, we know nobody owns you. Pity you're not still working for them, Hugh. Maybe you could have pushed Ellen's books.'

'I'll be helping. That's why I'm here.'

'That right? Tell me how.'

'Didn't Ellen say? I'm working in a bookshop now. Texts near Frugo where I used to be.'

'Found your way back there, did you? That could be useful. We'll talk.'

'What kind of television series?'

'One your books could tie in with, pick up on, anyway. It's going to be big and controversial. *Psychic Challenge*, they're calling it. Each show has two magicians going up against each other like they did when that stuff was new.'

'Not real magicians. Not like Pendemon.'

'You bet, Hugh. At least that real. No point otherwise.'

'I can't see what point there is anyway.'

'Same one your cousin's books have.'

'What are you making out that is?'

'If she was my cousin I'd say it was earning a living, Rory. I guess they aren't harming your bank balance either.'

'I only did the covers because it's Ellen.'

'Fine since it got them talked about, and we're looking at having you show us some ideas for another of our authors. On top of which we definitely want you doing more for our Pendemon books.'

'There's only one of those yet. What are you asking me for?'

'Now you're taking photographs it's a pity you can't go in his house.'

'Don't look at us. We didn't wreck it even if I thought we should.'

'OK, Hugh, nobody's blaming anyone. I guess we'll never find out who got in there with the gasoline. It might have been good if you hadn't told anybody what was there till we had a chance to film it, though. Even with your mobiles would have been useful.'

'We had other things on our minds.'

'I said I wasn't blaming anyone. You can tell Rory how it was down there, yes? We're figuring on using illustrations in the first book of the series to see how they work. The more they look like photographs the better. Work your magic, Rory. Bring it to life like Ellen is.'

'What do you think, Ellen? It's your book.'

'I'm sure Glen knows what's best for me.'

'That's why I'm here. Tell you what else we'd like – more author photographs.'

'Isn't the one Rory took enough?'

'You put on weight since then. Hey, no bad thing. We don't need the author looking like a ghost even on your sort of book. Maybe he can take some shots after we've all had lunch.'

'Does Charlotte know about the things you're asking me to do? Isn't she still Ellen's editor?'

'Sure thing. I'm just trying to help their books along. Makes sense for all of us.'

'What's keeping her? Shouldn't she be here by now?'

'She was finishing something off downstairs. I guess it's taking longer than she thought. She could catch us up at the restaurant if you're famished, Ellen.'

'No, I want to wait for her. We shouldn't leave her on her own.'

'She isn't, believe me, not down there.'

'Shall I go and find her?'

'You can't do that, Hugh.'

'Why not? Why are you telling him that, Glen?'

'Because nobody gets to go behind the scenes by themselves unless they're part of us, not just your brother. Here comes the elevator. Maybe that's her now.'

'Gee,' Rory said, having turned to watch that letter rob its neighbour of the light. It continued to glow, if somewhat fitfully, as the metal doors parted below the display. The inside of the lift seemed dim, perhaps by contrast with the street, where the window of a taxi caught the sunlight, flaring in his eyes. The blank patch it left on his vision appeared to loiter behind Charlotte as she stepped into the lobby, so that he couldn't immediately tell whether somebody was at her back. No, the gaping gloom was deserted, and in a moment the doors shut before the light shifted to the lowest number. Rory rested his hands on the upholstery to push himself off the settee, so fast that the blank patch engulfed his vision. He mustn't start imagining that it had wiped out Hugh and their cousins or the editor, let alone the place Rory had taken ages to reach. 'Now we're all here,' he said.

The Grin of the Dark

by Ramsey Campbell

Tubby Thackeray's stage routines were so deranged that members of his audience were said to have died or lost their minds. When Simon Lester is commissioned to write a book about the forgotten music-hall clown and his riotous silent comedies, his research plunges him into a nightmarish realm where genius, buffoonery and madness converge. In a search that leads him from a twilight circus in a London park to a hardcore movie studio in Los Angeles, Simon Lester uncovers a terrifying secret about Tubby Thackeray and must finally confront the unspeakable thing he represents.

9780753513811

Teatro Grottesco

by Thomas Ligotti

In this peerless collection of dark fictions, Thomas Ligotti follows the literary tradition that began with Edgar Allan Poe: portraying characters that are outside of anything that might be called normal life, depicting strange locales far off the beaten track, and rendering a grim vision of human existence as a perpetual nightmare. Just to enter his unique world where odd little towns and dark sectors are peopled with clowns, manikins and hideous puppets, and where tormented individuals and blackly comical eccentrics play out their doom, is to risk your own vision of the world.

9780753513743

My Work Is Not Yet Done

by Thomas Ligotti

When junior manager Frank Dominio is suddenly demoted and then sacked, it seems there was more than a grain of truth to his persecution fantasies. But as he prepares to even the score with those responsible for his demise, he unwittingly finds an ally in a dark and malevolent force that grants him supernatural powers. Frank takes his revenge in the most ghastly ways imaginable – but there will be a terrible price to pay once his work is done. Destined to be a cult classic, this tale of corporate horror and demonic retribution will strike a chord with anyone who has ever been disgruntled at work.

9780753516881

The Unblemished

by Conrad Williams

Enter the mind of a serial killer who believes he is the rightful son and heir to an ancient dynasty of flesh-eaters.

Follow the frantic journey of a mother whose daughter is infected with the stuff of nightmare.

Look through the eyes of Bo Mulvey, who possesses the ancient wisdom a blood thirsty evil needs to achieve its full and horrifying potential. A man upon whom the fate of the human race depends.

One of the most powerful horror novels of our time, *The Unblemished* is an epic tale of history and destiny, desperation and desire, atrocity and atonement. It is a savagely beautiful tale of a mother's determination to rescue her daughter, which plunges you into the monstrous world of serial killers and a cannibalistic apocalypse that rips through modern Britain.

9780753513514

One

by Conrad Williams

This is the United Kingdom but it's not a country you know or ever want to see, not even in the howling, shuttered madness of your worst dreams. You survived. One man.

You walk because you must. At the end of this molten road, running along the spine of a burned, battered country, your little boy is either alive or dead. You have to know. One hope.

The sky crawls with thick, venomous cloud and burning red rain. The land is a scorched sprawl of rubble and corpses. Rats have risen from the depths to gorge on the carrion. A strange, glittering dust coats everything. The dust hides a terrible secret. New horrors are taking root. You walk on. One chance.

9780753518106